# RISE RED KINGDOM
by Kerstin Espinosa Rosero

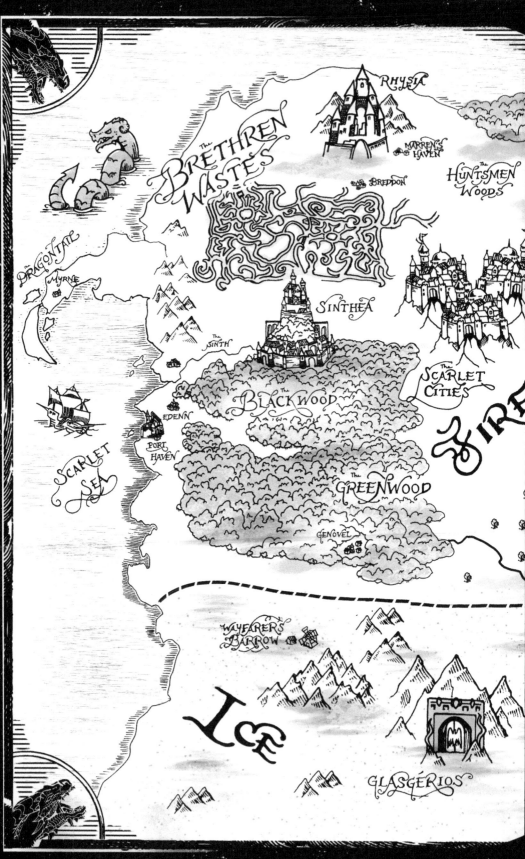

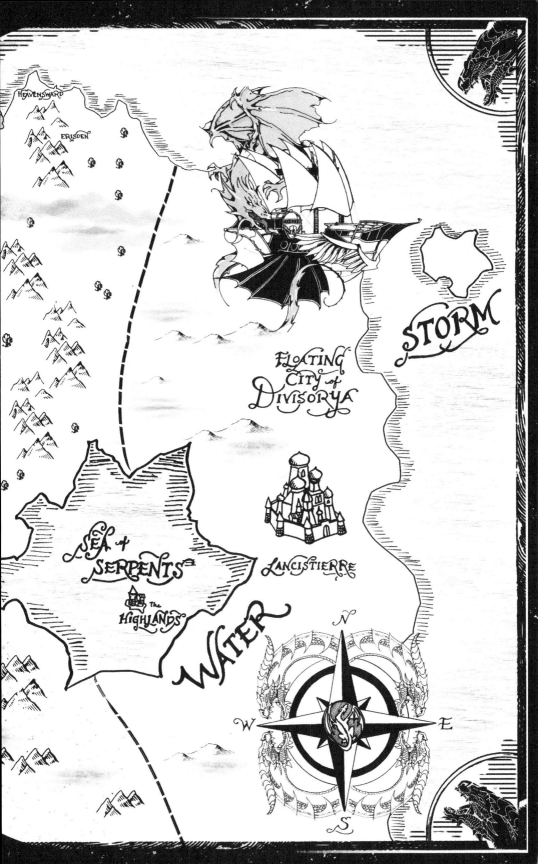

*First edition in English 2022*

Cover Design and Book Design by Franziska Stern
www.coverdungeon.com
www.instagram.com/coverdungeonrabbit

Map Design by Kerstin Espinosa Rosero
Illustration by Kerstin Espinosa Rosero

Author photo by Agnieszka Surdyka

Print: Amazon Media EU S.à r.l., 5 Rue Plaetis, L-2338, Luxembourg
- using motifs from pixabay.com -
ISBN: 978-1-7361041-1-8

www.instagram.com/k.e.rosero
www.twitter.com/ke_rosero
www.ke-rosero.com

IN THE SHADOWS, IT LISTENED.
AND WAITED.

# RISE RED KINGDOM

KERSTIN ESPINOSA ROSERO

By Kerstin Espinosa Rosero

**BURN RED SKIES**

Book I

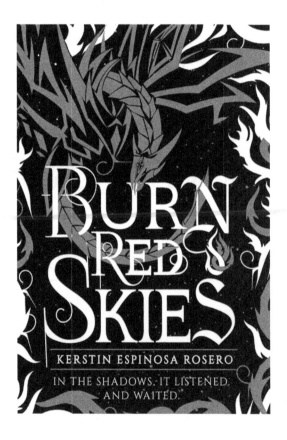

# BURN RED SKIES

KERSTIN ESPINOSA ROSERO

"[An] awesome book… the magic, worldbuilding, and politics of the story… made reading about the machinations of the world extremely interesting. And, it has dragons. What more can you ask for in a book!"—JENNIE IVANS, *Fantasy-Faction*

"Thoroughly gripping from the beginning. Well-done prose and well-developed characters that result in a great emotional hook. The worldbuilding is excellent… the story world grows beautifully through the characterizations."—LYNN K., *Fantasy-Faction*

"The story's unexpected turns and the author's crisp writing style keep readers flying through the book."
—ŁUKASZ PRZYWÓSKI, *Fantasy Book Critic*

"If you love epic fantasy, things that are… more light-hearted and have a great cast of characters… in a world you can't wait to explore, I highly recommend this!"
—*The Reader and the Chef*

*This one is for those*
*who breathed life*
*into the second dragon*

# DRAMATIS PERSONAE

## THE RED CITADEL

| | |
|---|---|
| Morian of Pyrrheas | *Reigning king of the Firelands* |
| Valerya the Fireborne | *Dragon Summoner and Summoner* |
| | *General of the Swordsworn* |
| Gryff | *Valerya's squire* |
| Lyra | *Castle smith* |

| | |
|---|---|
| Valk | |
| Diebold | |
| Skandar | |
| Oren | |
| Aidan | *Summoner's Army,* |
| Stane | *a band of elites known as* |
| Teo | *the "Spades"* |
| Weyan | |
| Justis | |
| Chuckles | |
| Jack | |

# DRAMATIS PERSONAE

## THE FALCONS

| | |
|---|---|
| Dove | *Dragon Summoner* |
| | |
| Wolff | *Captain of the "Smuggler"* |
| Decker | *First Helmsman of the "Smuggler"* |
| Merc | *Second Helmsman of the "Smuggler"* |
| Elayne | *Healer* |
| Marv | *Medican* |
| Sirian | *Devout of the Domeras* |
| | |
| Artis | *Mage; Valerya's former tutor* |
| Bard | *Thunderborne rogue* |
| Dancer | *Waterborne rogue* |

## RED SPEARS

| | |
|---|---|
| The Exalted | *Mage and scholar of the dark arts* |
| Daughter of the Exalted | *Leader of the Red Spears* |
| | |
| Danea | *Commander of the Red Spears; Pierce's older sister* |
| Pierce | *Danea's younger brother* |

# Avantys
### KING of DRAGONS

LAST KNOWN SUMMONER:

Bastyan the Cruel

CURRENT SUMMONER:

Valerya the Fireborne

# Rhysar
## KING of the FORESTS

LAST KNOWN SUMMONER:
*Baley the Kind*

CURRENT SUMMONER:
*Dove the Fireborne*

*What have I done?*

Dove coughed as the ash curled in her throat. The forest around her was a swirl of angry flames. Red fog misted over torn earth. She tried to prop herself up on her elbows, but the dragon had drained the strength from her arms. *Is... anyone there?*

She hoped it was all a bad dream, that her brother had not joined the enemy, that she had not just accidentally summoned an ancient beast. But no dream was capable of such exquisite cruelty. Her friends were probably dead. Her brother had abandoned her. And Valerya...

*Gone like the others.*

Soft flames rose from the ground and crawled at her from all sides. *It is not so bad*, she thought as her body settled into the dirt. She turned her gaze skyward and watched her dragon rain fire on the forest. In truth, it was almost peaceful. At least the screaming had stopped.

Her vision blurred at the edges until it threatened to darken. But just before she closed her eyes, she heard a voice.

"Stay *alive,* you fool."

*Valerya?*

Dove used the last of her strength to sit up, but she saw no one. Disappointment crushed hope fast. *No,* she thought as the world around her grew black and still.

*Please don't leave me... again.*

# FIREBENDER

The dragon… complicated things.

The Red Spears had been doing just fine before the dragon came along. Their ascent had been slow and painful, one that took years of careful planning, until their momentum finally created enough ripples to get the Sovereign's attention. Of *course* the gods saw fit to throw another dragon into the mix. If the royal general didn't have enough reason to double down and wipe them out, she did now.

Pierce shivered and thought of better times. They'd told him the Exalted threw a fit of rage when he heard. He was said to be a powerful man with a sorcerer's air, but old and getting older. By the time Pierce and his sister arrived, his daughter had taken over leadership. Pierce had never met her in person, but judging by the state of her camp, he didn't have to. People kept their heads down and kept walking, and every step was laden with urgency. Distrust. No one paid attention to the starving ten-year-old waiting for his sister at the mouth of the Exalted's cave.

*Can't rely on anyone but Danea,* he reminded himself. A lesson he'd learned early.

He cast swirls of Fire in his hands to pass the time, knowing full well how stupid he was being. The more he cast, the more his energy took a hit, but seeing the Fire bend perfectly to his will gave him at least some modicum of comfort. Flames swirled around his wrists like snakes, and when he imagined them twirling into a neat ribbon, they obeyed. He could even make them write pictographs if he wanted them to. It was the one thing he could do better than Danea, so he made sure to practice every day. According to her, casters in the royal army trained for years, but even they did not wield such precision. The Hounds were known for a great many things, she said, but art was not one of them.

Pierce glanced nervously at the mouth of the cave. *What's taking her so long?*

He'd heard rumors of the Exalted, but only a few people in his camp had seen him up close. Some swore the Exalted had sold his soul to claim an empire, and others claimed his elements cast black and purple flames. Of course, they were usually Danea's flings who liked giving Pierce a hard time, but he still wondered if the two were connected.

*"One, two... one, two..."* He sighed and gazed longingly at the forest. It was hard not to think of all the deer roaming freely when his stomach was threatening mutiny. It wouldn't take long, either. Danea had taught him how to hunt, and his Fire burned so fiercely that his family often told him to hide it. The Hounds were always looking for strong Fire-casters, but his parents didn't want him fighting for an empire that let them starve. He wondered if it was different now that he and Danea were fighting *against* the Empire, but he didn't want to take any chances.

*No.* Danea had warned him time and time again not to go into the forests alone. She was a beast, so he always obeyed. He didn't know anyone else who had fought the royal army on every coast, in every province—even the wastelands!—and survived. She would disappear for weeks at a time and return with another scar, another story. They covered her face like the webs of a spider.

He flexed his fingers as his stomach growled, and hunger triumphed over fear. *It's not like she'll need me for a while.* Just a rabbit or two. Even Danea wouldn't be able to say no that.

*One, two... one, two...* Pierce swung a leg over the fence and pulled himself to the other side. He paused to listen for sound and trudged to the mouth of the forest. By now, he could navigate it blindfolded, but recruits were always building new trapping pits. They stopped putting spikes at the bottom in case one of the younger Spears got careless—or in case fleeing Spears seeking refuge didn't see—but he had never been good at getting out of them. Even when Danea commanded her drudges to throw ropes down each pit, he stayed vigilant. One wrong move and he would spend days in that miserable hole.

He laughed bitterly. *At least Danea wouldn't have to dig a grave for me.*

Despite his sister's protests, the Spears deemed him too young to fight in raids, so he stayed behind and… dug the graves. It was a morbid pastime, but it wasn't like he was itching to go against the royal general any time soon.

Pierce shivered. He didn't know when it all went wrong. The Spears were always careful, really careful, but the royal army had been torching hideouts across the country for months. Someone must have been feeding them information. He and Danea were on the move every week now, it seemed—at first to avoid detection, but now they were running for their lives.

He reached their old hideout, hoping something had been spared, but his sister was right. The Hounds left nothing behind. They scraped their supplies clean, and when they were done, they torched the camp. Crimson flags fluttered restlessly like dying flames desperate for firewood. *The Swordsworn,* he thought. Danea made him memorize all the emblems of the royal forces, but he had never seen the dragon emblem of the General's Army. It was a dream of his to see it one day. From afar.

*One, two... one, two...*

He blinked as snow fell on his hair, blurring his vision. He shook it off his hand and frowned. *Since when does snow smear?* It wasn't even cold enough for it. If anything, it was getting warmer, and the winds had stopped completely. He tried brushing it off his arm, but it only stained his sleeve black.

"WHAT ARE YOU DOING?"

Pierce didn't even know he had collapsed, but an arm grabbed him by the shoulder and lifted him up. He knew only one person who could do that, even with a broken shoulder.

"Why are you... why are you here?" Pierce demanded, but his voice faltered. Even when he stood at his tallest, he was no match for Danea. A sharp glance from her fire-bled eyes crumpled his confidence like old parchment. "Your shoulder!" was all he could say.

He couldn't even tell it was injured. Danea would be out there swinging swords if he hadn't begged her to listen to the medican— or rather, if he hadn't begged the medican to add more nightbloom to her drink. He'd heard the stuff could take down trolls in high doses. But apparently, it couldn't knock out Danea.

"How stupid can you be?" she snapped and used her good arm to force his head back. "*That's* what we're up against now. Not the Hounds."

Pierce watched as the sky tore above the trees, and for a moment, he thought the world had broken. Someone had set the clouds on fire. No, that was ridiculous. Skies couldn't burn, no matter how many times Danea swore she had seen it. Red tides cascaded from the flames, and for a moment, it looked like it was raining arrows. A rippling shadow crossed the sky there, and it was only when he heard the roar that he understood what was happening.

As much as he wanted to, he couldn't move. A lifetime of training hadn't prepared him for this. Reason gave way to panic, and all he wanted was for Danea to tell him what to do.

"Quickly," she hissed, pointing to a second tear in the sky. He hadn't even noticed it before. Its glow was weak but defiant, and it burned white like the Northern stars. "See that? There are two of them now." She pulled him down as a sheet of fire blazed through the skies, sending hot ash in their direction. Without her, he would have been thrown against the trees. Instinctively, he cast a protective shield around them. "Pierce!" he heard her yell above the roar. "It's time. You know what to do."

"ARE YOU CRAZY? I'M NOT DOING THAT," he screamed, sobbed, but she slapped him across the face.

"Listen," she snapped. "We've prepared for this. Listen!" She smacked him again. The nightbloom did nothing to weaken the blow. If anything, it probably gave her strength, because everything made her stronger. "The forest will be overrun with them soon. There's no turning back. No more hiding. You got this, little brother."

Pierce knew the answer, but he wanted any excuse to keep her there longer, to keep her talking. Now, more than ever, he did not want to be alone. "What will you do?" he asked. Against his better judgment, he threw his arms around her. Sobbed some more.

"Follow the plan." Danea shoved him off, but he knew she was trying to be cold. Even with a shattered shoulder, a raging fever, and more nightbloom than any one person should be allowed to take, she could not be persuaded otherwise. They had agreed long ago that when the time came—when war came—they would have to part ways. He had always wondered when that would be, but two warring dragons could not be a clearer sign.

Now Danea had to lead the vanguard, like she always did. And him?

Pierce shuddered. *I need to stay with the Exalted.* That was the reason they were there, after all. His powers were getting much too strong, and the Exalted was the only one who could help him. Danea did not trust him much, but they no longer had a choice.

"I will see you soon," Danea said as his world broke before his eyes. She grabbed at his armband and pulled until it tore. For half his life, it had been his identity, the only thing that kept him connected to his sister. It gave his life meaning. Purpose.

She tossed it to the side, and he watched as it caught flame. "This is our last hope for the Spears, little brother. Stay here. Learn to control your elements, and you'll be a greater warrior than I'll ever be. And remember. When the time comes." She pressed a Fire-forged blade in his hand before she turned. "Do what you must."

# 1

## GENOVEL

# FIRE REALM

Valerya halted her destrier in Genovel just as the crimson fog lifted. The houses were sculpted in stone and bigger than she remembered, not at all like the timber huts from her childhood. It had been a tiny, middle-of-nowhere hamlet, but after it burned to the ground, King Avander made sure Genovel was rebuilt to last. The Summoner's birthplace should be a place of inspiration, he had said, but he had gone overboard. Now only the wealthy lived here, and the village was full of retired nobles.

*He should have left it a pile of ash.*

At least her men were excited, like children smashing ants. The battle had had an invigorating effect on their morale. Chuckles, whose real name she had forgotten decades ago, went between snickering, stifling himself, and snickering again. Banter crumbled into curses and insults on all sides, but she didn't care. It wasn't every day they saw two dragons. Someone had a lot of explaining to do.

The men straightened in attention when Valerya rode before them. "Spades," she said. "Ride ahead and keep the Citadel under control."

They glanced at each other until Diebold broke the silence. "My General," he said dutifully, trying to make sense of her command. He had never been a thinking man, though far from dim-witted, and disliked surprises with no potential for bloodshed. Strangely, he was the pacifist of the group. "What will you do?"

She ignored the question. "Take charge in my stead," she said. In truth, had her men been anyone else, she would have already slaughtered them to preserve their silence. She would gladly sacrifice a few lives to spare the thousands they would end with spilled secrets. But her men never disobeyed, not even in the face of dragons. "As for the rest of you." She turned to the others. "You are sworn to secrecy. And don't forget your *command*."

The Spades pounded their fists on their chest plates, and Valerya's lips curled into a smile. These men were loyal, skilled, and fully commanded to hack and slash their way through the Citadel should Morian suddenly demand their heads on spikes.

Their faces brightened at the prospect of smashing their way through the castle, and Chuckles burst into that weird laughter as they rode off without another word. Only Valk and her squire stayed behind.

"With me," she said, glancing past her squire's helm. *I'll take care of him later.* Just looking at the boy boiled her blood, and he would have been foolish to think she had forgotten his insubordination on the battlefield. But he seemed to be well acquainted with Dove, who had suddenly become very interesting to her. Perhaps he would have his uses after all.

Valerya dismounted her horse and trudged towards Artis's house. She flung the door open. "We need to talk," she said as it slammed against the hinges. Normally, she would take care to soften her words around the old man, but her dragon was having none of it. The presence of another had threatened its reign, and it took all the patience she had to keep it calm. There was none left for anyone else.

"You do not take that tone with me," said Artis sternly, as though she had inadvertently set his garden on fire again. "Honestly, Valerya. That temper of yours."

For such an eventful evening, Artis looked well rested. Elated, even. "Why don't you sit down?" he asked, but his gaze was fixed on Valk.

She threw Valk a suspicious glance, but there were no answers in his eyes. She sighed. "Copper for your thoughts?" she asked him.

"Copper can't afford me," said the Spade with a chuckle, but the color had faded from his face. He shook his head and turned to Gryff. "If I may trouble you to ready our horses?" His tone was kind, but it was not a question.

The boy nodded wordlessly and took his leave.

"What's with him?" asked Artis innocently, but Valerya knew that tone well.

"Seen his first battle." Valerya massaged her temple. *And his friend is a Summoner.*

"He looks like he's seen a ghost, more like."

"Perhaps he has," she said coldly. "What aren't you telling me, old man?"

To her surprise, Artis chuckled. "Don't ask me, dear," he said, nodding towards Valk. "Ask him."

Valerya threw Valk a confused glance that lasted all of two seconds before she understood. They had often talked about what would happen if the world had gotten a Second Summoner, mostly contingency plans to keep the Firelands safe. Granted, she hadn't expected this power to fall in the hands of an unpredictable teenager who had allied herself with Glasgérios—and the Sore—but her age and temperament could still be worked with.

Valk remained steadfast as he spoke. "Do you even remember Sonea?"

The reprisal in his voice was subtle, but it stung. Artis busied himself by pouring tea for the two of them as if he hadn't heard. It had been years, but Artis still spoke of his daughter like she was still alive.

*Sonea. Of course.* Valerya tried to form an image of Sonea in her mind, but all she could recall was the freckles. As Lucien's wife, Sonea had been dutiful, but even a blind man could see the affection she had for his brother. Everyone at the Citadel had found it more fitting that she wed Valk instead, and Lucien didn't even want her to begin with. But as the firstborn son and commander—*Valerya's* commander, even—he was entitled.

According to Morian, at least. The king loved finding propriety in things, especially when it made everyone else miserable. *"He's getting too close to you, my dear,"* he had told Valerya once, a lifetime ago. *"He should be with his own kind."*

"I do." Valerya stopped herself before she could remember any more. "But I admit, we never shared words in private." *Sonea was terrified of me.*

Valerya was prepared for the silence that swept through the room, and she knew without asking what they were thinking. Lucien had never been subtle in his coldness, and it was often whispered in the halls that he turned his attention elsewhere—towards her.

An absurd farce, but one that Morian had believed all too readily. Many still believed that was the real reason Morian had ordered them all killed, but no one dared mention it in her presence. Still, she was sure some of her men believed the lies. Valk did.

She glanced at Valk and saw his face contort as he struggled to find the right words. "What they did to her and the children… *his* children…"

"I remember," she said solemnly. She may not have recalled Sonea with clarity, but it took great skill to get Lucien to shut up about his brats when they were born. Valerya had always used training as an excuse not to join them for dinner. He had invited her over so often that he was probably the reason she became a beast, defeating all the swordsmasters at the Citadel. *I think I even set a record.*

"Greaven and his men…" Valk paused, unsure of how to continue. "They…"

"I know." Valerya cut him off. Enough of Morian's men had boasted about it, but why they did it in her presence, she never knew. Each of them mysteriously resigned from service, some a limb or two shorter than before.

"The girl," Valk said.

"You said the girl had been killed by a falling beam."

"That's what I heard."

"But that's not the truth of it?"

Valerya knew the truth—the real truth—but did not want his hope to burn before his eyes. She let him continue.

"After the house burned to the ground, I searched what was left of it. Charred remains of… of…" He paused. "They never found a body. I mean, of course, it was crushed by the roof, but… because it was never found…"

"The name can still be claimed," said Valerya, finishing his sentence.

Valk cleared his throat uneasily. "That would likely be their next step."

"Does anyone else know about this?"

"Only Artis. He knows the Falcons, and… the North has kept the name unclaimed. I made sure of it." Valk dropped his gaze. "I did what I could to save my brother's child. Her memory, at least."

*"His* child?*"* demanded Valerya, spitefully. She knew her words hurt him more than any blade could, but her dragon's rage had fused with her own. But even when the beast bristled, shattering the glass on the table, he didn't look up. "Is there anything else you have to tell me?"

Valk avoided her gaze as tea spilled outwards across the table. "No," he said.

Valerya nodded and closed her eyes. It was the first time he had ever lied to her. "So we'll spin the story that the girl disappeared and ended up in the Dragontail. Of all places." She cursed to herself. *Well, at least it wasn't Genovel.* The Fates were kind enough to spare her that level of bardic justice, at least. "That's your plan?"

"It doesn't sound too unbelievable." Artis gave her a kind smile. "The commonfolk would believe anything if someone powerful enough said it. And I would argue that the three people in this room wield more power than the king."

Valerya felt the twinge of another headache coming.

"It's in your interest, as well," Artis continued. "Without the name, the girl won't survive by herself. Everyone will want her on their side. And do you really want her on *theirs?*"

*The Red Spears.* Valerya had almost forgotten about them. "The Spears are like the snakes in the Scrolls," she spat. "I cut off one and three more sprout in its stead. They're too busy eating each other to be a threat."

"Imagine hundreds of snakes following a dragon." Artis lowered his gaze. "Being underestimated is a great advantage in any war, my dear. Do not give them this gift."

*What isn't he telling me?*

Valerya closed her eyes, hating everything, as she contemplated what to do. "Valk," she said decisively. "You are no longer coming back with me."

The Spade blinked in surprise. Whatever response he had been expecting, it wasn't that. In truth, her own words wounded her. Since they had first met, there was rarely a day they did not see each other. It was like severing an arm. "Is this punishment? Because if it is, I…"

"It's not a punishment," said Valerya, insulted. Gods, did she *look* like Morian? "Once our King finds out I let a Summoner wander free, he'll go after you. You're a Northerner, after all. And it won't be long before he makes the connection."

Guilt tore at her insides. Valerya would never lie to him, but concealed truths bordered on deceit. Her dragon felt her unease. The table rattled, and the torch-fire wavered. She continued before the others could sense it too. "It is imperative that she claims the Northern name. It's the only way you'll both be safe."

Valk nodded. "I will ride for Glasgérios at once, then," he said.

"She won't be there," said Valerya. "If the girl's companions are smart, they won't stop at their headquarters. They'll have headed straight for the North. For Rhysia."

Valk frowned. "You're certain?"

"That's what I would do." She shrugged. It was not a lie. "I would send her closest companions to Glasgérios in a guarded caravan to throw us off the scent. That would allow her to slip away to the North undetected. It would be a small convoy, but her companions would know how to handle themselves."

"How do you know?"

*Because I've seen where she was.* "They need her to claim

the Northern name as much as we do," she said instead. Another concealed truth, but now was not the time to bring up sorcery. All she knew was that their dragons had created a connection between them. Whenever Dove was desperate enough to need her, Valerya found she could easily see where she was, like she was looking through the girl's eyes. *She would need to work on her defenses in the future,* she thought. But for now, it was good to keep track of her whereabouts.

Valk interrupted her thoughts. "What about you?" he asked.

Valerya cringed when she heard the concern in his voice. "You let me worry about our King," she said. "Now is not the time for blood. But should the time come for it, I expect you to return and fight by my side." She waved a hand dismissively before he could continue. "Just make sure she claims the name. And find her before the Red Spears do. In the meantime, I will double my efforts to crush them."

"The... Spears?" Valk frowned. "But they haven't been a threat in a while. Why now?"

*Because Artis seems afraid of them.* "We could afford to ignore them then," she said. "But Artis is right. If they get their hands on her, if they have that dragon, they'll become an unstoppable force. Our greatest mistake would be to *underestimate* them."

"We don't even know who they are. Who their leader is."

Valerya glanced at Artis, but he avoided her gaze. "Leave that to me. I have my ways." *Another thing I have to take care of.* Her list of problems was growing exponentially. "And where will you go?" she asked.

Artis rose from his chair. "Oh, I think our circumstances have improved remarkably. I'm ready to get out of here." His hands gripped the table for support, and Valerya rose to help him stand.

"I will join Valk in finding her. I'm the only one here who hasn't met her."

One less thing to worry about, at least. If these two found her, the girl would be the most guarded person in the Firelands. They could keep her safe while Valerya wrecked what was left of the rebellion.

She held out her arm, and Artis took it. He pulled her close. "I'm sorry they made you a monster, my dear," he whispered sadly, and released. "The gods be with you."

Valerya turned to Valk and held out her hand. He clasped her arm at the elbow.

"This is farewell," she said.

"For now, perhaps," said Valk, ever the optimist. His remorseful expression made her uneasy, and for a wild moment, it looked as though he meant to embrace her. Perhaps she wouldn't have minded, but…

No, she would have.

Much to her good fortune, they were interrupted when the door opened. Gryff trudged back in, silent as a shadow, and eyed them all in bewilderment. The dynamic had changed considerably since he left.

"Boy," she said coldly. "It appears that you have a choice. Will you ride with me to the Citadel, or do you want to find your… *friend* again?"

"Wouldn't it be dangerous for him back in the Citadel?" asked Artis as Gryff glanced back and forth between them.

Valerya gave Artis a bleak smile. The old man had grown fond of her squire after all. "Our King may turn his attention to Valk should he feel the need to punish me. But he may keep the boy alive just to annoy me." She turned to Gryff. "Well?" she snapped. "Are you coming or not?"

She headed towards the door, which flung open at her touch. Long farewells were not in her nature, and she was keen on ending the evening as soon as possible.

The boy stared wordlessly at Artis and Valk, and then back at Valerya. She could only wonder what was going on in his little head, but she spared him nothing. He had to grow up some time. If not now, she was more than willing to leave him to the wolves.

Gryff's jaw clenched in determination as he threw the old man and the Spade a regretful glance—and trailed after her.

# 2

# THE
# OTHERWORLD

Even before Dove opened her eyes, she knew she was somewhere else. It had been happening every day now. For a moment, the air hissed and flashed like something had breached an invisible barrier, and the stars rippled above her like silk. The moment the pain lifted, even in the slightest, something stronger took over, filling her head with thoughts that were not her own.

This time, the dragon had taken her mind back to the Citadel, but the colors were all wrong. Not just the banners, which no longer boasted the red and dark red sigil of Morian's house, but the *colors*. Fire raged, but it burned a dull gray, and darkened skies bled crimson. It must have been magic, but she could not trace its source. It did not take her long to realize she was trapped in another memory.

*Who am I now?* The body she was in was not hers, but she still felt its pain. It was pinned down by fallen bricks, and arrows were lodged in its ribs. Blood gushed from its nose in spurts. Torn muscles tightened and seized, locking splintered bones into place. As bad as she felt for this man, this stranger, his pain should not have been hers. And she hated him for it.

"Don't let him. *Don't let him.*" The man sobbed, a blade's edge closer to madness. She saw the emerald of his ring glimmer weakly in the fire. A walking stick lay splintered at his side.

She tried to find anything she recognized, but the dragon had taken her centuries before her time. The walls around the main keep had not yet been built, and spears were still a primary weapon. The man turned his gaze skyward and shielded his face, the stupid emerald still shining. Men were screaming all around him. At him. *"Stop him!"* But there was not much he could do.

And then she saw it: Avantys, burning redder and fiercer than the dawn. It spewed angry fire that made each scale glow like dying coals. Archers shot at it. Mages blasted it with all the elements they had, but whatever they launched at it dissolved in its blaze. Even in this alternate world, it could not be touched.

Dove had never burned before, but now she knew how it felt. It was torture in its finest form. At least in the real world, there existed the very real possibility of dying, but in her head, it could go on and on like this forever. *This is what Valerya left me to,* she thought as the man's breath crackled in his broken throat. *She should have just killed me.*

Sometimes the pain made her so desperate, she tried to make a connection herself. Never mind that Valerya had become her greatest enemy; Dove had to see her, and on the rare occasion she did appear in her hallucinations, the pain stopped. For a time, that is, until the dragon found her again. *It will fight me for control,* she remembered. *Until I want to die.*

She did die. Over and over again, in different bodies, in different times. She had been stabbed, hanged, drowned, and she was pretty sure she had been fed to a dragon. After a while, she stopped resisting and tried to piece together who they were, but it was difficult when she could only glimpse their final moments. And those were often full of terror.

"You're burning up." She heard a voice, a woman. And a man. *Where am I this time?* She opened her eyes and saw Marv wipe her forehead with a wet towel. Tinted candlelight blurred his features, but she recognized the scent immediately. Even when on the run, he always smelled like an apothecary. It was usually faint, but now it was so strong, she wondered if he had bathed in herbs. "I'm afraid I can't give you any more nightbloom, *Sintger.*"

His voice was barely a shade above a whisper, but his tone was seeped in doubt. *A least he is real,* she thought, flexing her fingers to make sure they were really hers. Moved her head to see him better. He saw it but pretended not to notice. Something was making him nervous.

*Probably a giant, undead dragon.* Dove had been so busy dying that she forgot others could feel its presence. One by one, her own memories returned, settling into place like sand in water. Most of them, anyway.

"We'll have you on your feet in no time," said Marv, and Dove sighed. She always admired his confidence, but it had suffered a spectacular misfire. *"You'll be fine,"* he had said. *"It's just a bit of adventure,"* he had said. Easy for him to say. He did not have to deal with a spiteful reptile.

"Sintger? *Sintger.*" Marv snapped his fingers. It was only the two of them in the room, and Dove realized she did not know where she was. The dragon had thrown her into so many memories, she could not place her surroundings. "Stay with me," he whispered. "Don't let it control you."

It. That *thing*. The Northern dragon they now called hers. *Of course it had to be a dragon.* The gods needed a laugh, she supposed.

She wondered how many people prayed for a savior against Valerya the Fireborne, only to be answered with her.

Dove wished she at least had a name that inspired fear. Respect. Across the Firelands, Valerya was known as the Blood Queen, the She-Jackal, Conqueror of the Realm. And her?

*I was named after a white pigeon.*

Dove groaned and shielded her eyes as more of her memories returned. She recalled Valerya and worked her way backwards. Decker and Merc were there in the forest with them. She remembered Decker was bleeding—but why?

"Stay with me." Marv's voice was calm, but his eyes spoke of fear. She could tell he did not want to be alone with her, with *it*. Suddenly, all the confidence in the world could not help him. Hells, even she did not want to be alone with it.

*Where are we?* Dove had assumed she was in Glasgérios, but the walls were paneled in dark timber and polished around a window that creaked with the wind—not exactly the mark of an underground cavern in the Icelands. More shapes settled into place when she squinted, giving form to Marv and her bed, but not much else. Dim candlelight did not make it very far.

"We're in the heart of the Greenwood," said Marv, reading her face. "According to your blue-haired friend, we're in a town called Waird. Fortunately, I have an acquaintance not too far from here who can brew more of this for your fainting spells…" He took a vial from his pocket and held it in front of her face. When he shook it, she saw liquid that shone as bright as Rhysar, the ascendant star, named after the dragon that was now hers.

"They call it Tears of the *Rhysandir*. But don't tell anyone. It's not strictly speaking… *allowed*." He left it on her bedside table. "This is the last of it, I'm afraid. I have to pick up some more."

Dove sighed and struggled to sit up. The *Rhysandir* were dragon riders, or so the Scrolls claimed. That was the most accepted translation, but it was more or less a Summoner in the common tongue. Nowadays, at least. She wondered if her own tears counted. She would have barrels full of them by nightfall.

Marv adjusted the straps of his cloak. "I'll be back soon, *Sintger.* You can take off the tinted glass when I'm gone." Soft flames wavered in his auburn eyes and sparked into mischief. He threw her a crooked smile as he pulled up his hood. "Do take the Tears if you go for a stroll. You'll feel a bit better."

Dove grabbed his sleeve and traced "woman?" on her blanket.

"Woman? What woman?" His brow deepened in concern. "Sure you're all here?" He felt her forehead. "If you're not feeling well, just rest up a bit. I'll be back soon."

Dove tried to stay focused after he left, but her vision began to blur again. Her surroundings throbbed with each heartbeat, and she knew she was going to be catapulted into another memory. *Damn it.* She threw a desperate glance at the Tears glowing on her bedside table. Valerya would know what to do, but whenever Dove tried to make a connection, all she got was a blinding light across her field of vision. A sharp slice in her skull. Wherever the General was, she did not want to be bothered.

*Give me a sign,* thought Dove to the Fates as she prepared for the plunge. She was so tired that it took less effort to feel pain than actively avoid it, and since the skirmish at Wayfarer's Barrow, it had been a bad time for everyone. *Just a little hope.* But before she could close her eyes, she heard tapping on the window.

*Raehys?* Even in the dark, Tomá's falcon was hard to miss. Since the death of its master, the falcon had never been far from her side. It did not respond to anyone else.

*Good enough for me.* Dove reached for the vial. *Here goes nothing.* She closed her eyes and lifted it to her lips. Sighed.

And drank.

# 3

## THE GREENWOOD
# FIRE REALM

W*aird, I am officially impressed.*
Bard took a swig from his tankard and stared out the tavern window. They had rebuilt the brothel absurdly fast. The last time he was here, the entire left wing was in flames. Whores and whore-mongers ran through the streets claiming foul play, pointed fingers at each other. The guards didn't know who to arrest, so they tackled everyone. In the mass confusion, he and Dancer had managed to slip by unnoticed, but not before Dancer set all the destriers free. That night may have been a giant blur in his mind, but the brothel was definitely roasted by the time they had left. *Amazing how fast it was rebuilt.*

Then again, he wasn't surprised. It was not the Fireborne way to ask questions. The masters told their dogs to build, and now the façade shone like polished wood. Still, the whores were skeptical and insisted on staying in the guest-keep. The innkeeper didn't care. As it turned out, the whores—no, former whores—had ample coin and always paid cash. The rooms in the guest-keep were much more comfortable, so they decided to work there instead. Since there was no room for anyone else, travelers had to stay in the brothel. Dancer would have loved this turn of events.

*She would have called us heroes.*

"Why do you think she set the horses free?" A voice tugged him from his thoughts.

Bard blinked. *Oh, right.* He had been talking to Prim before he drifted away. She was one of the—former—brothel paramours who now lived at the guest-keep, but her talents were wasted in Waird. He had only started talking to her because he felt bad for his role in her unemployment, but as it turned out, she was a wonderful listener and gave sage advice. Prim said the brothel burning down was the best thing that had ever happened to her, and for the past few nights, they stayed up talking in the guest-keep tavern. It was hard to say who was more indebted to whom. They had been buying each other drinks all night.

Bard shrugged. "Don't know. She loved animals, I guess."

Prim smiled and tucked a lock of her hair away from her eyes. "So let me get this straight. She didn't hesitate to take out a gang of bandits with her bare hands… but didn't want to leave the horses hanging? That's oddly sweet."

*Yeah.* Bard felt a pang of pain in his chest. *But she left me hanging.*

"It must feel like she left you hanging, though," said Prim. "I bet that hurts." She had a plain face that did not attract attention, but her beauty grew the more he listened to her voice. It was deep, soothing, and full of clever things. Bard could listen to it for hours.

*Damn. She's good.* Bard took another swig. "Didn't say she left me hanging. I just said she left. Just… gone, just like that. After all we'd been through."

"Huh." Prim smiled.

"What?"

"Oh, nothing. You're cute." She sipped at her tea, but Bard was pretty sure the cup was empty. "So you were raising a poor orphan girl together. Lark was her name, right?"

Bard nodded. Grunted. Wished he had been more creative with names.

"And dangerous people came looking after Lark, so you took her and ran."

"Yeah. That was when she left."

"She left Lark *in your care.* But what makes you think she's gone?" Prim shrugged sweetly. "Maybe she's just taking care of them while you're watching the kid."

"Them?"

"The dangerous people," said Prim, bringing a hand up to her chin. "She won't leave *horses* hanging. Why would she abandon her child?" Her eyes were so dark, they were almost black, but when she looked at Bard, she saw everything. "Be on the run forever, or neutralize the threat once. And from what you say, Ballerina is a woman of action."

Bard shrugged. "Shmaybe."

Prim laughed, but it was a sweet sound. The lock of hair fell back over her face. "Well, I only know her based on what you tell me, but I've met a lot of women in my life. Ballerina sounds like she has a lot to fight for. She wouldn't let someone she loves go so easily."

Bard choked back tears. *No more ale for me.* "Love?"

"Of course. Lark," said Prim coyly. Her dark eyes swallowed him whole. "Her *child.* Speaking of..." She nodded towards the entrance.

*Damn it.* Bard wiped his face and sat up straight. He hadn't expected Dove to be awake, and now that she was there, he was no longer allowed to be vulnerable. He threw Prim an apologetic glance, but she only smiled as she rose and took her leave.

"See you soon?" he asked hopefully.

"I'll be here," said Prim, throwing Dove a wink as she passed. Dove stared back in surprise. Prim was tall and broad but moved with grace, confidence. It was oddly alluring, and even the kid got drawn in.

Prim passed by the two kids he had hired to stand guard at the entrance. They were half his age and duller than their blades, but it wasn't like Bard had grabbed a sack of gold before they made a run for the North. He got what he paid for. All he needed was for them to report any suspicious activity—aside from the sudden appearance of a Thunderborne, a brood of fire-haired warriors, a medican allergic to light, and a teenage girl who kept passing out. Oh, and a night-wolf. Should be easy enough in a village like Waird.

Bard cleared his throat and tried not to look too concerned when Dove sat across from him. She had been knocked out for days. To make up for it, Marv hadn't *slept* in days, running around and collecting herbs or whatever it was medicans did. Bard almost felt guilty for being so well rested, but Dove looked like she was ready to run laps around the Scarlet Cities. *What did Marv give her?* He frowned. *And why does she have Tomá's falcon?*

Bard still did not know what had possessed Tomá to challenge Valerya to a duel. It was the best fight he had seen in years, but he knew before it began who would lose. Anyone who saw it did. Still, he hadn't expected the falcon to bond with a new master so quickly.

Dove had created a sling around her shoulder to protect the bird, but it still glared out at him from the openings in the folds. Tomá had never been his friend—Tomá had never been anyone's friend, really—but Bard swore he saw a bit of the domeric in his bird. *No wonder it hates me.*

"Here." He passed her a tankard. "I need a new drinking buddy." He took another sip to hide his cringe. Even saying it hurt. He hadn't seen Dancer since their first night back in Waird, but that was what she was—a master of secrets. All the weapons in the world were no match for the things she knew.

They would have to move fast now. Rumors were spreading like wildfire, and the more they waited, the more they closed in on them. A thousand absurd rumors, each with a kernel of truth. It was only a matter of time before people pieced it together. Bard glanced back at Dove.

*Of course she doesn't drink.* He didn't know why he was surprised. He had only met one other Summoner in his life, but even in her human form, Valerya was a beast. At Dove's age, she had already been twice her height and width, bedding swords and swinging maidens... or was it the other way around? *Dove made a fucking sling for an injured bird,* he thought, shaking his head. *Valerya would have let it die in the snow.*

He sighed. They had bigger problems now.

Bard had overheard Wolff and Sirian talking about the kid when he was pretending to be asleep in Wayfarer's Barrow, and their hushed tones only convinced him that he should eavesdrop. Nothing special; just more rumors sprouting from the scholars of the Scarlet Cities that as the Northern Summoner, the kid had a right to claim a Northern name. There were a few open, however that worked, so Sirian had convinced Wolff to send her north.

The plan wouldn't have been so terrible if the name hadn't belonged to Lucien of fucking Rhys. *Really?* Bard downed his tankard. He didn't know if the commonfolk would buy it, but people believed anything in a panic if it meant filling the gaps, especially if it came from the Scarlet Cities. If Dove wanted to be smart, she would use it to her advantage. All the gold in the world could not buy loyalty, but a name had substance, history. Money bought armies; respect commanded it for free. Hells, if she didn't want to be Avriel of Rhys, he would.

"Feeling all right?" he asked. *Stupid question.* Marv had said she was hallucinating and running twenty fevers at once, and that was *after* her brother stabbed Decker in the heart. He doubted she was feeling up for small talk.

Dove shrugged and traced letters on the table with her finger. *D. E. C. K.*

"Decker?" He set his tankard down. "Haven't heard from them since the last falcon, but I imagine that's a good thing." In truth, he had no idea, but Decker was in Elayne's hands. He knew no one else who could do better, and he suspected Elayne spent all her time on him. She may have sworn the Healer oath, but for him she would let the Icelands burn.

Dove sighed and rested her chin on her hand. Looked out the window. For a moment, she looked like she had been abandoned too. *She must be thinking of her brother,* he thought. Bard wished he had words of wisdom, but it wasn't like he was in the position to talk. Being dropped *stung.* There was no way to get over that wave. Best they could do was ride it out.

"This is the most depressing table I've ever seen in a tavern," said a voice, deceptively frail. Bard threw a hopeful glance towards the entrance, not daring to believe it.

*Artis.* His mood lifted when he saw him. *You lovely mage of an old man.*

For a moment, he wondered if Dove had laced his drink with

nightbloom. It had been so long since Artis left Genovel that his presence in Waird felt like a hallucination.

The two boys standing guard at the entrance blinked back surprise as though they had just remembered what their jobs were. They squared their shoulders and raised their arms. The black-haired one spoke first. "Hey, old man. You can't just be in here…"

The taller one tried to pull Artis back, but the old man dragged the tip of his walking stick along the ground and whipped it upwards, flinging pebbles in the boy's eyes. There was no time to protest; the stick came after. "Where are your manners?" Artis scolded, and his hard eyes shifted to the other. Artis let the momentum of his staff whirl him in a circle turn, and he twirled the tortured wood in his hands before jabbing its end into the shorter boy's chest. It was more of a warning than anything, but it served its purpose.

The force may have shoved them back, but it was Fire that kept them down. Artis raised his hand up to eye level, and flames curled around his arm like serpents. Spread upwards.

"In my day, even the most brutal sentinels had manners." The more the serpents swirled, the darker the rest of the tavern became, like they were feeding off the surrounding light. "Will we have a problem?" he asked as the flames danced circles in his cold eyes.

"No!" the kid yelled and turned to his companion, who lay unconscious next to him. He must have thought he had to answer for his friend, because he yelled it again. The kid let out a sigh of relief when the flames shrank back down and disappeared around the old man's wrists. When Artis made no move to attack, he sprinted out the door. Bard had never seen anyone run so fast. *He even left his friend behind.*

Bard rubbed his eyes, making sure he was awake. His gaze fell on Artis's travel companion, who was weighed down by sacks and satchels like a pack mule. In the chaos of the moment, he was easily overlooked in Artis's shadow. Everyone was.

It took a while for Bard to recognize Lucien's brother, who most people only knew as the second son. Or Lucien's brother. Valk seemed to like it that way, though. Even then, Valk had a curious distaste for attention. He was so agreeable that he had given Bard the creeps at first, but at least he was consistent. It was Lucien who tended towards coldness, even cold-heartedness. No wonder Sonea…

Bard frowned and glanced across the table. Blinked. The ale may have slowed his senses a bit, but Dove's eyes were a shade lighter, a shade fiercer… but…

*Now you're buying into the rumors,* thought Bard, suddenly overcome with the bizarre urge to laugh. It was reassuring to know that the highborn were just as messed up as the lowly mortals down below. Even the best of them caused more drama than a stage play.

Dove regarded Valk with mild alarm, but it faded fast, and she gave him a soft smile. Nothing would get her down today. Whatever Marv had given her for the pain, Bard wanted it.

"Good to see you again, my boy." Artis gave Bard an encouraging smile. Valk trailed behind him, taking in the sights of the guest-keep. Bard couldn't imagine the Spade ever setting foot in a tavern. Neither he nor Valerya looked like the type to indulge, and he wondered what they even talked about in their free time. "Where is your lovely companion? Dancer, is it?"

Bard shrugged. Tried not to care. "Gone," he said, failing. "Don't know where she is."

"So she figured it out," said Artis with a hint of a smile. "I never doubted it for a second."

Bard straightened. "What do you mean?"

"In good time, dear. There are a few things we have to tend to first." Artis laughed to himself. "She's so good that not even my falcons can find her. But hers always seem to find me."

Dove tugged at Bard's sleeve and pointed to the thug lying on the floor. *Are we just going to ignore this?* she said with her eyes. Her gaze darted between Artis and the Spade.

Prim reappeared from behind the counter, clicking her tongue at the mess. She asked no questions as she dragged the body away. *How strong is she?* Bard wondered in awe. She threw Valk a subtle glance as she passed. Winked. No one said anything until she was out of sight.

"They raised a hand against innocent civilians," said Artis sweetly, ignoring the thuds behind the curtains. "In my day, that was enough to get twenty lashes. These may be turbulent times, but we are not barbarians."

"What are you *doing* here?" Bard whispered. He and Thornbeard had made sure they covered their tracks. Wolff and the others had headed back to Glasgérios in a fortified caravan accompanied by their most able-bodied fighters. In the chaos, there was no way of knowing who was where, and betting on Waird would have been a stretch, especially since Bard still had no idea what it was really called.

*Could Dancer have told him...?* Bard sat up, hope renewed. If anything, at least that meant she was on their side. Sending two of the most powerful Fire-casters in the country had to be a sign of good faith, right? He asked again, this time politely. "What are you doing here?"

"I should ask the same of you," said the old man indignantly. "I imagine our goals aren't so different, so my companion and I have decided to accompany you on your travels."

Bard glanced down and watched Dove size them up. She stared

at Valk with renewed interest. *It must be strange seeing a dog without its master,* he thought. If it had just been Valk, Bard would have drawn his sword. The two of them would have been smashing their way through Waird by now, but he trusted Artis with his life. There was no way the old man would put them in danger. The kid was claiming his granddaughter's name, after all.

*But he still has some explaining to do,* he thought bitterly.

For an uncomfortable moment, everyone sat in silence. Bard started on his fourth tankard and sighed. It was just his luck to share a table with the worst conversationalists in the Realm. All they needed was Valerya to complete the circle.

*Nope. Not gonna do it,* he thought, eyeing Artis, challenging him to talk first. He took a long sip and made sure they heard it.

"What happened to your other companions?" asked the old man curtly.

Bard gulped down the ale. "What makes you think there are others?"

"A short and stout fellow with a handful of sons, a night-wolf, and a... Glasgérian medican who's not too fond of the light," Valk said. "Have I got that right?"

"Schmaybe." Bard tried to keep his expression impassive. He couldn't imagine Dancer telling them *that* much. She loved spreading juicy bits of information, but never in too much detail. *The surprise is half the fun,* she used to say. She would never rob them of the experience. But how did they know who was there in the first place?

Dove glanced up in surprise. Her eyebrows furrowed as she turned her gaze to the bottom left. Her thinking face, as he had come to know. Finally, her eyes met his. *I have to tell you some-thing,* they said. Urgently.

Later, he shot back with his eyes, but he didn't know if she got it. No one ever understood his expressions. "We can trust them. For *now*," he said. "To be honest, I wouldn't mind them with us when we hit the Brethren Wastes." He glanced at Valk. "Still remember the way? Or has Valerya beaten the North out of you?"

"Of course I do," Valk said, ignoring the quip. *Agreeably.*

Artis turned his attention to Dove, and she shifted uncomfortably in her seat. The kid may have summoned dragons, but even she crumpled under his gaze. Bard tried not to laugh when he remembered the days Artis sent *Valerya* to her room without supper. But this time, there was nothing but affection in the old man's eyes.

"Count me in," was all he said.

# DEATHBRINGER

Pierce had never considered himself a quick learner, but his Fire never failed him. It was the one thing he excelled at, really excelled at, and he mastered his training with ease. He reckoned if the Exalted told him to rain fire from the sky or turn rivers into molten slush, he could. All he needed to do was imagine where he wanted his elements to go, and they usually obeyed. Usually. It came so easily to him, like drawing circles in the sand.

And still he felt like sobbing.

The Exalted himself was a cold, unforgiving man whose features were carved in severe lines and set in pale stone. His eyes were so dark there was no room for mercy, and despite the folds in his face and the white in his hair, he moved with the vitality of a man in his prime. A lifetime of study had polished the edges off his accent, and he spoke with the wisdom—and cruelty—of a thousand years.

It was no wonder Pierce found himself panicking when the Exalted had him summoned to the cave one morning. For all the hours he trained near the entrance, Pierce had never actually been inside before. Small, dark spaces made him nervous, and even the thought of it sent his heart beating in jagged rhythms. He swirled threads of Fire between his fingers and counted to himself in twos, but not even that was enough to distract him today.

By the time the Spear came out to collect him, sweat had already matted Pierce's hair to his forehead. "I... the Exalted... the Exalted... Pierce, my name is..." *One, two... one, two...*

"Pull yourself together, kid," said the Spear, and Pierce recognized him as one of the scouts. Badge, his name was. Scouts spent most of their time away from the camp, but when they did come back, they were treated like royalty. They all had nicknames, usually something to do with their tasks, but Danea thought it was stupid, so she never bothered. Pierce wondered if they knew each other.

Badge spat. "You're lucky he's in a good mood."

Pierce walked past him without saying anything. He knew it was rude, but his stomach was knotting itself into little ribbons. It wasn't like vomiting on the Spear would have made it any easier. "It's fine. It's fine," he whispered to himself, spinning faster threads. He counted twenty-two steps from the entrance to the double doors. "Twenty-two. Here. I'm here."

*One, two... one, two...* Pierce swallowed and entered the Exalted's chambers.

The door opened into a circular hall lined with bookcases. Most of the light came from a small garden in the middle of the chamber, but Pierce couldn't locate its source. It looked like someone had bottled rays of the sun and focused its energy on the flowers. *An alchemy garden.* He recognized deathbell and the purple shades of nightbloom, but the others did not look native to the Greenwood.

"Fascinating plants. Wouldn't you agree?" The Exalted's voice cut through the silence like a blade. It was dry and bled of humor.

*One, two... one, two...* "Mmhh," Pierce forced himself to focus on the garden, on the conjured daylight rotating above it like a chandelier. It was the only thing that distracted him from the walls of the cave, which were starting to close in on him. *It's all in your mind. In your mind.* He had lost feeling in his hands, replaced by an unpleasant tingling in his fingers. "I... I like... I like plants."

The Exalted's shadow appeared in the light, and Pierce wished he could sound braver. Out there, he was hailed as the strongest Fire-caster in the group, but in here, he was bested by a cave. Worse, its walls. The one thing that didn't move.

*"Calm,"* whispered the Exalted. With a gentle motion, he used two fingers to draw a circle in the air. Shadows of the cave faded into a blue sky, like someone had wiped them away with a damp cloth. The garden expanded until the entire floor was blanketed in grass, and Pierce felt like he had just been dropped in the middle of a field. The only thing that anchored him to reality was the hard stone he felt through the soles of his boots. That and the desk next to him, which the Exalted probably left for Pierce's orientation.

"A conjuration, clearly," said the Exalted, whose black robes and dark gemstones were suddenly out of place in a summer field. It looked much too warm for him to be there. "But a useful one. Does it help?"

"Yeah... yeah, it actually... it actually does."

"Good. Now let's begin." The Exalted relaxed his element hand and waited for Pierce to catch his breath. "Do you know why I called you here?"

"Have you... have you heard anything from my sister?" Pierce asked hopefully. It had been weeks since her last message. Danea could be out slaying trolls, for all he knew, but she had never gone this long without writing him. Letting him know she was all right. The more time she spent away, the scarier his world became.

"I have not," said the Exalted softly. "Though if you're so consumed with worry, you should accompany her on her next journey. I imagine you would be of great help."

Pierce frowned. "How? I'm just a... I'm just a..."

"A *heinously* powerful Firebender."

"But I have no... no skill with a blade, or with... fighting."

"So the swordsmaster tells me." The Exalted turned to face him, and Pierce was surprised to see a smile on his face. It was more of a sneer, and a cold one at that, but it was the most the Exalted had ever given him. "No talent with a blade. Yields at the first opportunity. *Afraid.*"

Pierce winced at the last word. "Yes," he said. "That's... that's all true."

"Honest, at least." The Exalted regarded him with cruel eyes. "The solution is simple, my boy," he said. "You've got a gift that no one else has. It would be foolish to waste your time on your weaknesses. A prime swordsman does not lament his skill with a bow."

Suddenly, Pierce felt his head hammer. "I don't... I don't understand," he said as blood trickled down his nose. He wiped at it furiously, hoping the Exalted wouldn't notice.

The Exalted ignored it completely and pressed his palms together. "Then let me *show* you." He pulled his hands apart, creating lines of coarse flames between them. "This is raw elemental energy. Any beginner could cast it. Now see what happens when I concentrate its power." His brow deepened, and Pierce saw the swirls narrow into needle-thin threads.

*Not unlike the ones I make.* Only they were... more, somehow. The finer they got, the brighter they burned. "Quick. Throw me that blue book. It's outdated, anyway."

*Ethics in the Dark Arts.* Pierce grabbed it from the table and tossed it to the Exalted.

The Exalted held his arms out, catching the book in the threads of his flames. They sliced through cloth and paper like butter upon impact. For a wild moment, it rained pages. "If you condense the energy enough, your Fire will have the same effect as a blade. Better, even. You'll have the chance to melt your opponent's insides."

*Huh.* Pierce wondered why he'd never thought of that. Until now, his threads had been harmless, mostly used to take his mind somewhere else in unpleasant situations. He never thought they could cause much damage that way.

Eagerly, he cast a single flame between his palms and focused its energy like the Exalted had shown him. That part was easy, but creating one long thread was more difficult than he thought. The Fire wobbled the thinner it got, threatened to break past his palms, but he pretended it was like gripping the handle of a shovel. He had dug enough graves to keep his wrists steady. No one had ever told him to be quick about it, but the longer he took, the longer he had to look at the bodies of his dead friends. Day and night he used to dig, like something had filled his muscles with divine strength. Just like now.

Pierce had gotten his flame down to the width of a needle, but it was inconsistent. Sometimes it flared back to its original size, but he didn't mind. He had an idea.

Pierce dropped his left hand, but before the connection could break, he swirled his fingers around his right wrist. The flame extended into serpent-like bands, wrapping themselves around his arm like a hilt. He held the blade in front of his face and admired its glow. For effect, he added extra tongues to the blade, making it look serrated on both sides. But why stop there?

Pierce extended the tip until the blade was longer than he was.

*"Good,"* said the Exalted. His tone didn't change, but Pierce could tell he was pleased. It was a wonderful feeling. Danea had left him alone so often that he often forgot what it was like being useful. Really useful. As in, preventing dead bodies, not burying them.

"Now test it." The Exalted threw an apple in the air, and Pierce whisked his Fire-blade forward. It sliced through the apple, sending both halves soaring in different directions.

The Exalted nodded in approval. "You see?" he asked. "Now you have a blade of immense power at your fingertips. One that needs no sharpening. And it weighs *nothing.*" He snapped his fingers, and the blue sky disappeared around them.

Pierce's glory was short-lived as the walls of the cave came crashing in all around him. The rush of panic forced him to his knees. "I… I'm sorry… I can't…" He shook his head. *"Showing weakness is human, little brother,"* his sister had always told him, *"but admitting it may be your last mistake."* He steadied his breath before he continued. *Deflect with humor.* "How… how can you stay… stay here all day?"

"You mean instead of finding glory in the sun?" The Exalted closed his eyes and smiled. "I'm afraid warmth and sunshine aren't really my flavor."

"But isn't… being outside… out on the field… with your daughter?"

The Exalted jolted forward like Pierce had just interrupted his nap. "My daughter?"

His reaction was so sudden that Pierce wondered if he'd said something wrong. "Yes?"

This time, the Exalted's laugh was genuine. "My *daughter* can take care of herself," he said as he took his seat. The waves of his robes spilled over the armrests, which made it look like he was leaking ink. "She knows exactly how to hit the Royals where it hurts. Some would say she was born for this."

"What?" Pierce gasped, half in shock, half for air. "She's out there fighting?"

"Indeed. Probably with your sister, now that I think about it." The Exalted ignored Pierce's sputtering. "And I'm watching over her camp while she's away."

*One, two... one, two...* "My sister..."

The Exalted waved a hand dismissively. "Go on, my boy. I am pleased with your progress, but I have other matters to attend to."

*Gladly.* Pierce wanted nothing more than to see the sky again. The real sky. He stumbled towards the entrance, not even muttering goodbye to Badge at the doorway. "Watch it, kid!" he heard behind him.

*Sweet, sweet freedom.* The outside air tasted so good, Pierce thought he would cry. He threw himself on the ground, gasping like a fish out of water, and the others in the camp did what they did best—ignored him. When he finally caught his breath, he rose and dusted bits of earth and pebbles from his shirt. Straightened his collar. Good as new.

As was his wont, Pierce took a quick stroll around the perimeter before dinner. He liked saying hello to the patrolling guards, though they probably considered him more of a nuisance than anything else. The Exalted had forbidden Pierce from leaving the camp, so everyone else did the heavy lifting. And hunting. And water retrieval.

Pierce made a mental note to talk to the Exalted about that— such treatment was not good for team morale—but that was before he saw the blood leading to his tent.

Instinctively, he cast a small blade of Fire and snapped the flames around his wrist like a hilt. He was armed now. *I can melt their insides,* he reminded himself, forcing himself to be brave. No matter what, he had the upper hand. He took a deep breath and threw open the flap of his tent.

He dropped his element hand when he saw the source of the red trail. "Danea!" The Fire disappeared from his hands as he ran to his sister.

"Hey, kid," she said as blood gushed through her fingers. Three arrows were lodged in her, even in the shoulder that was already shattered. He did not know how she was still breathing. "They... they torched our camps. The Royals... their general... they're doubling down... we're no match for her. Gods, we're no match for her."

"WHAT? We need to—"

"Shh... keep your voice down. I hid here... so they... wouldn't find me." She groaned, and it took Pierce all his willpower not to sob openly. His mind was already flaring in different directions, wondering where to take her. *Who can help us? Who?* He could only think of one person.

"Listen," said Danea softly. "There's something I need you to do."

"ARE YOU CRAZY? WE NEED TO SEE THE EXALTED."

"NO!" Danea may have been bleeding, but she still had enough energy to smack him with her good arm. "Listen. The *only* reason we're here is because he's the only one who can help you control your Fire. I knew he was... a wicked man... but his *daughter* is not who she seems. You need to... you need to join the Royals *now.*"

"WHAT? I'M NOT DOING THAT!"

"We talked about this. It's the only way to beat them." In a defiant bout of fury, Danea screamed against the death that was taking her. Even for the Spears, it was difficult to ignore, and they began crowding around the tent. Someone had gone to get help, but their shouting already faded into the background.

"Stay with me," Pierce begged as he grasped her hand.

"Trust no one, little brother." And just like that, the fire in her auburn eyes burned out.

# 4

## GLASGÉRIOS
# ICE REALM

Decker woke up and wondered why he was feeling so comfortable. The sheets felt crisp and gentle against his arms. The walls surrounding him were paved in stone, with shadows that grew and shrank in the candlelight. *Where am I?* He lay there for a few moments, trying to remember if he was in trouble. The cane they made him use lay on the floor, just out of reach.

It hit him hard when he hoisted himself up against the headboard. Something sharp hammered behind his eyes, reminding him of his younger days. He pressed a hand to his chest and felt bandages. *Ah, yes. There was that.* Elayne had worked wonders on him, considering he was almost speared in the heart. He barely felt a thing after that, but they insisted on keeping him stowed away like an invalid. *Was my room always this nice, though?*

Then he remembered. The nightbloom had made him groggy—that mixed in with whatever the night-shift graces were experimenting with—but he vaguely recalled Merc playing the best hand of his life, recalled the cheers... drinks were bought... more drinks... and then nothing.

It had been a while since he'd had the fog. He remembered swearing off drinks after the last time, but now something was sloshing back and forth between his ears. *I am made of ale.* When he looked down, he even saw it seep through his bandages. *I don't remember it being red.*

"Is anyone there?" he shouted. Something was wrong. More wrong than usual. His heart was pounding abnormally fast, and his head throbbed with each heartbeat.

Elayne burst in, trailed by two night-shift graces who spoke no Sinthean. Indignantly, he pulled the blankets closer to his chest. The bandages around his ribs were the only thing he was wearing, and he didn't want Elayne to see how much he'd enjoyed the good life on the *Smuggler. Then again,* he thought, relaxing his grip. *She's already seen me.* He really needed to stop drinking with Merc.

But Elayne's mind seemed to be elsewhere. She gave commands in perfect Glasgérian—better than his—and the graces fanned out and surrounded him on both sides. With clockwork timing, they placed a hand on his shoulder and shoved until he was lying back down. Decker screamed as his lungs threatened to burst from his chest. The graces flung the covers to the floor. One pulled a scalpel from her apron pocket.

"What's happening?" Decker asked.

"Your wound is fine." Elayne kept her voice steady, but she avoided his eyes. The graces drew back and retreated to the foot of his bed as she approached. *She owns them,* he realized as she hovered a hand over his chest and whispered a few words under her breath. Waited.

A sharp coldness pierced through his ribs and spread outward, numbing the pain. He felt his insides pull from his body. Blue-white drops rose from his chest and swirled around her hand like stars. *So that's what my elements look like.* They circled once, twice around her wrist before they returned to him. Decker had never seen anything like it before. Suddenly, he felt ashamed.

*This is what she spent her life studying. Doing.* His heart slowed as he felt himself relax. *And I missed all of it.*

"I couldn't extract the Ice," she said softly. "Whenever I tried, it kept ripping your wounds back open. So I closed the wound, but…"

"But it's still in me?"

She dropped her gaze. "You were…" She cleared her throat and straightened. Turned to the graces. *"Segnes,"* she said. They bowed in silence and took their leave.

"Now I'm really scared," joked Decker, hoping he wouldn't have a reason to be. He reached for her hand. "What is it?"

"You were dead," she said, drawing it back. "You died in Way-farer's Barrow."

If Decker had control of his heart, it would have stopped. "What do you mean? You healed me. You…"

"I did what I could," she said, "but not even the best healers can stop you from dying. Not even if I tore all the magic from the earth. And I would have."

Decker let her words sink into his memory. It had been a while since anyone cared about him like that. It was nice. "I'm alive because of you," he said. "I…"

"Elements *want* to stay alive. When I tried to remove the Ice, your heart stopped. The only way you survived is because it bound itself to your blood."

"I've always had Ice in my blood."

"Yes, but this is different. This is…" She lifted her gaze, and fear graced her features. "That kid attacked you with powerful Ice. I don't know how, but it latched onto you. If I try to remove it, you'll… you'll die. Again."

Decker sat back up and leaned forward. Put his hand to his chest. "Is that why my heart feels like it's going to explode?"

"Your body just needs to get used to it."

"Does that mean I can cast it now?" Decker smiled, but it was mostly for her sake. Might as well find some fun in such bleak times.

Before she could react, Merc threw open the door and strutted in. His clothes looked new and freshly pressed, and his cloak looked made of velvet. *Velvet.* The confidence in his eyes burned fierce but faded fast when he saw Elayne. "Ahh, hey..."

But Elayne was having none of it. "YOU TOOK HIM OUT LAST NIGHT?" She lifted Decker's cane and pointed it at Merc like a sword as he cowered under her gaze.

"Just for a little bit!" said Merc, throwing his hands in front of his face. "Just a bit of a stroll through the tavern..." He threw Decker a desperate glance. *Help me,* it said.

"You combed your hair?" Decker frowned and pointed at Merc's head. His hair was slicked back and neatly brushed over, fire-colored swirls that arched perfectly over an angled face. Decker blinked the surprise out of his eyes. "Are... are your eyebrows thinner?"

"It was just a quick drink!" Merc bellowed, avoiding Elayne's cane. "And there's no time—" He ducked. "Wolff wants to see us *immediately.* All of us."

Elayne lowered her cane, and even Decker blinked, surprised. After Elayne, Wolff had been the most adamant about keeping him in the infirmary. It must have been something big if Decker's presence was warranted. In *public.* "What, like in the main cavern?" he asked.

Elayne and Merc looked at him with a shock that made him forget Merc's eyebrows. "Does he not know?" Elayne asked Merc incredulously. "What were you *doing* last night?"

"What?" Decker threw a pillow at them. "Where's Wolff?"

"Ahh..." Merc scratched the back of his head and stared at the ground. His admission of guilt. "He, ahh... wants to see us in the throne room."

"As in, the *castle?*" Decker was finding it hard to close his mouth. How long had he been out? "He wants us to see him in the Glasgérian *castle?*"

"No," said Merc. He shrugged and let his arms fall to the side. "Mate, we're already *in* the castle."

***

*Well, that explains the first-class rooms.*

Decker hobbled uneasily next to Merc and Elayne as they passed into the black-stoned wings of the castle. The walls were high and foreboding, gray swirls embedded in dark marble. They were simple in form but masterfully executed. The cooperation of builders who burned in daylight had ensured the creation of something unique.

But the Scrolls painted a bleaker history. Back then, it had been common practice to set prisoners loose in the castle for domerics-in-training to hunt in darkness. Their walls were built to reflect even the slightest of sounds, and domerics needed to see in the shadows. Each time Decker's cane hit the ground, it echoed off the sides and doubled back, loud as a cannonball.

The Servant leading them through the corridor was draped in a robe that hid everything save for long, white strands of hair. He stopped in front of a doorway sealed in iron and turned to Elayne.

"Are you ready?" he rasped in Glasgérian, revealing white eyes that saw everything.

Decker made sure the wolf clasps of his cloak were properly visible. Merc cleared his throat as he lifted his hood. Even Elayne took a few deep breaths, but out of all of them, she had the least to worry about. Healers were held in high regard no matter where they went, and her soft blue robes commanded respect in the castle. Even the Servant spoke only to her, ignoring Decker and Merc completely. She nodded.

"As you wish." The Servant bowed and opened the door.

Into another world. Decker's eyes felt like they were ambushed by spears. A column of light poured in through a hole in the ceiling. There was no way of gauging the size of the throne room; bright as it was, the light ended so sharply that the surrounding darkness could have been cut with a compass.

He blinked, but the brightness only increased in intensity. *How long has it been since I've seen daylight?* It set off the fury of a thousand hammers in his head, and they took turns pounding, pounding, pounding. It was enough to make the shadows around him swirl.

He felt Elayne edge closer, and Merc closed the distance between them. "My eyes are playing tricks on me," Merc muttered, but his whispers amplified tenfold in the throne room.

As Decker's eyes adjusted, he saw Wolff and Sirian seated at the long table. Wolff rose at the sound of Merc's voice. "Hurry up," he said. He looked uneasy, but Sirian sat calmly. Poised.

*Ah,* Decker remembered. *The only one who feels home in the shadows.*

Curiosity burned more holes in his heart as he approached the table, and he took his seat across from them. "Wolff. What's going on?" Decker tried to keep his whispers as soft as possible, but he knew it was stupid. The walls revealed everything.

"We'll talk later. Now sit down and shut up, all of you." He nodded towards the front of the hall, and Decker kicked Merc under the table to stop him from yelling out. "We are in the presence of the queen's interpreter."

Decker hadn't even seen her. The woman wore the same black-scaled armor as a domeric, but it was a strange choice of outfit for her profession. In any proceeding, it was considered sacrilege to attack the interpreter, so they often showed up in formal gowns and cloaks. Diplomacy was their armor—not actual armor. *Then again...* Decker frowned. *She could be a domeric.* Her movements glided in the shadows, just beyond the reach of light.

"My first and second helmsman are here, along with our Healer," said Wolff to the interpreter in Glasgérian. Decker could speak it fluently—he understood it as well as Sinthean—but still had difficulty with formal conjugations. No wonder they needed an interpreter. "Now I urge you to reconsider."

The interpreter translated it to Sinthean with the utmost precision. Her words were heavily accented but flowed with ease. After she spoke, she waited for a response.

"We know what playing safe has done." Another woman's voice. She glided next to the interpreter, and Decker saw that she was also clad in shadowed armor. She *flew* into the throne room, but something else struck fear into his failing heart. *I didn't hear her at all.*

Even when she landed, she made no sound, but her voice was clear and demanded urgency. Silver hair lifted and fell around a gaunt face with eyes that glowed red like wine. It was impossible to tell her age, but she was terrifyingly beautiful—like Tomá had been.

*Is that the queen?* He frowned and glanced at Wolff.

The interpreter translated and glanced in Decker's direction. "The queen's voice is too pure. She never speaks at these proceedings," she said, reading his face. "This is Kerys. She has been keeping us updated on your activities in the Underground."

Wolff cleared his throat uncomfortably. "I've never seen you there, Kerys."

The woman who now stood next to the interpreter threw them a jagged smile of crooked teeth. "I would hang myself in shame if you did," she said. No one said anything else.

The interpreter waited long enough to be courteous before she continued. "Who is the one that's been touched by Ice?"

Decker cleared his throat. "I am," he said, trying not to let his fear show.

"Ah, yes," said Kerys. "Tomá has told me a great deal about you and your... friends." She gave a solemn bow when she said Tomá's name, but when her gaze lifted, cruelty returned. "I see some of them didn't come back with you. A medican. And a young girl."

Decker tried not to notice Merc go pale. *How long has she been keeping tabs on us?* He kept his face impassive, the one thing he learned from playing cards below deck. "A lot of lives were lost," he said, a concealed truth. He heard himself misspeak a formal conjugation and hoped he didn't insult anyone.

The interpreter gave him a diplomatic smile as she translated. Kerys's grin widened in amusement. *Damn. I didn't know I was that rusty.* The interpreter gave another courtesy pause. "Yes, a lot of lives were lost when the King of the Firelands attacked our border. This is an unforgivable breach of the Stalemate, and we must act."

"I urge you to reconsider," Wolff said. "This cannot be solved by more fighting. Glasgérios will not stand a chance. Not even if you forge alliances with Lancistierre and all the mages of Divisorya."

*Good luck with that,* thought Decker. Divisoryans lived in the floating city for a reason. They wanted nothing to do with squabbles on land.

"One dragon was enough," the interpreter continued. "But two? We cannot allow this thing to happen." She glanced behind her and listened to something Decker could not hear. "Are you certain?" she asked. "Very well." She turned her gaze forward and nodded. The curtains around the opening in the ceiling drew back, and the column of light widened. The shadows behind the interpreter receded.

Decker kicked himself to keep from yelling out.

The figure behind her could have been a statue. Their queen looked like she had been carved into her throne, which looked forged from glass. Her dress spilled outwards in waves of white, and from the circlet of her crown sprouted crystals that resembled sharp branches. But the cold did not stop there. Her face looked like an empty wound out of which all the blood had been drained.

And then it started speaking.

*"Min vras."* Two words that silenced the throne room like a knife to the throat. He felt his heartbeat quicken out of control. *Damn it.* He pressed a hand to his chest. *Not now.* He felt the corners of his vision tremble, and another shadow rippled across the darkness around him.

The queen dismissed the interpreter with a single wave of her hand. "No matter," she said, but her tone was delicate like a fine blade. "There is a second Summoner out there. *A Sint'mys.* And not one of *them.*"

*We're fucked,* thought Decker when he heard the daggers in her voice. Word traveled fast. Not surprising in a city of messengers.

"And you," she continued, addressing Wolff. "Why should I trust the words of a man who abandoned his own kind to join thieves and plunderers in the skies?"

If Wolff felt affronted, he hid it well. It was not the first time he had been accused of treason. Decker had lost track over the years.

"Please reconsider," Wolff repeated firmly. "Lancistierre is wrought with civil strife, and even if they agreed to ally, you wouldn't have the numbers to go against the Firelands."

Once again, the darkness around them wavered, and Decker tried to control his stupid heart. But when he looked closer, he was surprised it didn't stop completely. The throne room was not shrouded in darkness, but in shadows. As in, *shadows.* Flaking apart layer upon layer until Decker understood why his companions looked so terrified.

Wolff's speech was swallowed by a sudden crash. Darkness had donned a human form. *Deception,* Decker recalled. *That was their strength.* Wolff had once said that shadow guards may wander, but they were always, inevitably, where they needed to be.

He would never forget it again.

"My queen." He heard Wolff's voice. "What have you done?"

Decker would have wept openly had he not been so captivated by the sight that unfolded before his eyes. *There must be... hundreds of them.* Hundreds of domerics trained since birth to see with their ears. And whether by the Fates or the gods or the *domeras,* they had returned. Them and a hundred of their falcons, each flying around the column of light.

"You see?" Sirian rose from his seat and pointed at the falcons. "It's the will of the *domeras,*" he said as Wolff tried in vain to pull him back down. *"Vra vinsaehras doméras."*

His words were followed by a hundred and more voices, the only sound they made. *"Vra vinsaehras doméras!"*

"A shadow cannot fall alone," said the queen's interpreter, "for all darkness falls as one. *Vra vinsaehras doméras.*"

"Vra vinsaehras doméras!" the shadows repeated, and their voices echoed off the walls. The tension tightened between them.

Decker did not need telling twice to know what that meant. There was no cage for this darkness, no light that could beat it back.

The shadows had risen.

# 5

## RED CITADEL
# FIRE REALM

Morian knew of the Northern dragon long before the messengers came.

Nothing else explained the state of the world otherwise. A wound had torn across the skies and bled for days. Trees lashed about in a violent frenzy. The commonfolk flocked to the temples, repenting their sins.

"Greaven, why don't you look happier?" he demanded when he noticed his bodyguard huddled in the shadows. Morian hated it when he did that. Greaven was already a stone slab of black; it was hard enough finding him when he needed him. Yet there he was, shoulders hunched forward, Morian's personal raincloud.

Morian shrugged it off. *The curiosities of man are of supreme indifference in the face of greatness,* he thought. *The excitement must have dulled his senses.*

*But it's a rogue Summoner. A threat to the kingdom.*

*No. We just need to find him before the Red Spears do.*

*What if he is already one of them?*

*We still have one.*

*One.*

*Marvelous.*

*But dangerous.*

*And where do her loyalties lie?*

*Where do her loyalties lie?*

Morian felt his blood boil beneath the surface. Sometimes the voices came without warning, and only rarely did they agree. He hated fighting with himself.

The Spades had returned days ago, grimy and sweating, but none of them had reported even seeing the Second Summoner. Valerya hadn't been particularly talkative either, uttering a quick "your Highness" before heading to her chambers. No one had the stomach to reply when she was in that mood, especially after a long journey. He often allowed her this lapse in manners.

It was the first time Morian had reached out to the scholars of the Scarlet Cities of his own accord. He had last seen them as a child, back when they were researching day and night for a cure to the mystery illness that had swept the Firelands. His mother's death had been the second and last time they would fail him.

To be fair, no one had expected them to save his sister. Not even the best of Healers could heal a broken neck. *Mystery illness, indeed.* At least, that's what they had told everyone, but he was old enough to understand what happened. What really happened.

*Oh, well.* He shrugged. No use dwelling on the past.

Since then, the scholars had been useless to him, but these were different times. Now all students who passed their novice exams, young and old, were pouring into libraries all over the capital. Who could this Second Summoner be? There were many theories but no substance. Still, the scholars kept researching, eager to crawl their way back into his good graces.

*Of course it had to be the Northern dragon.* He sighed. This wasn't going to be easy. There were dozens of clans that breathed life into the North, and combing through them would take at least another couple of centuries. Northerners sprang from the ground like weeds.

Morian suddenly found himself with much to ask of that Spade who constantly trailed behind the General, but Vilas or Vargen or whatever his name was didn't return with the others. Shame, really. If the Spade had indeed been connected, as the running theory went, he would have at least served some purpose at the Citadel. Leave it to the Northerners to vanish once they became useful.

"Greaven?" he called after a moment of silence, forgetting yet again that Greaven was standing sentinel in the corner. "Please have our General summoned to my chambers."

"Yes, your Highness," said Greaven dutifully.

Morian sighed as the man took his leave. In truth, Greaven and Valerya could be the best of friends. They would simply sit there like slabs of stone, sharing the same words that boulders did. A pity they didn't like each other, really.

A knock at the door interrupted his thoughts, and remorse instantly gave way to delight. "Come in!" he shouted, straightening. When he stood tall, they were of a height, and he always wanted to show her his best side. Now that there was another Summoner in their midst, he needed to keep her close.

"Your Highness," said the General. No smile, no bow, nothing. She gave him *nothing.*

Morian forgave her this lapse of judgment. He turned as though he hadn't expected to see her there. "A pleasant surprise." He cast a smile to mask his mood, but his eyes immediately took in her lack of armor. Not like she looked much smaller without it. Even in plainclothes, she outmatched him in size. He motioned to the chair across the table. "Do have a seat."

Greaven must have woken her up. She looked only marginally resentful when she took her seat, but not even the most charitable of bards would call her gracious.

"Tell me about the other dragon, Valerya," he said. *Surely she would give me that, at least.* "I've been *dying* to hear it from you."

Valerya frowned, charming as ever. "It was white. I couldn't see who summoned it, only that it must have been accidental." She leaned back. "Probably triggered by heartfire."

*Heartfire.* That first, uncontrollable burst of Fire that was often likened to losing one's maidenhood. It was an expression that often came from the backwoods, and he was certain she was using it just to annoy him. "Do you remember your first... heartfire?"

She almost smiled. "I set a wardrobe on fire."

Morian laughed, endeared. "I set fire to my wet nurse's gown," he said, shrugging off the memory. "I admit, I expected a livelier description." He took a seat across the table and waited for a response. *Nothing.* Shifting topics was difficult when he was the only one talking. "The Northern dragon," he said after a courtesy pause. "You know, I couldn't help but notice that one of your Spades did not return. Where is he?"

He had been hoping for even the slightest trace of surprise, but Valerya's face remained impassive. Tired folds creased around stone-colored eyes. "I ordered him to look for the Summoner. I imagine he's still looking."

Morian ignored the quip. Sharing words with her was like being drawn and quartered. "I also notice that Genovel has been left spectacularly unburned."

"There were more pressing matters at hand... your *Highness,*" she said. "When your soldiers broke away from camp, I assumed they were deserters."

Morian cursed to himself. Perhaps sending them over had been for the best. If anything, at least it rid the Realm of their incompetence. Had the Blood Queen been able to train jackals and equip them in armor, he would have preferred them to the dregs dangling at the bottom of the Swordsworn ladder. Still, he had expected them to be able to besiege a group of farmers.

*Well. The other side did have a dragon.*

"How's your shoulder?" he asked instead.

"Intact."

"Valerya," said Morian curtly, deciding this dance was not for her. He stood and walked over to her end of the table. Leaned in. "You wouldn't lie to me, would you?"

Valerya's gaze was unfaltering. "Your Highness."

Anger welled inside him, but a playful smile returned to his lips. "Forgive me," he said, feigning empathy. "I often forget how tiring it must be for you, ordering people around day and night. But you know… there *is* a way to make it all end."

The torch-fire lighting the chambers burned low, cowering from their moods.

Morian closed his eyes and tried to think calming thoughts. Anyone else in the Realm would have been ecstatic at the prospect of ruling by his side, and he would have given her everything. The scars didn't bother him, and he could overlook her unsavory manners. Her face may not have been delicate or soft, but it had strength. And as relentless as she was on the battlefield, he often found himself wondering if she loved just as fiercely.

If anything, their alliance would put to rest those repulsive rumors once and for all.

"Will that be all, your Highness?" she asked.

Unwillingly, events from his birthday flashed through his mind. "Look at me going on and on. You must be exhausted," he said, allowing mirth to lift his tone. "I trust you will return to me first thing in the morning." He cleared his throat, deciding he had all the answers he needed. "Good night, Valerya."

She rose. "Your Highness," she said, bowing.

"Wish me a good night, General," said Morian, making his way back to the window. "Now that there's another Summoner in our midst, we need all the well wishes we can get."

Valerya frowned. "Good... *night*. Your Highness," she said.

"Call me Morian."

*"Morian,"* she said sharply. He pitied anyone who got in her way in the corridors.

"Greaven!" he called when the General took her leave, knocking Greaven back as she passed. Two boulders, speaking.

Greaven entered silently and shut the door behind him.

Morian drew in a deep breath and straightened. "Have our General followed," he said. "Make sure you note every move she makes, every falcon she sends. She does not leave her chambers without me knowing. And report to me if she meets with anyone. Is that understood?"

*And if she is sharing her bed with anyone. It will end badly, for the other.* He smiled. *Just like the last time.* "And this time, make sure she doesn't find our man."

Morian cringed when he remembered what happened to their last spy. Valerya did nothing to him, instead setting him loose in the Spade's quarters. Her men found a more appropriate punishment for him.

"Yes, your Highness," said Greaven and bowed.

And when Morian heard the doors open and close for the last time, he sighed, suddenly feeling lonely. *Oh Valerya,* he thought ruefully. *Why do you lie to me so?*

# 6

## RED CITADEL
# FIRE REALM

I t was the fifth time that night that Gryff found himself falling asleep over piles of old books and manuscripts. One of them was the archemage's journal. Gryff had been avoiding the last pages, savoring the last moments with the only friend he had left at the Citadel.

The past few weeks had drained the color from his life, but it sharpened his focus. All he did was eat and train, even seeking guidance from Valerya's personal medican, Aela. Different scholars swore by different diets, but if his goal was strength, Valerya's medican was probably his best bet. All he had to do was take recipes to the kitchens, and the cook would prepare whatever Aela had written up for him. Sometimes it paid to be Valerya's scribe.

Most times, it didn't. On the nights Valerya took over his training, she broke him, and no recipe in existence—not even with Aela's magic—could save him.

Gryff closed his eyes. The Citadel felt vast and lonely now that he had no purpose. At least before, he had Valk, and out there, he'd had Dove. Dove, who he stupidly thought had been looking for him the entire time. *She sure found a replacement fast.*

He set the book aside and pulled the next one closer—a beast of a tome on Northern lineages. He flipped through the pages and sighed. They really were one of the largest families in the Realm, and every pairing seemed to have at least five children. But if Dove's next move was to claim a Northern name, he wanted to know which ones were available. Especially in Valk's family.

*She'll be adopted into one of the most powerful families in the Realm.* He laughed when he tried to imagine Dove married to some Northern lordling, but the thought was more painful than sun-born wounds. Instead of a lordling, instead of *Gryff,* even, she had chosen…

Him.

The entire time he was thinking of her, training at the Citadel so he could be at least half the man she deserved when their paths crossed, she was… she was…

*What does he have that I don't?* So what if the blue-cloaked Falcon was tall, handsome, and brave?

He shook his head as he went through the names. There was one that seemed likely, and for her sake the most strategic. *Avriel,* he read, leaning against the bookshelf. It was a pretty name, but he couldn't find himself warming to it.

A knock at the door made him drop the book in surprise. The volume cracked and split in two, sending pages scattering in every direction.

Gryff cursed. If this chaos ever ended, on his life, he would organize and restore all the books in Valerya's tower. He glanced warily at the door. At least it wasn't Morian or the General; one knocked in song, and the other didn't knock at all. He felt a pang of regret when he realized that it wasn't Valk, either, nor was it likely to be in the near future.

Another thing he had lost to Dove.

Gryff decided he'd had enough of dragons and dreams for one night. He left the pile of papers on the ground and pulled on his helm as he made his way to the door.

The voice betrayed the figure in the shadows before her fire-red hair did. "Gryff!" it shouted. It was enough to lift his mood. At least someone was happy to see him.

*Those dimples,* he thought when Lyra darted past him. They dented the sides of her face as her eyes lit up. "I didn't know if you were in your chambers, but I thought I'd stop by for a bit and see how you were doing. But I understand if you're tired. I've heard all about the... the dragons. And, well..." She stopped herself and looked at him expectantly.

*She looks well.* Without the bruises that outlined her cheekbones, she looked happy, more like the girl he had met when he and Valk rode into the capital for the first time.

"Um," said Gryff awkwardly, reddening inside his helm. "Hi, Lyra."

Lyra brightened and threw him a playful glance over her shoulder before heading deeper into the library.

"How are you?" he asked, finding his courage.

"Better than ever," she said, beaming. "Our General let me sleep in Valk's chambers while you were gone, so I've been making friends and hearing all *sorts* of rumors and gossip." She grinned. Her new life suited her well. "Did you know Valk keeps toy bears by his bedside table? There are more than a few rumors going on about him and..." She caught herself. "Aahhh. I'm talking too much again."

"No, no," said Gryff hastily, placing his hand on the door handle. The last thing he wanted was for her to leave him alone with his thoughts. He frowned as her words sank in. "Valk collects toy bears?" His frown deepened. "Our General lets you sleep in his quarters?"

Lyra grinned. Clearly, she and Gryff had gotten to know very different people. Perhaps the General had more patience for the daughters of blacksmiths. Perhaps Valk felt a natural urge to protect small, fire-haired maidens. Not so surprising then, after all.

"How are you?" Lyra asked, breaking the painful silence that followed.

"I'm... well, I'm good."

"That's good." She let her gaze drop.

*Come on, Gryff,* he thought to himself. *You're not that hopeless, are you?*

"What are you doing?" She brushed past him. "Reading about dragons?" She laughed when she saw his helm jerk upwards in surprise. "Everyone forgets my father is the former swordsmaster of the Citadel. Of course I can read. And I've read all about the Northern dragon. Everyone has by now."

"Sorry," said Gryff, embarrassed. Reading may not have been commonplace in Myrne, but the capital was a different story. Even stonemasons could read basic words and numbers, at least enough to write and decipher their own ledgers. "Did you now?"

"Its last known Summoner was Baley the Kind. Rhysar has a history of choosing kindhearted masters. I wonder what our new Summoner is like."

Gryff shrugged. Pretended. "Kindhearted, I suppose," he said absently.

Lyra squinted as she tried to see through the slit of his helm. "Why are you still wearing that thing? I mean, I'm flattered you like it and all, but I imagine it's uncomfortable indoors..."

*Shit,* thought Gryff as Lyra approached. Mischief gleamed

underneath the guise of good faith. There was no escape. It would have been weird to just leave her there.

"C'mon," she teased. "What've you got to hide? I promise I won't laugh."

Gryff suddenly felt like a novice dancer who had suddenly forgotten all his steps. Her smile lost its playfulness, and she dropped her gaze again. "Sorry," she said. "I'll stop distracting you from your reading."

Feeling a sudden burst of renewed confidence, Gryff grabbed her arm. Not to be outdone, Lyra's hands moved up to his helm, and her fingers worked furiously to unfasten his visor. Instinctively, Gryff brought his hands up to stop her, but his fingers rested on hers.

*Don't,* he wanted to say, but he was tired of hiding. Aside from the General and Valk, no one else at the Citadel even knew what he looked like. He wasn't even sure *Morian* knew.

Gryff held his breath when Lyra pulled off his helm, and her eyes widened when she saw wounds that no Fireborne could possibly bear—the burns, the sun-born scars etched onto skin paler than parchment. But where he expected fear and disgust, he found none.

"Who did that?" she asked softly, tracing the lines of his burns with her fingers.

Gryff fell silent. *Daylight. Torch-fire.* He had already forgotten which one.

"So you're a… you're one of them." Her eyes shot up to his hair, and her gaze lingered in awe. "You have the… blackest hair I've ever seen."

Gryff laughed, relieved. Her eyes burned a shade of auburn—fierce, like Dove's, but they held no secrets. He leaned in and kissed her, awkwardly at first, until he found a sort of rhythm to it. It started out cold and wet, and he wondered if he was doing it right until he felt the warmth spread to his fingertips.

*Was this how she did it?*

Lyra winced, bringing him back to the urgency of the moment. "*Gryff.*"

"Oh," said Gryff. He was gripping her arm more forcefully than he had intended. In other, perhaps less intimate situations, she would have punched him in the face, but she looked afraid. Not in the way maidens were said to be on their wedding night—at least, from what little Gryff had heard about them—but *frightened.*

Gryff closed his eyes, suddenly angry with himself. "I'm sorry, Lyra," he said softly, releasing her. She sat at the edge of his bed, and he took the opposite end. Before long, they found themselves talking. Laughing. *Joking.*

They talked until the candles burned out, until weariness slurred their words and sleep finally intervened. And when Gryff found her curled up next to him, their heartbeats aligning in the most captivating of ways, he decided the rest of the world—the gods and Fates and all their dragons combined, and *Avriel* most of all—could wait for once.

# 7

## BRETHREN WASTES
# FIRE REALM

Dove wondered if she had slept through another war. Not long ago, she had been looking for her brother and fighting the Swordsworn at Wayfarer's Barrow. Thornbeard, the stout beast of a man riding in front of her, had cleaved countless assailants in two with his battle-axe, and even Bard had taken no prisoners. The Hounds were their *enemy.*

What had happened since then?

She had accidentally waged a dragon war, Gryff had become her enemy, and now she was riding north with the General's closest confidante, cushioned awkwardly between his arms. Had she joined the side of the Hounds without knowing it? Gods, had *Bard?*

She looked over the Spade's shoulder and scowled. She had wanted to ride with Bard, but he insisted on taking his pony, which was already struggling under all the weight. Thornbeard and his sons formed the head and tail of the convoy, and for the life of her, she could not stomach riding with Artis. Anyone who radiated that much power put her on edge.

No, Valk was fine. The lesser of all evils.

"Are you uncomfortable?" he asked.

*YES,* Dove thought, but she shook her head and turned her attention back to the front. If she ever made it to safety, she swore on her life she would learn how to ride alone. Until then, she did not want to provoke the only people who knew how to navigate the wastelands.

Dove understood at once why no one wanted to travel north without the right company. The Wastes were vast wildlands of untamed possibility, split into craters and shadowed roads that branched off in all directions. Nothing grew there; even the mountains had lost their courage. They looked shriveled and deflated, weathered by years of windstorms.

Valk, at least, looked unfazed. He followed her gaze and chuckled. "Time and time again, clans have tried to settle into the Wastes," he said. Teased. "But survivors claimed the smoke drove them mad, told them to eat each other..."

"You're the worst," Bard bellowed behind them. "Don't listen to him, kid."

"Mm," said Valk curtly.

The Spade was otherwise sullen, a smile as rare as a laugh, and Dove wondered what he and the General even talked about. She had so many questions, and he promised to answer them once they reached Rhysia. What made him leave? What was it like in Rhysia?

What was Valerya like?

*Shut up, Dove.*

But Valk always sensed her curiosity. "Valerya was fond of my brother, you know," he said once, breaking the silence. He must have figured the other Summoner was never far from her thoughts, and she wished she could be less obvious about it. "Not everyone was. Beyond the surface, at least. At first, she wanted nothing to do with me."

Dove glanced at him, surprised. Even now, it was hard imagining Valk and Valerya away from each other. She suspected Valerya was never far from *his* thoughts, either.

Valk smiled to himself. "I was scrawny, sickly, and on my way to being a scholar. But I suppose outcasts find comfort in each other, especially at the Academy." He shrugged. "She helped me become a better swordsman. And I, well..." He laughed. "Without me, she would have failed all her classes. She was always late, and some days, she never showed."

Of all the stories he told, that one stuck. The General was nothing if not disciplined, and it was hard to imagine her as a terrible student. It was almost... endearing.

Dove bolted upright when she heard a clash and felt the Spade's grip tighten around her shoulder. "Careful. It's the Huntsmen," he whispered into her ear. "They're a bit far from home, but they bring the forests with them. It looks like the She-Warrior is training her apprentice."

Her companions steadied their horses to give the Huntsmen a wide berth, but the warriors regarded them with little interest. They were too focused on each other, waiting for the right moment to strike. The forests wavered around them the more her eyes wandered, conjured by the light. A trap for careless travelers.

Dove had seen fights before, but there was no steel between the Huntsmen. It was easy to tell who the She-Warrior was—she moved with the ease of water and earth, and even the air swayed to avoid her path. She picked a branch off the ground and held it away from her as it came to life. Awakened. Green vines snapped twice around her wrist to form the hilt, and once the branch was bound to her, it glowed a deep green. Dove could not help but stare as the She-Warrior condensed the air around her into a solid emerald shield.

Her opponent tried to do the same, but his movements were much clumsier. Dove saw traces of a shield, but its edges were undefined, its color hazy. The barriers between them burst, and the man's shield broke into a fury of blue splinters that vanished in a hiss of smoke. He fell back, and his branch unsnapped from his wrist. Before he could retrieve it, the She-Warrior held up a hand in warning—and turned her golden eyes in Dove's direction.

"Don't listen to her," warned Valk. "Don't talk to her, not even in your mind. Ever." She felt his grip tighten around the hilt of his sword. "They won't harm us as long as we stay away."

Dove blinked. *Then why are you reaching for your sword?*

"Now look at her," he whispered in her ear.

It was hard not to. The She-Warrior wore light armor the color of old bronze, and it rippled in the sun when she moved. She eyed the travelers with suspicion.

"The last guardians of the Blackwood," said the Spade. "The trees bend and break at their command. Do you recognize them? Quickly, now. The trees will vanish once they leave."

Dove squinted, confused. *They look like...*

"You've seen them around the Citadel," he said. "Blackwood trees don't burn." He nodded towards the She-Warrior, who took off her helm. "Now quickly. A'delun will chase us away in a bit, so I want you to see what we're up against."

The She-Warrior was a rock encased in armor, with dark skin and amber eyes that glowed. Her hair was short, like she had sliced it off herself, and its ends were flushed with shades of embers. Dove had never seen that before.

A'delun stared at Dove and pointed the branch in her direction. For a moment, it looked like she wanted to advance, but she stayed where she was.

Valk's grip on Dove's shoulder tightened. "Come on," he said. "We've had a love-hate relationship with them for years. Only their gods know what they really want."

They continued along the Wastes in silence, but the She-War-rior's gaze burned softly in the back of Dove's mind. Even when her entire body ached in hunger, pain, and dizziness rolled into one, they were all she saw when she closed her eyes.

Soon, nightfall swallowed all rays of light, and it was hard not to fall asleep with each blink. "This is as good a place as any," said Valk when they reached a shallow cave. "We've already passed the heart of the wastelands. Danger will not follow us here."

To that, Dove opened her eyes. *Sweeter words have never been spoken,* she thought as Valk released the saddlebags.

\*\*\*

Dove and Bard sat in the cave with Valk and Artis while Thornbeard and his sons scouted the surrounding area. "First lesson, kid. You always, always set up a perimeter first," said Bard. He, Valk, and Thornbeard had drawn straws, and Thornbeard picked the shortest. "Better tired and hungry than dead."

Dove was glad she got to stay in the cave. Artis had cast a faint light above their heads, and it was just enough to stay warm. She huddled closer to Bard, and together they stared at the orb in awe. They must have looked stupid to the Fireborne, who sat on the other side of the cave. *It is still us versus them.* Even in a miserable pit in the middle of nowhere. Except…

*Except now they are trying to convince me I am one of them.*

"Can you do the same?" asked Artis kindly, catching Dove by surprise. No one had ever asked her before. She stared at her hands, recalling the last time she had cast Fire. *Nothing too big,* she thought. *Only a dragon.* Since then, she had not even tried.

The old man laughed. He moved closer and took her hands in his, turning them over until her palms faced up. His face drew into a scowl when he saw the scars on her left hand, not-so-gentle reminders of her time at the Citadel. "Zan, if you will?"

Dove glanced at Bard. She had heard the name before, but it still seemed like an ill fit.

"Alezán," Bard muttered, devastated. "In case you were wondering. Don't let it slip, though." He glanced nervously at Valk, who met his gaze and smirked. "What, like 'Valk' isn't short for anything?"

Valk shrugged. "Valk is old Sinthean for *falcon*. Does *Alezán* mean anything?"

"Defender, I think." Bard shrugged. "Apparently it's a common name in Thoryngald."

"Really?" Valk sat up in interest. "But you're from Divisorya, right?

"Born and raised. But my parents are from the Thunderlands." Bard stretched his arm upwards. A surge of Storm erupted from his hand, wrapping itself around the ball of firelight. Dove watched, enamored, as the elements rotated in the air, casting colored shadows across the walls of the cave. "Go on, kid," he said. "Give it a try."

"I find it helps to think of something you would like to protect," said Valk. "Even if it's just an idea. Do you have anything like that?"

That gave her pause. *It used to be Gryff, but...*

"Hard, isn't it?" said Artis, coming to her rescue. "Zan, what's yours?"

"That's easy. My friends." Bard sprawled out across his sleeping sack. Dove glimpsed a flask under his pillow. He hid it well. "What about you, Hound?"

Valk watched the elements swirl above their heads until Dove could see them in his eyes. "Family." He turned towards her. "What were you thinking of when you summoned Rhysar?"

*I thought you wanted to kill Decker,* she thought sheepishly. She closed her eyes, trying to remember the battle in Wayfarer's Barrow, just when the two beasts collided. She sensed the air around her and commanded it to stillness. Her companions' voices dulled as the air condensed and cracked. Burst.

Silver Fire erupted from her hands, quick and unimpressive, giving way to a wisp of smoke. She tried not to look disappointed, but Artis was already fishing a wooden blade from his satchel. "Light that on fire, dear," he said as he tossed it to the ground. Bard sat up and rubbed the sleep from his eyes.

Dove stretched her arm towards the blade and volleyed another burst of Fire in its direction. The wood burned black as it crackled under white flames.

"Oh, shit," said Bard, tactful as always.

"Now it makes sense," said Valk thoughtfully, rubbing his chin. His curiosity had donned an academic layer. "Grayfire may not be able to burn me," he said, "but it can burn through the Blackwood."

Dove recalled A'delun's eyes on hers, how the She-Warrior held herself back from attacking them. *She knew,* Dove realized. *She knew before I did.*

She could see why Morian was looking for her. The Huntsmen

were the only ones standing between him and the North, and she was the only one who could destroy their home. She turned over the crisped piece of wood in her fingers as Bard cursed next to her. "All this time, I thought you were a stowaway who'd run off in a caravan," he growled.

Dove blinked, indignant. *I am a stowaway who ran off in a caravan.*

"Of course." Artis shrugged. "Rhysar is the Northern dragon. His flames ruled the North for hundreds of years."

"What about Av... Aviant... Valerya's dragon?" asked Bard.

It grew quiet. Valk and Artis glanced at each other until Valk spoke. "You don't want to know what crimson flames can do," he said softly. "I've only seen her cast them once, but..."

"Another time, perhaps," said Artis darkly. "That's a story for another time."

"Probably for the best." Valk laughed, but there was a nervous edge to it. He cleared his throat. "I should see how Thornbeard is doing."

"I'll join you. I need a bit of fresh air," said Artis, following him out of the cave.

*But I want to know what crimson flames can do,* thought Dove, but as usual, no one noticed. She sighed and leaned her head against Bard's arm, and together they stared at the Storm swirling weakly above them. She reached out a hand and shrouded it in grayfire.

"Would you look at that?" Bard smiled broadly. "Now that's something I've never seen before." He leaned back, taking her with him. *Rude,* she thought. They watched as blue and silver danced across the walls of the cave. When she closed her eyes, she could still see them, filling in the colors of her dreams.

***

The dragon screeched inside her skull, and Dove woke up surrounded by soft sheets and wolf pelts. Gold-threaded tapestries lined the walls. *Another memory?* She brought her hands to her face and saw that they were hers. She felt no pain, no exhaustion, and when she stretched, the aches in her legs were gone.

She was in the Otherworld again.

Dove sat up and looked around. Screamed inside when she saw.

Valerya had been leaning against the wall, looking out the window. "Finally," she said coldly as she turned. Her eyes were dark but spoke of fire. "We need to talk."

# LIFEBRINGER

Screams died fast in the cavern.

The Exalted had ordered the beast's death, but it did not go down without a fight. It was as big as a horse, but its fangs and fire did all the damage. *"It has to be an elemental,"* the Exalted had said. Pierce saw the night-wolf ward off the scouts with flames, and only the immune were left standing. Others were flayed by the creature's teeth, and those who tried to restrain it were rubbed raw by its hide. In the chaos of the moment, no one asked questions.

Pierce couldn't bear it. He looked away, but fire cast the shadow of the beast against the walls. Goats had not been good enough for Danea's cure. A fighter like her needed a wolf among men, so that was exactly what the Exalted demanded. Fortunately, half the camp owed their lives to Danea, so they brought back the biggest night-wolf they could find.

Pierce sat in the corner of the cavern, cradling Danea in his arms. He had given her root of the nightbloom to slow her heart and keep her breathing steady, but the Exalted had already foretold her fate. To change it would require… a risk of sorts.

"Whatever it takes," Pierce had said. But he did not know what his words cost.

After the beast died, it was easy clearing the cavern of people. Most of them left of their own accord, horrified by what they had seen. A few were curious about the Exalted's plan, but they escorted their wounded to safety. Badge was the last to leave. He crawled towards Pierce, strong arms dragging useless legs. "Don't do this." His words were strained but full of urgency by the time his friends caught up to him. Lifted him by the shoulders. "Your sister wouldn't want this. Just let her go, kid," he screamed as they dragged him away. "Just let her go!"

*One, two... one, two...* Pierce brought his hands to his ears until Badge's screaming stopped. He dared a glance over his shoulder and saw the wreckage. Claw marks gashed the stone. Blood grayed and brightened in the wavering torch-fire. Bookshelves were torn asunder. All that was left untouched was the Exalted and his enchanted garden.

"What's... what's happening?" Pierce stammered.

The Exalted regarded his ruined abode with annoyance. He cast a sweeping glance around the cavern and made sure they were alone. When he was satisfied, he took a pinch of herbs from a vial and threw them into a bowl of the beast's blood. It hissed and exploded into purple smoke.

"Quickly, now," he urged, holding out his arm. Pierce didn't know what he wanted, but the Exalted beckoned him closer, this time more impatiently. "Your arm, boy. Don't make me ask again."

"My what?" At that, Pierce felt Danea grab at his elbow. *Of course,* he thought. The dose he had given her would knock out a grown man for days. He had stupidly forgotten that his sister was a different kind of beast. She had only been gone for fifteen minutes, if that.

The Exalted saw her stir and spoke again. "You said you would do anything. Whatever it takes." He stood before the conquered wolf, before the fire, before the purple wisps of smoke, but his voice was as calm and cold as the winter wind. For a moment, Pierce wondered if it was another illusion. No one should look so composed in the face of madness.

Pierce gently set Danea's head on the ground, on the makeshift pillow he had made from his own cloak. He tried to rise, but her hand shot up to stop him.

"What have you done?" She didn't have to see the dead wolf to know what was happening. The smell of its blood, of the smoke, was enough to suspect the worst. "Kill me," she whispered. Urged. "Kill me *now*." Her own strength was leaving her, fading like a slow heartbeat. But for the first time in his life, she would not decide for him. He broke free from her grasp and stumbled towards the Exalted.

"Whatever it takes," the Exalted repeated softly. "You must choose now."

"Whatever it takes," Pierce repeated dumbly. He had barely extended his arm when the Exalted pulled him to the fire, beyond the smoke until he could see nothing at all. Charred ash scratched his throat, and he smelled burning flesh.

*Mine?* he thought wildly but felt no pain. Before he could say anything, he saw the flash of a dagger, saw it graze his arm. For a moment, he felt nothing and sighed in relief.

Then his head exploded in a cacophony of pain. Invisible hands wrapped around his neck and pulled, like something was being ripped from his body. *Whatever it takes,* he reminded himself. *Even if it takes me.* Danea had taken arrows for him his entire life. Whatever comforts he enjoyed were built on her pain and sacrifice.

Pierce grit his teeth until he swore they shattered. Something roared in his ears and flushed his veins with something that felt oddly warm and pleasant, taking the edge off his pain. It was strange feeling so calm when he was being torn apart. *That wasn't so bad after all.*

"Yes. Very good," he heard the Exalted say. "Now we begin."

More screams. This time, they did not fade.

# 8

## RED CITADEL
# FIRE REALM

Gryff felt the back of his cuirass snap shut and tighten. It felt smaller around his waist, and he tried vainly to hide his pride when he caught himself in the mirror. It had been over a year since he first arrived at the Citadel, broken and stammering, but now he looked like a passable soldier: taller, broader, with scars that had dried and settled into his face. Even his voice deepened, and new recruits began calling him "Sir" whenever he walked castle grounds.

"You've gotten bigger since the last set," said Lyra, distracted as she pulled on the straps. "I had to adjust the sides and add more padding underneath the plate…"

"It's smoother than the other one," said Gryff, frowning. "But what about—"

"I don't care how tough those blade-breakers made you look," she snapped. "They're more likely to get you killed than protect you. Only a handful of people can get away with it. Like our General, of course, which is why I always…"

"I understand," said Gryff quickly. As much as he adored Lyra, the girl could hold a conversation with herself for hours. He eyed his reflection, noting the curved edges of his elbow-piece. It flowed over his vambrace when he outstretched his arm. It hadn't taken Lyra long to realize she could best him in a swordfight, and she labored on another set for weeks. "I get why it's rounded. But why is it so *smooth?*"

"Less chance for a blade to get caught on something," she said in disbelief, as though he had just asked what a sword was.

Gryff laughed and glanced at her in admiration. He had often seen her sparring in the courtyard with the Spades. Unlike him, she held her ground against Valerya's elite, and they treated her like their little sister. *Her father probably trained most of them,* he realized.

He smiled as she handed him his helm, glad that she couldn't see him under all the armor—or any part of him, for that matter. Since his own return from Wayfarer's Barrow, she had shared his bed almost every night, sometimes until morning, and just the sight of her warmed his blood. It was hard to concentrate on anything else.

"How does that feel?" she asked, and he turned, surprised.

"The helm, Gryff."

"Oh." He grinned sheepishly. "Much lighter than the other one…"

In truth, it felt exactly the same. It was the rest of his armor that made it easier to move, and it looked close to standard issue. If he didn't know any better, he would have pegged himself as one of them—an idea that had disgusted him once, but now he was grateful. Better to be a Hound than the only outsider on castle grounds. Passing off as one certainly had its benefits.

Lyra glanced to the side, lost in thought. It was subtle, but Gryff caught it through the slit of his helm. "What is it?" he asked.

"What?"

"That look."

"Nothing."

"Lyra."

"Nothing."

*"Lyra."* Gryff pulled off his helm.

She met his gaze willingly, her eyes fierce with determination. "Who's Dove?" she asked, and Gryff felt his heart stop. Dove was never far from his mind, but it was a name he hadn't expected to hear so soon. Especially from Lyra's lips.

"Where did you…?"

"You say her name in your sleep sometimes." Lyra cut him off as though she had rehearsed it. Interrupting would have broken her flow. "And our King calls me that sometimes…" She coughed as she tightened his shoulder guard for the fifth time, suddenly deep in concentration.

If his breastplate hadn't been so tightly fastened, Gryff would have gasped. *So it was her.* He remembered when Valk told him about Morian's former squire. It felt like a lifetime ago, back when he barely survived his training. Back when he would have given anything to see her again. *Valerya was supposed to have her executed.* He frowned. The General did not seem like the type to fail in these matters.

"So… is she…?" Lyra began as she tightened his shoulder guard.

*Only the Summoner of the North.* "She's just some… highborn," he said instead, realizing with unease that he knew exactly how she felt.

"Like me?" asked Lyra, failing not to look like she cared.

"No, just… stop." He put his hand on hers to stop her from

cutting off the circulation in his shoulder. "Dove is... no one. No one you need to worry about." He forced himself to smile. "We grew up together, and I was like a brother to her. But she's gone now."

Lyra's eyes widened, and her hand shot up to her mouth. "Oh," she said, mortified. "I'm so sorry. I didn't know!"

"It's nothing," said Gryff, cursing himself in the mirror. "She's gone." He wrapped his arms around her, and her head rested on his shoulder. "See? There's nothing to worry about. I..." He paused, choosing his words carefully. "There's only you."

Lyra tried to hide a smile, and Gryff felt guilty for veiled truths. He cared for Lyra, but it was nothing compared to how much Dove had meant to him. Or how little he meant to her.

"You're not here anymore," said Lyra softly. "Where are you?"

He blinked. "Right here," he said, snapping himself out of his trance.

"You're not."

Gryff felt sick to his stomach as he imagined Lyra suffering Morian's affections, as Dove must have. "Lyra," he said solemnly. "Why haven't you told your father about...?"

"About what? About... our King?" She dropped her voice to a whisper. "He has a lot to deal with. He can barely walk, and knowing him, he'd try to storm the castle to come get me." Gryff caught the gleam in her eyes, but it faded fast.

"But why...?"

"Why not fight back?" Lyra threw him a not-so-subtle glance, and Gryff felt another twinge of guilt. It was easier accusing others of cowardice, but what about him? Was it not his own village that had been burned to the ground?

*Is it not my own lover being tormented?*

"Has Morian ever…?"

Lyra cleared her throat.

Gryff's face softened. "Sorry," he said as he unfastened his gauntlet, twirling a lock of her hair in his fingers. But before he could say any more, he heard footsteps outside his door. An executioner's pace, as he had come to know. Even before it drew near, Gryff knew the knock would never come.

Lyra reddened as she pulled away and threw him a playful grin over her shoulder. She dropped to one knee when the door opened, and Gryff did the same.

"Rise." The General frowned when she saw Lyra. They had returned over a fortnight ago, but Gryff had barely seen her on castle grounds. It was strange seeing her without Valk, but he suspected that she, too, was burdened by his absence. Instead of Valk, she cycled through the rest of the Spades. He had glimpsed Diebold on occasion, carrying out Valk's old tasks, and the next day, he would see Skandar or Weyan or Stane. Even *Chuckles,* whose true name Gryff still didn't know.

The General turned to Lyra. "Leave us," she said.

"Yes, Ma'am!" Lyra beamed as she scuttled past her. "Oh hi, Chuckles!" she exclaimed before the door shut behind her. Gryff could hear his weird laughter fading, fading, fading, along with his confidence.

Gryff got to his feet, but before he could open his mouth, she cut him off.

"You must do something for me," said the General. Gryff blinked in surprise. Outside of training, she had only given him one command since their return from Wayfarer's Barrow: *do not speak of Wayfarer's Barrow.* His presence was otherwise, for the most part, ignored.

And now here she was in his chambers, the Guardian of the Realm, looking as uncomfortable as he did. She strode to the window and glanced outside as if expecting to find someone scaling the walls. She turned and handed him a piece of parchment, rolled up and tied neatly with string. "You must deliver a message to the Second Summoner for me."

"The Summoner," repeated Gryff. "My General…"

But Valerya saw no need for pleasantries. "Use the peregrine at the top of the falconry. It's mine." She closed the window. "It recognizes my seal."

"Where should I send…?"

"It knows how to find Valk."

Gryff took the message carefully as though it would burst into flames at his touch. Curiosity burned in his mind with the same intensity. It took him all the willpower he had not to ask what was in it. "Should I go now?" he asked, tightening his fingers around the parchment. The dragon seal smiled back at him, showed teeth.

"When the night is at its darkest," said the General. She kept her gaze fixed on the sky outside, which darkened with her mood. "No doubt you have questions about your friend."

"I do."

"And no doubt you've figured out her role in all this."

Gryff paused. "I have."

The General stepped away from the window. "I told you about choices," she said coldly. "Answers won't make them any easier."

"But our King… she's been here before," persisted Gryff, "as our King's squire."

"A fun term for it."

"And did you… did you know she was…"

"Would it have made a difference?" She turned, and Gryff was surprised to see how tired she looked. Red veins branched across her eyes, with lids that grew heavy around them.

"But why did you let her...?"

"Are you seriously asking me why a terrified girl sent to her death escaped?"

Gryff nodded, almost hearing himself fall from her favor. It was as though Valk had convinced her to show some semblance of mercy for him, but now that he was gone, so, too, was her patience for Gryff's presence.

"The same reason you're still alive." Her eyes narrowed. "I see now that mercy has been a mistake." Gryff kept his gaze on the floor, but the General didn't admonish him further. "You were friends," she said after a painful pause. It wasn't a question, but it was close enough.

"Yes," he said awkwardly.

"How easily we make sure our allies and enemies are saved or sacrificed shows who we really are," said the General. "Remember that."

Gryff stared at the message in his hands, at a loss for words. Her initials were signed next to the wax. *V.t.F.* The letters of a commoner next to the most powerful seal in the world.

"When the night grows darkest," she said firmly. "Don't disappoint me this time."

\*\*\*

Gryff had never prowled the castle grounds so late at night. He had expected to find at least some signs of life, but aside from the patrolling guards, the entire castle slept in silence. *The Fireborne love their order.* Even in the capital, shops closed shortly after dinner, and on every tenth day—the day of rest—nothing was open. No one liked to break the rules.

Better that way, he supposed. The last thing he needed now was unwanted attention.

The falconry was easy to reach but hard to climb. Spiral stairs of uneven stone made it easy to lose sure footing, and he doubted Valerya could fit between the narrow walls in full armor. For all the sentinels posted around the keep, the falconry was sparsely guarded; most of the birds were trained to respond only to their owners, so spiders were easy to catch.

Gryff found it strangely inviting. He had almost forgotten how comfortable he felt in the shadows. As if he needed another reminder he wasn't one of them. Not really.

He threw a quick glance over his shoulder when he reached the entrance to the falconry, still not daring to believe that the General wanted to send a message to *Dove.* Dove may have been the Northern Summoner, but this was the Guardian of the Realm. Powerful words meant for a voiceless girl.

He sighed as he wrenched the doors open.

The first thing he saw was a staircase that spiraled around a massive cage. Hundreds of yellow eyes watched him in the dark and bobbed. The birds flew in through an opening in the ceiling and slept on branches until their next flight. The bottom floor sheltered common kestrels, used by trainees to send word home; the middle floors were used by castle servants and the Swordsworn. The higher the rank, the higher the floor. Only the top was reserved for royalty: black peregrines.

*My favorite birds,* he thought bitterly. They were greater in size and refused to mingle with the other birds, so they were housed individually at the top of the tower. No doubt the reason why the General found them so charming.

He climbed past shrieking birds that had suddenly sensed an intruder. There were only three black peregrines, but the General's personal messenger was unmistakable. He felt silly trying to coax it out of its cage, the way it glared daggers at him when he opened the door.

It screeched in protest but perched dutifully on his arm when he waved the seal in front of its face. Gryff made his way across the walkway leading north and opened a small door in the wall to reveal an even smaller chamber. He set the peregrine down, and it hopped into the chamber, waiting obediently for a message.

Gryff took the piece of rolled-up parchment from his pocket and hesitated. The wax had barely reached the tips of the parchment. *I can open this easily.* He'd opened loads of letters after sealing them, mostly to add a signature he'd forgotten in his days as a novice scribe and notary. It wasn't too difficult after a while…

*No. Only bad things come from black peregrines.*

But then again, this was Dove. What could the General possibly have to say to Dove? He knew Valerya was doubling down on the Red Spears, close to finding their leader, but he doubted that was why she wanted to talk to her. The more he thought about it, the more it infuriated him.

He didn't know how long he stood there, contemplating under the watchful eyes of the black peregrine, until it screeched him back to reality.

"All right, all right," he muttered. But just as he was about to tie the message to its leg, he hesitated. It was much harder to resist now that it was right in front of him.

*Dove has enough secrets to last a lifetime,* he decided. *What's one less?*

Gryff sighed, hating himself as he untied the string and worked around the thread of wax. Blood pounded in his ears and blocked out all reason. The peregrine shrieked in disapproval, but all he could think about was Dove, how she had tossed him aside the first chance she got.

He expected to find a message, but all he saw was one word scrawled on the parchment.

\*\*\*

IDIOT

\*\*\*

Gryff felt his sweat cool, hardening along his backside like the wax of the seal. Suddenly, it felt like Valerya's eyes were on him. But it wasn't her voice that approached him, nor was it her face he saw when he turned around.

"What's it say?" asked the voice raspily, a man.

Gryff wanted to scream, but the man's voice had already driven the birds into a frenzy of screams. He was thin to the point of grotesque and cloaked in rags stained black with blood. His faded eyes were sharp with moonlight, and though Gryff could see the whites of his eyes, he still didn't seem human. *A ghost.*

"Who are you?" Gryff demanded. He was taken aback by his own brazenness, but he didn't want to die in a falconry. It was a long way down. "What do you—?"

"I need this," said the Ghost, shivering like he had fever. The Ghost held a dagger out in front of him. "I don't care if you're one of *them*. I need this."

"What—"

But before Gryff could finish his question, the Ghost turned just in time to catch a fist to his face. Gryff heard the sound of a nose shattering, and the Ghost staggered in his direction. Before he could collide with Gryff, Valerya's falcon swooped down, swift as an arrow, into the Ghost's face. The bird shrieked and tore itself away with something dangling in its beak.

*OH GODS.* Gryff felt dread sink in his stomach when he saw the hole where the man's eye used to be. There was no blood, but the man screamed all the same.

"OH GODS!" Gryff screamed himself. *Why isn't he bleeding?!* His own eye hurt from just seeing it, and he could only watch helplessly as the peregrine swooped around the tower. The birds screeched in response, enraged. Hundreds of falcons, each trained to protect their messages at all costs. It was enough to make Gryff forget the second assailant.

The Eyeless Ghost cowered in the shadow of his attacker, but he soon recovered and raised his dagger. The hooded figure seemed to anticipate it; it imitated the flow of movement and grabbed the Ghost's forearm, swinging him down to his knees. He heaved his own arm down at the Ghost's elbow with a crack that sent all the birds shrieking, begging for more. The Ghost screamed as bone jutted through his arm, and Gryff's savior chuckled as he tossed the dagger over the railing. Gryff held his breath until he heard the clang.

*It really is a long way down.*

Gryff backed away instinctively, readying his element hand, but the figure laughed and pulled back its hood. Gryff almost wept in relief.

"Well, he isn't going anywhere," said Diebold the Pacifist over the sound of the falcons. "We've been hunting down our King's rats for weeks, now."

Gryff laughed nervously. A good thing, then, that he hadn't attempted to take on a Spade in the goddamn falconry. Of all the possible ends, being found face-down in a pile of bird shit was not the noblest way to go.

The Ghost sputtered and spat out blood between curses, clutching what was left of his arm. "You broke it!" he said, but Diebold ignored him.

"What are you going to do with him?" asked Gryff, catching his breath.

"Don't much like killing." Diebold shrugged. "Our General wanted this one alive... and she can make bards out of beggars."

"What does that mea—"

*"You fucking broke it!"* the man screamed.

"I'll make you forget your arm," said Diebold, grinning like he had just been waiting for an invitation. Without warning, he kicked down on the man's leg, twisting it at the knee.

"I... thank you," said Gryff, trying not to vomit as the man howled.

"Oh, I wouldn't rejoice too soon," Diebold sighed. His brow folded over his left eye, giving it the impression that it was permanently swollen, and Gryff found himself wondering if he even had an eye there. He recalled his eyeless assailant and felt the bizarre urge to laugh. *At least one of them would.*

But Gryff's relief was short-lived. His heart sank when Diebold's good eye glimpsed the message in his hand. "Ma'am told you not to read it," said Diebold the Pacifist, sighing.

# 9

## THE

# OTHERWORLD

It was not like Dove wanted to panic, but it was hard to stay calm in the face of the most dangerous commander in the world, especially one that had just invaded her mind.

The Otherworld did not make it easier. Even on a different plane of existence, Valerya looked fiercer than ever. Dove supposed it was not easy being General of the Firelands, but in a world where they could not feel pain or exhaustion, Valerya easily looked years younger. Something had renewed her strength, imbued her eyes with new life. In this world, they were flawless statues of their former selves. Only the scars remained.

"Where are we?" Dove asked, immediately regretting it. Her voice crackled in her throat like an old furnace coming back to life. It came out hoarse and sickly.

"Quickly." Valerya nodded towards the wall. "What do you see on that tapestry?"

Dove pushed herself to the edge of the bed and squinted at the golden threads, trying to ignore the deep slashes embedded in the wall next to it. Whatever made them, it was much larger than a bear. *Like a small dragon.* "Um... a castle with three towers, and above it... a phoenix on fire. And I think dahlias."

"You like flowers?"

"Yeah, I... like lilies."

Valerya ignored that. "What color is the phoenix?"

"Blue and green. Actually, it kind of looks like a peacock."

"Commit it to memory."

"But why...?"

Valerya uncrossed her arms, and it was only then Dove realized she was not wearing any armor. Instead, she wore a plain shirt spun of linen that opened at the collar. It was not dyed in colors of wealth. It frayed at the edges, like it had been worn and washed against the rocks too often. Her trousers were neatly pressed but simple, and her boots boasted no luxuries. "Not many know you're the Second Summoner, but they will," she said. "And when they do, they will send skin-crawlers far and wide to steal your secrets. Conjure illusions. This way, you'll always know it's me."

It was the worst reason Valerya could have possibly given, but no one looked to Valerya the Fireborne for hope—only cold truths. But a cold truth was better than an empty promise. At least Valerya would never lie to her. Dove sighed. "How do I know it is really you *now*?"

Valerya smirked. "Shall I tell you where your birthmark is?" she asked. "I seem to recall one right between your—"

"That's fine." Dove reddened. She hated how warm her cheeks got. It was a wonder they did not burst into flames. "But I guess for now we can say peacock?"

Valerya's mouth drew back into a thin smile. "Peacock it is."

Dove was mortified. She wished Valerya would turn those sharp eyes elsewhere. "But skin-crawlers would be able to see this, right?" she asked. "That we have... that we have talked about this. They will have seen the tapestry too."

"They can only see memories we form in the waking world. Not here," said Valerya. "Time seems to play by different rules here. Our minds may perceive it as a dream. I can't explain it otherwise."

"Then how do I know I am not dreaming?"

"When you wake up, offer Valk a copper. Just do it." Valerya waved a hand dismissively before Dove could ask why. "But more importantly. How are you?"

The words caught in Dove's throat, and for a moment, she wondered if she really was dreaming. "All right, I think. I do not... I do not really know what is happening."

"Unsurprising," said Valerya with a quick chuckle. "But you're here, so that means you're still alive. Keep it that way."

Dove was oddly touched. "Barely. Rhysar... my dragon... it is not easy..."

"I know." Valerya turned her gaze back to the window, and Dove swore she saw the shadow of a smile against the light of the moon. It gave her a strange sense of comfort knowing she was not alone. "And you've seen him?"

"Yes, of course," answered Dove. "When I summoned him."

"Not in *our* world. In this one."

*In this one...* Dove blinked. "They are here too?"

Valerya laughed like she had told a joke. "It hadn't occurred to you why we're the only people in this world?" She reached an arm out towards the torch and brought it to a softer flame. Dove felt blood rush to her ears when Valerya sat at the edge of the bed. "We're in *their* world now. And it is imperative that you keep this in mind."

*Their world.* "And... only Summoners can come here?"

"Yes. I've spent years in this castle, going over things my... our... predecessors have left behind."

"Years?"

"Hours in the real world." Valerya shrugged. "Bastyan the Cruel summoned Avantys before me, but he seemed to enjoy the solitude of this world. Surely you've heard of him."

"The... Last Emperor?"

"Yes. But it was your predecessor who studied here in peace. He spent decades here, and it was good he did. The library is filled with notes of Baley the Kind."

"My predecessor too?" Dove sat up. "And we can... come here whenever we want?"

"I can. Until you bond with your beast, I advise you to stay away."

*I guess never, then.* "How do I bond with him?" Dove asked. "I can barely stay conscious when he is in one of his moods."

"In due time," said Valerya. "As you'll find out, your... *relation-ship* with him will be largely out of your hands. But bond with him you must."

Suddenly, Valerya rose from the bed and brought the torch-fire to an even softer dim. "You need to leave now," she said, barely a shade above a whisper.

"What?" Dove did not want to go. Back in their world, she was constantly surrounded by people, but the dragon had placed mountains between them. Even her friends were afraid of her. It was in the world of the beasts, with Valerya, that she felt safe. "But what about...?"

"Valk will tell you everything you need to know. And Dove." Valerya turned to face her for the last time, and Dove tried to take in every detail of her sharp features. She did not know how long it would be before they saw each other again. Valerya shook her head and turned back to the window as Dove's surroundings faded around her. "Don't die."

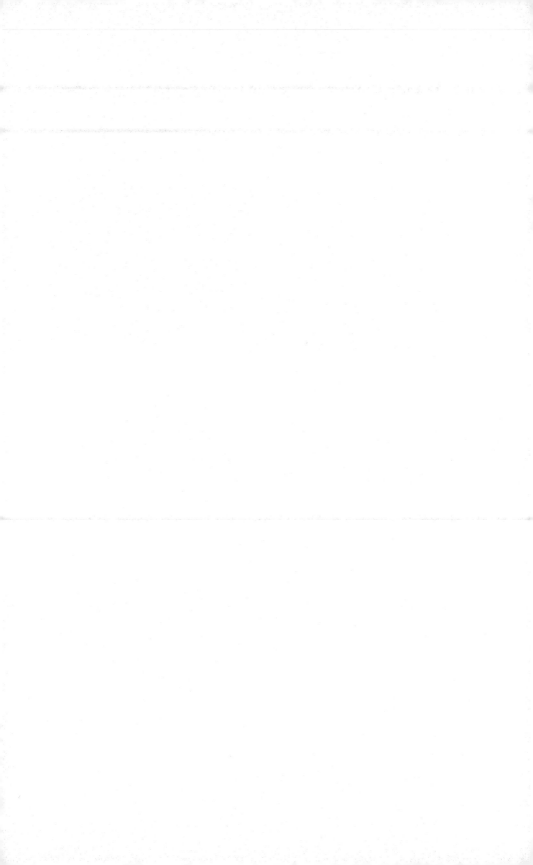

# 10

## BRETHREN WASTES
# FIRE REALM

"There's something majestic about the Wastes, isn't there?" asked Artis good-naturedly when they set off at dawn, but clear skies and gentle winds did not make them better. Somehow, the wastelands looked emptier than the day before.

Dove woke up feeling like she had gotten hit by a caravan. Valerya had warned her that jumping back and forth between worlds would feel like the fog. Dove had imagined giant clouds until the General told her it was what people felt after a night of heavy drinking. Dove still did not know what that felt like… until now.

Valk gave Dove a gentle nudge, and a white light burst across her field of vision. "Sleep well?" he asked, and she shot him a tired look. Marv had refused to give her more Tears until they reached Rhysia, and by midday, she was struggling. She sighed and handed him a copper.

"Copper can't afford me," said Valk. He gave a soft chuckle. "Well, I'll be damned. Tell me, how is our General doing?"

*So it was not a dream.*

Dove had decided to ride with him again that morning, and they took the lead over rocky terrain. She suspected he could lead the way blindfolded; he only seemed to stop for the others' sake, but he rarely spoke to them otherwise. If all Northerners were this sparse with words, she would fit right in.

She tilted her head to the left and listened. There was a faint rumbling in the distance that her companions seemed happy to ignore.

"Our General and I have ridden north together a few times," said Valk. "She hates the journey. And to think, this is the safest of the seven routes to Rhysia."

*What is making that sound, then?* Dove pointed to the distance. She could see the shadow trails of the Huntsmen Woods, creeping up from the earth like some sharp, malignant growth. Dark flames, frozen. The rumbling grew louder, but no one paid it any mind.

"That sound?" asked the Spade. "I haven't the faintest idea."

"Wouldn't do any good to think about it," said Bard. "Besides, my stomach is making worse sounds. When did we last eat?"

"An hour ago." Valk frowned. "Don't you have any discipline?"

"Valerya keeps you Hounds on a tight leash, doesn't she?" snapped Bard. "What, do I need permission to breathe, too?"

Artis chuckled as the two descended into mindless insults. It was like journeying with Decker and Merc, but more stressful. Dove felt like they were always one poorly timed remark away from a fistfight. "Twenty years," he whispered. "Twenty years, and nothing has changed."

And so they continued. Valk towered over Bard and his pony, but that did not stop Bard from slipping rocks into the saddlebags of the Spade's horse when he was not looking.

At long last, the mountains appeared before them. They were

not cold and jagged like the mountains of Glasgérios, but lush and green, with slopes stained yellow and gold by the rising sun. She understood at once why those colors made up the Northern banners. It was a stark contrast to the blood-red sigils of the capital.

She wondered how anyone had ever managed settling here in the first place. It looked so out of place after the Brethren Wastes, like someone had just dropped a castle up the middle of a mountain. Even from afar, Dove could see vines of black fingers climbing up the walls of the castle and spreading, like poison of the nightbloom, and the paths before her twisted and turned like thorns.

*Maybe they had help from the Huntsmen.* The thought provided no comfort.

"Rhysia," said Thornbeard, who had just woken up from a nap. How he could sleep without falling off his horse was a mystery to her.

Valk smiled. "The black vines you see are blackwood. They give the walls protection, which makes Rhysia the only castle safe from *Avantys*. And it's lovelier than it looks." he said.

But Dove heard what he did not say. *Safe from Avantys, but not from me.* She dropped her gaze as they rode on, wondering how many enemies she would make before the turn of the next star.

*How can anyone live with this power?*

# 11

RED CITADEL
# FIRE REALM

How the Ghost screamed when Diebold splintered his arm paled in comparison to when the General found out. Now, he was singing. Words flowed from his throat in different pitches and wailed for forgiveness. *"Our General can make bards out of beggars,"* Diebold had told him in the falconry. Gryff understood what that meant now.

Gryff's courage wobbled with each lash and shattered with each scream. The sobbing took care of the rest. People had assembled in the courtyard to watch, visibly curious. Valerya may have been the royal executioner, but she rarely dealt the lashings herself. The man must have committed a severe crime if she held the whip. *Only the attempted murder of the General's squire,* he thought. A crime that merited twenty-five lashes.

"A mercy if someone else held the whip," whispered Oren beside him, oddly alert. The other Spades had joined Valerya in the courtyard, but he stayed behind to keep Gryff company. *More like he wanted a better view,* thought Gryff bitterly, but he was grateful he wasn't alone. Oren spent most of his time staring out the window, and Gryff saw him cock his head after each lash, saw him whisper to himself. *He's scoring them.* Gryff didn't want to know.

Reluctantly, he forced himself to look out the window. The Ghost was bound to a wooden post, and his hands were raised high above his head. Gryff recalled with unease the hole where the man's eye use to be, how it didn't even bleed when the falcon tore it out of him. Now the Ghost himself was a dark red stump.

"Stop!" begged the man. *"Please! Please! I'll do anything!"*

Gryff's eyes fell on the General. *Royal executioner, indeed.* According to Oren, it had been ages since there had been a good old-fashioned public whipping, but she hardly seemed out of practice. If anything, years of not doing it seemed to have made her all the more unforgiving. She held the whip firmly in her right hand, and beside her was a barrel of red water.

"Dipping it in water makes the sting last." Oren took a swig from his goblet like he was watching a play. He feigned concern as the whip cracked. *"Oh, that was a good one!"*

The whip bit down on the man's flesh, and its tiny teeth tore away skin when the General whirled it back.

"Have you, um… have you ever been whipped?" asked Gryff nervously.

Oren laughed. "I was our King's whipping boy until Avander decided Morian was misbehaving on purpose." His eyes glazed over, and he smiled softly. "If she gives you the option," he said, offering him his cup, "always shirt off. You think it'll help soften the pain, but you see how the whip tears away at your skin? It'll hurt loads more with cloth attached to it."

Another lash, another cry. *"Seván!"* he heard the ghost screamed to no one in particular. *"My name is Seván!"*

Gryff took a swig. And then another.

"Not so much!" said Oren, half-irritated as he took his goblet back. "Wine thins the blood. You want to keep most of it inside you when you're up, don't you?"

Gryff closed his eyes and tried to block out thoughts of his own fate. Valerya had decided it was high time he faced the consequences of his choices. Reading the message despite her orders had merited ten lashes, away from public view, but he knew he was a goner. He sensed that she had wanted to have him flogged since Wayfarer's Barrow.

"Is he a Red Spear?" asked Gryff.

"Nah, one of Morian's rats." Oren tapped on the barrel of wine next to him and sighed when it rang hollow. He drank from his cup, slowly. "But I advise you not to bring it up either way. Ma'am is *pissed*. She suspects Spears on the inside and was hoping this was it."

Gryff frowned. "I didn't think they'd be so hard to find."

"Neither did we. We almost had them, too. Ma'am tracked down one of their camps, but a few dissenters managed to escape. Even their leader… and we had her cornered, too."

"Their leader? Escape *Valerya?"* Gryff

"Ma'am… I can't explain it." Oren frowned. Drank the rest of his wine. "We had her, but it was like Ma'am didn't want…"

"Gryff!" shouted Lyra from the end of the corridor. A welcome sound in terrible times, but the worry in her voice struck more fear in him than the lashes to come. "I… I just heard about everything, and that man who tried to kill you, and…"

"Don't worry about me," said Gryff, nearly staggering as she rushed into his arms. Oren cleared his throat uncomfortably.

"Oren!" said Lyra, just in time to hear Seván give his loudest scream yet. *A ballad for the gods,* thought Gryff with unease. After that, the entire courtyard went quiet.

He saw the General raise a hand, signaling the boy behind her to check if he was still alive. He did not look much older than ten, and Gryff had seen him working in the kennels.

*Today he's the General's lapdog.* The boy approached the man cautiously and pressed his golden head to his mouth. After a terrible silence, he turned back to the General.

And shook his head.

"That was the fourteenth lash," said Oren, who had clearly decided that now was not the time for comfort. "Remember, kid. Shirt off."

When Gryff turned his attention back to the courtyard, the General was already making her way back to the castle, parting the crowds as she went. A few of Morian's men rushed to cut the dead man down and clear the courtyard.

"Lyra," said Gryff. His punishment had arrived eleven lashes sooner than he expected. "I don't want you to see this."

Her eyes widened, threatened tears. "But Gryff, I…"

"Go on," interrupted Oren. His voice had gone uncharacteristically gentle, and Gryff stared. The Spades had a soft spot for her. Even when Gryff was scheduled for a beating, it was her they comforted. "Won't help no one if you stayed and watched. Least of all you."

"See?" Gryff tried to sound as reassuring as possible. "Don't worry about me. I'll survive." *Until the General kills me, at least.* "We'll see each other soon." *In the next life, maybe.* "Now go somewhere safe. Please."

Lyra nodded and turned just in time to see Valerya reach the mouth of the corridor.

"Go," said Gryff, this time more firmly, and she ran, glancing over her shoulder.

"Nothing personal, eh?" said Oren, slapping Gryff on the back as he bowed and opened the doors to the library. Gryff dropped to one knee, unwilling to break any more rules today.

"Up," Valerya commanded as she headed into the library. Gryff followed behind her miserably and winced when Oren pulled the doors shut.

"Let's get this over with." Valerya let the whip uncurl to the ground. It looked so harmless dangling there, like Seván's arm after Diebold had fractured it at the elbow. At least she had gotten a new one on her way up. "Shirt off or on?"

Oren nodded behind her as Gryff pulled off his shirt and dropped to his knees. He didn't bother saying anything. Begging would only make her hit harder.

"Oren," she said, and the Spade offered him a piece of black-wood wrapped in cloth.

"Bite down on this," he said. "It helps."

Reluctantly, Gryff obeyed. His teeth clenched upon the wood, and he took a deep breath as Oren eased out of view.

"Moving costs another lash," said Valerya. Her voice was as cold and sharp as the whip in her hand. "Maybe this time, you'll learn to listen."

\*\*\*

It must have been days before Gryff opened his eyes again. Outside his window reigned a complete absence of light, which could only mean the turn of the ascendant star. A single candle neared the end of its wick, and it took him a while to piece together his surroundings.

*I'm in a bed,* he realized, and his stomach knotted. *Better than lying face-down in a Sinthean gutter.* It was so cold he couldn't feel anything, but when he tried to move, the numbness flared into a world of pain. It stabbed through his neck and down his spine, and only then did he remember the kiss of the whip.

Gryff groaned. His bones weren't broken, but his flesh was held together by pulled stitches. He hoped it was sweat he was lying in. "H... help," he tried to speak, but his voice caught in his throat. Words disappeared into the void. "Is... is anyone there?"

He knew he was alone, but something tugged at the edge of his consciousness. It pressed against the sides of his skull, but it was far from a headache. When he closed his eyes, he felt like he was floating in a warm sea, calm and unafraid. *What did they give me?* he wondered as something pleasant washed over him. He let himself be carried by the golden waves, let the gentle water cradle his head.

*An opportunity,* a voice responded, pulling Gryff back to reality.

"Who's there?" he demanded. He was in no state to challenge anyone, but there was nothing left to lose but his mind, and even that dangled on the brink of possibility.

*Calm. Don't be angry,* the voice wheedled. *Let go, child. Look at me.*

Gryff found himself thinking back to the warmth of the waves and felt compelled to obey. He opened his eyes and forced himself to look, but the figure in front of him was anything but intimidating. He had seen her before. She was small with short hair and green eyes that glowed, but she usually kept to her tiny pocket of the castle. They had never spoken, but they were certainly making up for it now.

*Where am I?* he found himself asking.

*Everywhere. Anywhere you want to be.* She nodded to someone behind him.

Before Gryff could turn, something forced his eyes shut, and a scream tore between his ears. But when he cried out, he found himself another place. The last place he expected to be.

Daylight washed across his vision. After a lifetime of hiding from it, he felt the urge to run for cover, but he felt nothing. For the first time in nineteen years, he felt the sun on his skin. It tingled pleasantly but didn't burn. Something rough tickled the back of his neck, and he sat up, flexing his fingers in front of his face. *Nothing.*

He pressed his hands to his face and felt for scars. *My face.* It was whole again, like the feeling in his limbs. He looked around, not daring to believe his eyes.

*Sand-leaves.* The sun and the moon. Soon they would collide, creating a landscape of star-lit fields. *The blossom fields.* Just before the moon blocked out the sun. It was the sweetest scent he had ever smelled, one that instantly made him feel safe. Home. Like he had just woken up from a long nap.

"Hello?" he called, looking around for the woman who had summoned him there. He began to walk, effortlessly. Like he was gliding across the fields. As far as the eye could see, the land was empty, yet every detail was there—from the glow-flies getting ready to shine, to the tree where he and Dove had carved their initials. *G and D.* He smiled to himself. *G and D always.* He wondered what he would have given to stay there.

A soft shadow swept past his field of vision, rippling through his memory. The letters wavered in the wind. "Wait," he said, finding his voice. "Wait!" Even from afar, he could tell it was the woman by the silk of her robes. They trailed behind her like ink.

Without thinking, Gryff ran after her. It was easier to run when he couldn't get tired, but she was still faster than him. *"Come,"* she whispered. She took him down the hill and through the village, and as he ran, his mind filled in the emptiness with all the things he thought he had forgotten. The winding roads. The steep trails. The slanted houses with oaken doors. His house.

The shadow stopped in front of his door, sensing his connection to it.

*Don't you fucking dare,* he thought angrily, feeling the threat of hot tears. It was his home, his memory—the last thing in this world that was his. Now this woman, this intruder, threatened to take that from him, too.

She ran inside and slammed the door shut behind her.

Gryff cursed as he flung it open. Desperation surged. He was ready to draw blood, but when he entered, a light exploded in his skull. He leaned against the wall, unsteadied, but when he came to, everything was exactly where it used to be. Cluttered, no doubt Dove's doing, but in a way that only he could understand. The smell of stew, just the way his mother made on his birthday. To this day, he didn't know what was in it. He had always been too afraid to ask.

"Mother," he whispered to himself, forgetting the intruder. "Mother?"

His voice sounded younger, just when it threatened to break. He ran his fingers over the walls, over the table. Exactly how they used to be. It brought a smile to his lips.

Laughter from his room jolted his senses. He put his hand on the door and pushed it open. "Mother?"

Anger welled in him when he saw the cloaked figure. Her back was to him, but she knew he was there. She turned her head to the side, and the door shut behind him.

"Who… who do you think you are?" he demanded, feeling tears

roll down his face. Everything about this seemed wrong. Somehow her presence desecrated his memory. He gathered his courage and placed a hand on her shoulder, forcing her to face him.

And immediately let go.

"Dove?" he asked.

She laughed, a pleasant sound. "Gryff," she said, in a voice he never knew she had. She spoke. "I knew you'd find me." Her features were hazy, but they sharpened the more he remembered her. Before he could reach out and touch her, sharp pain returned to his limbs.

"No, wait!" he said as something seared the edge of his vision. He felt like he was being pulled from a dream, but his mind was still asleep. His thoughts became drowsy, unintelligible. His room faded, bleeding into the walls of the infirmary.

"What…" he began, but the words caught in his throat again. He coughed instead.

"Interesting," said the woman in front of him. "*Very* interesting. I've seen that girl before."

"WHAT WAS THAT?" Gryff screamed.

"Thank you. You've revealed so much," she said, ignoring him. She nodded towards someone behind him again. Gryff couldn't turn without ripping his stitches, but he sensed the man's presence long before he knew he was there. *Skin-crawlers,* he realized, but the woman continued. "We're offering you a chance."

"A… chance?"

"So much has been taken from you," she said. "They took away your family. Your home. They forced you into this life, and now they're even taking that away." Her words stung, but they were full of terrible truths.

*Don't listen,* Gryff thought to himself, but it was too late. They knew his secrets. His fears. *And now they know I know Dove.* "Get out of my head!" He forced his eyes shut. "I don't... I don't want it." He raised his hands to his temples and realized they didn't hurt. *Oh gods,* he thought. *I'm still sleeping.*

"*Child.*" A whisper before everything went black. "*We offer you the teachings of the Exalted. You know where to find us.*"

Gryff felt himself drift back to sleep, and when he woke up, he was alone.

# 12

## RHYSIA
# FIRE REALM

By the time they reached the gates, it was like someone had draped a curtain across the sky. The ascendant star had faded and cast no shadows. It was so black that Dove might as well have kept her eyes closed.

She sighed. Despite everything, she still had no idea what happened beyond the stars. She did not mind, though. The dragon still scared her, but somewhere in that fear grew a certain comfort in knowing it was there. It would never abandon her, like Gryff had, and it would watch the world burn before seeing her hurt. Slowly, painfully, Dove understood. No wonder Valerya trusted nothing else. It was hard to compete with that.

*You will love it. And you will hate it.* Truer words had never been spoken.

"Pull yourself together," whispered Bard. "We have to look presentable, now."

*Yeah, right.* Dove glanced over her shoulder. Only Valk and Artis looked like they knew what they were doing. The others stared at the walls, poked sticks at the cobblestone. She wondered if Thornbeard and his sons had ever seen a castle up close before.

Dove glanced up at the battlements and saw a single guard peering down at them, but Valk warned her not to be deceived. The City Watch lodged in barracks behind the gate, and it was common to send the drudges up to stand guard. She heard snickering on the other side.

The blackwood gates glistened against torch-fire, built to withstand fire and metal. She wondered if it could survive the other elements and was tempted to ask Bard to blast it with Storm. *Probably best not to start an uprising, though,* she thought, stifling a giggle. But when she turned to Bard, she saw to her amusement that he was wondering the same thing.

"H... halt," said the gatekeeper. His voice shook at the sight of them. "Who gggoes...?"

*"Disgrace."* A gruff voice took over, and rough hands shoved him out of sight.

The new gatekeeper was *massive.* It was enough to make Dove believe in ogres. Even from below, his neck looked wider than her shoulders and narrowed as it met his head, which was not much better. His jaw jutted forward like it was permanently displaced, his skin grayish behind silver bristles. He glared at Bard in suspicion.

Then he squinted past Bard for a better look. "Surely it can't be Valk? Well, what are you waiting for?" He spat at the boy behind him. "Inform our Lord! Quickly! *Quicker!*"

"You're tormenting him," said Valk as the boy scrambled out of view. Dove felt bad for him. She remembered jumping at Morian's command with the same nervousness, the same fear. Well... for his sake, she hoped it was not quite the same.

The ogre met them at the bottom when the gates opened. The Northerners had been smart to place him at the forefront. He and

Bard were of a height, but the difference between them was enormous. He must have weighed more than Bard and Valk combined. Dove too, with all that armor. Even the horses shied away.

"The years have made you more charming than ever, Gor," said Valk.

"Don't need to be charming." Gor's mouth widened into a smile, and Dove screamed inside. That face would give his own mother night terrors. "I still remember when they brought *you* here for the first time. Least you were better than Maxwell there."

"You gave us nightmares for years."

"Good," Gor growled, flattered. "Means I was doing my job right."

Valk lowered his voice and turned to Dove. "This man has been the Keeper of the Gates for forty years. Even in war, the gates have never fallen. Not to people, at least."

Gor laughed, a sound nastier than his smile. "Didn't know you liked them that young. Actually," he said before anyone could correct him, "didn't know this was the company you kept. A Stormhead, a dwarf, and a legless axeman? Is *this* what's been keeping you away from home?" He frowned as he tried to see underneath Artis's hood. "And..."

"Dwarf?" said Thornbeard indignantly, steering his horse in front of Valk's. "Ivan's a bit small, I'll admit, but he's no dwarf."

Bruin coughed. "I think he's talking about you."

"Talking about... what? Me?" Thornbeard sputtered.

Gor turned to the Spade smugly. He needed no further words.

Maxwell reappeared, harried and out of breath. "M... my lord," he said, and Gor gave them the signal to ride forward. Maxwell immediately helped Valk unload his horse.

"Can't imagine you've abandoned your queen for good," said

Gor gruffly as he approached, throwing Bard a distrustful look. Dove blinked uncomfortably. Their people had fought centuries ago, but the Hounds never forgot a grudge. Yet Bard's eyes lit up when he saw the gatekeeper, and she knew that he had found a new best friend.

Dove slid down from the saddle, eager to stretch her legs, and Valk clasped arms with Gor. She saw Maxwell struggle under the weight of the saddlebag from Valk's horse before he fell on his knees. She wondered how many rocks Bard had managed to sneak inside.

Bard tried not to snigger as he rode past him and swung down from his own saddle. "All right?" he bellowed as he extended his arm.

Maxwell did not take it. "I'm f...f... fine," he said, rising.

Dove frowned. If they knew were in the presence of a Spade, an Elemental Master, and a Dragon Summoner—and a night-wolf, though Marv and the beast had chosen to stay in a nearby village— perhaps they would not consider Bard to be the greatest threat.

Bard took the insult in stride. "Well, good man," he said with exaggerated propriety. "Forgive my presumptionness. It has been a most *burdenous* journey."

Dove bit back laughter. She liked Bard's nobleman persona, especially when he started making up words.

The messengers approached with equal caution. "Our High Lord has been informed of your arrival, my lord. He requests your company at once," one of them began. The sigil of the lone huntsman gleamed gold on his doublet. "Rooms are ready for your guests. They can rest in the meantime." He threw Dove a curious glance. "My lady can rest in your old chambers."

"Thank you," said Valk. "But she will stay in the upper chambers of the Guardhand Tower facing east. I'm sure no one has stayed there in a while."

The messenger blinked. "But my lord, those are…"

"That wasn't a request, kinsman," said Valk. His voice was courteous but left no room for negotiation. "Kindly show Thornbeard and his sons the cleanest rooms in the keep, and you can put Alezán wherever you like, as long as it's nowhere near the kitchens." A light grimace flashed across his face. "Perhaps… the *lower* chambers of the Guardhand Tower will suffice."

*Thank you, thank you, thank you.* Dove tried to hide her glee. She needed Bard. There was no way she was going to get through this alone.

The messenger bowed and turned to Artis. "And what would my lord require?"

"A bath," said the old man curtly. "And a word with Kayne. I believe he still resides in the Rhesán Tower?"

"The mage? Hasn't left the tower in decades." Gor frowned, squinted again with his good eye. "Have we met before?"

"Probably," said Artis, unfazed. "My trade used to take me to Heavensward and back, and I've seen many faces on my travels. Forgive me if I do not recall where we've met." He turned to the messenger, this time more firmly. "I'm afraid it can't wait."

The messenger bowed. "At once."

Artis dropped his voice to a whisper as the messenger headed back into the keep. "Kayne was one of my first students," he said. "Brilliant mind, terrible student. Got himself expelled from the Blackstone. Not a very outgoing man, I'm afraid. Bit of a recluse."

"How'd he get expelled?" asked Bard, and Dove smirked. *Of course he would be more interested in that.*

"Unfortunately, Kayne didn't discriminate. Knowledge was

knowledge to him, even in matters of… shall we say *darker* forms of magic. Even in teachings of the Exalted," said Artis. "I believe his son is studying at the Blackstone now. Bastian, I think his name was. Named after the Last Emperor himself. Terrible mind, brilliant student."

*Skin-crawler, in other words.* Dove recalled the gaunt, white-haired mage on her first visit to the Blackstone. Was his father one, too?

"Let's rest up, kiddo," said Bard jovially before she could react, stretching with no concern for social propriety. He belched. "I haven't stayed in royal guest chambers in ages!"

***

Dove stared at the furnishings with a twinge of guilt. The wardrobe was stocked with clothes, the drawers full of trinkets. If Gryff had been there, he would have likely poked fun at them, the wasted hours it must have taken the tailor to put the pieces together. Sometimes, he had the tendency to belittle the things she found fascinating.

*Such a giant room for such a small person.* She sighed and fell back onto the bed, letting herself sink in feathers. *When was the last time I was alone?* Even when she was by herself, the dragon's presence was constantly around her. She would never be alone again.

*Unless…*

Sweat iced along her back. Even thinking about it felt forbidden. The last time she felt at peace, even a semblance of it, was in the Otherworld. Going back was all she thought about, especially now that there was nothing else to distract her. *But can I?*

She took a deep breath and drew upon the air around her. *Come on,* she thought to the creature. *I know you are there.* Her surroundings sharpened and blurred in succession, like her eyes were sliding in and out of focus. They rumbled in her ears like a soft earthquake, but her body was still. *There is nothing to be afraid of,* she reminded herself, forcing herself to concentrate on the connection. It softened to a slow hum when she felt Rhysar's presence.

*Oh,* she thought. *That was not so bad.*

And then her world shattered.

***

*This is the dumbest idea I have ever had,* thought Dove when she opened her eyes to a black sky knitted together with silver stars. There was no sound, and the air was crisp and clean. She liked it here. She was in the dragon's world now, and for the first time since Wayfarer's Barrow, her head felt clear. Free. She felt no demands and heard no lies.

Dove stretched her arms upwards and felt the air curl around her fingers. Air was easier to bend in this world, and when she twirled her wrist, she felt a gust of wind lift her hair. *This is my world now too.* All this energy around her, and she was the only one around to wield it. She turned her attention to the ground, which was covered in rocks and rubble. She pressed her hands together and concentrated, condensing the air around the stone. When she broke her fingers apart, the rocks parted violently, clearing a path for her to move forward.

If Dove could move mountains in this world, she did not want to imagine what Valerya was capable of. She stacked the rocks on top of each other, marveling at how easy it was to command the winds. For good measure, she swept away the dirt in short, smooth gusts.

It did not take her long to realize that underneath the debris, she was standing in the main square of the capital, gazing up at the Red Citadel. But something was different. The streets of Sinthea had been stripped bare of life. There was no joy, no heart to keep it going. *It is not just empty,* she realized. *It is destroyed.* The roofs of all the houses had caved in, and the aqueducts lay in shambles around her. It looked like something huge had torn into the lower pillars, and down they went, one by one.

Dove felt a twinge of unease. Getting here had been easy, but she felt her connection to her dragon wane. *Did it just leave me here?* She did not know how to get back without it, and it was only her in this broken, forgotten world. Well, except for…

*Valerya.*

For a wild moment, Dove wanted to reach out to her but kept herself together. What did she think would happen? That Valerya would arrive and… what, tell her how to get back? She felt a pang of guilt when she realized that was exactly what she wanted. She needed to see her. But without Rhysar, she could not make a connection.

She halted in her tracks when her foot hit a boulder. She glanced down and cocked her head to the side. *Boulders do not have eyes.* She crouched until she could make out the head of a giant statue, and when she rolled it to the side, she saw that it was black like coal.

Fear beat from her chest and pounded hammers in her ears. *I am the dumbest person alive,* she thought. She was not alone, not by far. Out of all the places in the world, Rhysar had dropped her off in the capital of the Firelands, where an uncomfortably large creature used to dwell. She did not know how she had forgotten that.

The air felt like a warm breeze against her back as the ground began to tremble. *Oh gods,* she thought as the rumbling grew louder. But it was not the ground making those sounds. She turned her head slowly and looked over her shoulder.

The first thing she saw was her reflection. She had associated Avantys with crimson for so long that she was taken aback by its golden eyes, the black, oval slits that narrowed when they saw her. Before, she could not imagine anything more terrifying than the spirit of a dragon, but now it was easy. *The body of one.* One that watched her with cold amusement, that waited to see what she would do. A game of chess where she was surrounded by enemy queens.

*Is that even how chess works?* It did not matter. Even if they played by the rules, Avantys owned the game.

Its breathing curled into soft growls, and she saw its teeth glisten under armored scales. Blunt horns lined its jaw, but they became longer, sharper, as they made their way down its neck. *How can anyone even kill this thing?* Even if it just sat there, she doubted all the swords, crossbows, and catapults in the kingdom could dent its hide.

*Rhysar, come back,* she thought desperately. She wondered if she should stay still or run—or cast Fire, even. All the while, Avantys stared at her, challenging her to move. A streak of cruelty flashed across those golden eyes. The dragon tensed, ready to lunge.

Dove heard a screech in her ears. Rhysar had finally sensed she was in danger, and she felt the winds lift as their connection grow stronger.

Avantys bristled, affronted, when it sensed Rhysar's presence. It let out a roar and lunged at Dove. She saw rows of teeth as big as her face, jagged smiles coming at her from all sides.

She had heard herself speak only a few times in her life, with Valerya.

This time, she screamed.

***

Dove felt like she was drowning in a dark sea, and when she opened her eyes to the warm light of her chambers, she gasped for air. She inhaled so much of it that her chest threatened to burst. She keeled over, knocking over books and glasses in her struggle to breathe.

Someone kicked the door open, daggers drawn. "Hey, kid," the stranger said, sheathing them when she saw no intruders. "You all right?" She pulled Dove back up with unnatural strength and slapped her back until she caught her breath. Cried. It was not a dignified first impression.

The woman threw her a slanted smile, and her eyes were dark with mischief. "Mayet," she said. "Would've been my personal best if I lost you in my first hour as your swordmaiden."

Dove stared. Her skin was dark, like Elayne's, but Dove sensed the Fire in her without even trying. Her jaw was cut in severe lines, and she boasted strong features that began at her face and led all the way down to her…

Dove looked away, turning the same shade of red as her hair, but her embarrassment was politely ignored. Mayet's grin widened. "I'm sure we'll get along," she said as she got up and opened the door. "Now come on. They're calling us for food."

The main keep of the stronghold was across the inner courtyard, and Dove felt a chill the moment she set foot outside the tower. Two armed sentinels manned the entrance, but they relaxed when they saw Mayet. "My lady," they said in unison, and Dove realized they were addressing her. The left continued without his partner. "Your blue-haired companion is already inside." His voice was steady, but he could barely keep a straight face. "He was briefly detained for blasting the gates with Storm but granted reprieve by Lord Kai before Gor got to him. He wanted me to tell you, my lady, that blackwood absorbs *some* of its impact. Not all."

Dove struggled not to laugh as their eyes glinted, more mischief than honor. *Bard would make so many friends here,* she thought as she and Mayet entered the keep.

Dove had been in two castles before—in two capitals, no less— but she knew she did not like them. They were too massive, too bleak, too specifically designed to keep people inside. This one was no better. They turned the corner and almost swerved into Valk, who looked like he had been waiting for them.

"Evening," he said courteously. "I see you've met Mayet. She was swordmaiden to my cousin, Julieth, before she ran off to become a medican." They entered the dining hall, and Dove was relieved to see Bard already sitting there with two guards at his back, spears at the ready.

At the head of the table sat Lord Kai... she assumed. To her surprise, he did not look a hundred years old. His hair and beard had thinned and grayed, but his body was still strong. In truth, he looked like Valk with white hair.

"Welcome," he said, his voice soft in the grandness of the hall. It must have run in the family. "Your companion is still speaking with Kayne. This one and I, however, have been having a most pleasant conversation."

"Can you tell them to lower their spears now?" asked Bard.

Kai ordered the guards back with a wave of his hand. "I regret I cannot stand, myself. The medican would have my head if I disobeyed him again."

"You really must stop leading the charge," said Valk, taking his seat.

"I am the protector of this castle," said Kai. "I would rather be stripped of my title otherwise. A pity your king doesn't follow suit." He gave Dove a courteous nod when she approached. "Have a seat. You're under our protection now."

Dove took a seat to Bard's left as Mayet stood behind her chair, towering over her from behind. Bard bit back a grin, already smitten.

"No doubt your king is already aware of your existence," said Kai. "The question is, what will we do about it?" He kept his gaze fixed on Valk. "What will *you*?"

"Me?" asked Valk.

"It isn't Morian that keeps me awake at night. Your queen may have granted you leave, but she will never be on our side."

Dove looked into Valk's eyes. Then understood. Painfully. The Citadel, the Spades, and all the Swordsworn—that had been his life. He had fought side by side with Valerya, probably since he was her age, and now he had to choose.

"But let's not talk about that now," said Kai, taking pity on them. "For now, let's raise a goblet to all the years lost and regained."

# 13

## GLASGÉRIOS
# ICE REALM

Glasgérians considered it vulgar to talk outside, but it had been ages since Decker had seen such a quiet night. In the air, he could always count on the *Smuggler* to creak and groan through every mile, and on land, almost everything made noise. But nothing covered the silence tonight. Faint clouds clung to the sky like memories that refused to fade, and even the stars had abandoned them.

Life had been simpler with one Summoner. For better or worse, it created a dynamic in which a Summoner commanded and everyone else obeyed. With two, people had a choice. Choices created hope. Young Falcons suddenly found themselves facing a future unknown to them, and they were terrified. In the blink of an eye, they had so much more to lose.

Decker grunted and brought a hand to his chest. Elements worked differently than steel. They left traces, wounds that twisted and scarred on the inside. *That kid really did a number on me.* He could still remember the boy's face—burned, full of hate, covered in tangles of wild, black hair. The Ice might have missed Decker's heart, but his body didn't forget.

A group of Falcons parted when he approached, but he didn't let his pace slow. It had been happening a lot lately. Without Surge, he was second in command, and he hated it. When he was one of them, it was easy basking in the glory of his company, joining them in triumphs as well as defeats. But as a fresh-faced commander, especially one from the clouds—especially back from the dead—they looked to him for answers. And blame.

When he turned and saw another domeric looming in the corner, he understood at once why the Falcons were getting desperate. *Gods be damned.* He continued in silence. *Another one.*

The shadow guards had started spilling into the Underground, slowly at first, until they stood sentinel at every turn. They watched over them from the darkest corners of the tunnels, bits of night granted independent will. He was glad Dove got out when she did.

But as terrifying as the domerics were, it wasn't like they could go after her. Their numbers were low, and one attack from the Firelands would obliterate them from the Scrolls. They couldn't even get to Lancistierre without crossing a desert, and shadows did not thrive in the sun. No, they wouldn't risk leaving their capital defenseless. They protected the heart of the city, but an attack from either front would cut off their arms and legs.

No doubt the image would appeal to Morian, and it wouldn't be long before he turned his attention towards Glasgérios. Even if all the warring clans in the Waterlands united against him, their numbers wouldn't be enough. Throw in a dragon or two, it would be impossible.

Decker stopped at the mouth of the cavern, but instead of Chip guarding the entrance, a domeric was leering down at him. Decker sighed. He knew they'd been ordered to report on their activities, but it was a shame they came right when the Falcons had completely fallen apart.

Wolff was at his desk, signing parchment after parchment. "Rotten age to die," he grumbled without looking up. A warm welcome from him these days. "Rotten place, too."

"Are we really going to stay here?" asked Merc, sitting on a ridge of rock just above the river. The soft glow of the water colored his skin turquoise, and his hair exploded into odd shades of purple. Decker wondered if he knew how ridiculous he looked. Another thing for the domerics to report. "Even Kerys has abandoned us."

Merc didn't need to say it, but Decker saw the real question in his eyes: *Why haven't we received word?* They had received a single message from Rhysia. It only said "Hi," but Bard's handwriting was unmistakable. They had long since decided the fewer words, the better, but that didn't stop Bard from drawing a happy face next to his message.

"There... is no need... to worry about her," rasped Sirian. "Or your friends... for now."

"Thanks, Sirian," said Merc, not bothering to veil his sarcasm. "Thanks a million."

"Quiet." Wolff raised a hand before anyone could respond. "Do you feel that?"

For a moment, they stood in silence. Decker felt a shift in the air that he couldn't quite place. That was usually a bad sign. A chill bristled the hairs on the back of his neck, and he placed a hand on his dagger. Whatever it was didn't appear immediately.

But the figure that emerged was so incongruent to the suspense surrounding it that the words caught in his throat. The Underground was a place for ruffians, misfits, and armed mercenaries—not ladies in flowing silk and sapphires that shone like stars. *How did she even make it this far?* The Falcons may have stood together for a cause, but trinkets and jewels were fair game.

He blinked. *Damn.* He knew it was bound to happen sooner or later: he had gone insane. "Kiera?" He never forgot a face, let alone a name—especially in Port Haven, where there had been nothing else to do. Now here she was, smiling like he owed her another drink.

"Brunhilda," she corrected curtly. *Brunhilda unmasked,* he realized. She saw his confusion and ignored it with grace. "Is Bard here?"

"Good of you to ask. You only missed him by a couple of weeks." Decker hadn't meant for it to sound spiteful, but she didn't have to deal with a drunken, despondent Bard after Wayfarer's Barrow. "What are you doing here?"

"Not the warmest welcome," said Brunhilda, but she seemed to have anticipated that. There was a time he would have melted for that smile, but now he knew the only reason she was trying to see past his clothes was to work out which weapons he kept where. "I'd say I deserved it, but..." She shrugged innocently when their eyes met. She cast a cursory glance at the rest of his companions, sized them up. Eliminated them as threats.

"How did you get past everyone?" asked Merc. "How'd you even find us?"

Brunhilda laughed as though he had just told a joke and didn't bother responding. "I figured. I can find Bard some other time." She shrugged. "That's not the reason I'm here. Actually, I'm here to find *you.*"

"Me?" asked Decker. He was not used to being talked down to, especially by someone half his size, but Brunhilda didn't particularly look like she cared. "Listen, I don't know you, Kie... Brunhilda. Whoever you are."

She smiled. "But I know you. Our encounters have never been by chance. I've been keeping an eye out for the perfect sky commander, you know." She sighed dramatically before anyone could speak. "With dragons, domerics, and Red Spears... our fight is in the skies, now."

"The Hounds found their leader?" Wolff knocked over his cup in surprise. Ale spilled over the sides of the table. "Haven't heard anything about that."

"For some *inexplicable* reason, she keeps evading Valerya's grasp." Brunhilda put a hand to her chin. "You wouldn't happen to know anything about that, would you, good man?"

Decker frowned. Brunhilda must have dodged the detection of hundreds of shadow guards, but Wolff's reaction interested him more than her presence. The man looked *nervous.*

Decker opened his mouth reluctantly. "No one escapes Valerya," he said. Try as he might, he couldn't think of anything else to say. "Right, Wolff?"

"Why, it's almost like Valerya keeps letting her get away!" Brunhilda's face lit up, but she kept her eyes on Wolff. "Why is that, I wonder?"

The more Decker stared at Wolff, the more fascinated he became. Wolff was a large man with a past built from larger sins, but Brunhilda was making him squirm. Sweat pearled on his forehead and fell down the sides of his face. For a moment, he matched the desk and the dripping ale. "Ah, fuck," was all Wolff said.

"Valerya's figured it out, it seems," said Brunhilda coyly. "Now, who is this mysterious leader, and why can't Valerya touch her?"

"Yeah, Wolff," Merc joined, intrigued. "Who is she?"

"Shut up, Merc," Wolff growled, but he didn't answer.

"If Valerya figures out more, the world will burn." At that, Brunhilda's voice became stern. She cocked her head to the side. "Now what about it, Sky Commander?"

"Sky Commander?" asked Decker. "What, you need a first helmsman?"

Brunhilda smiled sweetly. "Kind of. In a way."

"Can Merc come?"

"I've seen him fly a ship. It was a disaster." She shrugged. "Sure, why not?"

"What's the plan then, Brunhilda?" asked Wolff.

"Kiera," she corrected, smiling sweetly. "I just need to borrow your sky commander. Just for a bit." She threw Sirian a knowing nod. "If this works, we might actually have a chance. Why, we might actually even... beat Valerya."

"Wolff, what aren't you telling us?" Merc asked incredulously.

Wolff wiped the sweat from his brow and turned to Kiera. "How long have you known?"

Kiera had the grace to cover a laugh with her hand. "Since you and Rey agreed to do King Avander a favor," she said. "That package really *did* fall into the wrong hands, didn't it?"

"Wait," said Decker. "You don't mean...?"

"It's good that Dove is claiming the Northern name," she continued, ignoring him. She pretended to ponder. "Gives their leader time to claim *another* one."

*Oh, shit.* Decker's heart stopped. Morian was not going to like that. Valerya was sworn to defend Avander's bloodline, but she couldn't crush the rebellion without...

Merc cursed, loudly. "Shouldn't we be... helping the Spears, then?" he asked. Coughed.

Wolff shook his head. "No. Valerya can still crush us easily. Only their leader is safe, but who knows how long that'll last. Which is why..." He glanced at Decker. "You should go with her, boy. You and Merc. This could be our only shot."

Decker glanced at Kiera, but she met stare for stare. Lifted an eyebrow. Despite playful appearances, she waited, disciplined, with the patience of a hundred years. Finally, he broke the silence. "*We* should go? What about you?"

"Can't leave the Falcons alone in this sorry state," said Wolff. "Man's only worth as much as his word, and Sirian and I are sworn to head the Order until the very end."

"*Until the very end,*" Sirian nodded.

"But one attack from the Hounds and…" protested Merc.

"Until the very end. Just do me a favor and, ah…" Wolff cleared his throat awkwardly. "Take Elayne with you. Should Morian attack Glasgérios, at least I can… well, at least you and Merc wouldn't be completely doomed."

A bunch of thoughts flooded through Decker's mind, but none of them formed words. Splitting up was blasphemy, especially now. It was hard enough when Surge left—again—and took Dove with him. They were family. A big, dysfunctional family, with hordes of brothers and sisters going on different adventures. But this was something else. This felt like… leaving.

Merc looked like he wanted to say something but stopped himself. His trimmed eyebrows lifted and fell. "All right, then," he said, glancing at Kiera. "I guess… we're all yours."

Decker extended his arm towards Wolff. It felt surreal, but Wolff took it without hesitating. They embraced. "Don't look so depressed. And don't let Merc die out there," he said.

Decker gave his arm to Sirian, who simply nodded. "You will be… fine," he said. "The *domeras* wills it."

And that was that. In the Underground, there were no goodbyes. Falcons simply flew until they didn't, but before that they always, always made it home.

"I'll take care of them," said Kiera as the sharpness in her eyes eased into playfulness. Decker understood at once why she and Bard had been such good friends. "Oh, and Kerys is coming. I don't know if that makes you feel better or worse."

"Kerys?" asked Merc, frowning. "But why...?"

"She's been my eyes and ears in the Underground," she said, cutting him off. "I never know where her loyalties lie. I love it." She turned to take her leave as though her last statement gave no cause for concern. Merc threw Decker a glance that screamed: *ARE YOU SERIOUS?*

Decker nodded and followed her, trying not to stare at the domeric sprawled on the ground near the entrance. Merc cursed as he stepped over the shadow guard's legs.

"Don't worry. He's not dead," said Kiera nonchalantly as turned to face them. "Pack only what you need and meet me above-ground at daybreak. And dress warmly." She smiled and nodded towards the domeric sprawled behind them. Laughed. "Would you look at that?"

Decker and Merc glanced over their shoulder at the fallen shadow guard. "What about him?" asked Decker, turning back to Kiera. But by then, she had already gone.

# SERPENT TAMER

*Not now. Not now.* "Not now!" Pierce whirled his arms around, creating rings of Fire around him. The whorls were enough to drown out the surrounding sounds, and he felt safe cocooned between the flames. *This isn't right. Not right.* "Not right!"

Pierce did not quite know what happened that night in the Exalted's chambers, but he returned to the waking world shattered and alone. Nothing felt the same. Something had stripped the soul from his skin and returned a shell. There was a presence in his mind that was difficult to place, like the Exalted had split it in two.

*But your sister lives.* "My sister," he whispered. Closed his eyes. *At least she lives.*

Not that he had seen her much since then. Danea had regained her strength faster than he did, because of course dying couldn't stop her, but she barely looked at him anymore. In truth, she made it a point to be gone by the time he woke up, leading charges along the border. Driving the royal dogs back. Whatever happened that night, she wouldn't tell him. *Monster. Monster. She thinks you're a...* "I'm not a monster," he said, intensifying his flames.

But it ended today. The Exalted had summoned him to his cavern, and Pierce was finally going to get answers. "Monster. *Monster*." He made his way back to the cavern, avoiding the others at the camp. It wasn't hard. They were avoiding him now, especially when they saw the twin flames swirl around his body like snakes. Pierce felt better that they were there, and he did not care that the others feared him for it. The presence of his own Fire had always comforted him, and it cost him nothing to keep it close.

The guards at the mouth of the cavern did not even bother stopping him anymore, and he made his way inside. The flames of his serpents lit the way, but he still closed his eyes and counted. "Twenty-two. Twenty-two steps. *Here*."

"Come in," the Exalted commanded from inside his chambers, but he barely looked up from his book when Pierce obeyed. Slowly, Pierce let his snakes return to his core. *Back to the source. Back to the source.* The Exalted's lips parted into a cold smile. "I have good news—"

"What did you do to me?" Pierce demanded. Anger shook his thin frame.

The Exalted snapped the book shut with one hand. "I saved your sister. You saved your sister. At all costs—those were your words, were they not?"

"They were. But I… but I don't feel like me."

"You gave up part of yourself to save her life," said the Exalted calmly. He spoke like he was soothing a child, but his eyes flickered in cold amusement. "It's not surprising that you feel different. I was the mere vessel who completed the connection."

"And the night-wolf?"

"And the night-wolf." He set the book down. "Your blood is strong, Pierce. Such *Fire* in you. In Danea, as well. We needed a strong, Fire-bound creature to strengthen the connection."

"She won't even look at me anymore." *Monster. Monster. You are a...*

"I imagine dying is an unpleasant experience," said the Exalted, unfazed. "Even a warrior like Danea must come to terms with the living now."

"The others think I'm a monster!"

"Their envy is a monstrosity." The Exalted waved a hand before Pierce could say more. "Now if you're quite done, I need to talk to you about something." His eyes narrowed, almost daring Pierce to interrupt him. "Our scouts have reported royal recruits in the southern villages. This is your chance, boy. You must join their ranks."

"What?" Pierce blinked. "I'm... I'm not leaving Danea. Not to join *them*."

The Exalted shrugged as though he was expecting it. "Very well," he said softly. Coldly. "Go, then. See to your sister. But I imagine you'll be back sooner than you think." He turned back to his book, looking more bored than disappointed. *"Go."*

Pierce scrambled out of the cavern and made his way to Danea's tent. He didn't know how long he waited there, sitting and hugging his knees in the far corner, but he refused to move until she came back. By then, the skies had darkened, and the tears had dried on his sleeve.

She paused when she saw him, but he rose and wrapped his arms around her. "I... why can't you look at me anymore?" he asked. *Pathetic. Pathetic. Monster. Monster...*

Danea stood, still as a statue, until he let go. She looked into his eyes but said nothing.

"What happened?" Desperation tore at him from the inside. "What did I do to you?"

"What you did to me..." she repeated, the first thing she had said to him in days. "What you did to me?" Without warning, she pulled the dagger from his sheath—the dagger she had given him when they first arrived at the Exalted's camp—and slammed it into her heart.

"WHAT ARE YOU DOING?" Pierce screamed. Instinctively, he tore it out of her, feeling her blood on his hands. *Monster. Monster. Murderer.*

But Danea kept standing. She glanced at the tear in her shirt, at the splash of crimson that spread outwards like ink, and after an uncomfortable silence, she pulled it down at the collar.

Pierce saw blood spill from a wound that was already closing. The scar whitened before his eyes. "What... I don't..." *Monster. Monster.*

"This... is what you did to me," she said, and Pierce was surprised to see tears on her face. He had never seen her cry before, not once. Not even when their parents died. Their friends. "It was my fate to fall that night, little brother. But something is keeping me alive now. I feel it. It's keeping me alive, but this... this isn't living."

"Danea, I  "

The reproach in her eyes was too much to bear. "I would have given my *life for* you, little brother," she said. "I never expected you to waste it so carelessly."

*Monster. Monster.* "What do you want me to do? I'll do anything," he said. Pleaded. He hated how helpless he sounded, but without her, it had all been for nothing. *It can't have been for nothing.* "The Exalted wants to... wants to send me away. He wants me to join the Royals. To be one of them. To infiltrate them."

But there was no comfort in Danea's eyes. There was not much of anything in her eyes, no matter how much Pierce tried to see it.

The fire had gone out, replaced by something cold and dark. Dead. She lowered her gaze. "Then *go,*" she said, cruelly. "And don't come back."

# 14

## GLASGÉRIOS
# ICE REALM

"What are we doing here?" asked Merc without bothering to lower his voice—a deliberate defiance of reason, as they had done their best to slip past detection at the first signs of dawn. After spending weeks in the Underground, daylight seared through Decker's eyelids, but it felt good against his skin.

Decker steered his horse down a ridge of granite that the winds had scrubbed clean of snow. He and Kerys—or the Ice Wolf, as he affectionately called their resident shadow guard—didn't feel the cold like their companions did, so he moved with little effort. Kiera seemed used to it. In any case, whatever frost-born wounds she would bear would heal a hundred times over. Only Merc was at a disadvantage, but for once, he stayed quiet.

"Do remember the way," said Kiera to no one in particular. "I won't show you again."

"Where are we?" asked Merc as she slid down from her saddle and tied her horse to the nearest tree. She walked over to the side of the mountain and pressed her ear gently against the stone... and began talking to it.

"I knew it," whispered Merc to Decker. "She's insane."

Kiera took a step back and pointed to a stretch of rock that looked too smooth to be natural. There was a carving in the stone, but had she not pointed it out, Decker would have missed it completely.

But he recognized the symbol.

"Uh, Elayne?" asked Merc. "Is that...?"

"The triangle used to guard the Blackstone!" said Elayne in wonder. She brushed past Decker and ran her fingers along the etchings. "But how...?"

"Don't look at me," Kiera shrugged innocently. "A good friend of mine sealed this place years ago, and its seal is bound to Water and Ice. He did teach me how to open it, but it would look far less clumsy if you did it for me." She smiled at Elayne, but it wasn't a request.

Elayne's jaw tightened, but curiosity got the best of her. She held her hand out against the symbol and whispered something to it, just like at the Blackstone. When she finished, blue flames shot out between the etched lines, and Decker heard a familiar click on the other side.

"Mm, thanks," said Kiera as the stone slab gave way. She entered first, taking a torch from its sconce and holding it out towards Merc. He lit it without question. "Good man," she said, pleased. "Stay close, everyone."

Decker followed her into the cave. She lit more torches along the walls until firelight spilled into every crevice of the corridor, but where he expected to find a cavern, he was met with a set of iron doors. "Help me," she said to Decker as she heaved her weight against them.

Decker threw himself against the doors, but they barely groaned against impact. It was only when Merc attacked them with a running leap that they opened wide enough for them to squeeze through. As Decker was the biggest, he went last—enough time for Kiera to run ahead and light the torches of the chamber, even the ones thirty feet up. He frowned. *How did she reach them so fast?* he thought as his eyes adjusted to the cavern. Widened.

"Fuck me," said Merc in awe, ever the aspiring poet.

No matter where he looked, Decker found himself facing weapons and armor. They lined the walls, piled on top of each other. His practiced eye took in everything from longswords to spiked maces, from axes to crossbows. Shields were propped up against the sides of the cavern, some small enough for children. A chain whip lay curled in the corner, forgotten next to sets of mail forged from chains and scales. They didn't look like anything local.

"What is this place?" asked Elayne, and Decker laughed to himself. Somehow, a Healer did not quite belong in a hall full of weapons, and he could almost feel her discomfort. She was likely imagining all the wounds she would have to heal.

Kiera shrugged. "Recycling."

Decker glanced around until he saw domeric gauntlets, still loaded with dart-blades. He swallowed his dread. "Is that…?"

"Tomá's? Goddess, no. What do you think of me? Like I said, I had this place sealed off years ago." Kiera laughed. "No, I hid Tomá's armor elsewhere. It's not like he was going to need it anymore." Her long, black hair swayed as she continued into the chamber. She pointed to the sets of armor piled in the far corner. "Those are all infused with blackwood. Since we can all burn, I suggest taking them. There aren't many, unfortunately. That kind of metalwork is not easily parted from its owner."

"How did you even… *begin* accumulating all of this?" asked

Elayne, who had stumbled upon a cupboard of what Decker assumed to be poisons.

Kiera laughed off the question with grace. "I've been stripping these off the bodies of dead enemies for years. I pilfered armories and smithies on my journeys. It's not so hard once you get the hang of it."

"Is this the only one?"

Kiera laughed louder. "That's cute," was all she said.

"This could arm a small army," said Merc.

"That's the idea," said Kiera, strapping on a bracer she had been eyeing on the wall. "Take what you want." Excitement turned to disappointment when no one made a move for the chain whip. "Shame." She sighed. "I've always wanted to see someone wield that thing."

Merc attempted to pass it off with a chuckle, but it died a slow death in the vastness of the chamber. Sighing, Decker made his way towards the blackwood cuirasses as Elayne examined a pile of daggers. Some of them were still stained with blood.

Kiera pulled a set of light armor from the wall. "I haven't worn this in years," she said, and Decker gaped. He supposed it was no surprise that she had been a *reyna*, part of the Lancistierrean elite, but he had never seen one in full attire before. He'd always wanted to know what the belt was for. It was thick and supported two holsters on each side, but neither held weapons.

Kiera followed his gaze and smiled softly. "This belt helped us defeat the shadow guards once. A lifetime ago," she said. "It helped us *fly*. Come with me and I'll show you how."

Decker unsheathed his own sword and set it aside in favor of a newer blade. Blackwood was by far the lightest, and he took to its feel instantly. Only the Ice Wolf didn't bother changing her gear.

Instead, she collected arrows.

"Kiera," said Merc over the clamor of dropping metal. "What exactly are you planning to do with this place once we leave?"

"I've already left Sirian instructions on what to do with this place," she said. "I just wanted us to get first choice before leaving it to his disposal."

"Sirian?" Merc frowned. "How is he going to get the door open?"

This time, Kiera's laugh was genuine. *"Children,"* she said, shaking her head. "You spend all this time with them, yet you know nothing about them. Tell me." She turned to Merc, the smile still on her face. "Who did you think sealed this door in the first place?"

Even if they had all the time in the world, Decker suspected the surprise would never fade. With all the knowledge she had, she must have been hundreds of years old.

"I'm not surprised your friend is the Second Summoner, you know," said Kiera. "Sweet little thing. But she's killed and fought and bled, and I doubt she's finished. Why, I believe her blood campaign has just begun."

"Blood campaign?" Merc repeated. "This is Dove we're talking about."

"Oh, spare me. Even Valerya wasn't born the She-Jackal. The first time we met, Valerya was a lamb," she said, pocketing a pair of hand blades that were shaped like stars. "Monsters are made, not born, and the sweetest can be just as terrible."

*No. Not Dove.* The kid had been wearing burnt rags when they first met, and her face had been covered in ash. *Such a harmless kid... who ended up summoning a dragon to save us.* "So where's the airship?" he asked, trying not to think about the devastation Dove's beast could cause. "Don't tell me you have it hidden away in another cavern."

"An airship?" Kiera stared at him blankly. Amusement curled the corner of her lips upwards. "You're cute, Deklan. Has anyone ever told you?"

"How do you know my—"

"I need a sky commander, good man," she said. "But not for an airship."

"For what, then?"

Kiera laughed as she strapped the belt with holsters around her waist. "You'll see soon," she said, handing him a thicker belt. "If we survive this journey, I'll teach you to fly."

# 15

## RED CITADEL
# FIRE REALM

Gryff wondered how long he had been knocked out. The illusion
had been so perfectly crafted, so flawless, that it was easy to
tell he was back in the real world. Everything hurt, and the cold walls
of the library provided no comfort.

"WATER," he shouted, but it came out a voiceless growl. His
throat was so dry, each breath felt like swallowing needles. The
graces may not have liked visiting him, but he had at least expected
them to leave clean water behind. *This cup has been here longer
than me.*

But Gryff could not afford to be choosy. He extended his arm—
and felt the burn.

"AAGHHH!" He jerked back instinctively as his stitches ripped
open. His weight knocked against the side table, and he watched
helplessly as the cup crashed to the floor.

Gryff groaned and rubbed his eyes. It was taking him too long
to recover, but nightbloom was the only way he could sleep after
the General flogged the skin off his back. It also made him groggy.
Disoriented. *Just my luck,* he thought. Not only did he burn in

daylight, he also bled longer than normal people. No matter what they gave him, his wounds refused to heal.

He heard the door open and glanced around the library, waiting for the blurriness to subside. "Whossere?" he slurred, hoping for a medican.

"It's me," came a voice, much softer and deeper than usual. *Lyra.*

He frowned. As welcome as her voice was in his pit of despair, she wasn't supposed to be here. She'd found extra work in the kitchens, eating everything she pleased, and fallen ill after the latest import from the fishing villages. Since Morian had begun summoning the warlords, even fishermen had more important things to worry about—like securing their own food supply.

In truth, Lyra had only accepted the job for the access to free food, but it was a complete disaster. Everything she tasted seemed to make her sick. But Lyra was stubborn, that much he knew, and he had only recently convinced her to seek help from the medican.

"I thought you'd still be with Aela," he said, relieved. It made him happy to see her well, and he was grateful to Valerya for letting Lyra see her personal medican. He moved aside, ignoring the pain. Outstretched his arms. "Why are you standing so far away? Come closer."

Lyra sat at the edge of the bed, and he felt the silence grow between them. *No,* he thought firmly. He couldn't lose her, too. She had already been distant lately, snapping at him one moment and sobbing in apology the next.

Not that he could blame her. There were so many things going on at the Citadel that it was hard to keep track. Recruits were pouring into the capital in droves, there was talk of storming Glasgérios... even Lancistierrean emissaries had been seen wandering castle grounds. For some reason, Lyra thought it was the perfect time to take on a third job.

"Of course you're feeling overwhelmed," he said. Valerya had commissioned her to rework the Spades' swords, and she had been slaving away at the smithy, desperate not to fall from the General's good graces. Not like him; he was so far down, he might as well disappear.

Gryff tried a different approach. "What did the medican say?" he asked, keeping his voice steady. It wasn't hard. The medicine was making him feel oddly relaxed.

"Nothing bad," she said.

"Lyra."

"What?"

"*Lyra.*" He placed a hand on hers and propped himself up on one elbow. Suddenly the pain became easier to ignore. "What's wrong?"

"I…" She turned away from him. "It's… it's not spoiled food that's been making me sick. Nor is it… nor is it being overworked. All right, the medican said all that work *might* have something to do with it, and that I'm doing too much anyway, but I'm thinking that if I had to choose, I should probably give up the kitchen because I can't very well say no to our Gen—"

"Lyra." He rested his head on her shoulder and let his fingers run gently through her hair. "What is it?"

"I…" She stared intently at the bookcases before she continued. "I'm with child, Gryff."

The words hit him harder, sharper, than the General's whip. "You're… with child." He took special care not to let his fear show. The words sounded so foreign when they escaped his lips. It was not something he had ever thought about at length, let alone dreamed of. Yet it was here, in this room, present in the shimmer of life she was carrying inside her.

Her voice dropped to a whisper. "What if... what if it's our King's?"

As much as he didn't want to entertain the thought, his mind was preoccupied with another possibility, far worse for them and the child.

"What if it's not?" He looked away, not wanting to meet her eyes. If the child was Morian's, his reign of terror would have an heir, and Lyra would receive the full brunt of his affections.

But if it wasn't...

"No... we'll find a way," he said. It was the only truth he could think of, but it didn't stop him from being afraid. "I promise."

"If it's his, he'll... but if not, then... our child, Gryff..."

Gryff thought back to the Sun-sworn priests, burning Fireborne children in their first month of life to strengthen the flames. *If the child has even a drop of Ice in his veins, or the slightest shade of night in his hair...*

He drew in a sharp breath. *Then we're all dead. And him first of all.*

A faint smile flickered across his lips. "Don't worry," he said.

"What if... what if we told our General?" she asked.

Gryff's hope soared and died fast. Valerya was the only person in the Realm who could change the tides, but she would not sacrifice dinner—let alone duty—to help Gryff. He did not even know if she was still in the castle. Last he heard, she had been torching camps, hellbent on crushing the resistance. Best not to bother her with thoughts of Morian's descendants.

Gryff closed his eyes and lay back down, stroking Lyra's hair until she fell asleep. He kissed her shoulder and draped the blanket over her before slipping out of the library. Suddenly, the halls stretched farther than the eye could see. An ominous breeze stirred the crimson drapes. The smell of rotting meat wafted after them.

"Mongrel," a voice boomed behind him as he closed the door.

*Of course,* he thought. Greaven. Gryff drew in a steady breath to settle the tremor in his stomach. His courage waned. *Well, better here than there.* If Morian's guard-dog had barged in on him and Lyra, they would have had a bigger problem.

It was unsettling to see Greaven away from his master, capable of autonomous thought after all. Malice burned black fire in his eyes, and a semblance of a grin flickered across his face. "Valerya's little whelp," he growled. "I could skin you alive with this blade."

Indeed, the dagger in his hand had an absurdly large blade. What he was hoping to encounter in the corridors in the dead of night, Gryff didn't want to know.

Gryff felt his body tense. He clenched his jaw and bowed respectfully.

"Ha!" said Greaven, amused. "I suppose they've given you enough beatings if knives don't scare you anymore." It was the most Gryff had ever heard him say at once, and he was surprised to hear a trace of an accent that placed him far from the capital. In truth, it sounded a bit like Valk. "I was hunting rats tonight when I heard a rumor. Concerning a certain *mongrel* and a Summoner."

Gryff blinked. "There are many rumors floating around the Citadel," he said, keeping calm. "Which one is it now?"

Greaven bared his teeth. Some may have mistaken it for a smile. "That you know her. That she grew up with you in some shit stain of a village in the Dragontail."

Gryff found himself thanking the graces for all the nightbloom they had given him; he was so relaxed, he couldn't even get angry. Under normal circumstances, he would have already panicked or blurted out some ludicrous lie. "I didn't take you for a lover of gossip," he said.

Cold, terrible fury broke out over the man's face, but Gryff stood his ground. "Our King believes it," said Greaven. "If he believes it, so do I. And he's going to *love* you." He straightened, and Gryff realized with dread that he wasn't wearing any armor. He'd assumed that armor made Greaven look bulkier, but even without it, the man dwarfed him five times over. "See, we've been wondering how to deal with the Second Summoner. And if this *gossip* is true, then you've suddenly become of use to us."

Greaven stopped and let his gaze linger on the library doors. "I trust you have no visitors at this hour," he said with a shadow of a smile. "Have a good night."

As Greaven turned and left, whistling a merry tune, Gryff felt the life leave his limbs. He bent over, suddenly short of breath. He was marked now. Morian had taken a special interest in him; only this time, it wasn't just his neck on the line, but Lyra's. And the child's. *His* child, if the gods wanted to spit on his grave. Desperation bit into his spine.

*Either I sacrifice them, or I sacrifice Dove,* he thought. If he could, he would just sacrifice himself. It was an impossible choice. *What do I do?*

Everything answered a voice, soft and soothing, deep within his mind. *You can save them all.*

# THE
# MAD WHISPERER

The Exalted had been half right.

Breaching the Citadel had been almost insultingly easy. Pierce's elements were so strong that the Royals didn't want him fighting for anyone else, and after a few weeks, he'd even gotten his own chambers. Well, it was more like a broom closet, but it was more than he could say for the other recruits who suffered in the barracks. It had a large window, at least, and if he kept it open, it didn't feel so suffocating. The other boys hated him for it, but he had fallen in favor with the Sovereign, so they left him alone.

"Alone. Left me alone. *Alone.*"

It was reaching the Sovereign himself—alone—that had proven to be a challenge. Pierce's elements often got him invited to dinner with the Sovereign and his trusted circle, but otherwise, the man was constantly surrounded by admirers. It was easy to see why. He was a charming man with a crescent smile, and his words were full of promises. If Pierce had not grown up on the other side, even he would have believed the lies.

The Sovereign's chambers were guarded by ten of his elite

guard. Pierce was afraid of them. Especially the big one with the black armor who smelled of death.

"Death. *Death.* Black death."

Pierce brought his hands to his temples. The headaches were becoming more and more frequent. It often felt like something was in there, watching him. *Whatever it takes.* He didn't care what happened to him as long as Danea lived, even if she hated him for it. His sister had given him everything. Gone days without food so he'd have something to eat. His pain was nothing in comparison. He recalled with sadness all the unanswered letters he had sent.

The next headache hit when he was sitting at his desk in front of the mirror.

"This again," he whispered to himself. Cursed. "No, wait. I have to finish. I'll just finish." His vision was swirling into colors, but he made sure to sign his name neatly on the last page. "Time to go. See this? Time to *go*." *Going. Going. Going.*

He had to do this before the medicans gave him more deathbell. His whispers had already been noted, and no matter how much leniency the Sovereign had shown him, he did not want it known that there was a madman in his castle. *The mad whisperer.*

He rose from his chair and draped his cloak over his shoulders. "Time to go."

It was well after dinner but not late enough to arouse suspicion. Pierce opened the door and made it down a few corridors until he almost crashed into Ulma, the head chambermaid. She was a stout woman in her forties, and for a servant of the castle, she wasn't very good at servitude. Not when it came to him, at least. In many ways, she reminded him of his own mother, but her brown eyes were flecked with gold. Even the servants called her 'Ma. "Oh! Sorry, very sorry, 'Ma..." he muttered.

"My lord?" Ulma's brow furrowed in motherly concern. "Are you all right, love?"

*Ulma is confused again.* They all were. Just because the Sovereign had shown him mercy and given him his own chambers, the entire castle treated him like royalty. "Yes. Yes. I'm all right. All right. Right, that's good. Say, Ulma," Pierce stammered. "Did you... did we find the Second Summoner yet?"

Ulma gave a patient laugh, but her smile didn't reach her eyes. *She thinks I'm going mad.* "Yes. We found the child, Pierce. You know this already. Why don't you go find—?"

*I need to talk to the child.* He shook his head. "Calm. *Calm.* Thank you Ulma," he muttered as he turned and continued down the corridor. "Need to talk to the child. The *child.* Need to talk to the child." The throbbing was getting worse, but he had to keep going. Sometimes, colors blurred together until he could no longer see, but it was only when they disappeared that his head exploded. Best to get things done before then.

"Stay with me," he muttered to himself as he glanced over his shoulder. "No one there. No one." He descended the spiral staircase. "Have to finish. Must finish. Then talk to the child."

The dungeons had been refreshingly empty this month. Pierce made sure to let the Exalted know exactly where the Sovereign was planning on striking, so the cells remained free of his fellow Spears. And now that the Sovereign was on a rampage, even small-time crooks kept their heads down. Pierce was alone.

"This here. This here. Remember." Pierce committed the stone to memory. There were hundreds making up this wall, and he had already lost track of some of his more valuable items. The ring the Exalted had gifted him was surely behind one of these bricks, but he didn't have time to take the wall apart. "Seventeen from the left.

Nine down," he muttered to himself as he traced the stones with his finger. "Seventeen from the left. Nine down." He pulled the loose brick from the wall and shoved his notes inside. "He mustn't. He mustn't read it. Avantys mustn't read it." *Mustn't. It mustn't.* It took him a while to realize he was sobbing. "Danea. Danea, I'm so sorry." *Monster. Monster. She thinks you're a...*

He allowed himself a good cry, as he often did when he was alone. But this time was different. "This is my goodbye message," he said between tears as he shoved the brick back in. "I have to go. I have to do it. It's the only way. The only way to kill a tyrant." He covered his mouth with his hand to stop himself from wailing. *It hurts so much, Danea.* He pressed his hand against his head and stroked his hair. Comforted himself. "Please, please forgive me. Please don't forget me. Now go. *Go.* It's time to go."

# 16

## RED CITADEL
# FIRE REALM

Three raps on the door jolted Valerya awake, and she stirred,
ready to draw blood.

Her dragon was growing more vicious with each passing day.
Long days of training drudges had once been enough to devour her
energy, but now she commanded the Spades to spar with her every
night. Even when it was all against one, they stood no chance. Anger
had taken root inside her, and it needed an outlet.

Valerya rolled over and thrust a pillow over her head, but the
knock returned. This time, it was melodic and teasing.

*Fuck.* Morian hadn't visited her chambers since his birthday,
but his absence did not make her miss him. She had barely hoisted
herself up when he entered. "No need to get up," he said, feigning
nonchalance as he inspected her chambers. He clicked his tongue
in disapproval when he saw her. "Really, Valerya. You sleep in that
thing?"

Valerya cursed herself for not locking the door. In truth, she was
surprised she had even managed to take off her armor before falling
asleep in her linens. The wealthy considered it poor taste, but she

had never understood why they made clothes made specifically for sleeping. If anyone stormed the Citadel, who would take her seriously if she wore silk shirts like Morian? Might as well command the castle guard naked.

With a flick of his wrist, Morian lit the torch closest to him. He made himself comfortable on the other side of her bed. "I just wanted to give you the *delightful* news," he said. "A rider from the Rhysian provinces arrived in the dead of night."

"I doubt they mean to invite us to Lady Julieth's wedding," said Valerya. There was no such wedding, but Julieth was the first name that came to mind. She was the only one of Valk's hundred cousins she had taken a liking to. There was something inherently appealing about a woman who abandoned her titles and disappeared off the face of the world.

To that, Morian laughed. "Northerners produce more whelps than all the whores in Sinthea combined. The last thing we need is another wedding." His eyes widened as though he had just remembered something. "Speaking of the Northerners and their brood... how many did Lucien have?"

"Two."

"Yes," said Morian absently. "A son and a daughter. But it's a funny thing, really. My men torched the house. Saw the roof collapse and everything. And yet..."

"I remember," said Valerya. "I saw the remains of that house."

"And some of the Spades before you, from what I recall. Oren and... *Valk,* was it? My mind isn't so sharp this time of day, so remind me: that was his niece and nephew, was it not?"

"They were."

"Because the scholars say it's *her* name that's being claimed in the North." He rested his head on her shoulder. His breath curled against her neck. "Do you remember seeing such a girl on the battlefield?" he whispered.

"I barely saw two strides in front of me."

"Sixteen, seventeen, maybe... not much older than you were," he continued. His voice had become unsettlingly calm. "Uncanny, really, how history repeats itself."

"Where did you hear this fantasy?" she asked.

"Little birds talk, especially falcons. And they told me everything." He turned to face her, and a repugnant grin split his face in two. "And they whisked her off to the North. Well played. *Gods,* I didn't know they had it in them. We need to keep them in the fold, Valerya."

Valerya thought she was going to be ill, but it wasn't because of the news. She felt his hand move under her shirt, felt his vile fingers run over the scars that textured her skin.

"Your Highness," she said, but his free arm moved forward, grabbing onto her own. For a peaceful moment, she tried to pretend he didn't exist, but that was difficult with his lips pressed against her shoulder, moving towards her neck.

Valerya closed her eyes, unable to envision a future that didn't result in regicide. "My *king,*" she said.

Morian stopped. "You know," he said after a thoughtful pause, his arms still draped around her. "The medican informs me the blacksmith's daughter is with child."

*Goodbye, Gryff,* she thought, unaffected. The two had been spending an inordinate amount of time together lately, and they were young. If they did it once, they did it twice or more each day. It wasn't ideal, but it kept them out of her way.

She frowned. *Goodbye, Lyra.* That was more troublesome. She hated her soft spot for blacksmiths' daughters.

Yet if the child was Morian's...

"I…" Valerya's frown deepened. "What… joyful news."

She felt the corner of his lips turn upwards. They grazed against the side of her face like sand. "Joyful, I suppose… to some," he said. He smelled her hair, hovering dangerously close to the edge of his life. But before murder seemed the most viable option, she heard Avander's voice ring in her ears. *Protect the bloodline.* She cursed her younger self.

"How long has it been since you've been… intimate?" Morian asked. He didn't bother waiting for an answer. "I suppose *Lucien* was a long time ago."

"We were never…"

"A good thing that was taken care of," he continued. "As for the brat, on the other hand… she can still be reasoned with."

"Forgive me," said Valerya. "But if what you say is true, the girl's lost everything. What makes you think she can be reasoned with?"

"Just a hunch," said Morian, shrugging. "After all… here we are. By the way…" His face broke out into another awful grin. "Why *did* you keep her alive?"

"A hunch," said Valerya curtly. If they were testing each other's limits, he would lose, and he might as well know it.

He seemed to understand her well enough. "I suppose I can't be too angry. Your hunch saved a Summoner, and who knows how many centuries we would have waited for the next one." Something dark flashed across his eyes. "I will forgive you this once, Valerya. Do not disappoint me again."

Inside, her dragon raged, and it took Valerya's remaining strength to quiet it. Morian took her silence for compliance. "Is that all?" she asked.

"I was hoping you'd ask!" Morian's face lit up. "I'm sure you understand my dilemma. I can't have a rogue summoner in the Realm, and I hear you can be… persuasive."

"Diplomacy isn't my strong suit."

"I'm aware," said Morian with a short laugh. "Gods almighty, I'm aware. But it's time we pay our countrymen in Rhysia a visit. And who better to represent the interests of the Empire than you?"

*The Empire.* He wasn't even hiding it anymore. No one was. In truth, Valerya didn't care what word they used. It was all the same to her, but throwing it around so carelessly would create a lot of enemies.

"A tiresome task," Morian continued, unaware she had stopped paying attention. "But you don't *have* to lead them. Stay with me, open yourself to me, and I'll get someone else to go north. And I could have your friend spared… a courtesy I never extended his brother."

"And the girl?"

Her hand shot up instinctively to stop his before he could reach her breast. It had been too long since she felt the sensation of human flesh on hers, but if this was the only alternative, she would rather join the Silent Sisters at the temple. It was a cruel world.

*Sorry, Valk,* she thought as Morian pulled away. Indignation brewed under a thin veil. "I am bound to my duties as Guardian of the Realm," she said.

Morian shook his head and chuckled to himself. Even without the dragon, she outmatched him in size and strength; she never understood why he kept pressing his luck. "You don't know how much it pains me to hear that," he said. "Very well, then. Prepare the Spades. You will ride for Rhysia at the dawn of the ascendant star."

"And if they don't give her up?"

"You'll think of something," he said. Smiled. "Surely a Summoner General can handle a teenage girl. No matter what the cost."

*Well played.*

She knew what was coming. Morian would not rest until she had given him everything. It was a tactic she had often employed against enemy strongholds. It was stupid attacking fortifications head on; stone walls did not bleed, and what did not bleed could not bend. Instead, she waited outside their walls until the city starved itself into chaos, ordering their fields burned, their water poisoned, their livestock slaughtered.

Now Morian was doing the same, cutting down her allies so she would be alone, defenseless. And for the love she bore his father, he knew she wouldn't slaughter him in his sleep. *A cruel world, indeed.*

"Oh, silly me. I've completely forgotten," he said, false mirth veiled over a cruel smile. "Your ally. That… Valk. He is guarding the girl, is he not?"

Valerya opened her mouth, but Morian cut her off. "Good," he said. "I want you to bring me the girl. And I want you to bring me his head."

She nodded solemnly. He would not get the satisfaction of outrage from her. "As you command," she said coldly.

Valerya stood there a long time after he left. She could think of nothing that would compel Valk to give into Morian's demands. He might even offer his head willingly if it meant the new daughter of Rhysia would live to see another dawn.

She sighed and slung her sword over her back. She would need to rouse her men—a task more daunting than war for most—but before that, she needed some air. The ascendant star would turn soon, which meant they only had a few days left.

"You fucking owe me, Avander," she growled as she left her chambers. The night was too cold to brave in linen garb that was thin and tattered, but her blood was boiling. *I'm going to fucking haunt you in the afterlife.*

She made her way through the halls, confronted with memories seeped into each stone. The corridor before her, where she had first shared words with Eithan the Archemage. And there, where it curved, was where that Thunderborne gave her her first ever lesson in proper pub brawls. She passed by the guest chambers, trying to recall those who once stayed there.

None of them mattered, though. They came and went and nothing changed because of it. Only the foreign beauty came to mind. She had married into Heavensward, a massive bastion in the northernmost part of the world, and was forced to pay her respects to the Crown. Valerya must have been seventeen then, but they had taken a liking to each other. *Jes'ka or Jez'ka or something else I couldn't pronounce,* thought Valerya, recalling more than a few warm nights.

She continued until she reached the stairs, where she once caught Valk and Sonea arguing about... Valk and Sonea. She hated it. Chambermaids and midwives prayed to the gods for gossip and scandal, but it was always Valerya who managed to catch the Citadel in its most dramatic moments. Fortunately for the two of them, she couldn't be bothered to care. They made each other happy, and there were enough whispers floating around the castle; lending them a voice would have gotten both of them killed. Not like it mattered though, in the end.

Valerya grunted as she swung the doors open and listened to the sounds of the night. The entire Citadel bathed in silence—a hollow, echoing quiet. Except for the hammer.

A flame flickered in the corner of her eye, amber sparks that came from the smithy. She frowned. The Swordsworn were always welcome to sharpen their weapons on castle grounds, but no one took advantage of it. Especially at this hour.

Except for...

"Lyra?" Valerya forced the doors open. Ash and smoke intertwined and rose to greet her, but she broke through their embrace, irritated. Fifty horseshoes lay scattered on the ground, freshly forged, as Lyra brought her hammer down. Mercilessly. Her determination was faultless. Sweat slicked her skin with each clang, and Valerya wondered how Gryff, of all the boys in the kingdom, had managed to gain her affections.

"Oh!" Lyra exclaimed when she glanced up, and she wiped sweat from her brow. Her joy vanished when she saw the ground scattered with broken blades. "Forgive me, I can't kneel…"

Valerya waved a hand. "What are you doing up at this hour?"

"I've… I've just finished Oren's sword," said the girl, embarrassed.

"Let me see." Valerya took it in her hand, and her face softened. "This is fine work," she said. "You will surely have his gratitude."

Though the smithy was filled with shades of dancing flames, Lyra reddened until her face matched the fire. She glanced away when Valerya caught her staring.

"Speak plainly," said Valerya.

"Your… your sword," said Lyra. "I've never seen anything like it before. Was it… was it Damien's work? I heard he was the castle smith under King Avander, so I assumed…"

"No," said Valerya. Rare patience steadied her tone.

"Not a lot of smiths can infuse swords with blackwood," said the girl, eyes sparkling. "Let alone reforge them. Even I… I can't reforge broken blades. Not as well, at least." She smiled shyly. "Who did it?"

Valerya turned Oren's blade in her hand. "After my first siege, I refused to let others touch it. I did it myself."

Her eyes widened. "You?" She caught herself and turned away. "Of course you did. I mean, your father was a blacksmith, too."

"Working metal ran in my family, but you'd be a fool to think my father was the smith."

Lyra's face broke out into a wide grin. "Still," she said. "You'd need a certain connection to Fire to be able to do it. But I guess it's easier for a Summoner, I mean, you're connected to a dragon and all, and their Fire burns the strongest. It's just… it's just really… fascinating."

It was almost painful to look at, knowing what awaited her in the months ahead. There would be no mercy for her or the bastard. If Valerya's fool of a scribe had any wits about him, he would kill the brat in its womb. A few pinches of deathbell would solve all their problems.

"Go to sleep, girl," said Valerya instead. "I will make sure Oren receives his blade."

Lyra bowed, clearly glad for the reprieve, but Valerya knew she would be headed for Gryff's chambers. "Good night, General!" said the girl before darting out of the smithy.

*A connection.* The girl said too many words for her liking, but that one stayed. *A connection.* She slid the blade in its sheath and made her way to the Spades' Quarters.

"Up, drudges!" she commanded, banging on every door along the corridor. She heard the familiar scuffle behind closed doors as her men grumbled and growled.

It was Diebold who emerged first, disheveled but at her command. "My General," he said dutifully. More and more doors opened as her men stepped out into the corridor. "My General," they said in a groggy attempt at unison. Chuckles snickered behind tired eyes. It looked as though he had been drinking the night before—with Weyan, who stumbled out of his own chambers, wishing, it seemed, that he had never been born.

"Act plainly," she commanded impatiently, and they all relaxed in posture. She tossed Oren's sword at his face, and he caught it, stunned. "Wake up," she snapped. "I have orders from our King. Diebold, are your chambers presentable?"

He glanced inside. "Yo," he said. Shrugged. After Valk, he had the biggest chambers, and she did not feel the need to use Valk's room for what they were about to discuss.

"Convene," she ordered, and the men filed into Diebold's chambers. "Skandar, bring me a map. And Chuckles." She turned to the man, who met her eyes with a broad grin and a stifled giggle. "Bring whatever you and Weyan had to drink last night."

Chuckles disappeared back into his chambers and emerged with a barrel of ale. They entered Diebold's room and gathered around his desk, where Skandar unrolled his own tattered map of the Realm. In addition to place names, he had marked differences in terrain. Skandar may not have had a soldier's charm, but he had a cartographer's memory.

"What's this about?" Skandar asked, placing stones at both ends.

"We are to ride for Rhysia," answered Valerya.

That woke them up. "*Rhysia?*" some of them asked. Then asked again.

"Oren, Stane, and Aidan," she said. "You're from the surrounding area, correct?"

"Yes," said Oren softly. "I trained at the stronghold in Rhysia. That's where I met Va..." He stopped himself with a dry cough and turned to Stane and Aidan for help.

"I'm from Erisden," said Aidan, taking the hint.

"North Reach," grumbled Stane, frowning. "But... why Rhysia?"

"There will be time for questions later," said Valerya sternly as Diebold handed her a tankard. "I trust one of you can navigate the Wastes without getting us killed by the Huntsmen. I want you to take us through the most dangerous path, past Bjarred." She pointed at the small bog drawn hastily on the parchment. "Chances of being sighted are lower there."

Valerya downed the tankard to stop herself from laughing. In truth, she didn't care if they were sighted, but Morian's men wouldn't last a day in Bjarred.

"How… but what will we do in *Rhysia*?" asked Weyan cautiously.

"Have a pleasant conversation," said Valerya dryly, "with the Second Summoner."

She didn't even wait for Chuckles to finish pouring before she pressed the tankard to her lips and drank. It was vile, but it washed out the sour taste in her mouth. "A *marvelous* wreckage built on hills, but they never bothered to level the ground when they built their walls." She circled the stronghold with her finger. "The walls range from ninety feet to thirty-five. Is there anything else that is useful to know?"

Oren cleared his throat. "Uh, my General," he said weakly, taking a tankard for himself. "Lord Kai… he's a hard man who leads every charge. I don't think he'll grant us audience…"

Valerya nodded. "I thought so." As much as she hated riding north, she could respect a lord who fought his own battles. Her men fell silent as she contemplated the map. "What about the surrounding area?"

"There's… Breddon a bit to the south," said Stane reluctantly. "And *Marren's Haven,* just outside the castle walls. It's not drawn on the map, but…"

"Good," said Valerya. Her fingers traced along the space that separated the stronghold from the Huntsmen Woods. Marren's Haven. No more than a few huts the last time she was there, but it must have expanded since then.

"Are we… kidnapping the Summoner?" asked Weyan. He was not the brightest of the group but the first to lend his thoughts a voice. If only it were that easy. Dove would be painfully easy to abduct—she was small, weak, and made no sound. Her dragon, on the other hand…

"The High Lord is all we need," said Valerya, ignoring his question. "Once we have him, we have the stronghold. They will listen to us then."

"How do we draw him out?" asked Aidan, but she suspected they already knew.

She clenched her jaw firmly. "Distraction," she said.

*And perhaps, just perhaps—a connection.*

# 17

## THE

# OTHERWORLD

Dove woke up in a cell, but she knew it was a farce even before she opened her eyes. For one, it was so cold it burned. It never got this cold in the Firelands, not even in its outermost edges. For another, her surroundings rippled like something seen through the waters of a lake. Something else was playing with her senses. The bars were made of twisted branches, thick and gray, and misshapen roots broke through paved stone.

"Hello?" she called, but her voice was met with deep silence. As she came to, her cell stopped wavering. It felt like a bad dream, but she did not remember falling asleep. Dead leaves clung to the bars and blurred her vision to the outside world. She brushed them away and slipped her arm through the branches.

"Don't do that," a voice warned. It was sharp and stern, but Dove had grown to like it. She followed it to the opposite end of the room, where she found Valerya leaning against the wall. Her eyes were colored with pale contempt, and Dove suddenly realized where the cold came from. "Your cell is the only thing separating your world from mine."

*So I am not dreaming.* "We are in the Otherworld again," she said softly. "But why am I in a dungeon?"

"Can't have you running around now, can I? After the last time?"

*She knows about that.* Dove shifted uneasily. "Should I even ask about our... our word—"

"Always," said Valerya curtly. "*Peacock.* Something about carnations."

"Dahlias."

"Whatever. Not the kind you like."

"No... I like..."

*"Lilies."* Valerya did not quite snort, but she turned away to chuckle.

Dove sighed. Somehow, her subconscious had been more pleasant. At least there was a field and fresh air; here, she was surrounded by stone tinged with a tired scarlet, branches withered by painful years. There was an edge to the air that made it difficult to breathe, and it shifted with the General's mood. Wherever they were, it was not a welcoming place.

"You should be thanking me," said Valerya. "I'm not locking you in. I'm keeping it out."

Even through the stone, Dove felt its presence. It drove the chill from the bloodied walls, but its warmth was far from comforting. Instinctively, she glanced at the ceiling, only to find that there was none—only a hole that opened outwards into the night.

A shadow rippled across the moon. In this world, Avantys's flames did not brighten the night, and there was no scar in the sky to signal its coming. Dove had not expected to see it again so soon. *But where is my dragon?*

"Avantys... cannot kill me here though," said Dove. "Can it?"

Valerya gave a short laugh. "Skin-crawlers have been trying to breach my mind for years," she said. "The last one is even staying in your castle, if I recall. Why don't you ask him what happens when you cross my dragon?"

Dove was sure Valerya did not mean to sound terrifying all the time, but she did. She felt her stomach knot as she backed down from the older woman's gaze. "Why am I here?"

"Do you ever pay attention?" snapped Valerya. "I hate being in the minds of others, as... easy as yours was to breach. That beast of yours should guard it better." She paused when she saw Dove's confusion. "You *have* bonded with it, haven't you?"

"What?"

Valerya cursed, and the walls trembled. "Until you bond with it, it won't protect you. Your mind is open game, and all sorts of things can breach it. Honestly, girl. I let you live, and you're doing everything in your power to get yourself killed."

Whether or not she agreed, Dove wished Valerya would calm down. The dragon's roar filled the silence, signaling its closeness. Its Summoner's shifts in mood attracted it like fresh meat, and soon, it would rush to her aid.

"It may have chosen you, but you must choose it. Otherwise, it's nothing to you. An uncaged dog." Valerya's tone was layered with strained patience. Sensing no immediate threat, Avantys lost interest, retreating once again beyond the clouds. "If you're wondering *why* I've called you," she said before Dove could speak, "thousands of scrolls have detailed the *mereyna* in-depth. I wanted to see how our connection worked. How Avantys would react."

"Does that mean you can find me whenever you want?"

"You are weak." Valerya was not one for veiled insults. "Your mind is undisciplined. Learn to control it, and it will be more difficult to breach."

"So that is it, then?" asked Dove, hurt.

"You have questions?"

"You... this... we are *connected,* but you..."

"Speak plainly."

"You took... everything from me," Dove said, finding her courage. "*Everything.* And now you say we're *connected.*"

There were few moments—not many, but few—where Dove was happy she was voiceless in the waking world. For one, she never had to endure false pleasantries, and for another, she never said anything stupid. Her thoughts could be dumber than hay, but they never offended anyone. It was just her luck that the first time she insulted anybody, it was Valerya, whose dragon was looming dangerously above them.

It took a while for a response to come, but Valerya stared. Glowered. "On the night we burned through the Dragontail, how many people did you consider close to you?" she asked.

Dove blinked. *Well, there was...*

"My scribe. But he survived, regrettably." Valerya threw her a spiteful glance. "And once the Northmen discovered your existence, they came to take you away. A wonderful loss it must be, then, if everyone who loves you is still alive." She strode to the other side of the chamber and gazed out the window. "But that's not what I came to talk about."

"What is it, then?"

"I have invoked the mereyna in the waking world. Do you know what that means?"

"No, I..."

"I thought as much." She crossed her arms. "In the eyes of the Sun-sworn priests, Summoners automatically outrank the highest commander. A stupid law, but we are the first of our kind in hundreds of years. No one saw the need to change it."

"Commander? As in… an army, with proper soldiers?"

Valerya acknowledged the question, then ignored it. "Soon you will be forced to choose a side, and you will be bound to it for the rest of your life. Join us and you will be my second-in-command. The Swordsworn and all those bound to the Realm will answer to you."

"And I will answer to you?"

"That is the idea of a second-in-command."

"And… Morian."

"And our Sovereign," she said softly. "Should you refuse or swear allegiance elsewhere, you will be branded an enemy of the Crown. We will come and crush you."

Dove sighed, recalling her life as a runaway with fondness. It was easier when no one knew of her existence. Her life was much more complicated now that *every*one knew. "What does that mean, 'invoke the *mereyna*'?" she asked instead, changing the subject.

Valerya grimaced. Her eyes narrowed. "Another stupid law," she said. "If I as a Summoner come to the North, your people will be obliged by law to grant me audience with you. And as you've claimed the name of a dead girl, they are bound to you forever. Given the circumstances, I suggest finding someone who can speak on your behalf."

Nothing about this conversation was comforting, but Dove nodded anyway. "What… happened?" she asked, grateful for the bars around her. "Something must have happened for you to invoke the—"

*"Silence."* The word carried so much force that the walls began to quake. Dove watched in despair as Avantys soared towards them, sensing a disturbance. "It's time for you to leave."

As Valerya watched her beast soar ever closer, her lips curled into a smile that lasted all of two seconds before she turned her attention back to the cell. But her next words were not cold, or distant. "Take care of yourself," she said.

# 18

## RHYSIA

# FIRE REALM

"**A**vriel? *Avriel.*"

Dove blinked. The waking world hit her like a hammer when she opened her eyes. Her head hurt, but she found herself in a much happier place: blue skies and a green courtyard, too rich in color to be real.

"She's not used to the name yet," she heard, and giggling followed.

*Ah. Now I remember.* Dove turned to Mayet for help, but the swordmaiden seemed to bask in the pleasure of her pain. It may have been her duty to shield Dove from physical harm, but this sort of misery was far above her paygrade.

She sighed. Valk thought it was time Dove got to know the fine men and women of high society instead of trailing behind Bard all day. Bard, that traitor, thought little of nobility and spent most of his time in the town just beyond the walls. Whether it was the cheap ale or brothel that drew him there, she did not want to know.

It would have been fine had the others left her alone, but Saire and Rina swooped in the moment they sensed weakness. They claimed to be distant cousins of Valk, talking faster than she could follow, jumping from one topic to the next with admirable frequency.

They were sprawled out on the lawn watching men-to-be train in the inner courtyard. The two decided to skip their sewing lessons, fashioning themselves as rebels. Dove might have found it interesting had the trainees not been so bad at training. Noticing the sudden presence of three girls—two of whom seemed to own the castle—the archers focused more on form and poise than technique. Skill.

"Avriel. *Avriel,*" repeated Saire, snapping Dove back to her bleak reality. "Don't you think he's dreamy?"

Dove had no idea who she was talking about, but she nodded anyway. She followed Saire's gaze to one of the archers, broad-shouldered and confident, with wild, black curls. But her attention drifted to the boy next to him. The one with the bow built from pulleys and rope, who hit his target with more force than the practice bows. With a rueful sigh, she thought back to her own bow, neglected and stuffed in a corner somewhere in her chambers.

"She likes that one," said Saire when she noticed Dove's stare linger.

*What?* thought Dove as Mayet drew her lips tight, trying not to laugh.

"Really? That one?" asked Rina, but she shrugged it off with grace. They did everything with grace. They even skipped lessons with grace. "I suppose he's not bad…" Suddenly her eyes lit up. "Come on, I'll introduce you!"

*No, no, no.* Dove imagined herself unwillingly catapulted into another round of forced conversation. If Valerya was right and Dove gained control of the Northern army, she would make this count as a form of torture.

"Come on!" said Saire as she dragged Dove to the line of archers. Dove threw Mayet a desperate glance—surely this counted as physical duress!—but she saw only delight flickering in those evil, sadistic eyes. *A wonder she and Bard did not hang out more,* she thought dryly.

"Silas!" called Saire, breaking the archer's concentration. His arrow soared past the target, and he glared as he turned. At first, all Dove saw was hair—dark, brown waves and eyebrows knitted into a permanent scowl. But before he could say anything, another voice cut him off, invasive as it was taunting.

"Good shot," teased the black-haired archer, and Saire had the grace to giggle to herself. *This was her plan all along,* thought Dove, feeling like bait. Valk's distant cousins were of a deep and subtle cunning; they would do well among the ladies in Morian's court. Had the Northmen and the Citadel not been at each other's throats, she suspected they would have moved there the second they came of age and found a lordling to order about.

Silas ignored him, turning his attention back to his target, but the black-haired archer regarded her like he had found a new challenge. "I don't believe we've met," he said, clearing his throat. "I'm Daved."

"Daved," Rina repeated breathlessly. She sang praises as she spoke, but her voice was full of envy. "This is Avriel. She comes all the way from the capital."

"The capital?" He cocked an eyebrow. "Not a lot of archers down there. Not even the elite bother to learn. Your people *insist* on using swords." He handed Dove his bow, but he held on for a moment longer when she tried to take it. "I can show you how to use it."

He ignored Saire and Rina when they pretended to protest.

Dove's fingers tightened around the blackwood grip, and she was surprised that despite its smooth appearance, its surface was rough like sand.

Daved finally let go. "The trick is to stand like this..." he began, but Dove threw him a dark glance. This was finally something she could do alone. She blocked him out and drew in a deep breath to quiet her thoughts. Even the slightest, uncalculated tremor would throw off her aim.

*"Children."*

Mayet's voice tore through the silence, and Dove lowered the bow in surprise. Her swordmaiden must have been ten strides behind them, but she released an arrow that hit dead center. Playtime was over. She smiled, making sure everyone saw. "You're... needed somewhere," she said to Dove, finally deeming it fit to rescue her from the wolves. It was not the most believable exit, but no one protested. Dove tried not to look too excited when she took her leave.

Mayet clicked her tongue in disapproval when they entered the main keep. "Never show your hand too soon," she said. A single banner rose to greet them—a flash of golden silk embroidered with thorns. "Trust me. That boy isn't worth being your first enemy."

Dove glanced out the window at the labyrinth that made up the castle gardens. It was built to match the layout of the Brethren Wastes, but no matter how many times she traced her finger along the paths, the dead ends seemed to change. *How did Valk ever lead us out?*

Mayet followed her gaze. "When Northern children first start navigating the maze, the guards line the hedges with roses to help them find their way. It's become a sign of weakness around here. Giving roses is considered an insult. Hence, the thorns..."

Dove's attention to Mayet's voice waned as she concentrated on other things. Like the armor she wore. It wasn't like what they wore at the Citadel, where thick, sturdy metal was valued over form. Instead, Mayet's armor bent to her will, and bandages wrapped around her knuckles and down her wrists. No one else had that, but the wraps did not seem to nurse any injury. Through them, Dove could glimpse the knots of hard muscle that lined her arms…

She tore her gaze away when Mayet held up a hand. "Wait," she whispered, halting. Dove did not hear anything, but her swordmaiden grinned and took a gracious bow when Valk turned the corner with Lord Kai. "My lords," she said.

"I trust she's not giving you too much trouble?" asked Kai, but Dove did not quite know who he was asking. "I remember when Julieth was your age. Quiet, proper… until Mayet replaced her swordhand. After that, all she wanted to do was kill things."

Dove frowned. *A questionable ambition for an aspiring medican.*

"Should I even ask how sewing lessons went?" Valk gave her a defeated smile. "Remember what I told you. We need to lie low…"

"My lords!" a voice called, followed by rushed footsteps. The messenger stopped when he reached them and bowed so hastily, Dove thought his back would snap. "I apologize for the interruption, my lords, but this is urgent. We received a peregrine…"

"A peregrine?" Valk repeated, frowning. "A black one?"

"Yes," the messenger gasped and handed Kai a red scroll.

"What is this…" Kai broke the seal, but his frown swerved into concern as he read. "Valerya has invoked the *mereyna,*" he said softly, showing it to his nephew.

Dove glanced at Mayet, but it was clear she had no idea what that meant. Dove raised her eyebrows, pretending she did not, either.

"Forgive us," said Valk with a distracted bow. "We must attend to this matter at once. Mayet, I trust you can show Dove to her chambers."

Mayet led Dove to her room but did not enter. She never entered, except for when she thought Dove was dying. Instead, the sword-maiden stood sentinel outside her room. Even through closed doors, Dove could feel the presence of her elements.

Dove let out a sigh of relief when her swordmaiden was out of sight and made her way to the window. *The mereyna*, she thought, trying to trace a path out of the labyrinth below. Not that it would help much. The General was marching north with the Swordsworn at her back, and because of some stupid, ancient law, the Northmen, wastelands, and enchanted killer forests would not be able to stop her.

She placed her hands at the edge of the window and leaned out. Frowned. The surface had looked smooth, but it fractured and split like normal bark. *Blackwood,* she thought immediately. And what did one do with such a natural ladder?

Climb down it, of course.

\*\*\*

Dove waited until nightfall to test her theory. She blew out the candle and sat on the ledge, making sure no one could see her before descending into a colorless world. She moved soundlessly above the sentinels, landing cat-like on the roof of the next building. Physical strength was not her greatest asset, but she knew how to use her body's momentum to fly.

It was not as difficult as she had expected. There were no grip-stones or branches jutting from the wall, but its surface provided bumps just wide enough for her to lean against while she caught her breath. She continued along the spine of the roof, and when it ended, she dug her fingers into its edge and let her body dangle from the side.

In truth, she could have done it blindfolded. She had taken in every corner, every hidden pocket on castle grounds, and she knew how tall and wide the walls were. If she had mapped it correctly in her mind, the twirled, tortured bastion in front of her should have been…

*The Rhesán Tower.*

Or Artis's tower, as she committed it to memory. She had never seen anyone else enter or leave it, even though a skin-crawler was supposed to live there. *The skin-crawler who crossed Valerya's dragon.* Curiosity seared through her body like a flame. The walls were pitted and cracked like the skin of a sleeping serpent, and the tower twisted and turned beyond the clouds. The holds were small, but so was she, and she climbed with ease until she reached the first window.

She pressed her ear against the wall when she heard voices speak in hushed tones. Artis, she would recognize anywhere. But the other—Kayne, she assumed—had an edge to his voice that set her heart hammering.

"The Realm is bound to the mereyna. There is no other way," he said.

*The mereyna.* There was that word again.

"Don't tell me the safest place for her is at the Citadel," said Artis softly. "That's what I told Valerya once."

"So this is all your doing, then." Kayne laughed, a terrible sound.

"Maybe." Dove heard the sound of a chair push back from the table. "I'm afraid I must discuss this with Lord Kai."

"Indeed. But there is something I must do first."

Before Dove knew it, an arm lunged out the window and grabbed onto her shoulder, pulling her inside with unnatural strength. She barely had time to resist, let alone fight back, but something fierce flared inside her. *Rhysar,* she thought desperately. *Help me.* But she could not feel her dragon's presence anywhere.

"Kayne!" she heard Artis shout behind him, to no avail.

Kayne's hands had already moved up to her eyes, and his fingers wrapped around her temples. His gaze was not on her, but his tortured eyes spoke volumes. She tried to look into them, but a sound beyond her threshold of hearing exploded against the sides of her skull.

*Who are you?* she heard his voice ask, but his mouth did not move.

Suddenly, her world dissolved into whiteness. The ground disappeared beneath her feet, and even her shadow abandoned her in the blinding light.

Part of her knew it was conjured, but something in her chest tightened as she felt him triumph over her. Her connection to Rhysar had faded completely, and with it, her confidence. She forced herself to run, but there was no sound of footfall, no indication her path would end.

*Ah, I see. The new daughter of Rhysia.* The voice resounded in her skull like a dull echo. *But if you claim the name, can you also claim the memory?*

Suddenly, color began filling in the spaces. Another world unfurled around her, one she did not recognize. It was a memory, but it did not feel like her own. As her surroundings sharpened into stone and timber, she found she could no longer move.

*Where am I?* Whatever creature she had been transplanted into this time took a step forward and fell, soundless tears that darkened the stone below her.

A voice spoke out to her, but it was muffled, blurred, like her head was submerged underwater. But the child felt at ease. Hands lifted her up, up into the sky... until she saw a face, much kinder, freckled, than any stone likeness she had seen in the crypts.

It was strange feeling her own emotions collide with the child's joy. She could not remember the last time she felt it, not even before this started, not even in her old life. The skin-crawler was showing her a memory, and now he was making it hers.

"I told you no running." The voice sharpened as the child relaxed, and Dove realize its hearing was fading. Its mother's features blurred, slid in and out of focus. *A conjuration.* Dove tried to will herself awake, but she knew it was useless.

The woman kissed the child's head through untamed strands of hair. Dove wished the child would focus, but it was at an age where it could barely form memories. It was a bizarre feeling, cursing a two-year-old for not concentrating.

The woman was all smiles, but she frowned when she glanced out the window. She yelled something, which sent the child panicking. Once it panicked, it no longer listened. The woman opened a small cabinet and set the child down. "Stay here," she whispered, but her voice broke and trembled.

The child tried to stand when the door closed and locked. Dove could see through a crack in the blackwood, but its tears blurred her vision.

The knocks came when it grew quiet. A courtesy, as the door broke down a few seconds later, blown clear from its hinges. She heard a voice too familiar for her liking. "Find them," it growled. Drudges fanned out through the house, taking up positions between pieces of furniture.

It did not seem particularly challenging to storm a house with a woman and small children inside, but they still donned helms, save for Greaven himself. His image rippled, and the longer she stared, the more his color wavered. *Something is not right.* Of course everything felt wrong, but now it *looked* wrong. The child stared, dumbly captivated by their arrival. *It has no idea what is happening,* she thought, cursing it again. *Pay attention.* But it was no use. The child was content seeing its mother through the cracks and did not seem to care about the large man or his drudges. Or their blades.

"My father," said the woman between sobs. "What about my father?"

Greaven ignored her. "Enough," he spat, but even his voice came out garbled. "Now where are your brats?"

"No. No, not them. Please, let them..."

But her pleas fell on deaf ears. "Call out to them," said Greaven, crouching until they were face to face. "Make it easy for everyone. Make it *quick.*"

His voice was finally enough to scare the child, and it turned its gaze back to its mother. A terrible time to start paying attention.

After a defiant silence, Greaven sighed and gave his men a nod. They dragged the woman forward, right in front of the cupboard, and forced her hand on the table. "You can make it so much easier for them," he said. "How old is the girl again? Two? It would be easy to make her feel *the worst fucking pain* of her short, miserable life."

The woman spat in his face.

Greaven laughed and nodded again, and one of his men brought a hammer down on her finger. She stifled a cry, biting into her own arm, as Dove screamed inside. It was only when they shattered the third finger that she screamed.

"I hear something," said one of the drudges.

"Shh," said Greaven to Sonea, bringing a finger to his twisted smile. "I hear it too."

*I do not want to see this.* The child may not have understood what was happening, but Dove did. Greaven tortured them. A mother and her child, defenseless in their home.

*Help me,* she thought suddenly. Not to the toddler, not to Kayne. She did not care if the dragon scared her. If she had to decide between it and Greaven, she would take her chances. It was too much for her to feel the child's happiness in the face of something so cruel.

Then it came. *Rhysar.* It had taken a while, but her dragon finally came to her rescue. The walls began to tremble, but the figures in her memory did not react. A sudden shriek tore scars into the colors, and they faded like a flame burning through a piece of parchment. She felt her memory split at the seams, detaching itself from the child's. Soon she found herself trapped in another void, another space from which all color had been drained.

*Be still,* said Kayne's voice. *It will be over soon.*

But Dove had had enough. Kayne was an invader. And she wanted to see what would happen if the skin-crawler crossed another dragon.

*Burn him,* she thought, collecting herself. *Burn all of him.* Suddenly it became so hot that blood sizzled in her ears, and when she opened her eyes, all she saw was fire.

*What are you doing?*

But the roar cut him off, tearing through the barrier between them. Kayne was in her domain, now, and he must have realized it. She felt his presence pull away, but she held on. Cruelty was foreign to her, but his fear felt better than she thought.

*Gods, what am I doing?* She released her hold and found herself back in the tower. Her heart was beating so fast, the desk behind her trembled, but it was her rage that tightened the air around them. Drawers slid from the desk and onto the floor, and the wood began to crack and splinter.

"What did you do to her?" demanded Artis.

Dove felt her anger soften at his voice, and the air slackened.

"Forgive me," said Kayne. "I didn't know she was yours."

"Are you *completely* insane?" screamed Artis. It was the first time Dove had seen him lose composure. "The first rule is..."

"I did not *know*," repeated Kayne, but his tone had turned cold and humorless. "This is nothing compared to what they'll do to her. They've always wanted the blood of a Summoner."

Dove glanced at Artis. *Who?* she asked with her eyes.

Artis face softened. "My dear, you must forgive my student." He threw Kayne a dark look. "But from now on, you must never go anywhere without your swordmaiden, or Valk, or Alezán. Only those three. Do you understand?"

"And keep that *thing* away from me," Kayne interrupted. "Do you understand *that*? KEEP IT AWAY."

Dove threw him a defiant glare but looked away when she saw dead eyes, pale blue that faded into white. She should have known when she saw no books in his chambers, no maps or manuscripts, like she had imagined a "lover of knowledge" to have.

Though he had seen everything within and inside her, she understood at once.

The man was blind.

# 19

## BRETHREN WASTES
# FIRE REALM

Valerya fucking hated traveling north.

They had taken the most dangerous path, one that took them along high ridges overlooking the heart of the wastelands. Valerya enjoyed the complete absence of life down below. It wasn't as cold as Glasgérios, nor was it scorching and humid like Lancistierre. If only it wasn't bewitched.

Valerya may have been the Summoner General, guardian to an ancient beast, but nothing unsettled her more than sorcery, and the Wastes were full of it. The Scrolls recounted droves of convicts that were banished to the wastelands and never found. The rivers ran dry no matter how much it rained, and daylight broke through the clouds but cast no shadows. It was a world so devastating that no other reality could compete.

Valerya turned her gaze to the horizon and tried to gauge distance in the dark. At their pace, they would probably hit Rhysia by nightfall. She had given the Northerners ample time to prepare for the *mereyna*, and if they were smart, they wouldn't resist. Both sides were entitled to peace, after all, and violence was forbidden against the other side. Steel was not even allowed inside the negotiations chamber.

*The negotiations chamber.* Valerya laughed. It was easy to negotiate if the other side couldn't talk. Zan would likely speak for the girl, but Valerya could handle him.

She allowed the men two more hours of rest before rousing the camp. She and the Spades were used to long campaigns, but most of Morian's men wouldn't make it to the end of the journey. Best give them a good night's sleep.

They had been riding all day when they reached the boglands.

*Bjarred,* she thought dryly. *We meet again.* "Dismount," she commanded. A single strip of mud led across murky waters, just wide enough for them to cross one at a time, but it was sturdier than it looked. She and her men jumped down from their saddles as Morian's men eyed each other with uncertainty. "Stay on your horse if you want," said Valerya as Diebold bit back a grin. She took the reins of her destrier in her left hand. "And don't fall in."

Valerya threw her men a knowing glance before turning her attention to the mud strip in front of her. She kept her hand pressed firmly on the hilt of her sword as she led her horse across, making sure her foot was planted on solid ground before taking the next step. It was slow, no doubt, and painfully cautious, but there was no way she was going to fall in the water. She thought little of rumors and even less of fairy tales, but if there was even the *slightest* possibility they rang true, she had no desire to take on a fucking three-headed anaconda.

Diebold waited until she had taken five strides before he began, keeping his voice low for the sake of his steed. Seven more of the Spades followed, while the others stayed at the rear to prevent desertion. Chuckles trailed behind one of Morian's men, cackling unhelpfully.

*Maybe he does it on purpose,* she thought when she saw the drudge in front of him refuse to dismount. When the horse jolted in fear, the drudge slid from its saddle, breaching the shoreline with an ungracious thud. Even better, some of his companions rushed to his aid without seeing the ripples widen all around them. Patterns in the waves betrayed something large and barbed, and whatever it was uncoiled as though it had just woken up.

It circled around them with unsettling speed until a ring formed in the water. It was so perfect that she doubted there was only one. *Dinner time.*

The ring broke. One of the men screamed as something whipped through his legs, but before he could hit the ground, he went under. The others soon followed, and whatever attacked dragged them into deeper waters until all movement stopped.

"Continue," she said, unfazed, and turned to a particularly young Swordsworn. *Why do they do this to me?* She sighed. "You. What's your name?"

"Me?" he asked, more reflex than reason. "I'm… my name is Robian."

"It appears that horse has lost its rider," she said as Chuckles tried to calm a frightened palfrey. It was thin and scrawny, but so was the boy, whose ill-fitting armor bore no sigils. It had probably been handed down by an older relative. She liked that; if he made it this far, it must have been through merit, not wealth.

Chuckles shrugged and handed the reins to the boy before mounting his own horse. He stifled a giggle with his hands as he watched the others stare at the water, fear renewed. Valerya frowned. She couldn't remember the last time Chuckles actually spoke.

"Kill it!" one of the men screamed, but Valerya patted her

destrier's neck. It had charged war bears and night wolves without flinching, but it was getting nervous now. A terrible sign.

"You have my permission to," she said coldly, waiting for her own men to cross. Only Skandar and Weyan mattered to her, and they were already shouting for the others to make haste. It could have gone so smoothly.

*What... what the hell is that man doing?*

It was times like these that made her wonder why she didn't just throw down her sword, strip off her armor, and dive headfirst into the water. When she saw the flames erupt in the corner of her eye, she knew one of Morian's drudges had resorted to casting Fire.

"Don't move," she commanded. Chuckles could no longer suppress his laughter, and she could see Skandar on the other side of the bog glare daggers at him. Valerya smiled to herself. She wondered how she could have ever hand-selected this elite band of goons.

And then came a shriek, ear-splitting as it was terrifying.

Valerya leaned forward in interest. As much as she wanted to avoid the Twins of the Boglands, so named for begetting their offspring in twos, she had always wanted to see them. *Twin serpents,* she thought, recalling the blood tales. *Water drakes.*

The shriek came again, this time from the other side of the bog. The men on the mud strip turned, and Oren approached her cautiously.

"Have you ever seen them?" she asked.

"No," he said with a quick shrug. "My sister and I used to play in the boglands, but we've never been stupid enough to wake them up. Just hearing them scream was enough."

Stane and Aidan were already backing away from the shoreline, but Valerya remained steadfast. Ten drudges were standing on the mud strip, still as stone. If she were them, she would have been in

Rhysia by now. *Well,* she thought, *at least this will be educational.*

The first serpent lunged out of the water, displaying rows of serrated teeth. Valerya was pleasantly surprised. It looked like it could be related to a dragon. Wingless, smaller, and long, but undoubtedly reptilian.

Still, for all its teeth, the creature did not bite. Instead, it pummeled its weight against the men's legs, toppling them forward as it disappeared on the other side of the mud strip. Its twin took its place, finishing off what the other had started. Soon, the water was teeming with arches, spinal crests that ran down their backs. One of them leapt in the air, provoked by blasts of Fire. The flames slid off its scales as it whipped past them, and its barbed tail lashed through the line.

And then, as sudden the serpents came, the waters grew still.

But Valerya knew better than to be disappointed. Twins always hunted in pairs, and these pairs hunted in packs. Amongst hundreds and hundreds of children, there had to be a matriarch.

Before the men could rejoice, a head emerged from the surface, big enough to swallow a child. Spines protruded from its face, lined its snout with scaled armor. It rose from the water with poise and contemplated the men with scarlet eyes.

It turned its attention to a particularly unfortunate Swordsworn and opened wide, displaying fangs the size of Valerya's hand. It was more of a signal, if anything; the moment the man reached for his sword, eight serpents sprang from the water, each taking a man with it as it landed on the other side. The matriarch herself descended upon the poor man. She clamped its jaw around his torso, and Valerya heard a sharp crunch as his body broke, as his skin ruptured. The matriarch pulled back, dragging the rest of him into muddied waters.

No one disobeyed Valerya after that. The rest managed to walk across the mud strip, significantly more respectful towards nature than before. Some pissed themselves as they walked, but as long as they moved slowly, she didn't care. In truth, she had spent long hours with them, enough to gauge their character. Their deaths would mean nothing to her.

The twins had annihilated a line of drudges in an instant, but Valerya had no need for insubordination in her ranks. They had already lost twelve to the narrow crossings of the canyons, seven to the night creatures that attacked their encampment, and now ten to the boglands. Six had managed to escape and desert, but she had no doubt the Wastes would take care of them for her.

By the time they crossed into the Rhysian province, it was the dead of night. She cautioned her men to stillness, and they slipped past Breddon with ease. Declaring siege was traditionally considered a daytime activity; it was crime and mutiny that plagued the cities at night, so guardsmen often turned their attention inward.

Their mistake.

"Remember," she said once she caught sight of the castle. It was the only place she couldn't stand more than the Citadel, aesthetics wise. It looked like an enchanted fucking forest, and she hated it. "All we need is Kai or the girl. If we get one or the other, we own the castle. But we need them alive, and the *mereyna* has bound us to peace."

"General," one of Morian's men spoke. "Wouldn't it be easier to... take them by force?"

*Are they even fucking listening?* Valerya bristled. "The *mereyna* binds us to peace," she repeated coldly. She turned her attention to Marren's Haven, the sleeping village just outside the walls. Her men had studied the stronghold and its surroundings, mapping out each room and corridor, but all it would take was one half-wit from Morian's camp to ruin everything.

"It is *imperative* we maintain peace," she said, more to Morian's men than her own. "If you wound either of them, I will flay you alive." She steered her horse to face the castle. "And remember, Spades: if you see a raging Thunderborne, don't cast Fire. His Storm is strong, and he will put up a fight. Is that clear?"

She heard fists pound on breastplates. "Boy," she said cruelly, turning to Robian. "Make yourself useful. Knock on the gates. They're less likely to spear a child." She gave the Spades a nod. "Ride ahead. You know what to do. Chuckles, you stay with me."

Robian bowed and obeyed while Chuckles glanced back in surprise. She couldn't have him spoil the surprise, not this time. Skandar took off, relieved, and Chuckles rode up beside her sullenly, betrayed. *In time,* she promised him silently.

Valerya nodded to Diebold, and he rode off with the other Spades.

A tense silence fell over them as they waited. Whenever Chuckles threatened a laugh, she backhanded his ear—a sign of disrespect to others, no doubt, but it was known in her company that it was the only way to keep him quiet. He never took it personally. The men behind her shifted uncomfortably, but she would behead anyone who moved without her command.

She felt the dragon rage inside her, eager to make itself useful, but she commanded it to silence. *I need you to do something for me,* she thought to it. This would be a Summoning she had never tried before, but she wanted to send a message to the Northmen.

She cursed when she saw the gates open. She had expected it, but it still made her next move all the more difficult. Painful. *You idiots.*

And when she felt the bloodfire of the dragon seep into her

veins, so much that she swore she could feel it burn from the inside, she knew. There was no turning back.

She wondered if Valk would ever forgive her, in this life or the next.

*Just a moment longer,* she promised as the dragon filled her blood with Fire. She kept her gaze fixed on the slumbering town and thought of all the lives she would claim tonight.

Valerya stared at the castle a long time before deciding that the Spades were ready and waiting for her signal. "Stay behind me, Chuckles," she whispered. He threw a hand to his face to keep himself from snickering, but he nodded in response.

Valerya closed her eyes, already feeling the bloodfire take its toll. *Forgive me,* she thought, the closest to regret she had come in years. The Northmen had opened their gates to the wolves, and her dragon didn't need to be asked twice to attack.

The ball of light looked like a star returning to the skies, but one that quickly swirled with fierce intensity. It was only when she felt a sudden coolness wash over her that she knew Avantys had arrived.

*Kill them,* she thought as she forced her heart to harden. *Kill them all.*

# 20

## RHYSIA

# FIRE REALM

D ove opened her eyes and felt... Fire.

The castle was full of strong casters, but this Fire was different. It prickled across her skin like she was standing close to burning coals. She had never felt that before. Instinctively, she pulled the curtains from her window, expecting to see the cool, dim colors of the dying night. But the stars burned a fierce red today, and the landscape bathed in the glow of gods.

And then she saw it. *A dragon.* Avantys, but angrier. *Is this... bloodfire?* Her skin was so hot she thought it would melt. The creature's head snapped towards her, sensing the other, and Dove felt a pang of fear that was not entirely her own. *Shut up,* she thought desperately to Rhysar. But they were beasts. Dominant beasts that shared space would never tame. She gripped the edge of the window as she searched the horizon for the other Summoner.

Valerya may have been standing beyond castle walls, but now that Avantys was unleashed, her presence was everywhere. The air tightened with invisible threads that severed when the beast found its target. For the first time in her life, Dove was afraid of fire.

*It cannot be.* Valerya may have thought little of the *mereyna,* but she was not one to break her word, much less a sacred tradition. Hells, even when she sacked ancient cities and burned them to the ground, she left the temples standing.

Dove tried to create a connection, but all she got was a numb ringing in her ears. *How does she do it?* she wondered as her head began to throb. She was running out of excuses. If she survived the day, it was high time to bond with Rhysar.

"Hey, kid!" A voice tugged her back to reality. Mayet had climbed the stairwell from the main keep, but Dove only now realized she was there. Her words were slow, muffled. Drowned out by the ringing. "They're summoning you to the throne room. Let's go."

Dove tore her gaze away from the scarlet beast. They hurried out into the courtyard, but to her surprise, there was no fighting. No shouting. Avantys had claimed the skies, which looked like they were on fire, but the Northmen stood their ground. The intruders beyond the walls made no move to attack. Both sides just… waited.

*The first mereyna in hundreds of years,* Dove remembered. No wonder no one knew what to do. But if a blood dragon was their sign for peace, they were all dead. *Then again,* she thought wildly, *maybe this is part of the formality.* Was she expected to summon one, too? Was that what they were waiting for?

But Mayet kept pulling—carrying—her across the courtyard. When they reached the throne room, Mayet unsheathed her sword and handed it to the guards. "No weapons in the negotiations room," she recited, but her eyes said: *not like we'd survive that thing anyway.*

Dove took a deep breath and entered, surprised to see the hall already filled with people. On one side, the Spades stood on command with the Swordsworn at their back. They looked so orderly, so disciplined, especially when compared to the other side—her side. Bard had taken his seat in the front and was eyeing everyone with disdain, but he rose when he saw her, relieved.

Dove immediately felt at ease. She did not care if she had an army behind her; as long as she had Bard, she would not be alone, especially since Gor, Kai, and Valk were nowhere to be seen. As Keeper of the Gates, High Lord, and fellow Spade, it must have been their duty to receive Valerya, but Dove could not imagine that going well.

"C'mon," Bard grumbled under his breath. "I'm speaking for you today."

*What?* Dove wondered until her eyes fell on the center of the hall. Four chairs were separated by a measly wooden table, and a lone orb sat perched on the corner. For the negotiations, she reckoned.

"I'm not qualified for this shit," Bard muttered as Mayet took her seat in the crowd. "If it were up to me, Valk would've done it, but I guess having a Spade as your speaker would've rubbed people the wrong way. As for the old man, well..." He glanced over his shoulder, making sure no one could hear, and threw her a knowing glance.

Dove understood immediately. Artis had been Valerya's tutor. *If they get into a fight,* she thought, *there goes the stronghold.*

Bard grinned. "I guess I was the next best thing. To them, I'm harmless. A lamb."

The line of Spades did not react when they passed, not even when Bard stopped to look each of them in the eye. "Fascinating," he whispered to himself, waving his fingers in front of their faces, but something silenced the words in his throat. "Fuck!" he said when he moved to the window.

Avantys had been lingering there for so long that Dove assumed it was there to signal the mereyna, but when it spread its wings and roared, she realized she had never been so wrong.

It began its descent.

The ground trembled beneath her feet, and she forced her eyes shut as hot air blasted through the window. Bard pulled her back, his element hand at the ready, but the Spades stood their ground. They only reacted when the double doors opened, but instead of Northmen, Dove saw two Spades carrying branches made of blackwood. Before Bard could stop them, they cast a shield of Fire around their group. Dove immediately felt the strength of twelve casters, each of them fierce. A single man's Storm would not breach it.

"What the fuck are you doing?" Bard screamed over the flames. "YOU'RE IN DIRECT VIOLATION OF THE *MEREYNA!*"

It sounded stupid when he said it like that, but he was not entirely without reason. Most present in the hall could not burn, but enchanted branch-swords tipped the scales.

The Spades let their shields down and drew their branches in perfect unison. Some glowed violet or emerald, whatever ascendant star they had been forged under. *Just like the Huntsmen.* Branch-hilts snapped twice around their wrists. Their glow intensified.

*We are dead.* Dove threw a panicked glance at her side of the hall. Mayet, she recognized. A few guardsmen, but mostly bystanders. Thornbeard. The legless twin. Even Saire. Unarmed against the General's elite, they stood no chance, and they knew it.

"Diebold!" shouted Valk over the panic that had erupted in the hall. The new guardsmen must not have let him in with a blade, and he raised his arms in peace. "What is this?"

The oldest Spade drew in a sharp breath as he turned. He was a powerfully built man but aging fast; Dove barely recognized him.

"Sorry, Valk," he said, "but our King has asked for your head." He looked seasoned and scarred but avoided Valk's gaze. Suddenly, Dove wondered why the hell she and Bard were standing so close to them.

"Kill them," Diebold commanded.

He stepped forward and shoved Dove towards one of the Swordsworn, who caught her just before they both tumbled down. She elbowed him where men said it hurt and sprang to her feet just in time to see the General's men raise their swords against her companions—and turn.

Twelve blades cut through twelve Swordsworn and withdrew. It was done with such precision that it did not seem human. Even when their victims refused to die, they kept their gaze forward. The dead did not matter to them. They were instructed to deliver a killing stroke, no more. Thornbeard rushed forward, picked up a branch, and cleaved through one of the dying like butter before throwing it down. He glanced off to the side. It was an incident that never happened.

Dove took advantage of the moment's respite and darted back to the window. Burning men dotted the field. They thrashed about wildly and sank into piles of ash.

She squinted. In the distance, the Huntsmen Woods glowed a soft white. The trees had created a wall to shield their servants. They did not know what was happening, but they would sleep safe from Valerya's fury tonight.

It was not like Dove's side was any the wiser. Saire eyed the Spades in both outrage and interest. Valk did not know whether he should be relieved or angry. Thornbeard glanced at the Spades with skepticism but did not want to provoke them.

"What is the meaning of this?" Valk demanded, opting for angry.

"Wouldn't be making demands just yet. Negotiations haven't started," said Diebold. He threw Dove a quick glance, like he was looking for a resemblance. They all were. "Take a seat."

Before she could react, he and his companions formed two lines that led halfway from the double doors to the table. They stood at attention, ignoring all the dead things they had made.

Bard shrugged and sat. Reluctantly, Dove followed suit. She noticed a dagger in front of her, and another on the other side of the table. *What are these for?* They looked old but freshly cleaned and sharpened. She doubted they had been overlooked.

It was only when the silence settled that Dove realized how delightfully unfit she and Bard were to represent Northern interests.

Finally, the doors swung open. Northern guardsmen spilled into the hall and took their place along the walls. They were visibly shaken, and rightfully so—they must have ridden out to defend the castle, but Dove supposed they had never once feared fire. Even those who had sustained minor burns looked on fearfully as though they might have to be amputated.

Inside, the beast raged. *Quiet!* she snapped, matching its anger. Not now. It could screech and whine all it wanted when they were alone, but it would not break the first *mereyna* in hundreds of years. Destruction was not the first thing she would be known for.

"Dove. *Psst,*" Bard whispered, frowning. "You're bleeding."

Dove blinked in surprise and held a hand to her face. Blood gushed from her nose and trickled down her chin. Bard offered her a piece of cloth, and she wiped her face hastily.

That, at least, seemed to incite a reaction in the Spades, and they glanced at her with unease. *A nosebleed,* she thought dryly. Of all things, the savages were unsettled by a fucking nosebleed.

*Stop it.* She forced her eyes shut and took calming breaths. This was not like her. This temper came from somewhere else.

Bard glanced around, but even he straightened in his seat when the throne room fell silent. All one hundred Northern guardsmen stood at attention. They may have been welcoming a foreign commander into their halls, but they had never seen a meeting like this before. Some had never even seen the She-Jackal up close, and they wanted to be on their best behavior.

Lord Kai entered, followed dutifully by his guardhand. Natural nobility. Even under attack, he had donned a dark, silk coat embroidered in elaborate gold. The craftsmanship was subtle, but it established the hierarchy. He made his way between the two lines of Spades, but he stopped at the end, instead taking his seat in the crowd. *A meeting for Summoners,* Dove remembered. Not even lords were welcome. Valk took his seat next to him and gave Dove a solemn nod.

"Make way," barked Gor as he entered. He was covered in ash, but it did not seem to have fazed him. It barely took him twelve strides to cross the throne room, and even the Spades had to glance twice at the tower of a man. He took his seat behind Kai.

Suddenly, twelve fists pounded against twelve breastplates, and two heralds unfurled a crimson banner. Dove turned just in time to see the General enter, leaning heavily against a Spade she had never seen before. He was a head shorter than the others, and together they looked like they had just crawled out of the wreckage of some collapsed building. Still, the Northmen dropped their gaze, fearful she might burn them again. Even in her worst state, the hierarchy was redefined.

Artis followed closely behind, ending the procession. He raised a hand, and the guardsmen shut the doors behind him. A book was tucked underneath his other arm. Dove could tell it was important;

she had illuminated enough manuscripts in the Scriptorium to know that its gold-gilded lettering meant there were only a few of its kind in the Realm.

"Leave me," Valerya commanded, and the Spade took his place next amongst his brothers-in-arms with a short-lived chuckle. She continued to her side of the table and took her seat without glancing at Bard or Dove. Her breathing was slow and heavy. "Let's get this over with."

Artis cleared his throat as he placed the book on the table and carefully lifted the cover. "Today marks the 47th *mereyna* in the history of the Scrolls," he announced. "According to custom, a *mereyna* is divided into three sessions. The time in between can be used as each Summoner sees fit." He gave a courtesy pause. "Now if the Summoners could declare their presence..."

Without hesitating, Valerya grabbed the dagger in front of her and slashed her palm. She held her hand over the book and watched as drops of blood spilled onto the pages. "Your move," she said cruelly, throwing Dove a sharp smile.

*Would it be weird if I just used my nosebleed?* Dove wondered as she took the blade in her hand. Just thinking about it nauseated her. Something cold trailed down her spine.

"Just a little," whispered Bard. "Enough to break skin."

*Why is it always the palm?* Dove could think of few places more inconvenient. She took a deep breath and drove the tip of the dagger into her hand, withdrawing it when she saw blood. It was less dramatic than she had hoped, but she was able to force out a few drops.

At least Artis looked satisfied. He said a few more things, but their surroundings caused Dove's attention to waver. All eyes were on them, eyes that mirrored fear and uncertainty. No one wanted to be there, least of all her, but it was still a better alternative to being crisped or captured. So they put on their best smiles, hid their unease like they were bred to handle awkward situations. She sighed and turned back to Artis when he said, "Let the proceedings begin."

"What did you do?" Bard demanded, an ideal start. Dove kicked him under the table.

"I will keep this short," said Valerya, ignoring him. "Two hundred of our men died tragically outside your walls. I can tell our King one of two things: either I had them killed after they threatened to attack your castle." She turned to her audience with distaste she did not bother hiding. "Or *you* did and broke the peace to which we were entitled. A hundred Northmen opened the gates and rode out to meet us in open battle tonight. Some would call it a declaration of war."

"What?" Bard said, affronted. He was not alone; the onlookers in the hall turned to each other, shocked. The *mereyna* could have gone in many directions, but no one had expected civil war. "What do you mean, we…"

"Watch yourself," threatened Valerya as the air around them tensed. "Breaking the mereyna is an act against the gods."

*This was never a negotiation,* Dove realized. This was a demand, pure and simple. She supposed she was not surprised. The General had never been one for compromise. Valerya's eyes glazed over the walls of the throne room, layering them with disgust. "Our King wishes for you to join the Citadel," she said. "Together, we will govern the Swordsworn and guard the Realm."

"Build an empire," interrupted Bard. "Kill anyone who doesn't fit your ideal."

"I apologize if I gave the impression this was negotiable," said Valerya, leaning forward. "This is the ideal. The North will remain untouched, granted autonomous rule, as long as it continues to pay its yearly tribute. Our King is even willing to overlook a few... forgotten debts. A peaceful solution. Some actually consider it smart to join the winning side."

"Led by a madman," said Bard. "I've heard people are getting tortured for simply *having* a different opinion now. Brainwashing kids..."

"Mind your tongue or lose it," said Valerya coldly, and Dove wondered how they could have ever been friends. "You will not insult our King in my presence. That goes for everyone in this hall." She turned to the onlookers. They tried to avoid her gaze, but there was no escape. She was addressing them directly now. "Refuse and you will be branded an enemy of the Crown. Breaking the *mereyna* is a sacred offense. Even now, I would be sanctioned to take the castle by force."

Dove wondered why no one else was saying anything. Artis sat silently, and a few guardsmen had to stop Thornbeard from shouting out.

*No one else is allowed to speak,* she realized. Valerya and she—through Bard—were the only voices allowed in the hall. *My, how the tables have turned.*

Bard turned to Dove before she could enjoy it too much. "Well," he said bitterly. "Shall we call for our first break?"

Dove sighed and shrugged. She had expected them to have more bargaining power before the first round was over, but they were being backed into a corner. Dove followed Bard to their side of the hall, where Valk and Kai sat. The High Lord nodded towards his guardsmen, who kept the crowd at bay. The last thing they needed was more panic in the halls.

"We're getting our asses handed to us," said Bard, diplomacy spent. Dove glanced back at the table, but Valerya had not moved from her chair. She simply sat there, flexing the fingers of her element hand. A terrible sign.

Bard cast a swift glance at the Spades before turning to Valk. "*Spade,*" he said. "What the fuck just happened? I thought violence wasn't allowed at these precious meetings."

"Against the other side," Valk corrected him curtly.

But Bard was not having any of it. "Oh, is that all?" he asked. "Doesn't exactly make me feel better that she burned 200 of *her own men* outside your walls."

"They weren't ours."

"Weren't ours, either."

"They were dispensable. She wanted them dead," said Valk, incapable of providing solace.

"*We'll* be dead if we refuse now, won't we?" said Bard. Valk's words had not made him hopeful. "But she wouldn't kill you now, would she?"

"Unwillingly, I suppose." Valk shrugged. "But I won't fight her."

Bard blinked. Several times. "Excuse me, what?" He ran a hand through his hair, glanced at Dove. "Not even for her?"

Valk gave a grim smile. "I dare say she has the best chance of making it out alive."

If the aim had been comfort, he had missed his mark completely. The way Valerya sat at the table and glowered at everyone in the hall did not make Dove hopeful for a bright future.

"So either we lose Dove, or we all die and lose Dove anyway." Bard frowned. "Those are terrible terms. Why aren't you more upset?" He stopped, and his dark eyes flashed in anger. "Unless... you knew about this."

Dove glanced at Valk, but his expression revealed nothing of his thoughts. He turned away from Bard. "It was the only way we could ensure her safety. Though I admit, I didn't anticipate the means." He kept his voice solemn, but it was seared with regret.

"Why not just *hand* her over to the dogs?" Bard demanded. "Why all this?"

"We needed to claim her name," said Valk. "Morian is less likely to defile a Rhysian ally."

"No. He can just *marry* her now."

"Once she accepts these terms, she will be under Valerya's protection," said Valk. "As such, she may be exempted from matrimony, even to a kin—"

"I'm touched at the faith you have in our enemy."

"*Your* enemy," said Valk coldly. "I trust my brothers-in-arms with my life."

"Once a Hound, always a Hound. Seriously, couldn't we have just done this via falcon?" Bard asked, exasperated. "Join us! Check yes or no. Better than burning everyone alive."

"The North needs to remember what she is capable of. Our King's men, most of all."

"Two. *Hundred*. Men."

"Two hundred deserters. Killers. Rapists."

"That makes it all right, then?"

"Better them than you," said Valk, but his tone had turned uncharacteristically cold. "You are free to question our General's motives, but she is offering the greatest alliance to the North the histories have ever seen. *And* spared 200 of our men at the expense of criminals."

Valk glanced at Artis, unsure of how to continue. "There was another matter our General wanted to attend to," he said, looking past the old man's shoulder. He gave a solemn nod.

Valerya rose violently, silencing the hall like a knife. "I request counsel as well," she said.

Artis blinked, taken aback, but he regained composure quickly. "As is your right," he said. "Who will you name?"

"The skin-crawler."

"Kayne?" asked Kai, his first contribution to the day's events. "I'm afraid he has not left his tower in years."

"Then I will go to him." Valerya stopped herself, and her lips drew back into a thin line. A half-hearted attempt at courtesy. "My *lord*."

Dove blinked. Even when she tried, the General could not sound like a subordinate. She supposed their relationship was unclear. The Spades had just invaded the North and unleashed a blood-beast that burned through a horde of men. Granted, none of them had been Kai's, but Dove could see why her presence had become awkward. Between the High Lord and the General of the Realm, it was unclear who outranked who in the stronghold.

The guardsmen threw their lord a questioning glance, but Kai gave a reluctant nod, sending two of them scrambling to the table. "M... my lady," one of them stammered to Valerya, who stared back, unimpressed. "Please follow us to the... to the tower."

Bard watched in fascination, but his gaze fell on the boy Dove had pummeled into earlier.

"Baby-Faced?" he asked, baffled.

"Franco?" rasped the boy weakly, choking back tears when he recognized the Thunderborne. "I... I must..." He nearly tripped over himself in his attempts to escort Valerya and the guardsmen out of the hall.

But it was Artis's reaction that Dove found intriguing. He had fallen completely silent. Everyone else in the hall seemed relieved when the She-Jackal took her leave, but it was fear that creased his confident features. Dove thought back to Kayne and doubted that Valerya meeting him would be such a good idea.

"Does the no-killing-thy-enemy thing only apply in the negotiations hall?" asked Bard, lending her thoughts a voice. "Because we might be short a skin-crawler soon."

"No," said Valk firmly. "Everyone in the stronghold is granted protection."

"Damn."

Valk ignored him. With more than moderate effort, he turned to Dove. "This is for your own good," he said. Dove could see in his eyes that he believed what he said, but he was making it difficult to trust any of them. Her grip on Bard's arm tightened. "And our General can help you tame that... *thing.*"

"Yeah," scoffed Bard. "And then she can use that thing to burn down the rest of the world. And here I thought you cared about her."

"I care a great deal," said Valk. "More than you can imagine."

"Uh huh. And what about you, then? What will you do?"

"My life would be in grave danger at the Citadel," said Valk. "Of course I'm going back."

They waited a long while before Valerya's absence made them nervous. For a moment, Dove wondered if she really did kill the skin-crawler.

The guardsmen looked uneasy, but the Spades had not moved at all. Twelve dutiful slabs of rock, all standing at attention. A few stole glances at her side of the hall, but Valk countered them with a glare, and they continued being boulders. *Valk is one of them,* she realized, half-expecting him to join them. *This is the only life he knows.* Made sense, then, that he thought she would be safe with them.

Dove almost felt relieved when she heard the doors swing open. Valerya strode back to the table with the two guardsmen trailing behind her, jogging to keep up. Without a word, she took her seat and waited calmly. Nothing on her face betrayed how her meeting with Kayne went.

Artis nodded as Bard and Dove approached the table. "Shall we proceed?" he asked. Valerya gave a dismissive wave, signaling her approval, and Dove wondered if the stronghold had indeed lost its resident mage. Slowly, Dove nodded.

Bard cleared his throat. "So, just to get this straight... Dove goes with you, and everyone lives. *That's* your only condition?"

"You were expecting more?" she asked. She was addressing Bard, but her gaze was fixed on Dove. She owned her now. She and the crimson dogs. In the entire hall, only Bard seemed to be on her side. Everyone else seemed uncertain, their resolve wavering like the wind.

Valerya smiled curtly. "In return, we will station more men in the North as a token of good faith. Rhysia will remain autonomous and regain its spot in our King's good graces. From what I have seen..." She had enough courtesy to smile, forced as it was. "You are in dire need of powerful friends."

"Doesn't sound like autonomy to me," said Bard gruffly. "Sounds like Mor... your *king* wants to keep an eye on them."

"Think of it as looking out for each other." Valerya leaned back. "When the time comes, you will need our protection."

"Protection from what?"

"Anything. *Every*thing. You are isolated. Your forces are weak. A prolonged siege would starve you out in months. Rebels are gaining support abroad. Do not delude yourselves... these prosperous times will not last forever. It is time to unite our forces."

"An empire," muttered Bard under his breath.

Valerya ignored him. "You will learn how to sign, of course," she said. It took Dove a moment to realize she was talking to her.

*Sign?*

"I will not allow a voiceless general to command my army," Valerya snapped. "Surely you have other means of communicating. If not, we will find you an interpreter who will teach you how to sign. You *will* learn."

*I know how to sign.* Dove threw Bard a quick glance, but something had darkened his expression, making it hard to watch.

"You keep mentioning an army. Is Dove really... going to be one of your *captains?*"

His voice was layered with good intentions, but Dove wished it were not so full of disbelief.

Valerya chuckled. "Captain? I'm not letting her anywhere near our ships." She leaned forward again, eyeing her audience. "According to the Scrolls, a Summoner automatically outranks the highest commander. In that case, I will have to share my title. *However.*" She turned back to them before Bard could look too stunned. "Even among Summoners, experience dictates rank. She will be second to me."

"A... captain... general?"

Valerya sighed. "*Lieutenant* general."

Bard glanced at Dove. *Well shit,* he said with his eyes. *Maybe you should take her up on the offer.* "So... what are the perks?"

Dove kicked him under the table again.

"Safety," said Valerya. "Tentative command of Swordsworn battalions, which can increase, depending on how she fares. Move them here. Take them out. Think of the things you can do for this... *province.*" She grimaced. "Stay loyal to Rhysian interests if you must, but you cannot protect them with branches and twigs."

Oh no. Dove glanced around the hall. As harsh as she was, Valerya was winning over the crowd. Only Thornbeard looked more than marginally skeptical; he gazed at everyone in disbelief but had enough presence of mind to hold his tongue.

Bard frowned. "Come on. Surely there's a catch."

She threw him a derisive smile. "Well," she said. "No one said it would be easy. I expect her to accompany me on campaigns, and should the time come when she commands her own forces, she *will* lead them." She paused, and her gaze passed briefly over Dove. "You will be shown no special treatment. Those who harm you will lose their heads, but you are expected to keep up. Failure or unwillingness will have… consequences."

Bard glanced at Dove. *I take it back,* his eyes screamed. "But she will be safe," he said.

"I doubt she will be safer elsewhere," said Valerya. "And any Northerner who comes to the capital with us will be granted safe passage. Under my protection."

Bard tapped his fingers on the table. It seemed he had run out of questions. He glanced at the rest of the hall, looking for inspiration. Valerya, on the other hand, waited patiently. Her gaze was merciless but mesmerizing. She knew she had won; even if they refused, it would be their right to take over the castle.

Either way, Morian would gain full control of Rhysia. The Northmen in the hall understood that; at least if they agreed, they would avoid bloodshed. Dove sighed. For someone unskilled in diplomacy, Valerya had managed to turn everyone against her.

"I need a break," said Bard, shaking his head. He seemed at a loss how to talk to Valerya. Dove followed him to their side of the hall as Artis announced the second pause.

"All right, Hound," said Bard through gritted teeth. "What's the plan?"

Valk raised an eyebrow. "That *was* the plan," he answered, surprised he even asked. "Dove will return to the capital and help Valerya command the Swordsworn. You may join us if you wish." A faint smile played upon his lips. "This isn't an empty gesture. There is talk of rebel forces getting stronger. *Dark* forces. In the face of adversity, our Realm will unite as it once had."

"A joy," said Bard spitefully.

They traded insults until Dove lost interest. Her gaze wandered and fell on Artis. He had remained standing next to the table, waiting with Valerya in silence.

"My lady," she heard him say after a moment's pause. "Do you require further counsel?"

Valerya gave a solemn nod. "I request private counsel," she said, raising her voice so their audience could hear. "With the Second Summoner. *Alone.*"

Dove bristled as she felt everyone's eyes on her. Without another word, Artis made his way to the doors, and Valerya rose, falling in stride behind him. Dove glanced at Bard, who gave her a quick nod, and she trailed after them.

They left the hall and entered smaller chambers. It was only when the doors closed behind them that Artis began speaking. "Is there anything you need?"

"No," said Valerya, and Dove shook her head.

He bowed his head, coldly distant, avoiding eye contact. It hurt, especially since there was not much else in the chambers for him to look at. There was a table, some books, a few candles... a quill. It was so narrow they could barely fit. "Very well." He bowed.

Valerya kept her gaze fixed on Dove even after Artis took his leave. She broke it when she strode to the narrow window and studied the maze. "The North gave you up fast," she said, her words sharper than fractured glass. "As one of us, we will not surrender you so quickly. Their actions should therefore be of no great loss to you."

Dove flinched. *In what world is this no great loss?*

Valerya noticed her reaction. "You were born in the South," she said. "You grew up in the South. Like it or not, you are a Southerner no matter where you claimed your name." She smiled, almost cruelly. "Rhysia will not make you a Northerner any more than the Citadel has made me a lady. We are who we are." She grabbed a nearby book, flipped through the pages, and flung it on the desk. "Write on that," she commanded. "It's not important."

Dove obeyed reluctantly, trying to ignore its gold-gilded lettering. It almost hurt dipping her quill into the inkwell.

"We do not have much time," she said, lowering her voice. "You're only alive because of the name you've claimed, whether it's yours or not." She narrowed her eyes. "When the time comes, you must ask Valk for the truth. The whole truth. Or better yet…" A sharp smile cut through her face. "Ask your dragon."

*You can tell me,* thought Dove, but she knew she would not. For someone who hated secrets, Valerya seemed to harbor more than a Scriptorium.

"I'm telling you this because I need a Summoner, not a title," she said coldly before Dove could finish writing. "I don't need a weakling. Oh, you're offended?"

Dove clenched her jaw and nodded. She was no warrior, but she had fought and killed like the rest of them. She lost like the rest of them.

Valerya sighed. "I don't underestimate your suffering, but leave the needless dying to the rebels. It would be a shame to sacrifice your life for a doomed cause."

*What about you?* Dove thought defiantly, not even bothering to write it down. *You are serving a tyrant, you are killing thousands to serve someone else's needs...*

Valerya placed her hands at the edge of the desk and leaned forward. "*You have no idea,*" she said, and everything in the room quaked. Dove heard the sound of cracking glass. "I made a choice. I chose to swear my life to the kingdom. What *choice* have you ever made?"

The narrow window shattered. Dove brought her hands to her ears as the table shook and splintered. Books rattled. A cup of water crashed to the floor. "In a stunning lapse of judgment, I made a stupid promise," Valerya said, ignoring the chaos unfolding around them. The windowpane snapped. "Now here we are. But the Realm is flourishing. And it still stands."

Valerya took out a piece of cloth and put it to her nose before it started bleeding. "This is what happens when it gets temperamental. I believe you've experienced it before."

*The dragon's temper?* thought Dove. *I am pretty sure it was yours.*

Valerya waited until the bleeding subsided and leaned back against the wall. "Let's get back to your situation. The first choice you will make for yourself."

Dove tried not to look affronted. It did not feel like a choice.

"Refuse to join us, and we will take control of the North. We will take down your... *allies*... in Glasgérios. And don't look so dumb, I know exactly where they are." She laughed. "You're young. Choose poorly, and you will live long enough to see everything you've fought for turn to ash. However," she said, straightening. "You can save them. Tell them to stand down. Tell the *Swordsworn* to stand down." She turned away. "Of course, your friends will brand you a traitor. They will take advantage of your mercy but hate you all the same."

Dove's heart sank. She had not even thought about that.

Valerya seemed entirely unaffected. "And now you've gotten your first glimpse into guarding the Realm. Congratulations." She nodded, but not unkindly. "You will be hated. Feared. But still, the Realm stands."

Dove sighed in relief when a knock at the door broke all tension. "Are you all right?" Bard's voice demanded. He tried opening the door, but part of the doorframe had caved in. "What's going on in there?"

Valerya almost smiled. "Speaking of old friends," she said dryly as the knocking grew more persistent. For a moment, she looked almost nostalgic. "Well, then. Shall we return?"

Dove nodded, eager to leave. She rose and headed for freedom, but Valerya placed a hand against the door before she could attempt to pry it open. Her gaze was uncomfortably sharp, especially now that they were standing so close together. Dove felt her breath on her neck. "If I find you communicating with the Spears without my knowledge," she said, dropping her voice to a soft whisper. "I will have you hanged for treason. Do you understand?"

Without waiting for a response, Valerya flung the door open. It looked so effortless that Dove almost missed the hinges that flew past them. "After you," she said as Bard stared, dumbfounded. He quickly recovered.

"Are you all right?" He put himself between them as they headed back to the hall. It was not far, but he glanced over his shoulder. Gawked. When the guards opened the door to the main hall, Dove saw why.

A deep crack had formed from the door to the table, ripping through layers of stone and dirt. Everyone stood and watched the ground in horror, bracing themselves for another wave. Chairs were overturned, and banners had fallen to the ground. Only the Spades remained where Valerya had left them. They seemed to be well acquainted with their General's temper.

Dove saw from his expression that Artis knew what had caused it, but no one else seemed aware. For all they knew, it could have been an earthquake. Valerya pressed on, leading the way to the table. Her outburst had split the tiles, but she sat and waited with enviable poise. *She was made for this life.*

Two guardsmen awkwardly repositioned Dove's chair next to Bard's and stepped back as though nothing had happened. Everyone else pretended the same.

"Let us continue," said Artis, breaking the silence. He may have been a powerful caster, but even he did not want to risk the collapse of the stronghold. "Do we have any concluding remarks from either side?"

"No," said Valerya sharply, and Dove was taken aback. As cold as the She Jackal was, Dove had the impression that she had least respected Artis. Even that was gone now.

Dove glanced at Bard and shook her head.

To that, Valerya's face broke into a sharp smile. "Welcome to the Hounds," she said, and laughed.

# 21

## MARREN'S HAVEN
# FIRE REALM

Valerya laughed again. Despite awkward circumstances, the *mereyna* still granted the Spades guest right, but there was no way in hell she was going to sleep in the stronghold.

She had booked the entire guest-keep in Marren's Haven for the night and given each guest eight pieces of silver—enough for a month's stay—to get out. No one ever protested. Some were already sleeping on the streets by the time she stumbled out of the tavern. Her men wanted to stay behind and sample the local flavors, which was code for a brothel visit, so she left them to it. Normally, she would have joined, but the *mereyna* had dampened the mood somewhat. She had just taken over their territory in all but name; even for whores, it was hard to couple after that.

It was quiet in the guest-keep. The Lone Ranger was small and cozy, nothing too luxurious, but clean enough. There were eight rooms; she had one to herself while the Spades shared the rest among them, but she suspected most of them would sleep somewhere else tonight. She grunted when she reached her own chambers, feeling the ale settle. She shut the door behind her.

*Never again.* She took her time unstrapping her pauldrons and let them fall to the ground. "I don't remember ordering the local flavor tonight," she said when she heard the last thud. "You must be either very drunk or very stupid. *Speak.* Or you will not leave these chambers alive."

Valerya had immediately sensed the other's presence when she entered, but it was only when the intruder lit a candle that she saw her face. Scarred, like her. Broad-shouldered but unarmored. The woman was sitting in a chair next to the bed, but Valerya could tell they were of a height. There was Fire in her, and it burned fierce.

Attempts had been made on Valerya's life before, and often, but this was new.

"I'm not here to hurt you," said the woman, but her voice was deep and forceful.

Valerya laughed, taken aback. "That's very kind of you." She readied her element hand, but something felt off. Avantys would be raging by now, but she felt the beast curl around her core. Its sign of affection. "What do you want?"

"I am a commander of the Red Spears," said the woman.

*Really, Avantys?* The creature was soothing *her* anger now. "I can have you hanged, Commander," said Valerya, but the beast gave a warning hiss. She frowned.

But something else was giving her pause. Only desperation would drive someone to break into the Summoner General's quarters, but there was no fear in this intruder's eyes. No contempt. No life behind them. "What do you *want*?" Valerya repeated coldly.

"My brother, General," said the woman, turning her gaze to Valerya. "He was just a boy. A sweet boy when he joined your ranks. He didn't *know*..."

"Speak sense," Valerya snapped. "I don't have your brother."

"He's… at the Red Citadel." The woman paused between words, like she was choosing them carefully. They came out slowly, but Valerya felt compelled to listen. The woman glanced up and met her gaze. "Please. You have to find him."

Valerya had to admire the steel balls this one had on her. "Why in your wildest dreams would I do that?" *The boy means nothing to me,* she hissed back at Avantys, but its calmness unsettled her. It rarely showed mercy, especially to outsiders. Especially to rebel leaders. And here it was, staying her hand. She had never known it to be so forgiving.

But the woman seemed to anticipate Valerya's answers. "I can give you something," she said, closing her eyes. "I've followed our Queen for years. *Years.* Our true leader." She let her gaze drop. "You're looking for the head of the Red Spears, right? I can give you her name. Though I suspect you already know."

At that, Valerya's rage returned, overshadowing that of her dragon. Fools, drunks, and half-wits, she could disregard, but there was no redemption for turncoats. A silver snake was still a serpent, its honeyed words still tainted and twisted. "Why should I trust a traitor?"

"I am no traitor to my country." The woman pulled out a piece of parchment and set it on the bed. "I'm afraid her mind has been poisoned by the Exalted's teachings, and she is spreading nothing but lies," she said. "Ask your beast if I'm being deceitful. Avantys, is it?"

Valerya frowned. In truth, Avantys was the only reason the intruder was still breathing, but there was no way the woman could know that. With a sigh, Valerya glanced at the parchment, mystified. *Is this a trick?* Her dragon gave a low growl, urging her forward, but Valerya kept her eyes on the intruder as she approached. *One move and she burns,* she warned the beast, but it seemed to be satisfied. "What's your name, Commander?" she asked.

But the intruder's eyes followed her too. Eyes that had seen so much, there was nothing left. It gave Valerya the creeps.

"Danea," the woman answered. "I've been wanting to speak with you for a long time, Valerya the Fireborne. Born Valerya *Smyth*."

Valerya ignored her and snatched the parchment from the bed. "You realize once I have this information, I will stop at nothing until your queen is in shackles, or dead. Whichever comes first."

"You've already let her go. I saw it with my own eyes. Even when I led her *exactly* where I knew you would be, you let her go. Why is that?" Danea leaned forward. "Because you *know*."

*What the hell?* Valerya frowned and turned away. "She escaped."

"No one escapes you. Even the Summoner girl, you let her—"

*"Don't."* The ground trembled, and something cracked in the distance. Valerya hoped it wasn't anything important, like a beam. But she was too focused on Danea, on the intruder that was confirming her worst fears.

Danea kept her eyes locked on Valerya's. Candlelight flickered off scars that sewed her face together. "I'm counting on you to stop her," she said quietly.

"You realize the resistance would be crushed."

"With all due respect, General. Capturing her will not crush what we stood for. Back then."

Valerya frowned. She did not know what to make of this strange commander. The fiercest rebels—and Danea looked like one of them—would give their lives to their cause, to their leader. They did not actually sacrifice their leader. "I could just take this and have you hanged anyway. Have your *brother* hanged," she said. "Are you not afraid?"

This time, it was Danea who laughed. But there was more surprise than spite, more heart than defiance. "I suppose I can be," she said. "I do not underestimate your cruelty, General. I have seen firsthand what you are capable of. But I also believe you want to save the Realm, and I am not the enemy. My *brother* is not the enemy." Her lips drew back into a resigned smile. "Your dragon knows this to be true."

Valerya was perplexed. She could not explain why Avantys showed this stranger mercy. *Is it because we look alike?* But that would have been stupid. "Your brother. What's his name?"

"Pierce," said Danea, but her smile faded. "But you won't find him by yourself. You need Dove. You need her dragon, especially since she hasn't bonded with it yet—"

Valerya bristled. Her element hand shot back up. "How do you know about her?" Skillful spies may have gotten a name, but no one could have known about the girl's ineptitude in bonding with that thing.

"I just… feel it," said Danea. She glanced at Valerya's element hand, at the angry flames swirling around her wrist like snakes. Danea gave a weak smile, and for a brief moment, light flashed across tired eyes. She was not afraid. "I just—"

"You do not touch her." Valerya cut her off. "You do not *speak* to her. I don't know what sorcery this is, but…"

Danea laughed again, but there was no malice behind it. She shook her head in disbelief. For a moment, her eyes glistened, but there were no tears. "Do you think we are capable of change, you and I?" she asked. "We think we are, but no matter what we do, history seems to repeat itself. Time and time again, in different places, with different rulers."

"What?" Valerya did not know what else to say. "I thought I was the drunk one."

But Danea only smiled. "My brother believed we were, that we could fix this broken system. He always believed the best in people. And it…" She paused when her voice broke. "It will get him killed." She eyed the parchment in Valerya's hand. "You've torched our camps but let our leader go free. Several times. I suspect you've known for a while who our leader was."

Valerya felt something cool wash over her. Instead, she sighed and unfurled the parchment in her hands, read the letters that spelled her fate.

*I'm going to murder Artis.* For a moment, she wished Avander were alive so she could kill him again.

"Ah, fuck," she said. And her dragon roared inside her.

# THE
# FUTURE EMPEROR

A falcon came to him a few nights later.

Pierce took the message from its leg and sent it on its way. His hands were calm, and his voice no longer shook. He and the voices had become one in the dungeon, and since then, life had been simpler. It was everything else that couldn't make up its mind. Winter nights were as warm as summer, and dry winds smothered the flowers in their beds. The past few weeks had turned them into dark, wilted blossoms.

Pierce knew who the message was from before he tore the seal.

He had already received one from the Exalted, telling him to finish his task, so this must have been from Danea, urging him otherwise. Funny how it took her this long to write him, just when he didn't need her anymore. Not for this.

"I wish you had come to save me," he whispered. "Just one last time." He closed his eyes and kissed the parchment before unfolding it.

His eyes darted across his sister's handwriting. "*Our sins are not worth your life,*" she had written. A simple sentence layered with meaning, especially since it was probably the last thing he would ever hear from her. Better than nothing, he supposed. With a snap of his fingers, the parchment burned and swirled into ash. He opened the window and blew it into the courtyard, watched as it caught the wind.

Pierce pulled the curtains to a close. He held his arm out in front of him and cast flames around his wrists, waited until they grew into swirling serpents. They slithered diagonally from his shoulders to his waist and back, protecting him. Calming him. The dark gemstone of the Exalted's ring gleamed in the dancing flames, and he glanced at it before adjusting the collar of his crimson cloak. *The ring would make a fine present for the Second Summoner,* he thought. The Exalted would kill him, of course, but what was it he also wrote? *Gain the Northern Summoner's trust.* A fancy ring bought many things; perhaps it would work.

The corridor was well lit when Pierce stepped outside, and he sighed when he saw Ulma sweeping the hallways. He had hoped to reach the Sovereign without questions tonight, but it was like the woman had been assigned to his wing since that night in the dungeon. She approached him cautiously. "My... my lord?" she asked.

*No. Not 'my lord,' Ulma. Gods almighty, get it right.* "Evening, 'Ma," he said instead, softening the flames around him.

Her posture relaxed when they faded. "Are you feeling well?"

"Splendid," said Pierce coldly before she could say anything else. His eyes narrowed. "Ulma, I would like a hot bath after dinner. Can you do that?"

Ulma dropped her gaze. "Yes, my lord," she said without protest.

Pierce almost felt guilty for how afraid she had become of him, but there was little time to spare. "I will be dining with our Sovereign tonight," he said more gently, hoping it would soften his command. *I haven't become a monster,* he reminded himself. *Not yet.*

"My lord, he hasn't returned from the capital," said Ulma slowly. For a moment, her dark eyes focused on his. Saw everything. "But I'm sure he will return soon."

*Why is she looking at me like that?* "Thank you. I will wait in front of his chambers." Pierce gave a slight bow and continued along the corridor. When it dimmed, he cast the serpents again. They kept him company as he made his way to the Sovereign's wing.

It surprised him when he saw the Sovereign's guard-dog in front of his chambers, the one with the black armor. "You're early," he growled. A lock of black hair draped over black eyes, and his mouth curled around jagged teeth.

There was a time the man terrified Pierce. His very breath smelled of rotting meat, and his demeanor *reminded* Pierce of rotting meat. "I would like to sit in our Sovereign's waiting chambers. Please move aside."

The man in black spat but obeyed. "You'll get yourself killed one day, little lordling," he said, and something cold flashed across his eyes. "Your Fire won't protect you forever. I promise you that."

Pierce did not respond. He entered the Sovereign's waiting chambers, and his eyes immediately took in the tapestry in the far corner. *A peacock.* He liked that; it felt so out of place in a castle of dragons and wolves that it comforted him. He made a mental note to get one just like it if he survived. He took a deep breath as his hand gripped the hilt of his dagger.

The dagger Danea had given him to protect himself. *How long ago it's been.* It was the last thing of hers he had left, but it didn't matter. He had already lost everything else, and it was too late to turn back. There was still a chance the Sovereign would see reason. And if not him and his royal dogs, maybe the Second Summoner. Absently, he rubbed the ring with his thumb.

*If it comes down to it,* thought Pierce firmly. Reminded himself. *I choose blood.*

# 22

## SINTHEA

# FIRE REALM

E ven with the piece of cloth pressed to his face, Morian felt sick. It was no secret that dragons were territorial beings, and once in a while, they fought over the same stars. When that happened, everything on earth scrambled to take sides. Storms waged war against the sun. Blossoms shriveled and died in the rain.

Morian sighed. It was rare that he visited the city himself, but appearances had to be made. His people needed to know he was protecting them. With another Summoner in their midst, safety and strength worked wonders for morale, and the commonfolk was getting to experience the finer planes of prosperity. That was the first part of his plan, and it worked in his favor: sentinels reported fewer crimes, and his people were less afraid. Of course, Morian had also ordered the crime lords to lie low for a while, but no one needed to know they were associated.

*Now the people know we're on the winning side.* He slowed his horse to a trot. *We are invincible.* So many had been eager to join the Swordsworn that they didn't know what to do with them. The strongest, he had trained in arms. The weaklings and children, he put to good use. They patrolled the city in pairs, listened carefully for rebel activities. Anyone who even *spoke* positively of the rebellion was brought to the Citadel for questioning. It was unintentionally brilliant: those too weak to make it to the Swordsworn, he found, tried harder to prove their worth. The interrogation cells were over-flowing with dissenters. Most who spoke against the Crown were simple, easily swayed and out by the evening, but two had held their tongues for weeks.

*Valerya would have taken their eyes by now.* He would have gladly let them starve to death, but Morian needed their secrets, and Valerya had a talent for extracting them.

*Curious, curious woman.* He hadn't expected her to find a peaceful, bloodless solution for the North, but he supposed it was for the best. He didn't care much for Rhysian provinces, but granting them autonomy meant less work for him. And if it gave those barbarians a sense of purpose, then so much the better.

All the more reason to be seen, even if it meant in the seediest part of town. The Ironhands was full of armorer's and smiths— Valerya's people—but it only made up half the plaza; the other half was known to locals as Hacker's Alley.

A clever name that encompassed all of its residents, as those who lived on the "proper" end were butchers and fishmongers by trade. The rats who dwelled in the shadier sections, on the other hand... well, there were plenty of other things to be hacked off, to be sure. Debts had to be paid somehow, and if it cleansed his streets of gamblers and addicts, then far be it from him to intervene. Savage, perhaps, but there reigned a different kind of order in the slums; having the crime lords on his side was better than nothing, and their presence incited others to good behavior.

*Of course Valerya wanted to stay on the smiths' end.* To live, to breathe among these people… she might as well have taken up masonry. At least that way, she could speak with fellow rocks all day.

Morian prodded his horse further along the cobbled streets of the inner city, and the commonfolk stopped and stared as they passed. Even the thugs and thieves gave them a quick salute, a sign of prosperous times. For people who lived near such a central point of violence and corruption, they certainly seemed content with venturing outside alone.

Finally, he halted and waited for his entourage to fan out across the plaza before dismounting. The rest of his men fell into formation as Morian flung his crimson cape behind him, letting it flow dramatically as he made his way towards the smithy. There was no need to get sloppy with appearances. He may have been dressed modestly, but class could not be bought.

The guards bearing emerald sigils showed no fear, at once making themselves known as guardians of the Castell house. A sad sign of a dying name—while wealthy families ordered servants to receive guests, families of the old blood sent their strongest to the gates. They bowed and made way for their king, but their loyalties lay elsewhere.

"Your Highness," greeted a voice, hard as nails. Just the kind of welcome he had come to expect. "Been a long time." The man set his blade aside. At least his manners were still intact. "What can I do for you?"

"Lukan," said Morian courteously, trying not to look at his leg. It was nothing more than a stump now, muscle long since padded by the comforts of civilian life. Gods, he had changed. He was so old that Morian almost forgave him the tragedies of his life. "If I may have a word?"

"Of course," said Lukan, but his expression hard to read. Morian wondered how often Lyra sent word down the hill. He'd had the falcons at the Citadel monitored, but these *children,* they always found a way. Now the child had a child inside her, and there was no way of tearing it out of her without starting a civil war. *Noble names are indeed expensive,* he thought ruefully. He couldn't fix this like he had his past... problems... and the girl was starting to show.

Then again, it wasn't a complete disaster. Now that the Rhysia had renewed its fealty to the Crown, perhaps it was time to make room for the Castells at his table. They were of the old blood, worthy of producing his heir. And if by chance the rumors were true and the brat wasn't his, he could always have it thrown in the river and try again.

Lukan leaned his hand on the counter and propped himself up. "Cam!" he bellowed, it seemed, to no one in particular. "Make yourself useful!"

A boy no older than fourteen came scrambling at his command. He was dark-skinned and small in stature, but he would grow into his muscles in no time. *We could use him at the Citadel.* Short hair curled close to his head. He bowed clumsily and glanced between Lukan and Morian, wondering who to answer to. Giving up, he shrugged it off and sat at the counter, a prime example of baseborn manners.

Lukan groaned as he stood, grabbing clumsily at his walking stick. He headed down the walkway behind the smithy that led to his humble abode. Morian never understood it; Lukan could have lived comfortably in the Walls, or the Sunset if noblemen weren't his style—not within strides of some slaughterhouse, and certainly not on the same stretch of road that led to the black market.

Morian smiled, pure formality. The green-cloaked sentinels were never far away. They wielded old swords rarely found in other parts of the Realm, longer than a human arm and serrated on one edge. It curved and gleamed like a jagged smile. Lukan preferred it, the old beast. But Morian needed his fealty today, and he had just the right leverage for it.

All Lyra needed to do was fulfill her purpose and maintain appearances. He had even had her write home on occasion, keeping it light, joyous. Aside from that, she was free to live as she saw fit. He didn't even care if the rumors were true, as long as the child was his. Aside from that, she was expendable; there was no need to fear her loss.

"Has something happened to Lyra?" Lukan grumbled when they entered his house. There were two stories, though Morian supposed with the former swordsmaster's former leg, his servants had free reign of the upper floor.

"She is in the best of health," promised Morian, throwing a cursory glance at his home. Not bad, he supposed. Better than he expected. A well-stocked kitchen, at least, and *beds,* but Lukan kept the décor modest. Lyra wasn't exactly the type to prefer porcelain over steel, so he barely saw proof that a girl had even lived there. There was, however, a curious display of blades on the wall, starting with a toy blade no longer than a dagger followed by dummy swords of increasing length. "Enough energy for two."

That seemed to appease Lukan, and he nodded, waited. Coughed. No doubt he had already heard the news, but he had never been much of a conversationalist. Civilian life suited him poorly.

"I was thinking it was time to build an alliance," said Morian curtly. "I've come to ask for your blessing..." He tried to keep his eyes from wandering, but gods, it was difficult. Everything was slanted or crooked, and he felt that if he looked at it long enough, his head would burst. He already felt pressure swelling behind his eyes.

"I'd like to see my daughter first," said Lukan, shattering his concentration. "She seems happy at the castle. If that's the case, then you have my blessing. But I want to see her first. Here."

"Of course," said Morian. Reasonable enough. The girl hadn't been home once since she left for the Citadel, and Lukan couldn't leave his house for long periods of time. "She is healthy and happy, but the medican recommends plenty of rest. Once she gets used to her new circumstances, I will have her escorted to your home."

Lukan nodded, visibly relieved. "Is there anything else I can…?"

He was interrupted when the door burst open, nearly swinging clean from the hinges. Crimson meant it was one of Morian's, regrettably. Morian wished his men had more grace. *Then again,* he thought, looking closely. It wasn't *quite* one of his men. Not yet, anyway. It was one of the junior scouts he had seen patrolling the streets earlier.

"Speak," said Morian gently. There was no need to scare the child yet, and this was the future of his empire.

"She…she…" Words were punctuated by gasps. "They're *hanging.*"

As much as Morian tried to hide it, his lips curled upwards into a smile. "Who?"

\*\*\*

Two bodies hung at the neck, flung over the ramparts like broken dolls. Blood dripped down the sides of the tower, layering the walls with the colors of his sigil. He had seen them just that morning, but not there, and certainly not dead. The only thing that had given them purpose was a secret, a name, and judging by this lovely twist, someone else now bore its burden.

Morian chuckled to himself. Valerya had no concept of subtlety, but he marveled at her ability to skulk around the capital unnoticed. She must have ridden ahead, arriving well before her entourage. Probably spent the night in a Sinthean guest-keep. It wouldn't be the first time; she claimed it helped her clear her head, but sometimes he wondered if she did it just to spite him.

Still, he admired her diligence. *I must have been gone a couple of hours at most,* he thought. *The prisoners were still very much alive then.* She certainly worked fast, and based on the state of their new décor, she had been running dangerously low on patience. But she wouldn't be in her chambers now. The carnage was fresh, hastily done. A signal that she was waiting for him.

Morian dismissed his own entourage and made his way up the tower. Valerya's back was turned to him when he reached the top, curiously devoid of metal. It was rare that Valerya decided to forego armor, but he didn't understand why she insisted on lugging her massive sword around. It defeated the purpose of plainclothes. Even more puzzling was how her blade stayed clean while her clothes were steeped in blood. Her eyes were fixed to a spot beyond the Blackwood.

"When did you arrive?" he asked.

"Yesterday." She didn't even bother turning.

*She's in another one of her moods.* They were getting more volatile as of late. He had five more questions, maximum, before she retired to her chambers. He had to prioritize.

"The girl, is she here?"

"In the capital. She needs time to recover."

"Meaning?"

"I made her watch."

*She never fails to disappoint,* he thought, sighing. He had told her to make the girl feel welcome, especially after they had gotten off to a spectacularly terrible start the last time she was here. Only Valerya would take that to mean forcing her to watch an interrogation. Morian wanted to ask more, but he was already down to three more questions. He glanced at the blood trail that led from the top of the stairs to the edge of the tower. "Did you get a name?"

"I have. I believe it will interest you very much." She turned, her eyes cold. Her laugh was harsh and humorless. "But first, there is something I must do."

"How long will you need?"

"Give me a week to ready the men."

"I meant for dinner tonight," said Morian. "You'll be eating with us, I assume. I imagine you extended the invitation to our lovely new guest..."

"We made a deal," Valerya said sharply. Her eyes narrowed. "She comes when she is ready. No one talks to her until she is ready. Not even my twit of a squire."

"Of course," agreed Morian. The girl was a Summoner General now. She and Valerya could burn the Firelands down if they wanted. He would give her all the time in the world.

"Your Highness." Valerya bowed and took her leave.

# 23

## RED CITADEL
# FIRE REALM

Valerya hated secrecy. Had she possessed less discipline, she would have taken full control of the North and been done with it. The girl could have stayed there for all she cared. She probably would have let her, after a time, but Danea's warning had been hard to ignore. *Keep her close,* Danea had said. Avantys had trusted her all too willingly, so Valerya did not doubt her words.

"Keep the corridors clear," Valerya commanded as she passed the Spades. There were too many stupid looks otherwise, especially now that her clothes were soaked in blood. She had thrown a cloak over her shoulders, but crimson seeped through blackened wool. She had not expected that at all. The dissenters attacked each other like madmen when she spoke the name Danea had given her, accused each other of treachery. At least that meant Danea wasn't lying.

Valerya had three chambers to herself, and the girl had moved into one of them. She could not think of a better solution, and it was not like the girl wanted to stay in the royal guestrooms. It would have placed her much closer to Morian, and the last thing Valerya needed was for a rogue dragon to blaze through the Citadel. As long as she ordered the Spades to stay vigilant, no one dared approach Valerya's chambers. Her tower was cordoned off to anyone else; even the two witchborn freaks were banned from the tower for the time being. She did not want to know where they went.

Valerya's—now Dove's—room had its own entrance, which she kept locked, but it was also connected to Valerya's chambers by communicating doors. When Valerya opened them, Dove rose. Her gaze immediately fell on the blood on Valerya's shirt.

"What are you looking at?" Valerya asked when the door shut. "I spared you that lesson today. Now let's go. *Quickly.* Morian thinks you're in the capital." Normally, Valerya would have used force and dragged her out of the room, but her dragon had been showing a lot of mercy lately. *It must be getting old.*

But it wasn't just Avantys. The world felt different with another Summoner in it. The girl may have been a voiceless weakling, but she knew what it was like fighting the creature for control, waking up each morning a little different than the night before. It was easy at first. The changes were small, barely noticeable, but over the course of years, entire memories had disappeared. Valerya wasn't too bothered by it. If that was the price to pay for power, then so be it.

She led the girl down the corridor and into the former maids' quarters. She and Valk had turned it into a pantry years ago. It was less suspicious that way, and even sentries felt guilty tearing through food supplies without reason. The Realm may have reached prosperous times, but memories of hardship were never far behind. "Artis showed me these tunnels when I was a girl," she said, closing the door behind her. "Do you still remember how to get in and out?"

The girl nodded meekly, kneeling next to a sack of potatoes. She ran her hands against the wall, nimble fingers going over every stone. There wasn't a mark on her, save for the scars on her hand.

Valerya doubted she had ever broken a bone in her life. *The new face of the Swordsworn army.* She sighed.

Dove pressed down when she found the right stone. She was a fast learner, at least. There was a click before the door unlatched.

Valerya pulled the door open and descended first. She doubted even Avander had known about Artis's tunnels. Royals had their own paths in and out of the castle, and there was never a reason to believe that others existed. Valerya herself used them sparingly, mostly to spend a few nights away from the castle.

Halfway through the tunnel, she stopped and cast a ball of Fire in her palm. She made sure the girl was in sight and raised an eyebrow impatiently.

*I remember where we are,* Dove signed.

Valerya knew basic signs, as it was common to use them on ambushes and stakeouts. She had hired a tutor to teach her more, but it was like any other language—a subject she had always failed spectacularly. It was normal for the highborn to be fluent in Glasgérian, and Morian could speak several languages with ease. But by the third month, Artis had given up teaching her completely.

They continued in silence. *Quick learner, indeed,* she thought, vaguely impressed. She had stopped casting Fire, but the girl could move freely in the absence of light. Whenever Valerya turned, she was right behind her. Finally, she stopped when she reached a wall, casting another ball of Fire. With her free hand, she signed. *Do you know where we are?*

Dove blinked, and dim light washed over her features. She mouthed to herself as if trying to recount her steps. Realization hit her like cold water to the face.

*Come on,* Valerya beckoned impatiently, pressing against the wall. The air grew cooler as the slab of stone gave way, and she shoved her weight against it until it opened wide enough for them to slip through. She stepped into the chambers and lit the torches on the wall.

She made sure the door was shut tight before turning to the girl. "I was able to get a name from the Spears." She turned, expecting confusion, but the Dove's face had lost its color. *Right.* The crypts must have held another meaning for her.

For a moment, she considered explaining but decided against it. She had done too much talking today. Danea had given her a name in Marren's Haven, but it was so absurd that she had to... *confirm it...* with the two inmates. Even after she had flung their bodies from the tower, she thought they were lying.

*I'm going to kill him.* It would explain a great many things she had ignored over the years. The black peregrines that always came to Artis's window. The peregrines that came to *Avander's* window. If Danea was telling the truth, their leader was a far greater threat to the Crown than she had thought.

*What is this?* She pressed a hand to her chest, felt her heart beat in ragged rhythms. An unfamiliar sensation.

She walked to the far end of the chambers where Avander's likeness lay. It was the only statue that had been carved onto the lid of the coffin, like he was sleeping on it, covered in sheets. The sculptors had slaved for weeks to make stone look like silk. His eyes were peacefully closed, his hands folded over his torso. For a moment, she wanted to reach out and hold them.

"Do you know these people?" she asked coldly, turning to the girl. The likeness of Avander's wife stood next to him, as well as the child that was supposed to have been the crown princess. She had been three, Artis told her. Wild hair and always laughing. *Elarya.* It felt strange looking into the eyes of the child who had become...

*Let's get this over with.* "Well?" she asked.

Dove nodded, signing what Valerya assumed were their names. She couldn't remember the signs for letters, but the girl was sharp. She probably had their names right.

Valerya concentrated fury in her fingertips and pressed her hands together. When she pulled them apart, flames tore through the air between them. Loose rocks trembled on the ground, retreated in fear. Just looking at the statues made her angry.

She concentrated her elements into fine threads. They were delicate but sharper than a blade, and it took all the strength she had to keep her wrists steady.

*What are you doing?* Dove pulled on her arm, but Valerya brushed her aside.

"Avander," she said, bringing her hands above her head. Avander's words were ringing in her ears. *Protect my bloodline.* "His last words never felt right. Never." Without hesitating, she brought her arms down, catching one of the likenesses in her blade of Fire. The child's. Stone crumbled upon contact, leaving behind a cloud of dust.

Valerya brushed it away, pulling a coffin to the surface. It was small, barely half her height, but her fears solidified into something real. *Wooden.* Why would it be wooden?

Dove pulled on her arm once more, but Valerya barely felt it, intent on being proven wrong. She didn't care how many gods she was offending with this breach in etiquette. Only they knew how much she had bled for them.

*This is wrong!* the girl signed hastily. Her cheeks flushed red, but she took a step back when Valerya drew her sword, heaving it down on the lid.

Valerya grabbed the girl's shoulder and forced her to stand in place. "Look. *Look at it,*" she commanded. Even her dragon coiled in rage when it saw through her eyes what she saw.

When the dust settled, it all became clear. Where she expected the bones of a child, she saw nothing—only a scepter, and a Falcon's coin.

Valerya picked up the scepter and closed her eyes. Cursed Avander. *How am I supposed to keep my promise now?* For such an immense presence it had in the Scrolls, the scepter was insultingly light and crudely crafted. Her eyes took in the jagged tip that formed the head of a dragon. She did not know which one it was fashioned after, but it looked suspiciously like Avantys.

"Elarya of Pyrrheas," she said, "is heading the Red Spears now."

*"Sister?"* Dove signed. Hopefully.

"Yes. But get that look out of your eye." *There is no way I can keep both Morian and Elarya alive.* Valerya cursed; she did not want to get the girl involved, but she was running out of time. "I need you to do something. There is someone I need to find in the castle. And I need your dragon to find him. Can you do that?" She cringed. "For me?"

Dove stared at the broken coffin, then back at Valerya. Bit her lip.

And nodded.

# 24

# UNKNOWN

Dove had no idea what to expect, but she opened her eyes and settled into a memory. It took her a moment to realize she was looking into a mirror. Or rather, he was. *Pierce.* The name Valerya had given her; the person whose body she was in. He must have been someone important for Valerya to ask for a favor. That warranted at least some modicum of curiosity.

The man who met her gaze looked rough, like he hadn't slept in days. He looked to be around Decker's age, with a stern face and dark eyes that held no fire. His hair was thick and black but starting to gray, and jagged bristles lined his jaw. A scar parted his left brow.

Then he spoke.

"This again," he said, eyeing himself warily. His stern gaze fixed on his reflection, but Dove realized he was looking at her. His eyes were deep brown and almost black, and she was drawn to them instantly.

*Can he see me?* For a split-second, she panicked, ready to jump back to her own world.

"No, wait. I have to finish," he said. His voice was deep but lacked force. It stammered and broke when he spoke. "I'll just finish." Dove watched, flabbergasted, as he signed a piece of paper. She tried to see, but the colors were starting to swim together. They swirled in the corners of his vision, and she felt the pressure build behind his eyes. *This poor man is going to have a terrible headache soon.*

"Time to go." The man set his pen down and held a book in front of his face. "See this? Time to go." He rose and threw on his cloak just as Dove began to feel his head hammer. She had almost forgotten that she could feel his pain. "Time to go."

Whoever Pierce was, he was nervous, that much she could tell. *I would be too,* she realized. *How does he know I am here?* He continued down the hallway until he almost walked into a broad-shouldered woman with black curls. She wore the neat apron of a chambermaid that was pressed and folded at the collar—Dove could always tell which chambermaids meant business—but Dove had never seen her before. She would have remembered those eyes, which were dark and flecked with gold.

"Oh! Sorry, very sorry, 'Ma," the man muttered. The light of the corridor was too bright for his eyes, and he turned his gaze downwards. He must not have seen her coming.

"My lord?" The woman frowned in concern. "Are you all right, love?"

"Yes. Yes. I'm all right. All right." He stared at her as though giving Dove a chance to commit her image to memory. "Right, that's good. Say, *Ulma,*" he stammered. "Did you… did we find the Second Summoner yet?"

Dove tensed as the woman threw him a suspicious glance. "Yes. We found the child, Pierce. You know this already. Why don't you go find—?"

Dove felt a pang of panic when she realized Pierce was standing right outside her chambers. *Does Valerya know this man?* She would have never let him anywhere near her tower. Or this woman, for that matter. Suddenly, she felt pain ricochet in the man's skull. *Oh, gods.* The more she panicked, the worse his… *their*… headaches got. "Calm. *Calm,*" Pierce hissed at her. Dove still could not believe he could sense her presence, let alone talk to her, but she obeyed. "Thank you, Ulma."

The man turned and continued down the corridor. Dove wished the colors would stop swirling, but she was all too acquainted with this kind of headache. "Need to talk to the child," he muttered. "The *child.* Need to talk to the child."

Dove bristled. *I am an adult,* she wanted to say, but she was too busy trying to commit everything to memory. He took twenty steps and turned. "Stay with me," he said, glancing over his shoulder. "No one there. No one." He started descending the spiral staircase to the dungeons. "Have to finish. Must finish. Then talk to the child."

Dove eyes widened when she saw the empty cells. They had never been that empty before. Morian must have been busy concentrating his energy on hunting down dissenters, and she imagined there were not many left. Two dragons quelled rebellion spirits fast.

"This here. This here. Remember," Pierce snapped, tracing his finger across the stones. "Seventeen from the left. Nine down. Seventeen from the left. Nine down." He pulled a loose brick from the wall and shoved his journal inside. "He mustn't," he said. "He mustn't read it. Avantys mustn't read it."

It took Dove a few more moments to realize the man was going mad. In an instant, he collapsed to the ground, sobbing. "Danea. Danea, I'm so sorry." It was awkward, but Dove forced herself to focus as this grown man crumpled to the floor. In a strange way, she understood his pain. She felt the bizarre urge to comfort him, this stranger who was somehow speaking to her. *But where is he?* Tears and colors blurred his vision. *And who is Danea?*

"This is my goodbye message. I have to go," he said. "I have to do it. It's the only way. The only way to kill a tyrant." The man collected himself and stroked his hair, and Dove felt it like it was her own. He was comforting her.

"Please, please forgive me," he whispered to her. "Please don't forget me. Now, go. Go. It's time to go."

*I will find you,* Dove thought wildly. She could not leave this man alone in such a state. But before she could react, their connection broke.

# 25

# THE
# OTHERWORLD

Dove woke up gasping for air, like she had been submerged in water again, but her lungs felt fine. There was no pain, not even a post-jump headache. The first thing she saw was the peacock tapestry. *I am in the Otherworld again.* "Valerya?" she called out blindly. "Where are you?"

"Here." Valerya was leaning against the wall, like she usually did, waiting for her to regain her senses. Concern grazed stern features. "You started convulsing in the waking world. I needed to bring your subconscious somewhere safe before I woke you up."

"We need to… we need to find him!" Dove said. Her thoughts were all over the place, and she did not know which one should leave her lips first. "He… he saw me. Pierce! He spoke to me. He's dying!" She took a deep breath. *Calm. Think first, Dove.* "He *saw* me. He knew I was there. Who is he? He was talking about… stopping a tyrant. Is he talking about Morian? But he *saw* me."

"I know," said Valerya softly. Dove realized she had been staring at the wall, deep in thought. Valerya often looked like she was thinking about something, usually something serious, but this was different. She looked like she was going to be sick. "Did he have a scar on his face?"

"On his eyebrow," said Dove. "Do you... know him?"

"In a way." She closed her eyes. "Are you all right? Did he hurt you?"

"What? No. I mean... he had a headache, so I had a headache, but..."

"Good." Valerya turned her gaze to Dove. "I need you to listen to me very carefully. When we wake up, you will show me exactly what he showed you. Exactly where he led you."

"It was some sort of—"

"*Don't tell me,*" she said sharply. "Just show me. Can you do that?"

Dove nodded. "Yes. Of course." She caught her breath while Valerya thought in silence. "Valerya, what is going on?"

"I don't know yet," said Valerya just before she faded. "Just hurry up."

\*\*\*

Dove woke up slowly, already anticipating the pain. She felt a dull throbbing behind her eyes, a tingling numbness in her fingers. It was like Pierce's headache had become her own. She stretched her arms and found that was in her own bed. She turned her head to the side and her eyes fell on Valerya, who had taken the chair next to the window.

Dove frowned. *How long was I out?* Valerya must have carried her back, but she was already in full armor. It looked like she had been awake for a while.

It always felt like waking up from a nap, but there was no comfort in Valerya's gaze. Or in her words. "Quickly, now." She rose and held out her hand. Dove grabbed it, and Valerya hoisted her up. "Show me." It took a moment for the room to stop spinning, but Dove made her way to the door.

It was already dark outside when she opened it. She looked around for Pierce or Ulma, but they were nowhere to be found. Perhaps they had taken the tunnels?

But there would be time to look for them later. Valerya was waiting, and her patience had already worn thin.

*Pierce took twenty steps from my door, so twenty-five for me.* Normally, Dove would take more caution wandering down the halls, but with Valerya right behind her, there was no need to worry. She glanced over her shoulder. *This is what I saw through his eyes.* The stairs were not exactly where they were supposed to be, but Pierce's headache had made it difficult to concentrate. She glanced at Valerya before going down.

*The holding cells.* Dove had never been here before, but she had heard of people waiting months for a fair trial. Leave it to Morian to slowly starve his people of hope. Dove continued in silence, and Valerya lit a sconce when they reached the cells.

"They're empty," said Valerya. "I had the interrogation cells moved to the main dungeon. We're too short-staffed to man two locations, and I wanted this tower cleared anyway."

Dove frowned. It was not quite what she remembered. It was smaller, for one. For another, the walls were smooth and mortared. There was no way she could pull a brick from it. She ran her fingers over the wall the journal was supposed to be in. *Seventeen from the left. Nine down.* But it did not feel right.

Dove pulled at it to no avail.

Valerya sighed and pushed her to the side. She tucked her right elbow in, drew back, and heaved forward with all her might. Dove heard metal scrape against stone, saw her body rotate with the punch. Dark red flames spread outward from the impact and ate into the mortar. Valerya drew back and tried again. And again.

Dust spilled from the bricks as they loosened, and Dove stared dumbly as Valerya ripped out a slab and chucked it to the side. Dove realized it was not the same wall she had seen through Pierce's eyes. It must have been built over the stones. *But why?* There was no reason for it, aside from aesthetics. A strange priority for a dungeon.

"Stand back," Valerya said sternly as she worked on the rest.

Dove edged closer to the boulder and tried to lift it when Valerya's attention was elsewhere. But even when she threw her entire weight against it, it barely moved.

Valerya glanced over her shoulder, and Dove pretended to lean on it. "That's all I can do." She tossed another slab to the side, and Dove stopped to appreciate the hole Valerya had punched into a brick wall. Her awe evaporated when Valerya said: "You need to climb through."

Suddenly, the hole was dark and frightening. Dove felt a cool breeze waft through it, one that carried with it the scent of tombs. "You'll be fine," said Valerya impatiently. "The original wall is right next to it."

Valerya was more than a head taller than her, so she had punched a hole Dove could not quite reach. Dove cried inside as she pulled herself up to it. She felt Valerya's hand at her back, steadying her— or so she thought before it shoved her through.

Immediately, Dove cast Fire, but there was nothing but the wall in front of her. She traced her hands over the stones—seventeen right, nine down—and pulled at the brick. When it did not move, she dug her fingers into it and tried to wedge it loose. *Dear gods,* she thought. *Why are my arms made of pudding?*

"Do you need assistance?" Valerya snapped.

Dove tried to catch her breath quietly before she tried again. She kicked her foot up against the wall to give herself more leverage. She pulled and pulled... and lost her grip, crashing into the wall behind her.

*"Do you need assistance?"*

Dove tried again, finally loosening the brick from its stone prison. She grabbed the journal inside it, which...

*What?* Dove wondered how long it had been there. *Long enough to build a wall over it, apparently.* The leather was tattered and torn, the pages yellowed beyond her years. She shook loose pebbles from the engravings.

"Come back," Valerya commanded.

Dove hoisted herself back to the other side and held out the journal to Valerya.

"*No,*" Valerya snapped, turning away. "You must never let me read it. Do you understand?"

Dove was too shocked to respond. She had never seen Valerya so rattled before. "But *you* must," said the General, avoiding her gaze. "Just don't... tell me what's in it."

*Who... what is this?*

Dove flipped to the last page, the last page Pierce had written in—and her heart stopped.

"Pierce," said Valerya. She leaned against the wall to steady herself. "Back then, the Red Spears gave each other nicknames. I've read accounts from Badge. Blade. Whiskers. Pierce was good with arrows, so that was what he was called."

Dove tried not to look at the writing on the last page, but it seemed to call out to her. Suddenly, she understood why Valerya looked so afraid.

"When he was a boy, the historians claimed he was so good, they called him Firebender. And when he grew up, they gave him other names. Deathbringer. Worldbreaker. The Mad Whisperer. But we know him by a different name." She turned back to Dove. "The Last Emperor. Before me, he was my dragon's summoner."

*Bastyan.* The Last Emperor. Dove forced herself to look at Pierce's—no, Bastyan's—signature. *Why did I have to read this?* she thought. *Why is it always me?* Sweat pearled on her forehead. *I can just burn this right now.*

Valerya looked at her, troubled. "Bastyan lived hundreds of years ago, but he is helping us win this fight. Now come on. I'll have the builders repair this wall. They stopped asking questions a long time ago."

Dove heard Valerya's footsteps climb the stairs, but she let herself read the last page again. And again.

\*\*\*

*I will bond with Avantys tonight. When I do, it will be mine, and I will belong to it. It is the only way to control it. But even after I am gone, Avantys will find someone else. I beg you not to make the same mistake I made. You must find Avantys*

\*\*\*

Dove closed her eyes and took a deep breath before continuing.

***

*You must find Avantys and kill its Summoner.*

# 26

## RED CITADEL
# FIRE REALM

I t was a long shot, Gryff knew.

Valerya's tower was blocked off to everyone but the Summoners and the Spades, and outside, a blue-haired Thunderborne and his swordmaiden companion made sure no one got close. Even when Gryff introduced himself as Valerya's squire, the Thunderborne laughed and challenged him to a duel. For days, people had crowded around the tower and asked questions. They only left when Valerya threatened mass imprisonment. As far as Gryff knew, nothing got in, and Dove never came out.

*The castle looks so different from up here.* Gryff's breath misted as he watched Valerya's tower for a sign of life. He felt stupid, but even when the world was being torn apart by feuding dragons, there was still one hope he clung to fiercely: that Dove was still there. And whenever she felt afraid, or overwhelmed, she would find the highest spot in the Dragontail and watch the village from afar.

At the Citadel, the falconry tower was the highest point. Gryff had climbed the stairs all the way up and almost broken his neck trying to get to the roof. It had taken a while for him to find a weak enough incline for him to sit on without sliding off. It was a stupid idea, but he would wait all night if he had to. He hugged his knees to his chest and shivered.

He did not know how long he sat there, but his ears pricked when he heard footsteps. "Dove," he said, turning his gaze in their direction. "No, wait!" Instinctively, he tried to stand when she turned away, but his foot slipped and his body followed. Cold panic washed over him when he realized he was sliding off the roof, but Dove grabbed onto his collar. Her free arm had latched around the spine of the roof, like she had seen it coming.

Gryff used his legs to back up from the edge, cursing. He kicked a few tiles loose, but they did not fall. He hoped no one would be walking around the base of the tower the next time it rained.

Dove sat awkwardly, watching him catch his breath. Her eyes were cold, layered with anger and something else, but the lids around them were swollen.

"I'm... I just wanted to see how you were doing," he said, but she held up a hand in warning. The noise had caused a few sentries patrolling on the castle walls to stop, and for a moment, he held his breath. No one ever thought to look up, but the last thing he needed was for anyone to find out they were sneaking around castle grounds at night.

*As if Lyra needed more grief...*

Dove relaxed her stance when the guards went back to their duties. Her tired eyes narrowed, and a for a moment, Gryff felt afraid. Dove was a Summoner now. In the blink of an eye, she had become one of the most powerful people in the Firelands. Part of him wanted to beg her to help Lyra, but he couldn't bring himself to. Not when he was being so monstrous.

Dove sat away from him and stared into the distance, clutching her knees to her chest. There were no pleasantries between them.

"I understand you're… that I messed up. Big time." He glanced at her. "I'm sorry. Genuinely. If I could take it back… if I could take it all back…" *Calm down.* He drew in a deep breath. "I wasn't there for you. And for that, I am truly sorry."

But Dove did not meet his eyes, and her expression did not soften. *I have a lot on my mind,* was all she signed. *I need to be alone.*

Gryff lowered his gaze. "Just a few minutes," he said softly. "*Please.*"

She frowned, caught off guard. *What?*

"Just a few minutes. Of us sitting here and looking at the stars. Not saying anything. Dove, we…" Guilt tore at his insides as he tried to find the right words. "This may be the last time we can. The last time we can even *pretend* things can be the same."

He turned his gaze to the sky, to the stars that pierced through the clouds like diamonds. After a short while, Dove slackened her shoulders, and together, they watched until the stars faded. He did not know if she accepted his company or if she had just given up, but he let himself drift back to the Dragontail, to the last memory that made him feel safe. He did not even recognize who he was anymore.

He allowed himself a quick moment, until Dove glared at him to leave, and climbed back into the falconry tower. And when she was out of sight, he had never felt so alone.

"*She may trust you yet,*" he heard after a while, but Mina's voice in his mind did not make him feel less lonely. "*You will get better, child. Until then, you must be patient.*"

Gryff wiped tears from his cheek. "*Why am I doing this?*" he thought to her, crying. Skin-crawling was a sin, but it came easily to him. Dove did not even notice he was trying. But he stopped himself before he could go too far; he did not know what would happen if he crossed paths with her beast, but he had no desire to find out.

"*Because once she trusts you,*" she whispered, "*you will see everything.*" Mina gave a soft chuckle. "*Patience, child. It will all be clear soon.*"

# 27

## THE GREENWOOD
# FIRE REALM

Dove had to hand it to Valerya—she was, if nothing else, a woman of action.

Since Dove's foray into Bastyan's mind, Valerya's wrath was swift, and it was felt in every layer of the castle. Servants kept their heads down. Morian and his entourage stayed on their side of the castle. The Spades sensed their purpose and saw nothing else; the few times she saw them in the castle, they were packing, training, or readying the horses. Dove had desperately wanted to talk to Valerya about what happened, but she rebuffed every attempt at conversation. All the General saw now was Elarya. All Dove thought about was Bastyan's message.

*Kill its Summoner.* Bastyan's words of wisdom had survived hundreds of years, and as the emperor who doomed his empire when he lost control of Avantys, it was not entirely without merit. *But even if I wanted to, I could not,* she thought. *And even if I could, I would not.*

Valerya and her Spades had ridden out soon after she discovered Bastyan's journal. Dove did not know where, but Valerya made it easy for them to follow. Absurdly easy.

Dove may have been a commander now, but she was no less afraid. In truth, her fear broke past its limits. Back then, she was terrified of the legend, of the conqueror they crowned the Blood Queen. Now she knew that the legends were true.

She wished she had not looked. Bard and Mayet and all the Northmen under her command had warned her not to look. If only she had kept her gaze to the east. Fire-red pinpricks dotted the silhouette of the forest, laying constellations on the lake like fallen stars. It would have been a peaceful image... had it not been for the smoke.

"This was a rebel camp," said Mayet, but her voice faltered. She hid it with a dry cough.

*A rebel camp.* Dove repeated the words in her mind, but they did not settle. *The enemy.* It should not have filled her with so much dread. Indeed, anyone would have rejoiced to be on the winning side, but victory was such an abstract thing to those not fighting. For one side to reign, another had to lose. Looking around, Dove had no doubt Valerya had won.

Crosses rose as high as the sun, almost higher than the smoke that settled in the clouds. People dangled from the wooden posts, their limbs ripped to the bone. One gasped, barely on this side of consciousness, and Dove realized when they failed to speak that their tongues had been removed. Some were still alive, but there was nothing she could do. The bodies were too high up; cutting down the posts would likely kill them, and even if her men built ladders and carried them down, there would be nothing left of their future. She could not take them along, and they would be food for the wolves once she and the Northmen left.

Bard did not say anything. He simply looked away, rode on.

*Kill them,* Dove signed to Mayet, who nodded grimly.

"Silas, *q'arl kroysh*," said Mayet to the dark-haired archer who had ridden south with them. It stung every time Dove heard their dialect; she may have claimed a Northern name, but she understood nothing, not a damn thing of the men she was supposed to command. They had followed her out of deference, but respect without substance was as thin as a veil. Soon they would realize that she, too, was a foreign commander, as strange and unknown to them as Valerya the Fireborne. She even thought in a different accent.

The archers glanced at Dove and followed suit when she drew her bow.

*Where the eye goes...* Dove repeated to herself as she took aim. She felt her own breath tremble, her hands shake, but she forced herself to grip tightly. Wide eyes stared back at her, but they spoke of relief. The man was so close to death, he could almost taste it. *I am so sorry,* she thought when she released her arrow. Movement ceased. Round eyes narrowed. Dove turned away and steered her horse towards Bard as the next arrows hit.

"I told you not to look," he grumbled. All the warmth had gone from his face. He had trimmed his beard before leaving the Citadel, but it only accentuated every frown, every crease that darkened with his mood. Dove always thought he looked better clean-shaven, but his jaw was clenched so tight, she thought it might burst. "Val's temper has always been sharper than her blade."

That was an understatement, like saying snow was colder than the sun.

By the time they had reached what was left of the camp, Valerya and her company had already gone. The General had only needed two days to mobilize a battalion, and her company led the campaign to cut down the rebellion at its roots. Of course Dove did not know where that was. No one ever told her anything. Valerya had only given her command of several divisions—mostly the Northmen who had followed her, along with several others—and told her to wait a day before following the smoke.

Dove knew it meant something ominous, but this was another plane of cruelty. There were seven posts that surrounded the camp. One of the dissenters had already died by the time they got there, but the others prayed for death. The rest of the camp was torched, covered in ash. Valerya must have had the bodies burned. She hated rebels and dissenters, but now she wanted them to know. With the way things were going, there would soon be none left.

"Well, kid," said Bard, chewing on a piece of dried meat. He nodded towards the distance, where smoke rose from black sand like snakes. "Ready for the next one?"

***

By the third camp, Dove was too tired to sit upright. Exhaustion came suddenly and without warning. They rested not too far away, setting up their own camp. Mayet had the Northmen dig trenches well into the dawn. That was Dove's first lesson. Before anything else, one always had to secure their defenses first. Better go to sleep a little cold, a little hungry, than not waking up at all. Mayet had a keen eye for danger, even when it was not present.

*I wonder if I will ever get used to this,* thought Dove. Bard had joined the Northmen in scouting the premises, hoping for tips. Rhysians were the best huntsmen in the Firelands, after all, and he was always hungry. Only Silas stayed behind to keep her company.

They were closest in age, and the silence did not seem to bother him.

"You should get some sleep," he said, unrolling a sleep sack for her. They had packed light, ready to leave at a moment's notice. "Must be tiring with that burden."

That *burden*. Dove knew what he was referring to, but in truth, her dragon had been curiously calm. The forests had a soothing effect on it. It had not bothered her once throughout their entire journey.

*Just a quick nap,* she signed, but he stared back, blinked. Everyone in the Firelands was expected to learn signing now, but for some, it was a slow and painful process. *I sleep short,* she signed instead. That he understood, and he nodded. "I'll stand guard, then," he said awkwardly, clearing his throat. Dove saw his skin tinge red behind dark curls. Not too long ago, they had practiced archery together. Now she was his superior, his commander. Everyone's commander. No wonder they watched what they said around her.

*At least I can take advantage of it,* thought Dove as sleep tugged her to the other side of consciousness. It may have been in poor taste to sleep in the presence of company, but one of the few perks of being a Summoner was not having to feel bad about it…

\*\*\*

"Took you long enough." A sharp voice tore through the darkness, but it was a welcome sound. In truth, even after seeing what was left of the rebel outposts, Dove could not help but feel a twinge of relief. She had been journeying with hundreds at her command, but fear created a distance between them. Back in the waking world, she had never felt so alone.

*But not here.* Of course she was a dungeon cell, but it was better than nothing. Dove opened her eyes and sat upright. She blinked and forced her vision to sharpen, but where she expected iron bars, she found damp stone. They were indoors, but she felt light winds through the cracks in the walls. Even without the likenesses in sight, she did not have to guess where they were.

Before she could say anything, Valerya turned to face her. "How many times have I told you to bond with that thing?" she snapped, and Dove sighed. Some things never changed. "Once it binds itself to you, it will do as you command. That *includes* building our connection."

Dove was not sure she liked Valerya's new location of choice. As much as she feared the dungeons, crypts were not much of an improvement. Dove tensed. "Why did you…?"

"They were rebels," said Valerya curtly. She seemed to have anticipated Dove's question but saw no need to layer her answer with tact. "Letting them live is not merciful, it's craven. You would only be leaving the killing to somebody else."

"But you *decimated* them," said Dove. "Some could have been…"

"What, spared?" said Valerya mockingly. "Survivors regroup. Imagine if they fled and attacked your entourage with reinforcements. An easy win for you, but there would have been casualties on both sides. Better them than us."

*Us.* It sounded so foreign to Dove, but she tried not to let it show. Valerya's mind was quick to categorize: either she was with them or against them, and the shades in between were reserved for weaklings. "And the crosses?" Dove asked, finding her voice.

"Were those necessary?"

"They certainly make people think twice before joining."

"Well, I can see why you are a conqueror..."

Valerya gave a derisive laugh. "You can see why we're *alive*," she said. "If you want to do the same, I suggest ensuring your own survival before anyone else's. You are..." She paused, and her eyes narrowed in regret. But Valerya always finished what she started, and she told no lies. "You've become too important to lose."

Dove looked to the side and hated how warm her cheeks got.

"Where are you?" asked Valerya, moving on.

"The... third rebel camp." Dove hoped the answer would suffice. She lost had track of their whereabouts less than a day after they left the Citadel. "We've set up camp several miles away."

"Good," said Valerya. "Before the dawn, ride north until you reach a fork in the road. Fill your flasks at the stream but take the path leading away from the water. Follow the line of broken trees and ride until you see our camp."

Dove blinked. She had been wondering how Valerya intended to get in touch with her should things go awry. In the Otherworld, there was no safer way to ensure no one intercepted their messages.

"How..." Valerya began, pained. "How... *are* you?"

"Good, I think." Dove did not know why she said that, but she went along with it.

"Have you encountered any difficulties on the road?"

"No."

"Anyone giving you trouble?"

"No."

Dove could not think of anything else to say. Valerya was a terrible conversationalist to begin with, but she was not exactly much better. "You?" she asked, stupidly.

Valerya laughed. "My men are well rested. They're glad you are taking so long."

Dove braced herself for the answer. "Are there... any more rebel camps?"

"I suspect any remaining rebels will pack up and make it back to their headquarters."

"Which is where?"

"You leave that to me."

Dove sighed. More secrets. "Are you planning on... killing Elarya?" she asked instead.

"If I have to," said Valerya grimly. "If she surrenders, she will receive pardon. But if she refuses, royal blood or no, she must be eliminated." She paused. Laughed again. "Morian is expecting a child."

*What?* Dove did not know what was more horrifying. "What?"

"Gods help us if it's a boy. But even if it's a girl, she would be the next in line. Bastyan changed the laws of succession to include female heirs." Somehow, Valerya seemed oddly pleased at the news. "There will be a royal wedding soon. I'm glad we're out here hunting rats instead."

*Me too,* thought Dove, but she said nothing. *Better a hundred of them than a hundred of us.* Was that really true?

Valerya watched her for a moment. "Once you get there, go to my tent immediately. No one else," she said, changing the subject. "Outside my camp, you must not go anywhere without that Thunderborne or your swordmaiden." Her gaze intensified. "There are dissenters everywhere. It would weaken our position if you were captured."

"Stop talking like I'm... a bargaining chip." It hurt enough that Dove did not belong anywhere, and it did not help feeling like they only cared about her dragon. "I am more than that."

"Not to them," said Valerya, irritated. "This isn't some street brawl. This is a fight for our future. You and I are *nothing* more than that." She turned violently and frowned, trying to figure out if Dove was joking. "Our value is determined by one of two things: how much damage we can cause, or how much damage we can fix. That thing in you makes you dangerous, and therefore high in value." The more she spoke, the more her eyes narrowed. "You would do well to stop taking things personally. How can you expect to defend yourself if *words* can wound you so easily?"

*Her* words shot through her like arrows, but Dove did not want to her to know. "I... understand," she said instead.

Valerya sighed. Her expression softened, but it was still stern. "It's been a long day for you. Get some sleep. Oh." She sighed, suddenly irritated. "And Valk sends his regards."

# 28

## THE GREENWOOD
# FIRE REALM

Valerya returned to the waking world just in time to watch Danea fasten the sheath to her belt. Scarred fingers worked leather laces with ease, and once they were fastened, Danea threw her coat over her shoulders. It was so tattered and torn, pulled together with different strings, that Valerya wondered how she had managed to sneak in and out of the camp without anyone noticing. No one wore frock coats anymore. The back of it dropped to her knees.

Valerya frowned. "You look like a pirate," she said.

A smile rippled the scars on Danea's face. "This coat is a few hundred years old. It belonged to a friend of mine, and I don't have the heart to replace it." She dropped her gaze when Valerya did not respond. "I imagine you still have questions."

That was an understatement. Ever since they had first met in Marren's Haven, Valerya had nothing but questions. "How are you not dead?" she asked.

Danea laughed as she tied her hair back. Strands fell over her eyes like a frayed rag, but she ignored them. "Are you this tender with everyone, dear, or is it just me?"

Valerya pulled on her own shirt and eyed the dagger on the desk. Blood had crusted and cracked over the blade, but Danea was still standing. Valerya had plunged it into Danea's heart herself, saw the wound heal before her eyes. Danea said it hurt like hell, but it left no scars. She didn't even wince; Valerya suspected it wasn't the first time she had to prove her immortality to non-believers. But something still did not make sense. "If the Exalted bound your blood to your brother's, why didn't you fall with the Empire?"

Danea gave a tired smile that did not reach her eyes. "Because it was never my brother I was bound to. It was only when he died that I realized I was bound to his creature. To yours. As long as that dragon lives beyond the stars, so will I. And it's too... cruel to let me go."

"Too cruel?"

She shrugged. "My punishment for trying to stop my brother, I suppose. Back then."

"Why not kill me, then?" asked Valerya. "I recall a few opportunities."

"It won't let me. And even if it did, it wouldn't change anything." Danea regarded the blood with disgust and sheathed her dagger. "You'd be gone, but not Avantys. If anything, it would be a waste." She grinned as she straightened her collar. "I quite like having you around. Though I'm surprised you're not... *allied*. I must say, celibacy is wasted on you."

"There's no time for that," Valerya snapped. "Even your brother died alone."

"He spent his life unwed. Not alone." Danea fastened the clasp of her coat. "His lover remained a close friend to both of us until the end. We both thought we could stop Bastyan, but... well, Avantys is a hard opponent. Even for another dragon."

"The other Summoner?" Valerya frowned, trying to recall all the time she spent in the Otherworld. She had pored over the notes of both Bastyan the Cruel and Baley the Kind, but they wrote mostly of wars and dragons. Court and politics. "The Scrolls write of their friendship, but anything beyond that was not recorded."

Danea shrugged. "I suppose it wouldn't be. I thought it would become more accepted over the years, but if there's anything I've learned in the past few centuries, it's that people find new ways to disappoint." She chuckled to herself. "But there's hope for you yet. The histories repeat themselves, General. Whether we'd like them to or not."

*Kill me.* Danea sounded like the matchmaker who had come to the Citadel when Valerya turned twenty. Valerya had woken up to a line of suitors outside her chambers, pre-approved and blessed by the Sun-sworn priests. By midday, Valk had to smuggle her out of the castle dressed as a jewel merchant. It was awful.

"When will your reinforcements get here?" asked Danea, pushing the tent flap to peek outside. Valerya liked the way her eyes caught the torch-fire. "I'd love to stay, but I don't want to be here when they arrive. Your men might ask questions, you know."

"The girl should arrive just before dawn."

"The girl?"

"The Second Summoner."

*"Ah."* Danea threw her a knowing smile. "See what I mean? The histories…"

"She's a child."

"She's well above the age of majority. If you were a man, no one would blink an eye."

"Get out."

Danea laughed. "Fine, fine. Don't say I didn't warn you, though."

But her smile faded fast, and her brow furrowed thoughtfully. "You know, Bastyan's greatest mistake was thinking that *thing* would always be enough for him. But in the end, he died alone, after all."

"And you call me tender."

Danea hesitated a moment before making her way back to the bed. Her eyes met Valerya's, and her lips parted hers. It was tender, unlike the urgency of their lovemaking that evening, and lasted more than a few heartbeats.

"What was that?" Valerya asked when she pulled away.

"I'm just saying," said Danea softly, looking back out the tent flap. "Don't make the same mistake my brother did."

# 29

## THE GREENWOOD
# FIRE REALM

They arrived just as the sun began its ascent, tinging the clouds with molten gold. Dove knew at once that they had reached Valerya's camp, which was right next to an abandoned stronghold. Aside from the sudden presence of Fire, the tents were so… organized. No stone was out of place. Spits had been used, but the pots were scrubbed clean. *The last time I was in her tent, I was a casualty,* she thought. *Now the men who held me captive are sworn to obey me.* Had she been a more vindictive person, she would have had them all killed. Valerya would have.

As she rode in, the men parted and stood at attention. She bore no banners, but they recognized her horse. It was not like Valerya's; the General's destrier was of a breed known for its temperament and loyalty. It only responded to its master's voice and attacked anyone else who got too close. Dove's was smaller, but from what Mayet had told her, equally expensive. It was much tamer and not easily agitated. Perfect for someone who did not know how to ride at all.

Dove dismounted and bristled when someone from Valerya's

camp came to take the horse. "I'll take him," he said when he saw her reaction, "my General."

Dove died inside. *I am not your General,* she wanted to sign, but her hands were busy with the reins. *Our General is in her tent. Our General is the one who burned down the rebel camps.* She gave up and handed them over. Head hanging, she made her way to the General's—the true General's—tent.

A single banner of crimson fluttered weakly at the entrance, and her natural instincts urged her to flee. *It's not too late.* Every time they were in the same room, something went wrong. In Rhysia, the floor of the castle broke. It *broke.*

"Come in," commanded Valerya from inside the tent.

Dove took a deep breath and entered. The tent was almost exactly as she had remembered it, but in more disarray. It looked like the Spades had set up in a hurry and did not mean to stay long. Her eyes shifted to the papers on the desk, to the crumpled sheets on the bed, before she tore her gaze away. *Pull yourself together.*

Valerya bit back a derisive smile. "Not bad." Only then did Dove remember the armor they had made especially for her. It was nowhere near as heavy as Valerya's—Dove doubted she could even bear that much weight—and made mostly of tanned hide, not metal. Speed was her greatest asset, not strength. There was no use pretending otherwise.

"I see the Spades enjoyed taking their time." Valerya laughed when she saw Dove's reaction. "What, you didn't think I would leave our most valuable asset completely unguarded? I counted maybe *seven* in your division who could hold their own, plus Zan. All it takes is one lapse in defense, or one turncoat. One."

*How many?* Dove signed.

"Six, in disguise. They knew where I'd be. Stane rode ahead

while you slept and informed me that all the... *survivors* we left behind are now dead."

Dove did not want to react. Valerya seemed well rested today. The air did not condense, and the ground did not quake beneath her feet. She wanted to keep it that way.

"There was a time you would have been too scared to do anything about it," said Valerya before turning away. "In any case, you look well. No longer sickly, or completely useless."

Dove was not expecting that. It was a compliment that bordered on insulting, but it had been so long since she heard a kind word that this elevated her mood to the stars.

"But we are not too far from a fight," Valerya continued, ignoring her reaction. "And I don't want you anywhere near it."

*What?*

"You're young and impulsive, and Valk would never stop pestering me if you died," she said, defaulting back to insulting. "I need you here for appearances. Your presence does wonders for morale. But my men and I can't fight and look after you at the same time."

*How do you even know where Elarya will be?*

Valerya paused, tried to understand. "You're asking how I know her whereabouts," she said after a moment. Her frown went so deep that it looked sewn onto her face, and her answer came out forced and pained. "Do you trust that I can keep you safe?"

Dove nodded reluctantly. Despite everything that had happened, the cruelties she had seen, she doubted anyone could keep her safer.

"Then leave Elarya up to me. She will not harm you."

Dove pointed to herself. *Where will I be?*

"You will be safe," said Valerya dryly. "That's all you need to know."

# 30

## GENOVEL

# FIRE REALM

*What the actual fuck, Valerya?* thought Bard as he peered out into the night. The stars dimmed and flickered in succession, diamonds that shone in the dark. Dove and the others may not have recognized where they were, but he did. Since the rest of their entourage consisted of a slew of Northmen and an unpredictable mute, no one else knew their way around, and he could see it was making them nervous. No one had the stomach to share words with the Swordsworn, who sat silently on the other side of the encampment. They might as well have built a wall.

Bard could see Genovel from where he was standing, quiet and still as a pond. He would never call himself faint of heart, but even he had felt a twinge of unease when he saw the wooden posts. *Now she's left us here.* He shook his head. *No. Val wouldn't put us in danger.* He shifted uncomfortably and took another swig. *Old fool. How many more must die before you realize Val is...*

*Gone?*

He sighed. A quiet night with cold-cut stars was perfect for recalling better days, back when Val and Lucien were still alive.

*It wasn't too far from here,* he realized suddenly, glancing over his shoulder. Probably thirty miles west at most, deep in the heart of the Greenwood. They'd had to scout a bandit camp, and Val had drawn the short straw. She came back claiming twenty bandits, so he and Lucien readied fifty of their own to scare them off.

There had indeed been twenty bandits… with a hundred of their friends. *Who knew the Realm's greatest general was the world's worst scout?* Bard laughed to himself when he remembered the panic on Lucien's face. Even worse, for years after, Val was convinced it was rigged, that he and Lucien already had the long straws in their hands. She'd always had a suspicious mind, and even then, she could hold a grudge.

*Avander was pissed.* That he remembered. Of course, Val must have been around Dove's age, but she had forced them to take her along. And of course, Lucien could never say no to her.

Bard sighed, trying to forget how young they had been. Now one was dead, the other completely untamable, and he? Bard turned his gaze skyward. *A wandering, drunken fool.*

Val had ridden out alone before Bard could even unsaddle his horse. Her men—and women, he noticed    stayed behind, unfazed, retreating to their tents and pretending the others didn't exist. It did not shatter his morale the way it did with the others; instead, it left him with a feeling that more closely resembled dread. They may have been armed to the teeth, but most of the Northmen were not keen on watching Val ride off into the sunset. That left them smack-dab in the middle of unfamiliar territory, following the command of a voiceless girl and her blue-haired bodyguard. Two foreigners in their fight against outsiders.

Dove had settled into Val's tent, but he knew she was only following orders. *Well,* he thought. *She fits her new name well.* No one in Valk's family knew how to say no.

The Spades saw no need to disguise their identities, so they stood guard in their regular armor. Dragon sigils gleamed on their breastplates. Then again, they were still the General's men. Only a softer, kinder general who would break in battle. Dove's heart may have been made of gold, but it would still bleed red like the others.

His gaze wandered to Val's tent. *Dove has no idea what she's in for.* He wondered if she needed company, but he had never been good at comforting women. His solutions often involved copious amounts of alcohol or other, more scandalous means of relief, but neither of those seemed appropriate. Aside from the fact that he had already finished off the ale, she was much too young for his taste. Even if he did harbor dark thoughts, she and the Swordsworn army would burn him alive before he got close.

He shrugged. *No harm in saying hello.* Voiceless as she was, she was still better company than the General's men, who were now eyeing him with distrust. Maybe they had finally figured out who emptied all the wineskins.

He stumbled towards the tent, brushing past Mayet, who was busy sizing up the Spades. Strange as it was, she was the only Northerner there who trusted him, and he gave her a winning smile as he passed. Best to keep it light and friendly. Despite the bread and ale they shared, he had no desire to get on her bad side.

Bard lifted the entrance flap. "Hey, kid," he began, but drove all his energy into not jumping out of his skin when he saw Valk. *Fuck!* he screamed inside. The Hound had a knack for slinking in corners, popping up when Bard least expected it—an incredible feat for a man clad in metal.

Dove glanced at him from Val's chair. It was almost comical; her feet barely touched the ground, and the seat could fit two of her.

Still, she was a Summoner, and settling into the part faster than he would've liked. Something fierce was replacing her fear, and he could see her growing stronger every day. She could sit wherever the hell she pleased. Cold relief washed over him when her face brightened. At least it was still her in there, for the most part.

"You," said Bard, turning to Valk. He was not in the mood for pleasantries. "We've been here for hours. Where's Val?"

"Urgent business," said Valk curtly, cutting into an apple. He didn't seem overly concerned. Even when a horse screamed outside, followed by Mayet's shouting, he barely batted an eye. "I didn't expect them to come so soon."

Before Bard could ask, Mayet entered the tent. "A single rider with a message for your ears," she said. "Should I call him in?"

They waited in uncomfortable silence. Dove seemed to have forgotten that she was in charge, but she nodded when they turned to her. She nodded again when Mayet pointed at Bard. The swordmaiden bowed her head in response and opened the tent flap. "Quickly," she urged.

The man came in with his hands in the air. He seemed rugged, like he had been outside for days, but underneath the wild beard, Bard saw that he was young, tired. He dropped his gaze, embarrassed. "Apologies," he said. "I was ordered to share words with your General."

"This is our General of the Firelands, which I believe you are part of, Citizen," said Valk sternly. "Second Summoner and Guardian of the Realm. State your name and your business."

"You?" The messenger caught himself before his surprise could sound too insulting. "Apologies. I had not expected…"

"Your name and your business, *Citizen*."

*Ah, yes,* thought Bard, feeling the last of the ale fade. *Now I see.*

There was a reason Val left her men behind. She had even ridden out using Dove's horse, leaving her beast of a destrier at their camp. It was obvious now why the Spades had donned their armor, walking around and pretending to patrol. They wanted to be seen. They wanted enemy scouts to see their dragon sigils, to alert their own forces.

*They think Val is here.* They saw the men. They saw the horse. They probably even saw Valk enter the tent, knowing he was never far from the She-Jackal's side.

"My name is Jonn." The messenger glanced up at Dove. He clearly hadn't expected her to be sitting in Val's chair. "I come from a humble family, so my first name should suffice for now. I am only here to bring... the Summoner... a message from Elarya of Pyrrheas."

Bard would have laughed had it not been so sad. Ever since he had heard of her existence, he wondered what kind of leader Elarya was. At the very least, she couldn't have been worse than her brother. However, she was certainly... *new.* She probably had thousands of dissenters rallied to her side but didn't know how to use them. Jonn was lucky that Dove was in charge. Valerya would have had the poor kid skinned alive for his leader's incompetence.

Dove was certainly getting good at putting on a brave front. She nodded slowly and motioned for him to continue.

*Don't do it,* thought Bard, but having once been a Falcon—in the goddamn sacred Order of Messengers—he knew it wasn't Jonn's fault. It was never the messenger's fault. Perhaps if Elarya had come herself, or at least sent in one of her commanders, they would have had the power to retreat, to call the whole thing off.

Bard chuckled to himself when he saw the messenger's jaw tighten. At that moment, Wolff's words had never rung so true. "*A messenger has no need for a bag of gold,*" he recalled fondly. "*Only *balls of steel. Remember that, you little shit.*"

Jonn took a deep breath when he saw Bard, and his gaze briefly lingered on his blue hair. "I wish to inform you that you are outnumbered and that your camp is surrounded."

"Not very friendly, Citizen," said Valk. He seemed prepared for the threat, because he disregarded it with poise. "Elarya of Pyrrheas does not deserve our graces, but let me impart a friendly warning all the same. If you wish to engage us in open combat, you will be sorely disappointed. We have orders to stand down, and should you force us to defend ourselves, we will annihilate you." He extended an apple slice towards Jonn, who refused politely. Valk shrugged, put it in his mouth. "Can you relay that back to your leader?" he asked, chewing.

"I'm… sorry?" Jonn asked, and when he turned to Valk, Bard saw. Underneath the boy's cloak was darkened armor. It looked like it had been smeared with oil, but Bard knew what that meant. *Infused with blackwood.* No doubt his friends would be clad in it, too. Even if Val had been here, she wouldn't be able to burn through it, and the only weapon they had against it could not be controlled. *At least they did their research.* "Genovel is a valley," the boy continued, "and we have the high ground. If we descended upon…"

"Yes, we know what that means, boy," said Valk, but he remained composed, cutting into the fucking apple. Whatever Valk did, it was working. Bard cringed every time the blade bit into its skin, and he could almost feel the boy bristle indignantly at every crunch. "Kindly relay our message back to your commander. We will not raise arms against you unless provoked."

Jonn nodded, his courtesy forced. "Thank you for granting me audience," he said. "I shall return shortly with an answer." He bowed and took his leave.

They waited in silence until Mayet's voice pierced the silence. "Clear!" she bellowed.

"What the fuck?" asked Bard, irritated. "Tell me that messenger was joking."

"He was not," said Valk, shrugging. Eating. "An amateur move that told us all we needed to know about Elarya of Pyrrheas. Unfortunately, we baited such an amateur move... with an equally amateur move."

"Meaning...?"

"He is right. Genovel is a valley. If they have the numbers, they could swamp us easily."

"So basically... we're fucked?"

"Indeed, we are *fucked,* Thunderborne."

"You seem calm about it," said Bard, turning to Dove. "Dove, permission to fry this man?"

Dove frowned and shook her head. Bard sighed. "Well, Val... sorry, Valerya... sorry, your General seems to be missing in action. Where is she?"

"Think, Thunderborne. And listen, Dove, because this is important. To surround Genovel, you would need hundreds of men. Close to a thousand, really, but let's assume they have fewer. I doubt they have much more than that, so if they're all *here*..." He glanced at Dove, who understood at once. "Who is *there?*"

"So wait. Val's... your *General's* master plan was to lure them all here and... face Elarya alone?" asked Bard incredulously. He was not sure he heard correctly. As inexperienced as Elarya was, she wouldn't be sitting around in the open, unguarded. "Surely the leader of the Red Spears has hundreds of guardsmen surrounding her. Willing to *die* for her."

"Oh, I don't doubt it."

"Does no one else see how this plan could fail?" Bard raised his voice, but it was like talking to a wall. Even the She-Jackal couldn't defeat a hundred guardsmen singlehandedly, especially if bloodfire couldn't burn through their armor. *But then again...*

Valk ignored him and turned to the girl. "Our General has placed quite a lot of faith in you. I don't know what you did, but her trust is a rare thing. Without you, we will lose tonight."

*Unbelievable,* Bard thought. "What the fuck was she thinking?"

"I admit, she did not tell me everything." Valk gave a weak smile. "But there is one way to find out." He turned to Dove, and his tone gained urgency. "This was the only way she could force you to do it," he said softly. "You know what to do."

"What the...?"

"*Silence,* Thunderborne," warned Valk. "And follow me."

"Dove, what...?"

But Dove looked at him sternly. Nodded. Leave me, her eyes said coldly.

*C'mon, kid,* thought Bard before Valk took his arm, forcing him out of the tent. *What the fuck were you thinking, Valerya?*

\*\*\*

*What the fuck was I thinking?* thought Valerya when she dismounted, tying the reins of the girl's horse to a tree. This had been her home once. She still knew every shortcut, every secret path that led to and from the border villages. Her father had made sure of it. They lived so close to the Icelands that he had her versed in every possible means of escape.

*Lot of good that did him.* She watched a flame flicker in the distance. *At least it finally came in handy.* She had strayed from the beaten path, cutting across the banks of the forest until she saw torch-fire.

She sighed as it lingered. "Come on," she muttered under her breath. This *Elarya* must have been a novice commander. There was no way it should take this fucking long to get caught. *Amateurs.* What did Valerya have to do, call out to them? After a few moments, she sighed again, coughed loudly.

The torch-fire wavered. Hushed voices spoke over flames as their bearers turned and listened. A falcon soared overhead. *Any time now.* Valerya crunched a leaf with her boot.

"Citizen!" one of them called when they saw her. A soft glow sharpened their features as they advanced, slowly. One was an older man, and the other, a woman, neatly dressed. In the dark, Valerya must have looked like a wayward traveler. A cloak was draped over her shoulders, covering the greatsword strapped to her back. From afar, the bulge caused by its hilt could easily pass for a satchel. "What business do you have here in the dead of night?"

"Could ask you the same," said Valerya, trying to get a good look at them. She saw a gleam of blackwood underneath their cloaks. Daggers were strapped to the woman's waist, and the man sported a crossbow. They could have been smugglers or thieves, but no one wore blackwood unless they feared fire. Judging from their look and their accents, they were from the area, and the sudden presence of Fire she sensed meant they probably couldn't burn. Not the traditional way, at least. "Closest village is a few miles away. Dangerous to walk around alone."

The grim, dark-haired one gripped the hilt of his sword. "State your business," he said gruffly, and Valerya bristled at his words. It had been a long time since anyone told her what to do, and it took all the self-control she had not to take them down. *They had to be using one of the bunkers,* she thought instead, glancing past his shoulder. The Greenwood was scattered with them. Villagers had once used them to hide from Glasgérian soldiers. Now, they were mostly used by smugglers and criminals. Rebels.

*I knew it. I fucking knew it.* Her mind flashed back to the time she drew straws with Zan and Lucien. She knew she had counted twenty bandits. Now it made sense where the rest had been hiding.

Still, she was not one to mask her purpose. Judging by their reluctance to leave their post, they must have been close. There was no need to prolong the misery. "I seek audience with Elarya of Pyrrheas," she said. "I come alone."

Without warning, the woman gave a high-pitched whistle and turned her attention to Valerya. "What's your name, Citizen?" she demanded. Her voice sounded young, but her face looked rough around the edges. Nothing compared to her companion, whose whitened scars sprawled over half his face. Their wounds mirrored the ugliness they must have seen.

"I am Valerya the Fireborne. Your General, *Citizen.*"

Instinctively they stepped back and drew their weapons. "Prove it," said the man.

"You don't want me to," said Valerya. "Listen, *Citizen.* If I wanted to kill you, the deed would be done. My only wish is to speak with your leader. It is of the utmost urgency, so I have come to present myself personally. I have… *information*… that may be of interest to her."

"You wish to *kill* our leader," said the woman, who had raised her element hand. "We saw what you did to our comrades."

"I only want to talk," said Valerya, ignoring her. "I give you my word."

"We're supposed to believe that?" the man asked.

*Easy, now.* Valerya was reaching the end of her patience. She had heard the whispers behind her back. People called her cold and cruel. Merciless. But false-tongued, a *liar*, was not one of them. *At least get my sins right.* "I know every bunker in the Greenwood and would have no problem blasting through all of them for audience with your leader."

"With what army?" asked the man as a falcon landed on his shoulder, but his tone was marred with confusion, not contempt. His brow furrowed as he unfolded the message tied to its leg. "You did come alone," he said softly, turning to his companion. "Our patrols report clear paths, and our men have your forces surrounded in Genovel."

*So they use falcons to communicate,* thought Valerya, trying to take in her surroundings. Quick, but unreliable. She supposed it was safer to use them at night. Archers had poor aim in the dark, especially under the cover of trees, and arrows drew attention in dead silence. "All the more reason to take me to her," she said curtly. "I am alone, and you have the upper hand. Grant me safe audience, and I will not raise arms against you."

"The legends may have been written in the blood you have spilt, General," said the woman, finding her courage, "but you cannot take on a hundred men singlehandedly."

*A hundred men,* thought Valerya. *So they did fall for it.* Danea was a persuasive beast, indeed. They must have sent the bulk of their forces to surround her camp, leaving a few behind to guard their leader. Her mouth drew into a thin line. "I can take you on single-handedly," she snapped. "However, I have come to Elarya in peace. I will surrender my sword and thus be unarmed in Elarya's hearing, a gesture of my good will. It would not be queenly of her to call for my head... or is it a tyrant you follow?"

The woman understood first. Her brave front betrayed nothing of her fear, but Valerya could sense it like fresh blood. The air was drenched with it. Valerya sighed and spelled it out for the older guardsman. "Take me to Elarya of Pyrrheas," she said, "or *die*."

"I thought you came in peace..." the man began.

"I come to *Elarya* in peace," said Valerya, irritated. She hated repeating herself. "And you are standing in my way, Citizen. Take me to her *now*."

They were far from her command, but they obeyed. The forest blurred and glistened under warm light as they passed. Valerya hadn't set foot in this part of the woods in decades, but behind every corner, every rock, hid a ghost of a memory. But she didn't care much for nostalgia, and her last time there left nothing to celebrate. She was too busy sizing up Elarya's guards.

*The fool appealed to sentiment.* There was no other reason Elarya would choose this part of the world, and by accepting her taunt, Valerya would be seen as weak. She didn't mind much. Being underestimated was a great advantage in any campaign.

They walked in silence until they reached the entrance to a cave. Even before stopping, Valerya felt the dragon's impatience tear through her core. *Calm now,* she commanded it, but memories of the same cave flashed in her mind—memories that weren't hers. Whenever this happened, Valerya knew Avantys was close to a frenzy.

*Capricious reptile.* It had been too temperamental lately, much more than usual; its hatred for this rebel leader, for this cave, burned fiercer than her own, and even she could not calm it down. *Only Danea could...*

Two sentinels emerged from the cave and regarded Valerya with fear and respect. They bore helmets, and Valerya didn't bother looking at their faces. "We must ask you to remove your greatsword," one of them said. "Please understand."

"By all means," said Valerya calmly, unclasping her cloak. She raised her arms as the guardsmen unstrapped the sword from her back. "Satisfied?"

The guardsmen bowed their heads, but the old man saw need to reassert his authority. "See that?" He pointed to the distance where a tiny flicker of torch-fire burned. "If you try anything, they will light the pyre. That will give our men in Genovel the signal to attack your camp."

*Your body will be on it if you don't stop accusing me, old man.* But Valerya had given her word and intended to keep it. "If it is lit, it won't be from my doing," she said instead. "I promise no harm unless I am threatened. All four of you have borne witness to my words."

The guardsmen drew a deep breath and nodded as a fifth emerged from the darkness. Unlike his companions, he was completely clad in blackwood and did not attempt to hide it. He even carried a tower shield of the same infusion. "Elarya of Pyrrheas has been alerted to your presence and invites you to come in," he said.

*Finally.* Valerya nodded tightly, unaccustomed to being kept waiting. *Keep vigilant, Avantys,* she commanded the beast. *Stay close to me.* She felt its presence grow, and their connection strengthened as she cleared her mind of anger, of doubt. Her focus had to be sharper than a blade tonight.

The dragon gave a deep growl, sensing danger. *Don't worry, my love,* she thought, soothing its temper. *Soon, we will know the truth.*

The guardsman in blackwood armor led the way, and the others trailed behind her. Her mind flashed to Dove, but she stopped herself from building a connection. *No. It is imperative that she do it herself.* She kept her gaze ahead of her.

It was not something she could explain. The dragons were linked in their fates; the stronger the creatures grew, so too their connection. Their trust.

*Dove,* she thought to herself as they reached the double-doors. *Where the fuck are you?*

# 31

## GENOVEL
# FIRE REALM

D ove waited until Valk and Bard were well out of earshot, until she could no longer sense their elements around her. Then she waited some more. *Everyone says it is of the utmost importance.* She finally released a sigh. *If that is the case, then we are indeed... fucked.* This must have been the shortest term any general had ever served. Ever.

They all said she would not be harmed, of course, but none of them had been forced to confront a raging reptile in another world. Only Valerya had. Only she understood what it was like, and that was the only reason she was even considering such an insane plan.

*Stay calm.* She glanced at her left palm. Seeing the two cuts kept her anchored in reality, reminding her she was still awake. It may have been a bad memory, but at least it was real.

*And I have this.* She pulled the dagger from its sheath. Its hilt gleamed gold, and the mark of the Citadel was carved into the base of the blade. It had belonged to Lucien, Valk had said. She could tell that talking about him always struck some resonant chord, like a scar that had formed over an old wound. Given her own relationship with her brother, she could understand why.

She let out a deep sigh and shook the nerves out of her wrists. When she closed her eyes, she felt herself coaxed by the slowing of her own heartbeat. *Take me away from here, Rhysar.* She thought of home, the boring life she now longed for. *I... beg you.*

Suddenly, her fears faded like shadows in the sprawl of night. Everything went black until she began to walk. Colors emerged with each step, lending form to her surroundings. The more she adjusted to this new world, the more it revealed itself—the trees, the winds, the light of the moon. It even smelled like old seawater, so pervasive that it settled in her bones.

Dove did not recognize the place, but she knew she was in the middle of a forest, and one that had taken the gods incredible skill and artistry to design. The ascendant star had never shone so brightly, so close that it looked like a second moon. This level of detail went beyond anything her subconscious had ever created, and the surrounding sounds did not come from any animal she had ever known. Even the plant life seemed foreign. It was green and sprouted leaves where it was supposed to but withdrew when she got too close. Even the trees knew she was from a different world. *A different time.*

Dove felt a growing sense of dread when she realized that she was in the dragon's domain, long before the Age of Summoners. Perhaps it was trying to show her its world, or what was left of it. The memory of a beast.

*Stop it.* It was all she could do to keep from snapping out of this dream world. She trudged forward until she found herself in front of a cave, but before she could enter, she was greeted by a low, unwelcoming roar that sent a gust of warm wind in her direction.

She forced herself to squint into the heart of the cave—until her dragon lunged at her with a rush of grayfire, screeching her back to consciousness.

***

Dove gasped and felt the sting of sweat drip into her eyes. *This is ridiculous,* she thought when she found herself back in the tent. *What does Valerya expect me to do?* People could not die in dreams, but maybe memories were a different story.

She closed her eyes again and prepared for the second plunge.

*It needs me,* she told herself. *It needs me.* If she said it enough times, she might even believe it. And when the earth grumbled beneath her feet, she forced herself to stand her ground.

*Here we go.*

***

The head of the beast emerged from the cave, and it was all Dove could do to keep from screaming. She had seen the flames of its likeness, but never had she imagined seeing her creature up close before. Here, in its domain, body and spirit were once again whole. It may have been much smaller than Avantys, but it was hers, as much as a beast of its caliber could really belong to anyone. She knew because she felt an indescribable connection, perhaps similar to what only mothers of boys like Morian felt. As much she feared it, it felt like… home.

*This cannot be real.* Smoke trailed threadlike over its shoulder as it gave another low growl. Scales lined its snout like delicate, white shields, and its nostrils flared as it yawned. Part of her wondered if she had finally lost her mind, but everything seemed so real, so precise, that every leaf, every speck of dust, had its place in this world.

Rhysar bristled when she took a step forward, sensing an intruder.

*Oh shit,* thought Dove, falling on her back as it lunged forward again.

"No, wait! Wait!"

Dove glanced over her shoulder, surprised when she heard a boy's voice. Suddenly, she felt violated, and it was only then that she remembered she could talk. "Who are you?" she demanded.

Whoever he was, his presence seemed to calm the creature. Rhysar halted and nudged its head against him. Its jaws were bigger than the boy's torso, but he stroked the top of its snout like he would a cat. "There, there. Cranky reptile," he said soothingly as the dragon grumbled, its equivalent of a purr.

The boy was taller than Dove, but scrawny, with thin brown hair that bore no luster. In his free hand, he held a scepter, and when Rhysar gave him a playful shove, his leg give way.

*Where have I seen that jewel before?* The green gem in his ring shone bright, and realization hit her like cold water to the face. She had read about this boy—this Summoner—before. *It cannot be.* The dead stayed dead, even in memories, and the boy should have been in his fifties when he died. "Baley?" she asked incredulously.

"I am he," he said, and when he smiled, she saw that they were clearly around the same age. Freckles lined his cheeks like constellations in the night, and his eyes glowed a warm amber. "You have to excuse him. He hasn't met anyone else in centuries."

"*Baley?*" Dove repeated. She was so stunned that she did not know what else to say. It explained everything, from his clothing to his odd inflections. He spoke Sinthean like it was bound to him, but it was different. Separated by hundreds of years. "You are… you are…"

"I summoned him before you," he said, finishing her sentence.

"I wanted to say dead. Does that mean you are… still alive?"

Baley laughed. It was a kind laugh, one that made her feel safe. "No, I left your world a long time ago, sweet girl. I am just a shade of my former self, called here because you were. And I must say, I'd forgotten what I looked like at this age." He chuckled when he saw her reaction. "I was fifteen when I bonded with this creature. Trust me, I was even more terrified than you."

He spoke strangely and his mannerisms were foreign, but Dove felt that in another time, another life, they could have been friends. *This is another life,* she reminded herself. "I saw that ring… in a memory. I remember it," she said.

"Bastyan gave it to me when I came to the capital," said Baley. "He was a bit of a bastard sometimes, but I could never bring myself to throw it away." He laughed and shook his head. "But what do you mean, you saw it in a memory?"

"I saw it. I might have seen you die." It sounded stupid when it left her lips, but she was convinced she had seen it somewhere before.

The answer seemed to surprise him, but he gave her a resigned smile. "That doesn't surprise me. I felt you there, you know. In my head. But I, ah… didn't have too much time to think about it." He glanced at Rhysar, who was sleeping soundly in his arms. "We're connected through him."

"But the dragon hates me," she said instead, envious of their bond. "Do you think he… he made a mistake in choosing me?"

Baley smiled. "He doesn't hate you."

"He attacked me."

"It's… well, it's a bit hard to explain," said Baley. "You have to get a bit closer to him."

*Oh, is that all,* she thought, feeling stupid. How the hell had Valerya done it? Her beast was at least five times bigger, with a temper ten times as short. Cautiously, she stepped forward.

The dragon bristled and moved its head to the side so she could look it straight in the eye. A translucent layer slid back into its lids to unveil a deep red. It did not seem to see her, though. Instead, it gave a low grumble to let her know it was still there. As if she could forget.

It moved forward and swayed its head to the side, nudging her with its snout. A soft roar curled in its throat.

*Okay,* she thought as she closed her eyes. Let her guard down. Whether she liked it or not, this thing, this creature inside her, was her only chance of survival. *It is time.* She felt it course through her, binding its Fire to her core. Suddenly, every nerve came to life, every sense sharpened. Cascading images flooded her mind in a silver flash, memories in an unknown succession.

Except this time, she was seeing what it had seen. She felt it soar high into the heavens, and when it opened its eyes, she recognized the Wayfare Forests.

But instead of hills and trees, the shapes looked hazy and un-focused, emanating rays of light instead of color. *It is blind,* she realized in shock. But where its eyes were weak, its hearing was impeccable. Each time it roared, figures sharpened as sounds rever-berated back from the trees. When they began to fade, it screeched again, bringing them back to life.

Light twirled into darkness, replaced by another with startling speed. Another swirl, another time, but not one she recognized. For a moment, all she "saw" was flaming arrows raining down from the skies. All around her, things were exploding, and Storm rushed up to meet the skies instead of the other way around. *Where are we?* Explosions were followed by screams, each sharpening Rhysar's vision. And then a roar, a roar from Avantys…

"*Come back,*" Baley's voice urged her back to reality—or wherever the hell she was.

Dove felt the forest rush back as Baley grabbed her by the shoulders and pulled her up. "What was that?" she demanded, but her sweat had run cold along her back.

Baley looked at her grimly. "As your connection grows stronger, you will find it will transcend time and space. But go too far back before your bond is strong enough, and you may get lost in it forever. You might… lose yourself."

It took a moment before Dove could catch her breath, before she convinced herself she was safe again… next to a murderous serpent and its dead Summoner. "What was it like?" she asked instead. "For you, I mean. And him."

Baley shrugged and went back to stroking the dragon's snout. The creature closed its eyes, lulled to sleep by its Summoner. "Rhysar is quite tame for a dragon. He was the guardian of the forests, and the forests bowed to him once," he said. "He and I were one, and we braved the rest of my life together. And it was a… colorful life. As I'm sure you can relate."

"More than I would like to," Dove admitted, rising. "So what happened?"

"I was a Summoner during the reign of Bastyan the Cruel. I don't quite know what became of him after I passed on, but before I died, before he became truly cruel, we were the best of friends."

"Bastyan?" Dove gasped. *Pierce.* Her heart stopped. "As in, the Last Emperor?"

"The last?" Baley lifted his eyebrows in surprise, but his face eased into relief. "So the Empire fell after all. As it should have, but…" He smiled weakly. "Well, that's another story. If you're familiar with Bastyan, you surely know of his dragon."

"Avantys."

"Very good, yes. Avantys is… well, Avantys is cruel. Merciless."

"I know. I have seen him."

Suddenly, Baley turned. Relief faded fast. "You've what?"

"I have… seen him."

"It's back?"

Dove did not know what to say, so she just nodded.

Rhysar opened his eyes, breaking out of his trance, and rose. "Whoa!" Baley threw out his arms to stop him as he screeched. But when he saw Baley, he calmed down and folded in his wings. Baley kept his voice soothing as he spoke. "Do you know its Summoner?"

"Yes," said Dove softly. "I do."

"What's he like?"

"She is the opposite of me," she said without thinking. "Strong and… ruthless. I grew up afraid of the stories they told about her. And now that I have met her, I am afraid of her anyway." She sighed. "But we are both generals of the Realm, now."

That made him laugh, to her surprise. "That doesn't surprise me. You know, despite our differences, Bastyan was my closest friend. He was older, and the greatest Firebender of our time, and I… well, I was the son of a fisherman. He was an excellent sportsman, and I, ha…" He pointed to his leg. "I had one working leg. But I had Rhysar, and he, Avantys." He smiled, thinking back to centuries past. "He wasn't a bad man. At least, before I… before it happened, he wasn't."

"Before what happened?" asked Dove. There was much she wanted to know about Bastyan the Cruel, about Pierce—about the boy in her dreams whom even Valerya feared. But they were interrupted by a roar.

A dark expression swept across Baley's face. "It's not important," he said, but his voice had donned a hard edge. "For now, at least. When your bond to Rhysar is stronger, perhaps you can ask him yourself. But whoever is in control of Avantys is looking for you now." He held out the scepter. "Come, now. Quickly."

Dove rose and edged closer to Rhysar, who no longer seemed to mind her presence.

"Ready?" He pressed the scepter into her hand. The dragon carved into its tip looked like Rhysar, but it did not have the scars. "Once I let go, he'll be all yours."

Dove nodded, but she was still sad to see him go. "Will I ever see you again?"

"Depends. Every once in a few decades, Rhysar summons me back, the brute."

Baley gave her his last kind smile, but there was sadness in his eyes. "Bastyan was my everything, but I couldn't save him. Maybe you can still save your friend." He nodded. "The gods be with you, sweet girl." Slowly, he released his grip and closed his eyes, like he was drifting off to sleep. The scepter glowed as he sighed his energy back into the air around them, and Dove saw him fade back, back into the stars.

Rhysar screeched, turning his full attention to her. She felt something inside her snap into place, like she had known this creature her entire life. It had only been a few moments since they bonded, but she could not imagine braving the world without him. *He chose me,* she thought, finally understanding what it meant. *And now we are one.*

"Come on," she whispered. She had so many questions, but there would be more time for that later. She let out a deep breath, the first command she had ever given. *Take me to her,* she thought grimly. *Take me to Valerya.*

# 32

# THE
# OTHERWORLD

When Dove opened her eyes, she knew at once she had succeeded. The entire world was cast in fog, but it did nothing to mask the silence, the complete absence of life. The tents had vanished, the people gone, but she recognized the village nestled deep in the valley. It was smaller than she remembered, but it was probably because she was looking at it from the top of a surrounding hill.

That may have explained the difference in size, but she knew of no natural occurrence that turned stone to wood. Tired as she was, she distinctly remembered houses made of brick, not half-timbered huts propped up by braces and beams. Log houses with abandoned gardens were separated by rough, uneven paths. It was more of a hamlet than a village, sprawled across a sorry patch of meadow. Even Myrne had been bigger, and that was saying something.

A single light flickered from one of the bigger houses. It was the only thing that moved in this world, and Dove approached it with caution. She reached the house and peered around the corner. A smithy was attached to the back. The forge looked neglected, but the grindstone had been recently used.

It was only after she knocked that she realized how meaningless the gesture was. *Who else would it be?* "Valerya?" she called when she opened the door.

"Come in," a voice answered, and Dove followed it into the next room.

*At least one thing that sounds familiar,* she thought, feeling her spirits lift. "Are we in your world now?" Dove asked. A single candle cast shadows across the walls, revealing the General's form sitting at the end of a wooden table. She had turned her chair to face the window, and her face shadowed against the moon. She was flexing the fingers of her left hand, watching the scars shrink and shrivel.

Dove continued. "But I made the connection."

"We're in a shared world now," said Valerya, giving her the briefest of nods to acknowledge she was there. She turned her gaze back to the window, where there was nothing in sight but the hills. A single tree. "As I have the stronger connection, I determine where we meet."

*Of course she does,* thought Dove. Even when it was only the two of them present, Valerya still had the upper hand. "But out of all places… why here?"

"It displeases you?"

"It scares me."

"It's my *home.*"

Dove was not sure she had heard correctly. "Sorry, what?"

"This was my home before I burned it down." Valerya spoke in harsh tones, but her face threatened a smile. Dove did not know if she was joking, so she kept her face impassive until Valerya continued. "I don't blame you. Until recently, I'd never visited. Not once. Not even in dreams. But this…" She extended an arm towards the rest of the village, the rolling hills that unfurled into the night. "This was where it all started."

"I… see," said Dove.

"I don't think you do." Valerya turned her gaze skywards. "As much as I hate being back, this sorry piece of land is the last thing I know to be true. Not even Avantys visits me here."

"We could have met anywhere." Dove took a quick glance around the hut. It was very modestly decorated. There were not even beds, but cloth-bags freshly stuffed with straw, tucked away in the corner. The most lavish thing Valerya had owned was a wardrobe, but even that was slightly burnt. In truth, it reminded Dove of her old house, but she and Gryff lived in luxury compared to this. "Like a neutral lake," she continued before Valerya could take note of the silence. "Or mountaintop."

"I told you you didn't understand." Valerya shifted in her chair. She extended a hand and gently swiped upwards. Another candle lit on the windowsill. "*Elarya…* is supposed to be dead. If she isn't, if my suspicions are true, then this… everything… the world I have built and all the neutral lakes and mountaintops in it… have been based on a lie."

Dove did not know what to say, so she waited in silence.

"I dedicated my life to fulfilling an oath," said Valerya, but Dove realized she was talking more to herself than to her. "How could he ask me to protect his bloodline knowing Elarya was still alive?" Her eyes narrowed against the moonlight. "How could he not tell me?"

"What are you… going to do?" asked Dove, suddenly nervous. She was used to the ground shaking or glass shattering, but Valerya had barely moved from her chair. Her temper was usually as taut as a bowstring, but here, it loosened and eased into sadness. For once, she had made herself vulnerable, which unsettled Dove more than her outbursts. "Are you… going to kill her?"

"If she's of Avander's blood, I can't, now, can I?" said Valerya. She laughed, spitefully. Dove had never met Morian's parents or his sister, but his entire family seemed to cause Valerya grief. "In our world, I am miles away, about to walk into a hall alone with Elarya of Pyrrheas and a hundred of her followers. Each of them is clad in blackwood. You know what blackwood does."

"It resists Fire."

"Not just that. It deflects it."

Dove blinked. "If only we had some way to burn through it…"

Valerya threw her a slanted smile. "If *only…*" She turned. "Artis would curse my bones if I asked you to risk your life, so I suppose I must order you to stay at the camp. If the rebels move to attack, command that thing of yours to burn through their armor. I will take care of the rest."

"What?" Dove frowned. Valerya may have had the highest kill count in the Firelands, but taking on a hall full of armed and angry soldiers—especially those who could not burn—would be a challenge for anyone. "They will kill you."

"You leave that to me." She turned back to the tree, uncharacteristically calm. She kept her gaze fixed on her element hand. Soft flames swirled around a scarred palm. "Should you deliberately defy my orders…" Her tone softened as her fingers relaxed, "…my wardrobe provides safe passage that should get you past their army. But be careful once you reach the surface. They will have raised their vigilance after me. They use falcons to communicate."

"So I have to avoid the fal…"

"I thought you bonded with that thing," Valerya snapped, back to her normal self. "It has a great advantage that mine does not. Avantys ruled the skies. What did yours do?"

"It…" Dove thought, remembered. "It ruled the forests."

"Exactly." Valerya grabbed the chair next to hers and positioned it to face the window. "It ruled the forests. The *wildlife*. Now sit."

"I…"

"*Sit.*" Her tone left no room for negotiation. Valerya straightened in a paltry attempt to appear more welcoming, but in her eyes burned an intense fire that made them impossible to meet. "This may be the last glimpse you'll have of a peaceful world."

Dove sat all too willingly. She was not keen on returning to the camp just yet. Here, neither time nor people existed; it was as real to her as the waking world had ever been, but not something she could share with anyone else. "Would you… take it back?" she asked.

"What?"

"Everything. This."

Valerya smiled with moderate effort. "When I was younger, yes. I would have given anything to take it back. Lived out the rest of my days in the Ironhands with nothing but a hammer and a forge. Can you understand?"

"I cannot even lift a hammer," admitted Dove, "but I think I understand. I just want to go back to the way things were, and… I do not know… bind books forever."

Valerya laughed, this time genuine. "At your age, I couldn't even read." She turned away, laughed some more. "Binding books, really…"

They sat for a long moment until the skies began to brighten. It was strange, this shadow of someone else's memory. The clouds changed color, but the winds did not blow, and no one would rise with the dawning sun. In the silence, Dove found herself wondering what Valerya had looked like back then. No scars, no army… no Morian. Just a hamlet, cloth-bags, and a forge. *Probably still tall.*

Valerya frowned, caught her staring.

"How did you get the scars on your hand?" Dove asked quickly, turned away. Heat spread to her face. "You're looking at them a lot."

Valerya smiled to herself as though Dove had made a joke. "My father told me I sliced my palm open when I was three, trying to pick up a dagger by the blade. I don't remember much from it, though. Just the blood." She placed her hand on the armrest, away from view. "Just thinking about how different my life had been."

"Why did it... change?"

Valerya leaned back against her chair. "Let me give you some advice, from one Summoner to another. With every decision you make, two legends will be born. A hero in some parts of the Realm..." She turned her gaze back to the stars. "And a monster in others. Every mercy, every cruelty, has its place in the world, as does every gain and every loss. Our decisions will create a world much greater than either of us can imagine. And we can never take them back."

"You could have stopped any time," said Dove. "Retreated to the Ironhands."

"Yes," said Valerya, closing her eyes. "We could have gone back and bound their books and forged their swords. Retreated to a neutral lake or mountaintop. But for what?" She reached behind her and grabbed a loaf of bread. "We'd go back to sleeping on bags and eating bricks." She threw it against the wall and snorted when it clunked against wood. "Nothing would change."

*She was worse off than I was,* Dove realized. No wonder she had never come back.

"At any rate," said Valerya, breaking the silence. "History will be written tonight, one way or another. Are you ready to go back?"

*No.* Sitting in the hut that was once Valerya's home was peaceful. Not being thrust in the middle of an army was peaceful. "Yes," she said instead. "But how can I... get to your house? In theory, I mean.

I do not *intend* to disobey…" *Oh, who am I kidding?* She tried again. "Your tent is guarded, and I doubt Valk would let me march off into the distance by myself."

"No, he wouldn't," said Valerya, but there was a hint of playfulness in her voice. "You're a general now," she said. "Surely I don't have to tell you how to do everything? Besides…" She faced Dove. "I am not one for stealth and secrets. I am the poor choice to ask."

"So you have never had to sneak around?"

"Never had to. However, I found I had the greatest mobility when I was Lucien's… *inofficial*… squire. No one cares about the messenger." She turned away, drew in a deep breath. "I'll stay here a bit longer. Try not to get yourself killed, girl."

Dove opened her mouth to say something, but her vision blurred at the edges.

Then Valerya kicked her out of the Otherworld.

# 33

## GENOVEL
# FIRE REALM

D ove was not prepared for being catapulted back into Valerya's tent. Colors and sounds attacked her in swarm as her surroundings settled into place, and the haze lifted as though someone had wiped it clean with a dirty rag. *I am definitely back,* she thought as she wiped blood from her nose. Going from zero to thousands of worldly sensations in just a few seconds felt like getting hit by a draft horse, and her body struggled, ill-prepared for the jump.

*Hurry up.* She groaned and massaged feeling back into her arms.

It was never a question. Of course she was going to defy the General's orders, but first, she would have to leave without anyone noticing. After that, she would have to slip into a village without anyone noticing, then past enemy forces without anyone noticing. It sounded better when Valerya had said it, but sneaking around was easier in an empty world. Now that she could feel pain and the sudden presence of hundreds around her, her confidence faltered.

Dove opened the desk drawer and examined her options. There was nothing but parchment and sticks of wax. A whetstone. Disappointing to some, no doubt, but to her, it was a beacon of hope. As much as she wished otherwise, she had to improvise using her strengths, and the drawer brought her back to a familiar sort of misery, a past existence of mindlessly copying and notarizing documents in the Scriptorium. But if the rebels relied on falcons, she had to make her message look as official as possible.

She ran her fingers over the sheets of parchment and sighed at the paper's thinness. *Do the Swordsworn care nothing for stationery?* She grabbed the quill, wondering what to write. It had to be short enough for a falcon to carry, but important enough to grant her safe passage once she reached their hideout. She practiced her fanciest penmanship in the air before bringing ink to paper.

\*\*\*

*Messenger. Permission granted.*

\*\*\*

She glanced around the desk and searched for a seal. Any seal. *Focus,* she thought, trying to ignore the hammering in her head. Morian had a signet ring he wore at all times, but Valerya hated adornment. She would have likely left it somewhere in the tent.

Dove opened all the drawers and cabinets, feeling around every corner until she found it—or rather, it found her. A ring with raised edges pricked her palm, and its seal revealed a dragon above crossed hammers. She could not believe Valerya had just tossed it in a drawer. The band was made of pure gold, which made it worth more than a horse. Dove blinked, suddenly afraid of dropping it. Without thinking, she folded the parchment and melted the wax where it threatened to open, smashing the General's ring into it.

*Now for the signature next to the seal.* A stupid, minor detail, but she would leave nothing to chance. If her plan to pose as a messenger failed, it would not be because of sloppy workmanship. She pondered for a moment and signed the first name that came to mind. *Franco.* That sounded like a proper Fireborne name. All she needed to do now was sneak past Valk...

Dove almost laughed as she tucked the parchment away in the pocket of her cloak. She might as well have tried to fly out of the tent, for all the good it did her, but a low growl reminded her she was not alone. Blood rushed to her face, resolve renewed. She had Rhysar, at least.

*I want to see the camp,* she thought to it, bringing a hand to her chest.

She closed her eyes, but the shadows were gentler, the silence soft. Pain faded on all sides. Something flickered in the corner of her mind, sharpening the more she concentrated. It was like sensing Fire, but instead of a subtle bristling at the back of her neck, she could see the elements everywhere, floating around like embers in a gust of wind.

Most were faint, barely stronger than a dying flame, but a few stood out, red and fierce like the rising sun. The stronger their caster, the more intensely they burned. The figure standing just outside the tent must have been Valk. It stood there like a slab of stone, growing and dimming with every heartbeat. As the flames gained a more human form, she saw that he was talking to someone smaller in frame. A woman. *Mayet.*

Dove kept her eyes closed and brought her hands to her face, saw white flames where they were supposed to be. She flexed her fingers and watched the flames dance. *Beautiful.* She could see the Fire inside her, inside everyone, binding itself to their blood.

*Enough.* It was no use trying to understand what was happening. She needed to find a way out, and time ran fast in this world. *I just need one thing...* She concentrated her attention on the camp until she found it. Past a slew of weaker flames burned the only Fire-bred creature with no human form. They had kept it isolated from the others, but she could tell from the way its glow raged a constant scarlet that it was brimming with anger. It matched its owner's temperament so well, it was a wonder Valerya had not left it in charge. If only it responded to anything besides the General's voice...

*If only.* She concentrated all her energy on it until the other flames faded, until it was the only thing in her field of vision. *Scare it,* she commanded. *Send it into a frenzy.*

Dove felt something that vaguely resembled a bludgeon to the head, but before she could cry out, she saw the horse jerk abruptly as though it had felt it too. She had not expected it to be painful. Being in Valerya's mind was calm, peaceful, but she supposed a connection was much easier when the other was willing. This creature was angry and distrustful—sensations that swerved into bestial terror when the dragon screeched. Dove opened her eyes when she heard the horse scream. She wanted to scream with it. What had started out as a headache exploded into a thousand bolts of pain and fear, but urgency eclipsed the throbbing in her head.

"Restrain it!" she heard Valk shout over the clamor. "No, don't get too close... you there!"

Dove waited until his voice faded before daring a peek outside.

It worked much better than she could have expected. If she knew anything about Valerya's destrier, it was that it hated everyone. The more others tried to approach it, the more it screamed, threatened harm. It thrashed against the sides of the fence and threw its weight against the tree it was tied to. It was still armored, as no one could get close enough to remove it after Valerya had ridden away from the camp, and its blade-breakers were denting the wood.

*Into the forest,* she commanded, bracing herself for another wave of pain. Another white light burst behind her eyelids when the horse panicked, thrashing at anyone who got too close. It was absurdly strong, but Dove held on until Valk finally gave up and went to help the others.

*Now or never.* Dove tried to ignore the red-hot blade sawing back and forth between her ears. She hugged her cloak around her cheeks and slipped out of the tent. Men ran around her but did not see her. She moved past them easily and only glanced over her shoulder when she heard the sound of splintering wood. The horse had ripped the branch clean from the tree and rammed through the fence, bolting for freedom into the forest.

Dove turned her attention forward. That had been too much for her. She would stick with this world for now, in all its pain and glory. Too much jumping and she might pass out.

She grunted. It was not hard to get to the village, and the paths had not changed much in twenty years. Even when they plummeted out of sight, she knew exactly where she was going.

It was almost insulting how no one saw her. She reached Valerya's old house with ease and found that it had been rebuilt in stone. It was in the same location, but nothing indicated that Valerya had once lived there. For one, the forge was gone; the space where the smithy once stood had been turned into a garden of wilted flowers. For another, it looked *expensive.* Stone houses were not uncommon, but bricks and slate were a sign of wealth. Whoever dwelled here led a comfortable life. It was certainly a step up from straw-filled cloth-bags, but judging from the state of the garden, no one had been home in months.

Dove opened the door and peered inside. The one room from Valerya's memory had been split into different sections and separated by stone walls. She walked over to where she and Valerya had shared words and glanced out the window. It took her a moment to place her surroundings. The tree was no longer there, but it looked like it had been cut down, not burned. For a village that bordered the forest, it was puzzling that they had chosen that one to get rid of.

She turned, trying to remember. If they had been here, that meant the wardrobe was in the far corner, in what was now one of those rooms. *But why would the wardrobe still be here at all?* She opened the door and blinked. Everything was so… *clean* that the burnt wardrobe caught her attention like ink against snow. As she approached it, she felt the back of her neck bristle.

*Oh no,* she thought as her nerves began to fray.

"That's enough, vagrant. Now face me. Slowly." She heard the voice, but fear faded fast, giving way to relief. She turned to its source.

Bard looked on edge, like he had been hunting a night-wolf and had finally trapped it in a corner. He looked like he had not slept in days. His mass of blue hair was swept up in waves, and his eyes looked like they had been sewn open.

"*Dove?*" He lowered his crossbow. He reacted quickly, countering shock with indignity. He glanced around to see if anyone was with her, angry when he saw no one. "What the fuck are you doing here? Alone?"

*I could ask you the same question.* She pointed at him, waiting for an answer.

"I was getting Dancer's crossbow," he said matter-of-factly, holding up the crossbow in his right hand. Its ivory gleamed in the scattered moonlight, but Dove still had no idea what he was talking about. "I mean, Brunhilda. She left it behind when we came to visit Artis, when I was still Franco, you see, before we made it to the Icelands…"

Dove gave up trying to follow him. Neither of them could explain their circumstances, so there was no use pretending to understand. She made her way towards the wardrobe and examined the burnt edges of the doors, careful not to snag her hand on a splinter. She opened it, expecting a magic portal, or something at least slightly shrouded in mystery. Instead, she saw plainclothes and boots. She closed it slowly, disappointed. Real life was boring compared to the Otherworld.

"Does Valk know you're here? Mayet?" Bard demanded as she began groping at the corners of the wardrobe. "What are you doing?"

*Help me,* she signed with her free hand.

If there was one thing she could count on, it was Bard's sense of adventure. His curiosity outweighed concern, and he placed a hand behind the wardrobe, pushing it forward with minimal effort. Dove crouched and felt for a handle on the ground. She reached down to open it.

"All right, young lady," said Bard indignantly, swatting her hand away. "You've got some explaining to do. Do you *know* how irresponsible it is to leave your camp? How dangerous it is when there are so many…" He stopped himself. Horror spread to his face like poison, and for a moment, it looked like he had swallowed some. "I sound like my mother."

He shook his head and pulled the hatch open in one swift motion. "C'mon, then," he said. "But don't think I'm letting you go by yourself."

Dove descended first, casting grayfire to light their way, but to her surprise, it spread much farther than she had expected. Instead of a tunnel, they found themselves in an underground chamber that spread out into several alcoves. Judging by the smell, they were stacked with barrels and sacks of rotten food. Storm drains lined the ceiling, most clogged or in disrepair, but it looked like the last owner had transformed it into living space.

There were shelves upon shelves overflowing with books and scrolls, but it was the stone table that caught Dove's eye. It did not take long to place it—she had seen something similar at the Citadel, in the skin-crawler's lair. *And in Divisorya,* she remembered suddenly. In the Blackstone, for student alchemists.

Bard seemed to recognize the etchings immediately. "That's how he did it..." he muttered to himself, tracing the five-pointed star carved onto the tabletop. "An alchemist's table." He turned to Dove and shuddered. "In Divisorya, we're not supposed to call it 'sorcery' anymore... but this mage stuff is scary shit."

*Agreed.* Dove continued forward. There would be time to explore it all later if she survived, and she did not want to linger too long in a mage's private domain. She followed the storm drains, walking past darkened alcoves until they reached a ladder leading up to another hatch.

Bard went first, heaving it open with his shoulders. He pulled himself through the opening and glanced around, making sure it was safe. "C'mon, kid," he whispered, holding out his hand. He wore rough, fingerless gloves that scraped against her skin, but she was grateful for his help. In truth, she was so exhausted from the jumps that she would probably pass out without him urging her forward. He pulled her up through the opening.

The moonlight that had bathed the forest in a soft, white glow had faded, covered by dark clouds. Behind them was a hill; on top of it, there would be rebel soldiers, no doubt, but they were safe on this side. The few stars that pierced through the fog revealed only the faintest suggestion of a path, and they continued until the silence got uncomfortable.

"So… what exactly are we doing?"

*Helping Valerya,* she signed.

"Slowly. I don't know my sign letters yet…"

Dove sighed. *Dragon lady!* she signed instead. *We are helping dragon lady.*

That, he understood. "Sounds like a solid plan," he said, glancing around. "We'll probably make it to her next week, at this rate. Wherever she is."

Dove ignored him, but truth sawed through his sarcasm. She had not thought this far ahead. Now that she made it past two camps, she and Bard were easy targets walking around in an open field. She closed her eyes and braced herself for another headache.

*I need a horse,* she thought, concentrating, but Bard tugged her back to reality.

"We're fucked," he whispered, pulling her down behind a bush. He pointed skyward, and she followed his gaze. An enemy falcon flew overhead, shielded by the trees. "I can't shoot it at night. Not with this thing." He slung the crossbow over his shoulder.

Feigning confidence, Dove rose and extended her arm, commanding the bird to land. To Bard's surprise—and her own—it obeyed without question, nuzzling its beak against Dove's cheek as it folded in its wings. It bobbed its head affectionately. Bard blinked furiously as she unfolded the message attached to its leg: *Jackal in lair.* She pocketed it and took out the message she had written in the tent. It was too big to tie to the bird's leg, but it took it in its talons without protest.

*Take me to her.* Dove pressed her head against the falcon's. *Please.* She released it into the night, and it flew in the direction from whence it came, waiting for her once it reached the clouds.

"What are you…?" Bard began, but his question was interrupted when Valerya's horse burst through the trees. Dove did not even want to know how it had managed to slip through the camp, but its pursuers had probably given up trying to capture it. "Careful," he warned, pulling her behind him. "That thing is dangerous."

The horse withdrew when it saw Bard, suddenly defensive, but Dove extended her hand and coaxed it to come forward. She pretended she knew what she was doing, but the beast really did terrify her. It was bigger than a normal horse and covered in slates of metal. Still, it lowered its head. *Get on,* Dove signed to Bard.

"One day, you'll have to tell me what's going on," he said, but he hopped onto its back all the same. He helped her up, and she settled into the space in front of him. "I've always wanted to ride this thing. Where are we going?"

Dove glanced up at the falcon, which had already begun flying forward. She motioned for the horse to follow, but something sharp tore through her senses. It burned fiercer than any headache she had ever experienced, and she realized it must have been Valerya. She closed her eyes, felt them water at the pain.

*All right,* she commanded her dragon. *Connect me.*

And then everything went black.

\*\*\*

"Where the fuck are you?" Valerya's voice demanded before Dove could see her.

"I am… on the way," said Dove. "Where are…?"

"Hurry up," Valerya snapped, and before her surroundings sharpened, the entire world went black again.

# 34

## THE HIDEOUT
# FIRE REALM

Valerya grunted as the hideout settled into place, filling her surroundings with cold, damp colors. Her connection to the girl had been quick, which made her return to the waking world all the more sudden. It smashed against her vision like a boulder. She had gotten used to the jumps a long time ago, but she would never get used to these fucking headaches.

"Are you all right?" asked the guardsman uncertainly, keeping his tower shield close to his body. Valerya stopped herself from laughing in his face. No one knew how to address her here. She wasn't their general, and she was as much a lady as Morian was, so they left out the niceties.

*Perhaps I should join their side after all.* "Wonderful," she snapped, waiting for the sting to subside. "What's taking so long?"

"Our leader must be briefed."

"What's there to say?" she asked impatiently. "I arrived and seek audience. Or does she need briefing on how to greet guests?"

They bowed their heads in strained deference, and Valerya sighed. She may have been on enemy grounds, but she had vowed not to murder anyone unprovoked. Instead, she closed her eyes, letting her thoughts drift back to the first time she waited to be presented... to Avander. She was sixteen and already bigger than most of the boys her age, but she remembered being scared. A common laborer in a king's hall did not follow the natural order of things, and she dreaded the moment the double doors would open. But now that the Red Spears were keeping her waiting, she fought the urge to blast them down.

*Calm*, she commanded herself, returning to the memory. Meeting Avander wasn't as bad as she had expected. He was old and proud and had all the power of the Firelands at his fingertips, but all he asked for was to see her hands. One could tell a lot about a man, he claimed, by the way his hands looked. Even then, her palms had been calloused, with a couple of slashes that had turned to scars, but he seemed more than pleased with what he saw. It was a strange, small gesture she had thought nothing of.

Until now.

*A fucking sham,* she thought, but she needed to stall for time. The girl was slower than she would have been, but at least she had managed to break away from the camp by herself. For a moment, Valerya allowed herself brief amusement in imagining Valk's re-action to an empty tent. She had seen him stay calm in the face of enemy soldiers, blood mages, even shadow bears, but a missing teenager would be the death of him.

Before she could laugh, a guardsman from inside the chambers opened the door. "You may enter," he said with a courteous bow. Cloth wrapped over his left eye.

Valerya didn't bother waiting for the others to lead the way. She entered the hall, brushing past the sentinels as rows of seats spilled out around them like an arena. It gave her the vague impression of a rundown theater, which would explain the shitshow this evening was becoming. Men and women, armed and armored, stared as she passed, but only one person was of interest to her. She stopped in the middle and scanned the hall until her gaze fell sharply on the woman sitting at the far end. Aside from her elevated seat, she looked to be roughly Elarya's age and had matted, brown hair combed out in neat waves. Her eyes were more a dull blue than gray, but they were bred for royalty. Command.

Anger bristled inside Valerya like thorns. *At least she looks the part.* From her posture, she was moderately tall. Valerya saw nothing of Avander, but the woman had more in common with his offspring, save for Morian's disgusting charm.

Her eyes fell on the woman standing in front of her, who was meeting her gaze forcefully. *Danea.* She saw lifeless eyes surrounded by scars, but now they were brimming with truth. *She's known all along.* Still in that tattered coat. Valerya almost smiled.

"Valerya the *Fireborne*," said Elarya. Her few words betrayed her origins no matter how much she had practiced the standard accent. Definitely from some forgotten patch of land far from the capital. "I must say, I am surprised to see you here. My men have told me you come in peace. My commander, Danea, has mobilized our people around your camp."

*Danea.* No wonder. Danea was their commander, but she had made it easier for Valerya and Dove to get through. She wanted this. "That is correct," said Valerya, forcing herself to cling to her manners. "I have no intention of harming the blood of my sovereign."

Valerya may have been talking to Elarya of fucking Pyrrheas, but all this small talk was grating against her nerves. It would have been clear to a blind man that they wanted each other dead. Valerya was the biggest threat to their cause, and Elarya… existed, falling into the fine line that separated lies and promises.

"Is there anything I can do for you?" Elarya straightened in her seat.

"Yes. But before we begin, it is ancient Sinthean custom to show our hands," said Valerya, reaching for her gauntlet. Archers stood on edge as she unbuckled the straps. "I'm just removing my gloves," she snapped at them. She turned to Elarya and drew in a sharp breath. "Your *Majesty.*"

"I'm your queen now?" Amusement lit those stupid eyes.

"You are the sister of our King," said Valerya, letting her gauntlets drop to the floor. She raised her hands to her face and showed her palms. "I believe it's your turn."

"Are you trying to say you have the hands of a swordswoman? Or of a smith?" Elarya glanced at who Valerya assumed was her advisor.

Valerya didn't bother following her gaze. *I'm not the one hiding in a fucking underground dugout.* But she shrugged it off. People had been trying to throw her origins in her face for years, like it was a weapon. But she was as much smith as soldier, and it was no insult to speak truth.

Elarya removed her own gloves. "Will this suffice?" she asked, showing her palms.

*Soft hands,* thought Valerya. *Smooth hands.* Hands that had handled swords, but never in the face of hardship or desperation. *Avander was right about one thing.* Her eyes narrowed as she contemplated the sad, sorry chain of events that led her here. *Her hands told me everything I needed to know.*

She glanced at Danea, who nodded slowly, confirming her worst fears.

"*I'm sorry,*" her eyes said.

Valerya should have felt something. Anything, really. But when she thought about all the times Avander had lied, something in her broke, and all that remained was anger. Avantys sensed it fast enough, and it rose to meet her rage. *I could destroy this entire bunker,* she thought, sorely tempted. Instead, she thought of the girl, and her temper stalled. *I'll give her more time.* Someone else needed to know the truth, and as much as she hated it, the girl was the perfect choice. She was the reason why they were in this mess, and it was about time she fucking well knew it.

"It suffices," said Valerya. People shifted uncomfortably in their seats, but she kept her gaze fixed on their leader. Elarya remained composed and met her gaze.

"Is there anything else I can…?" Before Elarya could finish her sentence, a guardsman entered, painfully out of breath. A falcon was perched calmly on his shoulder, opening and closing its wings to maintain its balance.

"An urgent message," he reported, and Valerya tried not to smile.

"Is the falcon one of ours?"

The guardsman nodded. "Yes, your Majesty," he said between breaths. "The message was signed and sealed. It looks to be authentic." He pressed the message in the falcon's talons, and the bird soared, delivering it to their leader.

Elarya broke the seal. "A messenger rides," she said, frowning as the falcon perched on her shoulder. "What's the meaning of this?"

"An urgent matter," said Valerya, mildly impressed. Even if Dove had gotten caught, Valerya wouldn't have let them harm her, but the girl had made it far on her own. She was already a clever one, making sense of things that Valerya was not capable of deciphering. Now that she was discovering her powers, she would get stronger by the day.

The doors opened, and the guards exchanged words. The one with the cloth wrapped around his eye cleared his throat. "Riders approach," he said. "What does your Majesty command?"

Elarya contemplated them for a moment. "Make sure this messenger is alone and unarmed," she commanded before turning to Valerya. "This had better not be a trick."

To that, Valerya smiled. "No harm will come to you unprovoked," she said with a courteous nod, unfeigned. "You have my word."

# 35

## THE GREENWOOD
# FIRE REALM

The falcon had reached the hideout long before Dove and Bard did. They were greeted by half a dozen armed guardsmen at the mouth of the cave. One was on horseback, but they all bore sigils, betrayed wealth. Whoever they were, they were making a statement. Family crests were never paraded in open rebellion unless their bearers had nothing to lose. The one with the horse wore the highest helmet and an expensive blade, and Dove guessed he was in charge.

The guardsmen stood at attention when they halted, and it was only when their commander forced his own steed to face forward that she realized how intimidating Valerya's destrier must have been. Its red eyes flared in the darkness, and its armor was probably more expensive than all of theirs combined. It certainly did not seem happy with the sudden presence of strangers, and it tensed when the commander drew near.

"I wouldn't come any closer, o' great... lorden soldier," said Bard in a convincing attempt at humility. Dove glanced back, impressed. He must have been practicing recently. His accent sounded regional, and with the hood pulled over his hair, he looked like he even hailed from the Firelands. "It doesn't like strangers."

"We received a message that spoke of messengers," said the commander, regaining control of his horse. Still, he kept his distance and threw Dove a quick glance before focusing his attention on Bard. He cocked an eyebrow. "How many?"

Before Bard could give the wrong answer, Dove elbowed him and held up one finger, pretending her silence was shrouded in secrecy, not voicelessness.

"Are you the messenger?" the captain asked, and Dove gave a single nod, hoping they would not notice how nervous she was. His sharp-eyed expression eased. She was small and harmless compared to Bard, who was already rubbing him the wrong way. "Then I'm afraid your companion must stay behind, as we only received mention of one."

Dove could feel Bard's head swivel slowly behind her, casting a glance at the line of guards. She felt relieved when his breathing stayed slow, consistent. His confidence was contagious and made her feel safe. "Are you… absolutely sure?" he whispered, laying a hand on her arm.

He relaxed his grip when she nodded and swung down from the saddle. Without her, Valerya's horse tensed back into its usual self, and Bard dismounted quickly afterwards.

*Stay,* she commanded, running a hand down the horse's neck. *Do not mind the guardsmen or the Thunderborne.* It was much less painful now that it was used to her presence, and it lowered its head to the ground.

Dove straightened and walked through the entrance with all the confidence she could muster. As much as she wanted to see Bard handle the situation poorly, she could not afford to look back and show weakness. Two of the guardsmen broke formation, trailing behind her as she continued. *That is unfortunate.* In these situations, it was a known courtesy for the first person to cast Fire and reveal their surroundings, but they lit the way when she refused.

*Better they think I cannot cast it, than to find out I can.* She wondered how furious Valerya would be if she got caught so close to her destination. On the bright side, at least she could burn through their armor.

*Twenty-two steps. I know this cavern from somewhere.* Fear crept down the small of her back, but it faded as Valerya's presence grew stronger. Finally, they stopped in front of a set of doors guarded by two sentinels. "Our messenger has arrived," said one of the guardsmen behind her, playfully. Dove tried not to let them get to her. She was half their size in height, probably even half the width, but she was almost there. The General was on the other side of those walls, and when she closed her eyes and concentrated, she saw Valerya's Fire burn brighter than all the stars combined.

The guardsmen at the entrance threw her a questioning glance but stepped aside as they swung the great doors open. *No one really does care about the messenger,* she thought, forcing her legs to carry her forward.

She had not expected to be welcomed into an arena. After spending the entire evening trying to slip through unnoticed, being watched from every angle put her on edge. Heads turned when they announced her presence, and she struggled to gain her bearings.

Valerya was standing in the middle, just past the long tables, and Dove stopped when she reached her. Valerya turned her head slightly, a quick acknowledgment. "Took you long enough," she snapped as she stepped forward, leaving Dove to glance around the hall.

Rows of faces eyed her with curiosity and scorn. A woman standing in front of Valerya looked down at her. Between the two, it was hard to tell who was more scarred, but her expression eased when she saw her. *"Baley,"* she mouthed softly so that only Dove could see.

But before she could react, Valerya nudged her and nodded upwards.

*That must be Elarya,* she thought when she followed Valerya's gaze. Her seat was considerably higher than the others, and she had the same hair color as Morian... perhaps the same desire to do harm... but not much else. Even in anger, Morian was always ready to smile. It was remarkable, and terrifying, how easily he could laugh at one's pain. Elarya, however, had been made for a cold world. She may have been no stranger to wealth, judging from her posture, but she was lean and hard and did not look like she found much joy in anything. If they had not been on opposite sides, she and the General would have probably gotten along.

"Welcome," said Elarya when the silence grew loud, and Dove forced herself to meet her eyes. The scarred woman in the strange coat had gone back to staring forward. "I hear you have a message."

*Not really,* thought Dove.

"She does not, but I do," said Valerya sharply, cutting between them. Dove knew immediately that something was wrong. The General's expression was beginning to crack, and urgency tore at the edge of her tone. "Everyone in this hall has been living a lie, and I don't know who the biggest fool is. I'm starting to think it may be me."

Elarya drew her lips back into a thin line, unaccustomed to ridicule. "I do not know what ruse this is." She glared daggers at Dove as though she were responsible for how the evening was turning out. "But perhaps you are correct in that regard, *General.* My scouts report that you really did come alone, save for this... messenger without a message. If the girl has no function here…" She raised a hand to her face and nodded towards the archers.

Dove understood at once why the arena was so effective. She was suddenly painfully aware of all the arrows pointed at her head.

"You promised us safe audience," said Valerya. The weight in her tone was unmistakable now, which shook Dove's resolve. Dove wanted to look into the eyes of the archers, but she stood as still as possible, unwilling to provoke them into shooting.

"Did you really think it would have been safe for you here?" asked Elarya, showing her true colors. "You fight for my brother. Some say his kingdom stands because of you alone." She straightened in her seat, and their onlookers did the same, waiting for further command. "Give me one good reason why I shouldn't have your head. Both of yours."

"You *promised* us safe audience," Valerya repeated coldly. "Is that not reason enough?"

"Come, now." Elarya leaned back as though she had told a joke, laughed cruelly. "You and I both know, *General*, that some things must be sacrificed for the greater good. My word is less important than saving the lives of thousands."

*Perhaps they would not be friends after all.* Dove tensed when she heard the draw bar lock the doors from the outside. When it slammed into place, a blast of sound echoed in the hall like a cannon. Before she could stop herself, Dove jumped back, startled.

"*No!*" she heard Valerya's voice, but something hot lodged itself into Dove's shoulder. Her dragon screeched, a sound that matched the pain that exploded down her left arm like shattering glass. It swerved into cold nausea, and she went down easy, letting the arrow guide her to the ground. The coldness spread. The impact muffled most of the sounds and blurred her vision. She knew that people were shouting but could not make out the words.

It was Rhysar who sharpened her senses, and when she opened her eyes, her vision refocused. The pain in her shoulder tightened like a pulled knot until it went numb. She could feel the dragon's rage as he clamored against the sides of her consciousness, demanding to be set free.

*No... not yet,* she thought, watching dark red wash gently over stone. She forced herself to her knees, feeling every muscle tremble, burn.

"You *fools*," Valerya snapped, but her tone faltered. It was quick, fleeting, and if Dove did not know her, she would not have noticed. Valerya turned to Dove, and a shade of fear graced her features for the first time. "Leave that in," she said when Dove reached for the arrow's shaft.

"I'd heard tales of your ruthlessness, but they were all lies, weren't they?" said Elarya, watching her reaction.

"Idiot! You don't know what you've done," said Valerya, but her breathing quickened. Dove recognized terror when she saw it, no matter how much the General tried to hide it. But even more than that, she also recognized the fury behind it. "*Open the door.*"

"And let you esca—"

"*NOW.*"

"You're afraid. As well you should…"

"I'm not afraid of *you*," spat Valerya. "I'm af…"

Dove braced herself as Valerya bent over in pain. No one had moved to attack, but she collapsed to the ground as though someone had fired a thousand arrows. Dove felt the stone beneath her tremble. The scarred woman watched Valerya in terror, but she immediately ran towards Dove. Before Dove knew it, she was being pulled towards the nearest wall. Not even the pain in her shoulder could distract her from what was happening.

*Oh no,* thought Dove as she understood. The others had never seen it, but she felt its intensity, brewing and simmering like a storm. Valerya crashed down on one elbow, and Dove heard the metal of her armor cut scrapes into the ground. Valerya's free hand clutched at her side as she dropped her head against her forearm, shaking as though hot knives twisted inside her. It made Dove's pain tickle in comparison.

"Open... the door..." Valerya managed to say when she looked up. Veins bulged in her neck and blackened. They spread to the corners of her mouth and eyes like webbing.

*Like scales.*

The onlookers were visibly shaken, and they glanced at each other, then at their leader. "What ruse is this?" Elarya demanded, but Dove could see she was unsettled.

"*RUN.*" Valerya turned to Dove, her eyes tearing in pain. One of her hands crawled across the ground. "Close your eyes," she managed to command between gasps. "Don't look."

Concern shrouded pain as Dove moved towards her. *What is happen...?"*

Valerya's eyes clamped shut, and for a split-moment, Dove thought she would pass out. Instead, she screamed, an inhuman sound, and when her eyes opened, Dove saw a sliver of gold where gray used to be. Before she could react, she felt the air tighten. Her lungs flared into pain so suddenly, she thought they would burst.

Valerya released her hold immediately, but only for her. The others in the hall were not so lucky, and when she opened her eyes, she saw them claw at their throats, struggling vainly to stay alive. Only the scarred woman stood calmly, but the ones sitting in the bottom row closest to her died instantly. Their bodies slumped over like broken dolls, battered apart by invisible hammers. Those closest to the doors were already banging on them, begging the sentinels to let them through.

"*TAKE HER DOWN!*" Elarya rasped at the archers, but the air severed her words. Valerya seemed to go easy on her, though. A promise was a promise, even if one side had broken it, but it did not seem like Valerya had any use for the others. They collapsed to the ground, gasping for air.

Those who were able readied their bows, but Dove could see their hands were shaking.

*No!* she thought, for their sakes. She gathered whatever energy she could and sent grayfire in all directions. Pure, unadulterated agony flared up every limb, but she forced herself to keep casting until she felt her strength leave the flames. White light washed over everyone like a warm bath and disappeared into the walls of the arena, but there was no time for anyone to be confused. She crawled until she reached the closest wall and slumped her back against stone.

The first crossbows fired, some even at her, but the arrows splintered before they left their bows. Tables ripped from the ground, thrown back with such force that Dove thought the entire arena had tipped over. Valerya rose, energy renewed. Cruelty flickered in those golden eyes, and it grew strong off their fear. *I know those eyes.*

Those who were not dead or dying reached for their swords and advanced, desperate to stop her, but Valerya extended an arm, condensing the air until it lifted them off the ground. They grasped at their necks, suspended mid-air, and for a split-moment, there was a complete absence of sound. Flying splinters slowed to a float.

For a beautiful, terrifying moment, time stood still, but when it returned, their bodies cracked and crumpled, spraying blood across the arena. Bodies hit the ground convulsing. Valerya wrenched a blade from one of them. "Is that all?" she roared past the screams, past the dying.

Dove could not find another way to describe it: it was a *massacre*. Blood pooled in deep places on the floor, joining her own. The soldiers left standing raised their blades, but they knew they were doomed.

Valerya reached out a hand and made a fist. When she heaved it back, their swords flew across the arena and crashed against the opposite wall. Some of the onlookers lost heart and ran for the door. By then, the lock bar had been removed from the other side. They even managed to open it, but it slammed shut when Valerya pointed in their direction.

"Stop! We surrender!" they screamed, cried, threw their weapons at their feet. Fear had driven their loyalty aside and crushed their resolve.

Dove felt a rush of hot air bristle against the back of her neck. *It is here,* she realized. A new strain of terror shot down her spine. *In the hall.* She could not see it, but she felt it linger. If she followed the splintered tables, the crumpled bodies, she swore she could see bones cracking exactly where the creature would have stepped.

*Make a connection,* she commanded desperately, but was met with a sharp sting that sliced inside her skull. *I do not care if she is rejecting it.* Her eyes watered. It was not like it could get any worse than the chaos that was unfolding around them. *Connect me, damn it!*

Blackness turned into a thousand rays of light. Wherever she was, Dove felt no pain in this world. She saw no land beneath her feet, no water, nothing even remotely recognizable—only the stars. *We are in the skies.* Just then, a tear opened in the blackness, and its edges glowed an angry white. Cold air rushed through it, strong enough to keep her down.

"Valerya!" she called into the wind, shielding her eyes.

"What the fuck are you doing?" The voice was sharper than usual, but Dove had never felt so relieved. She located its source, but Valerya stood, unaffected by the winds.

"What are *you* doing?" Dove screamed, trying to rise, but the tear only grew bigger, the winds fiercer. "Stop this!"

"They would have killed you." Her eyes were cold and still gleamed gold. But it was not her. It sounded like her, looked like her, even *felt* like her, but there was no trace of her in those eyes. Her creature was taking over in this world and the next. "They would have killed us. Would going slow have made it easier for you?"

Dove saw Avantys soar behind her, as real and terrifying as Rhysar had been—only worlds bigger. Its scales were not smooth plates, but jagged like broken glass, each blazing scarlet. *I have to do something,* she thought. Anything to pull Valerya back from the Otherworld.

She grabbed onto Valerya's arm and forced her to look into her eyes. "Come back," she begged. "Come back. Stop this. *Please.*" For a moment, Dove thought she would find out what would happen if one died in dreams, but she saw gold fade back to gray, saw color return to her face. Valerya blinked furiously as if coming out of a trance. She pushed Dove behind her when she saw the scar in the sky, shielding her from the oncoming dragon.

"Fuck," said Valerya as the tear grew wider. Beyond it was the distant image of the waking world. As Avantys passed through the barrier and into another realm, Dove saw its form turn to flames. "It will burn everyone in the hall."

"It is feeding off your anger!" Dove yelled, feeling her connection fade. *Oh gods,* she thought when she saw her hands, translucent against the night sky. Her physical body was losing consciousness, and her presence in the stars would fade.

"Go," Valerya commanded sternly when she saw.

"No, wait!" screamed Dove, but Valerya was severing the connection. Before Dove could protest, all the worlds as she knew them vanished in a rush of flames.

# 36

## THE GREENWOOD
# FIRE REALM

Bard spent a few moments trying to remember if he had ever been in a more awkward situation. The last time he masqueraded as a Hound had been for sport. Dancer had been there, and it was a contest to see who could last the longest without killing anyone. Now one wrong move might get his current accomplice killed. Dancer and Val could take care of themselves, but the kid might need a bit more help.

The one on the horse leered down at him. He looked like he came from good stock. Money and a life of comfort went into those muscles, and he boasted a chiseled jawline that women went crazy for. The only thing Bard would change was the soft tuft on his chin.

Bard sighed. He didn't know what was more depressing: that boredom drove him to check out the competition, or that, when all was said and done, they were actually on the same side. Well, similar sides. *It's not like I fight for Morian's sister,* he thought, *but she has to be better than her brother.* He frowned, wondering if that sentence made sense.

"What's your name?" the commander asked, breaking the silence.

Bard coughed. "Franco," he said, breathing new life into an old identity.

"Franco?" the captain repeated with a frown. "Like... the name of the messenger?"

"What?"

"What?"

Bard glanced over his shoulder and looked for answers but found himself face-to-face with Val's horse. It *growled* when their eyes met—fucking growled—and for a moment, he didn't know what the greater threat was. He turned back to the commander and took another stab at small talk. "So... tell me about your leader."

"Tell me about yours."

"I'm just the kid's bodyguard," said Bard, realizing that they probably took him for a Morian supporter. *Damn it, Franco.* There was no talking his way out of it. Silence settled on them again, but before he could open his mouth to insult the commander's beard, he felt something tremble beneath his feet. The others felt it too, but just as they were on the verge of disregarding it, the ground shook once more, this time with more conviction. Bard leapt out of the way when a crack formed from the mouth of the hideout, jolting the earth as it rumbled forward.

*Fuck me.* He had seen this before. He supposed he shouldn't have been surprised, but he had hoped that for just one gathering, no one would test Val's temper. But still, something was off. Her fury didn't just stop there; now it was splitting the world apart.

"Earthquake!" he heard one of them say, but that was before a rush of guardsmen emerged from the entrance.

"She's killing them," they screamed. "She's killing all of them!"

"What?" the commander demanded. "How is that possible? What happ..."

A gust of hot air pushed them sideways, cutting them off. Bard was about to yell something back when his eyes widened against his will. Sweat moistened his brow, but it froze when he saw it in the distance. They all saw it in the distance, and everyone stopped mid-panic to stare.

The red dragon soared through the night sky, the first time Bard had ever seen it move so elegantly. *Come to think of it,* he thought, feeling dread explode down his back, *I've never seen it soar like that.* Didn't it usually descend in a rush of flames and terror? Its appearance usually signaled a quick devastation, but this time, it just... flew, majestically, like a... like a...

*Like a king.*

The others seemed to be thinking the same thing, especially when it perched atop one of the hills overlooking the village. It sat and waited, shoving spears into Bard's resolve. *Well,* he thought with a sigh, *at least the ground stopped shaking.* Val was still alive, for better or for worse, wreaking havoc in the hideout. In a fresh bout of insanity, he felt relieved; if that was Dove's defender, it meant the kid was still alive, too.

"Light them!" the commander shouted over his concentration. He whistled once. Twice. "Destroy that thing!"

"That?" one of his men said incredulously. "How?"

"Not *that*... get... stop the Summoner!" He turned to Bard, spitefully. "And kill the messenger."

"Your beard... ugly!" Bard shouted as the commander turned, and his drudges stood at the ready. Bard could have done better. He had rehearsed several insults in his mind, ready to launch them in present company, but the dragon had caught him off-guard. He followed the commander's gaze to the torch-fire in the distance and saw it grow bigger, wilder. A pyre had been lit, but Bard doubted they were holding a funeral.

*That can't be good.* He sighed as the drudges in front of him unsheathed their swords. He threw his cloak over his shoulder dramatically before drawing his own. It had been a while since he fought anything, and he had been itching for some action.

"A fucking Thunderborne," he heard one of them say when they saw his hair, but the others slammed their helmets shut. Raised vigilance.

Fire came at him in all directions, but Bard cast Storm over his head to ward off the flames. He volleyed sparks in their direction. Screams ended abruptly, but he couldn't see what was happening past the rush of flames. Once, he thought he was being charged at, but he slashed a flank of darkness. *Damn it.* It had been a while since he dealt with a handful of Fire-casters at once. He yelled and focused his energy on a pulse of Storm that ripped through the lines like a whip, shoving back his assailants.

Bard caught movement in the corner of his eye and dodged a blade aimed at his head. He turned a slip into a controlled fall, but the commander withdrew his blade and thrust once more, quick as lightning. Bard countered with his own blade, and when the commander cast a burst of Fire with his element hand, he beat it back with Storm. *Fuck,* he thought, struggling against the strain. It was one of the rare instances Bard regretted not believing in proper form. The captain had clearly trained by the book, casting only with his element hand. He would not tire soon. Bard gathered his remaining strength and forced his opponent back with a concentrated surge. His elements sparked weakly, desperate for rest. *Better rely on brawn for now.*

More men scrambled out of the opening, and some of them were on fire. Bard tore the tower shield from one of them and brought it to his face when flames attacked him in swarm. But soon they found a new target.

Valerya came out, and for a foolish moment, Bard thought she had donned crimson armor. But the color dripped when she stopped and glanced to the side of the hideout, tossing her blade aside. She picked up her greatsword from the tall grass and cast a ring of bloodfire around the men, preventing escape. Fire bit into the earth and turned it into red patches.

*What the fuck, Valerya?* he wanted to scream, but decided now was not the best time to test her temper, especially when she was covered in other people's blood. Still, he made sure she heard him groan, loudly.

"A little help?" he asked as he turned to her, surprised to see that she looked tired. Blood and sweat slicked every line of her seamed face. A metal fist clenched Bard's sword hand in a vain attempt to get him to drop his blade. Bard yelled, part pain, part fury, and struck the man in the face. Bard withdrew his fist in agony, having just punched pure steel, and for a moment, they grappled until Bard kneed him in the gut, tossing him towards Valerya.

Unflinchingly, Valerya ripped his helm from his head and threw him back to Bard, who punched him again, this time more effectively.

"So how is good ol' Morian doing?" asked Bard as he blocked another incoming blow. "I thought you two would be wed by now."

"I'd rather wed *you*," snapped Valerya as she thrust forward. She doubled back, catching three in her sword's trajectory. "What about you? Any blue-haired brats running around?"

Bard giggled, a strange sound for a man of his size. "None that I know of." He drove back another opponent with a series of distracted parries. "Can't believe you and I haven't talked in twenty fucking years."

She drew back to steady herself and thrust an arm out, halting an arrow mid-air with a blast of Fire as Bard fried its caster. For a moment, Bard wondered why she stopped. Then he realized there were no opponents left.

*Magnificent form,* he thought as she turned to face the commander, who clutched at his side, aflame with agony.

"I HAD HIM," Bard lied, coughed.

Valerya ignored him. "You're the least useless of them all," she said to the fallen man. Her eyes narrowed. "What's your name?"

"Nate," he said, but his groans were filled with dignity and defiance.

Valerya didn't look like she cared much for either. "Get out of my sight," she said. "And leave the horse."

Nate didn't look like he was in the position to move, let alone flee, but he knew he had lost before he hit the ground. His wounds looked so precise, so calculated, that Valerya seemed to have missed his throat and heart on purpose. She needed a survivor. Someone to spread the fear.

Valerya waited, still as a shadow guard, until Nate hoisted himself out of earshot. "Go back and help the others, Thunderborne," she commanded. "They need you more than we do."

"What's with all that blood?" Bard demanded, still in shock. "Where's Dove?"

"She'll be fine. *Do it.*" She grabbed him by the shoulder strap of his armor. "I know you fight with the Falcons. It may even give you pleasure to see them swamp our camp. But everything we know has been based on a lie."

She let go and headed back towards the entrance. "The choice is yours. If you don't believe me, maybe you should ask your *father* one day."

*Fuck, shit, balls.* Bard heard the urgency in her voice, saw the blood dripping from her armor. He climbed atop the commander's horse. "WE NEED TO TALK LATER," he screamed as he rode off, but when he turned his attention to the hills in the distance, he realized the dragon had gone. Only dried, scorched earth remained, revealing that it was once there.

Nothing felt right about the evening. Valerya's dragon had even settled on hill, unwilling to lose its connection to the waking world. Dread grew and spread to his limbs, and he spurred the horse on faster. *Fuck, fuck, fuck.* He saw the Northern dragon from far away, turning the night sky into a tapestry of colored glass. It had not fully shown itself in the Wayfare Forests, but tonight it burned true, every flame bending itself to its form. It almost gleamed gold against the angry red flames that littered the world below.

A white underglow flushed the lowest clouds, forcing them to life with ivory crests and swirls. Bard covered his eyes as it lingered above the camp, swinging its head to and fro. *It's blind,* he realized, halting the commander's horse in a last-minute attempt to prepare for the flames.

But chaos had unfurled from all sides. Trees around him bent to avoid the flames. Night-wolves howled and emerged from their hiding places, and their fur bristled like spikes in the wind. Bard remembered seeing one in the Underground, but apparently, Bear was a goddamn *puppy*. These were wild creatures that were wider than the commander's horse, and centuries of being left to their own devices had primed every instinct towards the kill. They saw him, bared their teeth—but ignored him completely, charging to help the dragon. What should he do?

*Follow them, of course.* Bard was already convinced he had gone insane. What was one more adventure? He rode on, accepting his fate.

He knew they were reaching the rebel camp when the night-wolves veered in different directions, pummeling shoulder-first into unsuspecting horses and riders alike. They paved an opening towards the Swordsworn camp, and Bard didn't hesitate to take it.

Bard leapt from the saddle when he caught sight of Mayet. "All right there?" he bellowed as she mowed through oncoming assailants. Her blade was gleaming scarlet, but her face was remarkably un-besmirched. Strands of black hair, wet from sweat and strain, fell across black eyes. He wondered if she knew they had man-eating wolves on their side.

"Where's the girl?" she demanded above their screams, ignoring his question as she drove her sword down one of their throats. Bard stared, impressed.

"Where's the *dragon?*" he asked as she drew it back, suddenly aware of the silence that grew around them. A deafening screech turned their attention upwards.

Valk approached him, angrier and bloodier than Mayet. He grabbed Bard's shoulder, but Bard refused to take his eyes off the creature.

"*Where are Dove and Valerya?*" he demanded.

# 37

## THE HIDEOUT
# FIRE REALM

"**W**ake up."

Something hard smacked against the side of her face. Dove groaned, but no sound came out. *Where am I?* she thought as the brief burst of pain ended.

*"I need you to wake up."*

Another smack.

Slowly, Dove came to. Color spilled into the corners of her vision, giving form to her surroundings, but no amount of light could bring her to ignore the darkness around her. Blood splashed the walls. Bones and pieces of bones scattered like broken furniture across the arena. Valerya stepped in front of her, blocking it out. "Good," she said sternly. "You're awake."

She pointed the tip of her greatsword at Elarya, who was crouching on her knees. She did not seem to register what had happened, but Dove did not blame her. In truth, she was grateful for being un-conscious for most of the carnage. Her eyes wandered to the arrow still lodged in her shoulder, but its shaft had been broken, splintered down the middle.

The scarred woman was gone. Dove glanced around the hall, but she could not find her body in the wreckage.

"Truth is a wicked thing," Valerya said, turning back to Dove. "It was a whisper when we met, but now it screams. Do you remember?" She flexed the fingers in her element hand, and Dove saw the scars on her palm. From here, they looked more precise. Calculated. Valerya set her greatsword against the wall, opting for a smaller blade. "Tonight, she will sing the truth."

"Truth?" Elarya managed to sputter. She threw Dove a glance, her resolve replaced by desperation. *If she thinks I can help her, she is terribly mistaken.* "I'm not a liar."

"Who are you, then?"

Elarya frowned. Dove did, too; it seemed an odd question after an entire conquest to stop her rebellion. The woman stared back with renewed courage. "I am Elarya of Pyrrheas, leader of the Red Spears," she said, finding her voice. "I was a child when Eithan sent me away. He wanted to keep me safe from my brother after... after an accident. He knew I wouldn't be safe there."

"What accident?" Valerya asked, ignoring the bodies around her.

"I don't know I was a *child,*" said the Spear defiantly. "The men who brought me to safety told me of my purpose. Now I am here to take back the Crown from tyrants like you."

"Like me," said Valerya. Amusement tinged her voice. "But the crown isn't on *my* head. It's on your brother's, am I correct?"

"Yes, but..."

"Another *lie,*" Valerya spat. "Surely you don't want to go to the grave with lies on your lips?"

Elarya blinked, affronted. "I wouldn't expect you to understand," she said spitefully. "This is a matter of royalty. Of blood and nobility."

Dove cringed. A poor choice of words, given her current

circumstances, but she supposed she did not want to go down a coward.

Without warning, the She-Jackal grabbed Elarya by the shoulder and threw her back with such force that Dove could hear something crack. With one arm, she held her down, and with the other, she raised a blade. "You don't seem to understand your situation," said Valerya calmly as Elarya looked back in terror. Now that Valerya could touch her, fear had donned a form. "All I want is the truth. This seems to be an elusive concept for royalty. Blood. *Nobility*."

"Wh… what truth?" asked Elarya.

Valerya sighed, disappointed. "Just tell me who you are," she said softly, driving the tip of her blade into the woman's shoulder.

Dove's eyes widened. She moved to stop her, but Valerya glared daggers in her direction. "Stay where you are," she commanded as she drove it in all the more slowly, twisting the blade. Dove closed her eyes as though it would block out the sound. "WATCH," Valerya snapped. "I want you to remember. You must understand."

*Understand what?* Dove did not want to believe that Valerya found relief in torture, but nothing else could explain what was happening. She ran through that night in her mind, back when this all started, trying to remember anything out of the ordinary. *She fed me,* she thought, looking for meaning behind every gesture. *She gave me new clothes. I found a coin. Maybe before that? She clamped her eyes shut. She cut my binds. Showed me her caste-mark. And then…*

*And then she saw my hand.* Cold sweat lined her forehead. *Oh gods.* Even without the arrow lodged close to her heart, it became harder to breathe. A shadow of truth, but it explained everything. And the more she thought about it, the louder it screamed. *She recognized Wolff on the battlefield…*

Her oath was never a promise to protect her sovereign. She tried hoisting herself up, but her arms had gone numb, her bones weak. *Her hand... the scars...* Dove raised her own palm to her face. *Just like mine, but farther apart. Because she was younger than me. She closed her eyes. Wolff and Rey, fighting...*

Valerya nodded, satisfied at her reaction. She turned back to her captive. "Who *ARE* you?"

"All right!" Elarya screamed between tears. "I... I am... I am not..."

Valerya withdrew her blade, throwing woman and dagger to the floor.

"A fraud. A *double*," said Valerya as Elarya clutched her shoulder. Blood gushed between her fingers like a broken fountain. "See, the truth is not so hard for you nobles, after all."

"Please... my people needed someone... please have mercy."

*Another poor choice of words.* Dove let herself slump back against stone. There was no way she had enough energy for a connection. Her heart was furiously pumping blood out of her, and it was leaving her body in streams. But she understood now. She understood why Valerya could not break her promise. Why Artis felt so responsible for her wellbeing. *Everything.*

"Your people." Valerya cut through her thoughts. "*You* wanted the crown by impersonating a dead girl. You knew the real Elarya was in hiding, and there was a slim chance people would find out. Avander *wanted* his child to stay hidden. But something ruined his plans."

Dove gasped for air as she felt blackness cloud her vision. *Valerya was never meant to protect her sovereign,* she thought, crying, screaming wordlessly, watching Valerya grip the hilt of her sword. *She was meant to protect...*

The Spear struggled to her knees. "How... how did you know...

I wasn't…?" she asked.

Valerya raised her sword. The corners of her mouth twisted into a cold smile. "Because I am," she said, and swung down.

# 38

## SOMEWHERE IN THE
# ICE REALM

"This is impossible," said Decker, readjusting his belt. He had fired his right grappling hook a few seconds too late, and the rest of the momentum propelled him face-first into a tree. The trunks had been layered with cotton and cloth, but only barely—drudges had to learn from their mistakes, after all—and he felt the impact burst behind his eyes and ripple down his spine. His knees tightened around the trunk. *Easy for them to say.* He imagined this lesson was significantly less painful for people who healed instantly.

He closed his gauntlet around the nearest branch, but it snapped like a twig under his weight. Without anything else to grab on to, he went down flailing. Brunhilda had created a safety net between the trees, but she had tied the knots to sting. They dug into his side and bounced him upwards once, twice, until he flipped over to his elbows and knees. Groaned when the aches lingered. *That's going to bruise,* he thought, feeling like a peach. But when he saw the forest below, he knew to be grateful.

The foliage rustled as the creatures below raced to catch him. They made no sound otherwise. When the ripples of the leaves were right below him, they stopped. Waited. Wolves did not normally attack people, especially unprovoked, but the forest must have bewitched them. They sensed his presence and followed him wherever he went.

Decker glanced up just in time to see Brunhilda soaring effortlessly between the trees. Rabbits dangled from her belt, and they trailed behind her like feathers. He heard the swish of her grapple as she landed on the net. She sat cross-legged in front of him, and the ropes rose and fell like gentle waves.

"Stop admiring the view. We're almost there," she said, patting his back.

"Why are we here?" Decker tried to focus on something steady, like the clouds. He was used to flying, but this kind of controlled freefall made him dizzy.

Brunhilda watched him for a moment and chuckled to herself as she grabbed a rabbit tied to her belt. With a swift motion, she cut off its leg. "Watch and learn, Bright Eyes." She waved it in front of his face and let go, and they watched as it slipped through the net and disappeared into the forest. The growling and barking followed as the wolves fought over scraps.

"See?" Brunhilda sheathed the dagger Decker did not know she had. He squinted. *Is that mine?* Instinctively, he felt around his belt and found his sheath empty. Brunhilda threw him a knowing smile. "This is by far the best place for schemes and scheming. Not even Valerya can catch us here, and grapples are the only way to get to the other side."

*At least there's that.* Decker had no desire to see Valerya again for a long, long time. Not like it could get any worse. "Where's Merc?" He tried to stand, but Brunhilda stretched a leg out. The ropes gave a soft lurch, and he fell back down, feeling the knots. Brunhilda raised her arms above her head as she rode the waves. *Glad someone is having a good time.* He tried not to vomit.

Brunhilda sighed, disappointed, when the net stopped bouncing. "Merc is worse than you are." She shrugged. "I think he's crab-crawling across the nets."

Decker aimed his grappling hook at the branch of the nearest tree and fired. By now, he was used to the kickback of the firing device, and the hook met its target with ease. It wrapped around the branch twice.

"The trick is releasing once you're as high up as you want to be," said Brunhilda. "*Then* you fire the other hook. Wait for the hook to catch. Then release the first one. But never at the same time. Seriously. I've seen things." She shuddered. "We can heal a thousand wounds in an instant, but there are some things we just can't regenerate."

*Lovely.* "Any other tips?"

"When you panic, just release. Don't fire another. *Just release.* Now come on."

And just like that, Brunhilda was flying again.

Decker took a deep breath and looked at the firing mechanism in his hand. His finger tightened around the trigger… and squeezed.

"Ah, *fuuuuu*…!" His scream disappeared in the wind as the device reeled him towards the branch. The grappling hooks were a far cry from manning an airship. At least on the *Smuggler,* the only danger was falling off. This was not so much flying as it was falling in different directions.

The tree was approaching much faster than he had anticipated, and his body froze just before he remembered Brunhilda's words. *Just release.* He pulled his finger away from the trigger and felt the tension leave the rope of his grapple. The moment he felt his body fall, he fired his left hook at the nearest tree. When it settled, he pulled its trigger.

He made sure to release it before firing the next one, and the next, until he was soaring through the sky. It was rough maneuvering, and he could almost hear Brunhilda laughing at him from afar, but he enjoyed the wind in his hair, the feeling of being at nature's mercy. The squabbles of man almost paled in comparison.

Finally, Decker could make out a landing area in the distance. High, reinforced palisades kept the wolves out, but the forest behind it was cleared, save for two trees were marked with bright red X's and lines—presumably to tell novices where to fire and release the last hooks. Decker obeyed without question. The marks allowed him to lower himself to a safe distance, but he still tumbled forward ungraciously when he landed.

Brunhilda clapped. "Congratulations! You're about as good as a twelve-year-old in Lancistierre," she said, extending an arm. Decker took it without question and rose, and he was pretty sure his elbows and knees were bleeding. He didn't even care. For the first time in his life, he was happy to be on land.

They waited for the screaming to get louder until Merc crash-landed into the clearing. The ground had also been covered in soft cloths and cotton, but he still howled when he hit the ground. It took him a few minutes to catch his breath, and Decker let him gather his dignity before helping him up.

"They're only flesh wounds," said Brunhilda curtly as they walked. "Elayne can heal you when we get back."

Decker's heart skipped when he heard her name. They had set up camp not too far away, and Elayne was training new graces when they left at dawn. They would need more healers in this war, Brunhilda said. Valerya had started paying them a captain's salary and granting foreign medicans and their families free passage to the Firelands, so many flocked to her side.

*How can we even compete with that?*

Merc shook his head and wiped blood off his arm. His hands had already blistered from gripping the firing devices too tightly. "I'm not looking forward to the journey back."

"Lucky for you, then," said Brunhilda coyly. "We're not going back that way."

Decker frowned. "I thought you said that was the only way…"

The words caught in his throat when he saw. He stopped so abruptly that Merc crashed into him, but before Merc could start cursing, Decker grabbed his chin and pointed his head upwards.

Brunhilda was not leading them to an airship. Instead, what greeted them was a…

"A *dragon?*" Merc shouted incredulously. He ran a hand over his hair as though it would wipe the amazement off his face.

There was no other word for it. It was a monstrosity made of metal, masterfully tortured into the shape of a dragon. It gleamed in the sun but looked smeared with oil, which meant it had been infused with blackwood. "Brunhilda," said Decker, forgetting the pain. "What is this?"

She sighed. "Really? It's a dragon."

"I see it's a dragon," Merc sputtered. "But what… is it?"

The dragon was the size of a small hut. Wings were forged and attached to the body, layers of canvas sewn between metal fingers. Instead of a face, Decker saw a window and a ladder that led from it.

Brunhilda's eyes glinted as she looked at it, and Decker swore he could see tears. "The perfect construction of magestone and Storm," she said. "You're looking at the efforts of Divisoryan scholars, Lancistierrean builders, Glasgérian miners, and Fireborne smiths.

And the Thunderborne, of course. Did you know Storm capsules can create a new form of energy?" She pointed at the canvas. "They power the wings."

"This is *insane*." Decker climbed the ladder to the window and slid it open. He removed his gauntlet and ran his fingers over the helm. There were two levers to the right of it—to steer the magestone, he knew—and a third he did not recognize. Aside from that, the smaller switches and levers were arranged almost exactly like the control board of the *Smuggler*. Two seats were placed in front of the helm, but it made sense; the roof was too low for most helmsmen to stand.

Brunhilda cleared her throat. "Think of it as a mini-airship, but one that is faster and easier to maneuver," she said.

"And one immune to fire," said Merc, caressing the belly of the beast. He pressed his ear against it as if expecting a heartbeat.

"How did you even get the *idea* for this?" Decker asked, climbing back down. "Even the controls are similar to the *Smuggler*."

"Oh, I had a bit of help," said Brunhilda. She shouted something in Lancistierrean, and the belly of the beast opened outward. Merc jumped to the side and cursed, clutching his side.

A woman came out, waving a wrench at them. "Decker! Merc!" she yelled. Massive goggles covered half her face—were they Merc's?—but Decker would recognize that smile anywhere. The last time he had seen it was on the *Smuggler*, just before they parted ways in Glasgérios.

The kid who had nowhere to go, so she just lived on the *Smuggler*.

Nan lifted her goggles over her face and tossed them to Merc, but Merc was so surprised, he did not even try catching them. Even when she embraced him, all he could do was stare openmouthed like a half-wit. "You just missed Ieon and Bast," she said, throwing her arms around Decker. "They're working on the other stormships today."

"Stormships?" Decker blinked. "There are others?"

"See?" Brunhilda closed her eyes and breathed in the fresh air of the forest. Coughed it back out. "I told you this would be worth your while."

"I... thought you said you didn't need a helmsman," said Decker.

Brunhilda pretended to look surprised. "But I don't," she said, putting a hand to her lips. "I said I needed a Sky Commander. I meant what I said, kid. Come with me, and I'll show you how to *fly*."

# GOD'S END

The Sun-sworn temple was warmly lit with candles, and there was no torch in sight. It felt more like a funeral than a celebration of birth, but Dove had never been to a burning before. It was a highborn tradition that surpassed her level of understanding, like suitors' balls and public beddings—things that, she was told, would be in her future if she was not careful.

Dove was grateful for the dimness of the hall. She and Valerya stood on the uppermost level, on the balcony that had once been reserved for women and servants. Bastyan the Cruel had done a great many things, but one of his first decrees abolished segregated worship. Women and men must pray together, he had said. No one used temple balconies since then, which made it perfect. Valerya had simply ordered it closed off to everyone else, and Valk stood guard outside the only entrance.

It was the only way Dove agreed to attend. As much as she dreaded seeing Morian, even from afar, she did not think it would be a good idea for Valerya to attend his child's—her *niece's*— burning alone. No one could see them from down below, anyway.

The balcony was in the back of the temple, behind the pews and incense burners, and after centuries of disuse, most people forgot it existed. Dove and Valerya were safe from view behind red and gold clouds of smoke.

The only thing Dove could see clearly was the raised dais on the other side of the temple, where flames burned from sacred lamps. Nobles traveled far and wide to watch the royal heir burn, after which the child's name would be announced for the first time. To speak the name before the ceremony was an ill omen for the kingdom, so not even Valerya knew.

Dove squinted and saw the Sun-sworn priests bless the flames in preparation. She sighed when she heard them chant in ancient Sinthean.

It was going to be a long day.

Valerya had not said much since they returned to the Citadel. They had not even mentioned Elarya—not even the false Elarya—since then. Dove's was the only presence the General did tolerate, which was fine with her; it saved Dove from having to interact with anyone else. Even Bard. The questions, the *fear* in his eyes, were too much, his understanding too little, and all she wanted to do was disappear in her Summoner bubble... forever.

Dove glanced at Valerya, guiltily. As much as she hated to admit it, she loved their time together. It was easy to forget that Valerya was the She-Jackal, the Conqueror of the Realm—and now the Princess of Pyrrheas, to add to her titles—when they were alone. In this world and the next, they could forget it all.

*Pull yourself together.* Dove sighed glumly. Never had she been so confused about anything in her short, stupid life. She tried to distract herself with the rest of the proceedings and was almost grateful when something finally happened.

Then she ate her words.

The head priest stepped onto the dais with a child in his arms, and behind him, a woman Dove did not recognize. Followed by... Morian.

Something cold and sharp shot down Dove's spine. *Focus on the baby. The baby.*

She felt Valerya's hand on her shoulder. It was not particularly gentle, but it stayed.

It was enough for Dove to feel safe, and she turned her attention to the baby. The child slept soundly, and the king watched it with fear in his eyes, like the priest was going to drop it. For a moment, there was no cruelty, no malice. *Maybe he is human after all,* thought Dove dryly. Her eyes drifted back to the woman standing next to him, who looked understandably terrified. And not just because of the burning.

The priest proclaimed many things, among them the parents' names—Lyra of the Castells, Dove heard—and before she knew it, the child disappeared in a cloud of flames. Valerya leaned forward in interest, like she was half-expecting it to burn.

But the priest only smiled and lifted the child from the fire.

"Her Fire is strengthened!" he shouted. "Long live Andreya of Pyrrheas!" He shouted it again, this time louder, above the chanting crowd. Andreya's mother looked visibly relieved, and she took the baby in her arms.

Dove heard Valerya snort next to her. Dove bit back a grin and glanced at the General, who was struggling to contain herself. Her giant pauldron shook, and her crimson cape wavered like the wind. For a brief moment, their eyes met, and they burst into laughter that disappeared into the cheers of the crowd.

The smile was still on her lips when Valerya staggered back, clutching at her sides. The candles dimmed around them, and something blew through the hall, soft as a breeze. But when Valerya glanced back over the balcony, her hands gripped the railing, and her eyes gleamed gold.

*Oh gods.* Dove understood it at once. Andreya of Pyrrheas may have been Valerya's niece, but the child was another thing standing between Avantys and the throne now.

Before Valerya could melt the temple down, Dove did the only thing she could think of. Her arm shot up to the railing, and her fingers closed around Valerya's hand.

A fierce light exploded across her vision. Dove had been angry before, but this was fury like she had never experienced, and it was hungry. It ate at her from the inside and spread outwards into a thousand points of pain. She took a deep breath and closed her eyes. *I will take it.* She had already been torn inside out by Rhysar; this was only slightly worse. Okay, it was much worse, but Valerya should not have to bear it alone.

Dove felt her eyes water as her body took in the rage of Valerya's dragon.

Valerya bristled next to her. She glanced downwards and screamed into her arm, but when she opened her eyes, the golden gleam was gone. She blinked as if trying to remember where she was, and her eyes drifted to Dove's hand.

*I will... take it.* Dove felt the pain fade, slowly, until the smell of incense returned. The cheers and praises of the nobles. She felt the world settle around them like a shroud, felt its weight on her shoulders. They were back.

Valerya's breathing grew steady as her anger faded, and she turned her attention back to the dais. Dropped her gaze thoughtfully. After a moment, her hand clenched around Dove's. Her skin was rough and calloused, but her touch was surprisingly gentle. Dove did not mind.

*You fool.* Dove shifted her gaze from Valerya to Morian, then to the child in his arms. *So many problems in one temple.* The hall was full of people, past and present, who wanted to kill each other but could not. Avantys wanted Morian and the child gone. To save at least one of them, Valerya would have to fight it to keep it at bay. Dove could take the brunt of the dragon's wrath, but Pierce—no, *Bastyan*—begged her to kill its Summoner. And Baley, the past Summoner of her own dragon, wanted her to save her.

Dove sighed and wondered when the Realm was going to collapse.

But for now, Avantys had faded completely. It was just her and Valerya on the balcony, hidden from the rest of the world. Not even the King of the Firelands could see them from his raised dais, nor could the Sun-sworn priests judge them with their sacred scripts. For a peaceful, wonderful moment, they were alone.

That is, until Dove glanced out the window and saw a tear in the sky that closed.

A tail of red fire disappeared beyond the stars.

# ABOUT THE AUTHOR

Kerstin Espinosa Rosero is the author of SPFBO7 finalist BURN RED SKIES. Her quest to be a translator has led her to live all over the world, including the US, Germany, Taiwan, and the Philippines. When she is not writing or working, she is traveling, sketching, or kickboxing. It is her goal to turn her sketches into stories.

Twitter: @ke_rosero
Instagram: @k.e.rosero

# THANK YOU

Thank you for reading *Rise Red Kingdom,* Book II in the *Burn Red Skies* series. Without your support, writing this book would not have been possible. Dove, Valerya, and all the other oddball characters of this world would have stayed an idea in my head.

If you enjoyed your adventure with this ragtag group of characters, please consider leaving a review on social media or your favorite book site, such as Amazon and Goodreads. For an author, especially in the realm of indie fantasy, your words are more important than you know! Like hot chocolate on a winter day. Or courage in the face of dragons.

Regardless of whether you choose to leave a review, thank you again for taking the time to read *Rise Red Kingdom.* Hope to see you in the final installment of the *Burn Red Skies* series!

Best wishes on your own adventures,
wherever the dragons may take you,

**Kerstin Espinosa Rosero**

Printed in Great Britain
by Amazon

41428346R00219